Praise for the novels of

"A hunt for a lost manuscript, a cast [...] all bound together by a beautiful me[...] I highly recommend this sweet and suspenseful novel!"
—Lee Tobin McClain, *New York Times* bestselling author of *The Beach Reads Bookshop*

"Mollie Rushmeyer has gifted readers a story of sweet restoration. She takes us from the depths of unforgiveness and secrets, to the heights of renewed trust and love, while sprinkling a curious mystery in between it all."
—Lynette Eason, *USA TODAY* bestselling author of the Extreme Measures series

"Mollie Rushmeyer crafts a masterful tale of adventure, danger, and romance in *The Lost Manuscript* that culminates into a very satisfying ending! With nail-biting intrigue, readers will be entranced with this story of intrigue as well as the God of second chances."
—Tara Johnson, author of *Engraved on the Heart*, *Where Dandelions Bloom* and *All Through the Night*

"Rushmeyer has such a lyrical style that delights in every chapter. She's not afraid to tackle tough relationships and family situations, and manages to thread an engaging and interesting historical mystery through a story of healing and reconciliation. *The Lost Manuscript* is a lovely, heart-tugging story."
—Erica Vetsch, author of the Thorndike & Swann Regency Mystery series

"Book love, buried treasure, and a family mystery combine in a story of redemption, faith, friendship, and new beginnings. Where old pain once separated a wounded young woman from all she had hoped for, seeds fall like summer rain and broken places become the growing ground for new love in Mollie Rushmeyer's warmhearted literary debut."
—Lisa Wingate, #1 *New York Times* bestselling author of *Before We Were Yours*

"*The Bookshop of Secrets* has it all—mystery, history, romance, and more than a little literary magic."
—Laura Frantz, Christy Award–winning author of *A Heart Adrift*

Also by Mollie Rushmeyer

The Bookshop of Secrets

THE
LOST
MANUSCRIPT

MOLLIE
RUSHMEYER

LOVE INSPIRED

Stories to uplift and inspire

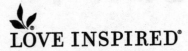

LOVE INSPIRED®

Stories to uplift and inspire

Recycling programs
for this product may
not exist in your area.

ISBN-13: 978-1-335-50842-3

The Lost Manuscript

Love Inspired
22 Adelaide St. West, 41st Floor
Toronto, Ontario M5H 4E3, Canada
www.LoveInspired.com

Printed in U.S.A.

For my husband, Mark, who has bolstered me and encouraged me throughout this writing process and who, after twenty years and the ups and downs of life, is still my best friend. You are home to me.

Acknowledgments

Thank You, Lord, for allowing me to continue doing this thing I love. I pray the words will have the impact You intend and the story will bless those who read it.

This story would never have been written had it not been for my life-changing trip to Alnwick, England, in college. So, I must thank the St. Cloud State University Centre For British Studies based at Alnwick Castle, as well as the Percy family for hosting American students and sharing their home, the magic and the history living in those walls. Please forgive any tiny changes to the castle for the sake of fiction!

A big thanks to Kate Tran (and Kate's dad) and Amanda Sanoski, fellow Alnwick program alumni, for jumping in to help me with my research and planning. It was so fun to walk down memory lane with you. I have the fondest memories of our time in Alnwick and wouldn't have wanted to experience it with anyone else!

Thank you, Mark, Rya and Nova, for allowing me the time to labor away at my fictional worlds and for encouraging me along the way. I love you each so much.

As I wrote a story about the far-reaching impact of our family trees, the many branches, how they grow and sometimes splinter or break, I realized not for the first time how grateful I am for my family. Thank you from the bottom of my heart to my whole big, loud, loving family—the McMurray, Rushmeyer and Neumann clans. I can't express how much your outpouring of love and enthusiastic support of my writing has meant to me.

I must also thank my fellow writerly people: my dear friend Michelle Sass Aleckson, Erica Vetsch, Gabrielle Meyer and the writing/creative ladies, Gail Helgeson, Julie Saffrin and Barb Marshak, who have helped me brainstorm this and other stories and have been a sounding board as well as confidants on many an occasion.

Thank you from the bottom of my heart, Kasey and Dustin Aune, for sharing with me the grief of your loss as well as the joy of your rainbow story, your precious Theodore. Your words were a help to me, but more than that, I know they will bless others. I love you all.

Thank you, Cynthia Ruchti, my agent extraordinaire. I can never seem to put into words exactly how grateful I am for you. I still have to pinch myself that you gave me a chance, but more than that, you believed in me. When I gained an agent, I didn't know I was also gaining a friend.

And thank you, Emily Rodmell and the Love Inspired team, for your patience and continuing to see the life and potential in these characters and stories from my heart.

Chapter One

Empty rooms are full of stories. Invisible memories. Silent echoes.

Ellora Lockwood's feet stuck to the floor in the living room she'd once shared with her husband. Her vintage-inspired saddle shoes wouldn't budge. The real estate agent may have to sell the original craftsman-style home "as is" with her body as the new owner's *Ode to a Failed Marriage* statue. A reminder of what not to do.

A life once lived seeped from every crack in the creaking floorboards, coalesced with the afternoon sunbeams pouring through the dust-covered glass, which was still on her closing to-do list, and pooled on the handwoven rug her grandmother had given her as a wedding/housewarming gift. The rug was the last thing Ellora would remove from this place of not-quites, open-ended losses and broken dreams.

"To keep your feet warm," her grandmother had said before handing the sturdy burnt-orange and turquoise rug to her—not exactly Ellora's colors—the night before the wedding.

Though she and Alexander, her now-estranged husband, had made it through four years of marriage, somewhere along the way, the cold had set in. Cold wasn't uncommon in St. Cloud, Minnesota, but this kind of chill could kill a relationship. That was bound to happen when one's husband chose to live an ocean away.

But it wasn't just a torn, almost-certainly-doomed marriage keeping her frozen in place. And it wasn't as though by standing still she could hide herself from the heartache and grief.

She worked to move her fingers, then opened and closed her fists. A slow, even breath whistled out in a steady stream. "This is it. The last tether to my old life." Well, almost. Pesky paperwork to deal with yet.

The smooth sound of Ella Fitzgerald and Louis Armstrong's "Dream a Little Dream of Me" sprang from her pocket. She dug her cell phone—the most modern thing about her—from the pocket of her A-line skirt. Had to be the Realtor.

She fumbled but caught the phone. "Hello?" It came as a half growl.

"You all right, Ellie?" Her soon-to-be ex-husband's English accent could still gut punch and send a flutter through her chest at the same time. "You sound a bit knackered."

"Call me Ellora." She caught her reflection in the window. Strawberry blond strands poked out from her low chignon, another nod to her love of all things historical and vintage. Smoothing a hand over it as if he might see her through the phone, she cleared her throat. "And yes, I'm fine. I was just expecting the Realtor."

Exhaustion pulled at her muscles, but she wouldn't admit it to him.

"You used to like me calling you Ellie." His words were low and mumbled.

She wanted to retort that "Ellie" was a nickname reserved for her grandmother and within her marriage. Both had gone missing. She crossed an arm over her chest. "I'm over at the house."

"Ah, yes. Everything shipshape for the sale then?"

No thanks to you. "It's a go. Buyers are firm and excited. I don't think we need to worry about them backing out." She pressed the little divot in her chin. "You're going to sign those papers, right?"

A rough *scritch-scratch* like fingers across his angled jaw. "I'm ready to sign the house-closing papers electronically. I've set a reminder and approved it with the Realtor. You do realize it will be the middle of the night here when we do the signing?" Some of the amused swagger—which once attracted her but later snagged on her last nerve—leaked into his voice.

"I forget about the time." Her feet finally unstuck. They carried her across the room and then back to the stone-and-timber fireplace. "Actually I was talking about the other papers. You know, the big *D*-word?" A stilted chuckle escaped that she would shove back down her throat if she could.

Nerves always made her awkward. Well, more than usual.

She rushed ahead before he could argue. "The divorce papers have been on your desk for three months, Alex. It's time." Oops. She had reverted to his nickname.

A gust of a sigh was his only response.

Her teeth clenched. He'd taken a job in Alnwick, England—pronounced like *ANN-ick*, she'd learned years ago on her own trip to the quaint little town—as resident coordinator of the University of St. Cloud study-abroad program based at Alnwick Castle. The university, for which both she and Alex worked, had hosted the program for many years with permanent faculty who lived and worked at the castle. He'd accepted a long-term position and left...sans wife. With no plans that she knew of to reunite with said wife.

She gripped her hip and paced away again, this time tripping over the rug. Brushing a hand over her skirt, she straightened. "Look, I know neither of us wants to talk about it, but you've been living in Alnwick for almost seven months now. You're clearly not coming back, and we're days away from selling the house we own together. What are you waiting for?"

"That's a brilliant question really, but I didn't call to chat about house papers or any other papers. I..." His voice, rough at the edges, held an emotion she couldn't place. Anticipation? Trepidation? Maybe both. "I want to ask you something. More like tell you something. I need your help."

Oh, this was rich. Needed her help? "With what?"

"One of our medieval history professors who was set to teach this summer can't due to a family emergency, and you're the only person I know who could step into this role even without a syllabus, so would you come, as we are... desperate?"

He'd spouted it all in one breath. Silence rang out over the thousands of miles between them. The reluctance in his voice stung.

Why her? And why did it seem like something else lurked between these words? "I don't know what to say." On the contrary, she had a million things she'd like to say starting with, *I'm still furious with you! Why would I want to be anywhere near you? And why would I ever do a favor for you?*

She clutched the back of her head and instead said, "I don't know. A person can't just pick up and leave everything—" she left out *and everyone* "—to move halfway across the globe. Life doesn't work like that." He had to have caught her deeper meaning. "Besides, I have my position here to consider."

"I understand. I do."

From his thick, gruff tone, she'd hit her mark with her words.

"This is all terribly awkward. But there's another reason I think you should come."

His tone made the hairs on the back of her neck stand on end.

"It's about Grandma June," he said. "I found a letter in the extra office she used here at the castle. It—"

"What? Where?" Of their own accord, her legs marched her forward.

"I was in her office to see if it needed to be cleaned out, but found I couldn't bring myself to remove anything, and there was this creaking like loose floorboards underneath the rug beside her desk. I lifted the rug and sure enough, a section of flooring could be removed and under the boards was an open space—"

Ellora couldn't help a dry laugh. "She always said that rugs were for more than keeping your feet warm. Things could be swept under them, but they'd come to light eventually. And she'd mentioned how there was a persistent squeak in the floorboards under her desk like no matter how big a rug she placed there it couldn't hide the secrets trapped underneath. I thought Grandma June was just being Grandma June, but I guess it was her secrets that couldn't remain hidden there forever."

"Subtle and literal, I suppose." His tone turned wry. "Anyway, that's where I found a letter from Grandma June. It was for you, Ellie. She wanted you to come to Alnwick."

She made a quick loop around the empty living room,

panting, forehead slick with cold sweat. This time she didn't correct the use of her nickname.

She raised a hand in the air. "I know she did. And there's nothing I can do to change the fact that I didn't go. I didn't help her when I should've. At the time, I was fed up talking about this thing." Her words frothed with the frustrations built up over the last ten months since Grandma June's disappearance, but beneath them percolated the guilt and regret shadowing her every step. All of the things she couldn't take back, and the things she couldn't do instead. "But you're the one who told me I needed to put her research away. To stop hoping for something that was lost long ago."

At the time, she'd been keenly aware he meant their marriage and any hope of finding Grandma June alive as much as finding the fabled long-lost medieval manuscript, her grandmother's obsession.

Her grandmother had traveled all over the north of England attempting to locate what she claimed was the lost illuminated manuscript created in the same birthplace as the famed Lindisfarne Gospels. But she'd gone missing in the process. Eleven months had now passed since she'd heard from Grandma June and ten since she'd been officially declared a missing person. Her grandmother had seemed to fall off the edge of a map. The rumored manuscript her grandmother had been chasing when she disappeared had supposedly been handwritten and "illuminated," or painted with brilliant colors, detailed with precious metals like gold and silver, the medieval style used to illustrate books of the Bible as well as other important writings of the day.

This particular volume, if more than a rumor, would be an exceptional find, according to her grandmother, because the pages had supposedly been colored with costly crushed brilliant blue lapis lazuli stone. And her grandmother believed that the bound manuscript contained hidden messages. Legends said the secret writings led to an even higher valued artifact. Other stories said the writings within the manuscript were a way for those on the run from Viking raiders to communicate with one another. Variations of the story abounded. But Grandma June had looked for so long, chasing down one lead after another, that it was hard to know if any were true.

Alex blew out a breath that rasped in her ear. "I recognize how ironic this is. I did tell you it would all come to naught because I didn't want you consumed over it like Grandma June. I didn't want to—" He stopped himself. "This is different. I know we were both concerned that she had become too fixated on this manuscript and maybe even lost a sense of reality, but her letter seems urgent and focused."

Something in his voice immobilized her midstride. "Read it to me. Please."

He cleared his throat and began,

"My dearest Ellie, I work hard at what I love and in this search to leave you a legacy of believing in impossible things. To remind you there is much we don't see that lies deeper. To show you the world isn't always fair and it doesn't always remember what really happened. It tends to bury what it doesn't want to see. In our own lives and in our love of history, we can be truth-tellers.

"That's what I'm attempting to do with this *Lost Manuscript of Lindisfarne*. I know you don't believe me. No one does yet. But you will. I've found mentions of it, echoing throughout history. A gong I can't ignore. And it feels all the more important to find these labored-over pages, which I'm now convinced were created by a woman's hand, and ensure their place in the halls of history—"

Alex broke off reading a moment, and there was a crinkle of paper. "I wanted to ask you, how did she know a woman was the author?"

"You mean scribe or illuminator?" She couldn't stop her inner professor and historian. Shrugging, she said, "Grandma June called me several times to tell me about some of her findings—not everything, just snippets here and there. She'd located writings from a monk who lived at Lindisfarne Priory before the holy men of Lindisfarne abandoned it—"

"Right, they left in 875 AD, because of the Viking raids."

Now he'd gone professor on her. He'd always been more of the Viking history buff, while the Middle Ages time period fascinated her.

She rubbed her temples, impatience needling to the surface. "Yes, and in a letter from Lindisfarne Priory to another monastery, a monk wrote that they had a book in progress rivaling the famed Lindisfarne Gospels in beauty and craftsmanship. The monk said the manuscript was not finished, but used the female Latin pronoun, saying 'she' would have it finished soon."

"'She'?"

"Mmm-hmm. And Grandma June was trying to prove not only the existence of another book that came out of Lindisfarne, this *Lost Manuscript of Lindisfarne*, but that it was written by a woman." She straightened. "Okay, what else did she say in the letter?"

There was a pause, then, "'What I'm doing isn't about accolades or making it into historical journals. It's about bringing light to the hidden places of the past to learn from them and make a better future. I've been underestimated, sneered at because I'm a woman, especially in my early years in this profession. This woman scribe had something to say with this manuscript and it's only fair, really the only decent thing I can do, to give her the voice she deserved 1,200 years ago.

"'I will do all I can to reach the finish line of this search. I'm tracking some promising new leads, which I'm keeping close to the chest, and I'm hopeful that the end is in sight.'" Ellora couldn't help her sigh. She'd heard that before. "'I know what you're thinking, but this is different. I can feel it.

"But I worry more and more each day that someone else is vying for the same goal though with different intentions. I know you may pass that off as an old woman's paranoia, but I've received several threats. And at every turn, I can't help but feel someone is either after me or the manuscript or both. Please, I'm asking you, not only as your grandmother but as a fellow historian—don't let this precious illuminated text fall into nefarious hands and be lost for good. If, for any reason, I'm not able to continue this search, come to the north of England where it all started and take up this mantle in my stead.

"Do what I taught you, my Ellie. Follow this trail I've laid out for you. Follow that wind in your veins. I'm sorry I'll often need to be cryptic. I don't know who might be watching. Regardless, I have every confidence you can find this manuscript. Pursue it with audacious faith and vigor, my dear girl.

"'And ye shall know the truth, and the truth shall make you free.' John 8:32. With all my love, Grandma June."

He paused, letting her soak in the words; then she heard the *shoosh* of paper again. "Inside the envelope was a key. I think this is the first clue she left for you."

Ellora bit her thumbnail, wishing for a place in this empty house to sit. "A key to what?"

"I'm not sure. I've never seen it before." There was movement as though he'd taken to pacing too. "Maybe if we can track down this lost manuscript or at least follow this first clue and the trail Grandma June said she left for you, we'll figure out why she disappeared. Will you come?"

She clamped her teeth together and swallowed a sob. Frustration and agony, in tandem, boiled to the surface. "Don't you think that's what I've wanted all along? I went to Alnwick, remember?" Her fingernails bit into her palms. Those weeks spent looking and working with local police while she and Alex crumbled to pieces rushed back to her. "It all ended with more questions than answers. I—I don't know if I can do it again, Alex. To look. To hope. All to be heartbroken when we hit another wall."

Or worse was her fear, not that they'd never find an answer, but that they would. A confirmation of her grandmother's death. While the not knowing drove her to endless sleepless nights, in a way it was its own sort of comfort. For now, she could keep her tenuous hold on hope that her grandmother was still alive somewhere.

"Ellora, if anyone can follow the clues to find out what happened to Grandma June, it's you. You know her best, you know how her mind works *and* you're the only one who has the early British history expertise—and that's saying something as a Brit and a bit of a history buff myself, if I do say so. No one knows this better than you do."

The pride he'd probably had to swallow would likely choke a whole herd of elephants. And while she could appreciate that, too many obstacles remained. Not the least of which was her fear and unwieldy grief, ready to freeze her in place for all of eternity if she made the wrong move.

"I can't do this. I'm sorry. I don't know if I want to solve this. What if—" She couldn't voice the potential gravest news she feared—that her grandmother was truly gone forever.

Alex's sigh crackled the silence. "I know if we find out the worst it will be difficult, but it might be what you need to gain closure and move forward."

He'd always been able to read her, know what she wasn't saying. Apparently, he still could, even through a phone and an ocean apart. Despite her sending the divorce papers to him, the "move forward" and his implied "without him" jabbed at her chest.

"At least think about it. All right?"

No was the correct answer, wasn't it? She couldn't go. It was absurd. But a little voice asked, *What if...?*

Her phone beeped to indicate another call. "It's the Realtor. Sorry. I have to go."

"Wait, will you—"

Her sigh was so heavy it likely could've been measured on the bathroom scale. "I'll think about it."

"I'm not sure this helps at all, but I hired Lanae. She'll be coming over for the study-abroad trip, so she—"

"What?" Lanae was her best friend in the whole world. Why didn't she know about this?

She circled the living room again, then plodded through the bedroom she and Alex had once shared. She pushed and shoved at the sudden onslaught of betrayal clamoring for validation.

"I, well—" his voice less sure now "—I hired her as a student adviser. Earlier today. She was in a pool of applicants to the international studies program."

"I knew she was applying for student adviser jobs. I guess I just didn't realize she'd applied to work abroad." The words were muttered, for herself.

"If it makes you feel any better, I don't think she intended to get a call from international studies, and less so from me. But she was the most qualified. Anyway, I didn't mean to spoil her telling you. I just thought with her here, perhaps making the trip wouldn't sound so egregious to you."

A nervous chuckle then a swallow.

"Try not to faff about," he added. "Summer term starts in two weeks."

Her spine bristled at this, but he followed it up with "Ring you later?"

"Sure," she answered before hanging up with him to switch over to the Realtor.

The conversation with the real estate agent brought her back to the present. Afterward, she kicked off her shoes and tackled the last of her to-do list before the house sold. She pulled on rubber gloves and her gingham 1950s apron and grabbed the bucket she'd brought from her month-to-month studio apartment near the university. It had been too difficult to continue living in this house once Alexander left. With haste, she'd moved into the cheap rental above an antique store and put the house on the market.

They'd have to talk about those "other" papers soon. Truth be told, she didn't relish dealing with it either.

She started scrubbing windows in slow, methodical circles. As she cleaned the glass to a crystal shine, it became clearer that traveling to England to search for answers that may be hard to take—answers that may not even be there—was a ridiculous idea. She needed to let go, not go back. Right? As hard as it was.

These goodbyes. First, the one she'd been cheated out of when her parents chose their addiction over their little girl, then the one she couldn't give her Grandma June—the woman who'd welcomed that little girl into her home and life. But was it goodbye for good to Grandma June?

Before she went missing, her grandmother had traveled to England on yet another expedition to find the lost manuscript and was there for several months. Grandma June wasn't always the best at staying in touch, especially when she was nose to the trail and close to a discovery, but she did usually check in with Ellora every few days.

Ellora's last conversation with Grandma June was different than the others. Less excitement and more anxiety had crept into her grandmother's voice as she'd shared her fear that someone might be after the lost manuscript and maybe even her. Her tone had matched that of the letter Alex had found. But Grandma June had been right—she was now sad to say—she'd written it off as paranoia.

Not to mention that Ellora was going through something traumatic in her own life at the time and no matter how hard she'd tried to be present for her grandmother, her heart's anguish had been too deafening and her mind had been somewhere else entirely.

But as several days turned into several weeks without hearing from Grandma June, Ellora calling and calling her with no answer, a heavy stone of dread had sunk to the bottom of Ellora's stomach. Her grandmother had gone missing without a trace. The police were still baffled, and with no body found, perhaps there was still hope but it dwindled with each day that passed.

Ellora blew out a long breath, her lungs and heart deflated. And now the goodbye to Alexander, the man she once thought she'd spend the rest of her life with.

Goodbyes left her drained. Weary beyond measure, far beyond her thirty-one years. Now what? *Should* she go back to England and finish what her grandmother started?

A snarl scraped past her throat. She took out her frustration on the "dust of disuse" until an ache crawled up her arms.

She still had her career at the university, but even there she faced reminders every day of Grandma June and Alexander, where they all three used to work together. The university held chances for advancement. But was it where she wanted to be?

Maybe she was hanging on to the roots of a life that was already felled and tossed to the flames. She was left with the stump where once had been a full and glorious tree, ready to add branches. To continue the story of their family.

But those would-be branches had splintered and broken apart when she'd lost her baby to miscarriage a year ago, two months before her grandmother had gone missing. In the store robbery that precipitated the miscarriage, she'd lost more than a baby. She'd lost her whole life and everything she thought secure and immovable. Alex had come out a hero, saving a woman in the grocery aisle of the department store. He had been all over the news. She'd been alone in her overflowing grief, unable to share what she'd lost, what they'd lost, with Alex or Grandma June before she went missing.

He didn't even know she'd been pregnant. Not that he'd ever wanted to be a father. He'd made that clear over the years. After the robbery and her miscarriage, a hollowness had taken up residence in their home, even before all of the furniture was gone. They'd shut each other out. And between all of that and later the unanswered questions about Grandma June's disappearance, the gulf between them grew until he'd packed and left.

A screech of tires and a blur of green out the window announced the arrival of her friend Lanae Reyes and snapped Ellora out of her should-have-beens. She'd teased Lanae that a drop-top hybrid Jeep wasn't practical for the middle of Minnesota, a place fortunate if it saw a couple of months of true summer a year. Lanae had replied, "You can take the girl out of California, but you can't take California out of the girl."

Lanae burst through the front door, the panes rattling. "Driving in this town is awful. It's a wonder I'm alive, I tell you." A face-framing lock from her just-the-right-amount-of-messy braids floated over her nose. She brushed it away with dirt-smudged fingers. Likely a little something leftover from the community garden she'd started in her neighborhood.

"Haven't you driven on a fourteen-lane freeway in California? And really, Nae, you've lived in Minnesota more than half your life now."

"Yes, but my life began in California, and Californians know how to drive."

Ellora chuckled. "I'm sure I could outdrive them on ice."

"Touché." She tossed an ombré honey-hued braid over her shoulder, teeth shining in the gloom of the empty house. "So ask me," she said, her smile expectant.

"Ask you what?" Ellora finished the last corner of the window she'd been working on and slid the rubber gloves from her hands.

"Ask what happened to me today." Lanae trailed after her as Ellora emptied the bucket into the kitchen sink. "You'll never guess, but that doesn't mean you shouldn't try."

As she leaned over the granite counter across from Ellora, Lanae's grin broadened.

Ellora cocked her head at her friend, heart already squeezing at what was coming. "I think I have a guess."

Her friend uncrossed her arms, but her expression flipped like a switch—dimming. "I don't think you do, El, and I'm not sure you'll entirely love this, but I hope you can be happy for me anyway."

For once, her confident, free-spirited friend seemed unsure. Ellora reached out and gave her arm a light squeeze.

"Of course. When something good happens for you, I share your joy. You know that."

"I hope so." Lanae buried her hands in the pockets of her overalls and shifted on her feet. "I—"

"Was hired for a student adviser position? With the Alnwick study-abroad program?" She tried to slow her rapid heartbeat with a slow breath. "Yeah, I spoke with Alex right before you arrived."

Lanae winced, her white-knuckled fingers gripping the edge of the granite. "Yeah, I—I mean, it's my dream job." Her hands twisted. "I'll see to the accommodations, food, coordinate outings and field trips and any other needs of the students. What are you thinking? Are you upset?"

Her heart pulled in two different directions, happiness for her friend and not anger or betrayal exactly, but more of a sadness at possibly losing another person she cared about to that all-too-captivating northern English village. "I know how long you've been waiting for an opportunity like this." She hoped her voice conveyed only happiness.

"I didn't tell you because I didn't think I'd get the position. I really didn't. It was a whim. I saw the posting on the staff website for advisers needed on the international study programs. And with the school year ending, I thought this would be the right time to give it a shot. I also didn't know—"

"How I'd react?" Ellora rounded the kitchen island so they stood on the same side, face-to-face.

Lanae's brown eyes creased at the edges. "I'm sorry. Maybe I was being selfish to apply. Plus, with the friend code—Alex being the one who left and everything..." She palmed her forehead then let her hand slide down her face. "I can tell him this won't work out."

"You'll do no such thing." Ellora managed a smile. "I

don't ever want to be the person standing in the way of your dreams." Tears welled against Ellora's lower lashes. She blinked them back. "I'm happy for you."

She meant it and prayed she'd mean it even more, but she hated the way her insides twisted and roiled. Not because of her friend's dreams coming true, but because of her own silenced dreams pleading for freedom. Traveling, teaching and making history come alive for others right at its source. That was an old, abandoned dream. Maybe she needed something weighted in reality. Steady. Like the head of the history department. There were rumors the current head of the department would retire and the position might become available.

But the conversation with Alex tugged at her heart's sleeve. Perhaps that lifeless dream could be dusted off, resurrected, and was just on the other side of accepting his offer and Grandma June's plea.

"You're happy? Really?" Relief flooded Lanae's face, lighting it with a wide grin.

"Really." She embraced her friend, pouring out every ounce of her goodwill, and swallowed before continuing, "I have some news for you too. But I haven't made up my mind yet, so no freaking out."

"What is it?" Lanae pulled back.

Ellora drew in a steadying breath. "Alex asked me to come on the study-abroad trip—"

Lanae clamped her mouth shut but a squeal escaped

"They need an extra history prof, but he also found something in Grandma June's office at the castle. A letter from Grandma June and a key. She said she wanted me to come and follow a 'trail' she left for me to find that lost manuscript she was looking for. Maybe if I follow it, we can finally figure out what happened to Grandma June." She filled Lanae in on her discussion with Alex.

Lanae dipped her chin, her expression somber now. "You have been in this frozen place of in-between since your grandma went missing, Alex left and after...you know." They didn't really talk about the baby much. It was too hard.

Reaching forward, Lanae squeezed Ellora's forearm. "I won't pressure you. I'll just say, maybe this could be good for you. Help you get 'unstuck,' you know?" Her shoulder lifted. "Besides, us traveling and working with students was always the dream, right? I can't deny that I would be ecstatic to have my bestie beside me on this adventure."

A swell of purpose made Ellora smile, but she had to be logical. She couldn't answer quite yet. "I don't know. Saying yes might be like opening a can of worms. No, more like a barrel of snakes. I definitely have more thinking to do—"

"You mean more pacing and pros-and-cons lists to make?" Lanae's smile was impish.

Ellora propped a hand on her hip. "Hey, those are very useful tools in making decisions, I'll have you know. Anyway, what do you say to celebrating *your* new job with too much Italian food and—"

"A trip to the mall for a little retail shindig? I saw they have this one hundred percent recycled fabric, sustainable and responsibly sourced clothing store I've been dying to check out, so we could—" Lanae's smile died on her lips.

It was absurd really. Ellora had yet to enter the shopping center or be near the store where *it* happened. The place was a death trap of negative memories and flashbacks to one of the worst days of her life and the beginning of the end of her marriage.

"Ellora?" Lanae's voice broke into her thoughts, calling

as though she'd been saying Ellora's name for a while. "Are you okay? That was stupid. I'm sorry. I wasn't thinking."

"No, that's all right. I'm fine." She turned away to gather her things and pull on her shoes. Before facing Lanae again, she swiped at the tear sliding down her cheek.

Lanae edged closer, her movements slow. "They have a remembrance service at Lake George for the victims of the shooting next week on May 21. I'll go with you if you want." As usual, Lanae's gaze seemed to cut right through any veil over what she truly felt or thought. "Maybe if you talked about it, El—"

"No." She hadn't meant to sound so harsh. "I mean, that's okay. Thanks, though." To reassure her friend, Ellora put on a smile. "Come on, let's go get that Italian food."

Her stomach rumbled in response and the air lightened. They both laughed.

One last glance at her no-longer home, and she rolled up the rug under her arm.

Loss was cold indeed.

Hours later, Ellora jiggled the door handle to her apartment and groaned. "I haven't been this stuffed since I sneaked a tray of Grandma June's homemade cinnamon rolls up to my room as a kid and ate the whole thing." Ellora patted her distended belly, her A-line skirt doing everything it could to contain it.

"Grandma June made the best rolls. I miss them. And her." Lanae sighed and followed Ellora into her second-floor apartment.

"She is the best cook. I guess I didn't inherit that. I could mess up a piece of toast."

Lanae smirked. "And you have. Multiple times. Remember in college when you set fire to the curtains with an overdone bagel?"

Ellora glared over her shoulder.

Lanae whirled into the room, flicking on the lights. A chandelier lit the eclectic, mostly open space. Many pieces she'd bought from the antique store on the lower level.

A mention of her grandmother, even if she'd been the one to bring it up, still sent a shock wave of pain through her chest. How had it been ten months? And at what point would she have to admit her grandmother must be dead? Was there a sell-by date on hope? Was there an expiration on searching for the truth? In her mind, no.

But after months of a police investigation with no trail to follow, even she had to admit an incremental fade in her once-robust belief that Grandma June would again burst through her door or call her up late at night to jabber about her latest historical discovery. And as the weeks turned into months, she'd tried to let go. She *had*. But it felt like a betrayal. Still did. And now, with this letter and key, was there once again reason to keep hope alive?

She pushed her toes to slide, then to shuffle forward. Guilt, like a snail's slime, dragged along behind her.

Lanae poked her head around the kitchen cupboards. "Tea?"

Ellora managed a nod.

"We might as well get used to the British national drink of choice, right?" Lanae beamed before ducking around the little corner alcove kitchen.

"I haven't decided to accept Alex's invitation to teach yet, Nae," she called, but Lanae was humming and clinking dishes.

She didn't want to fall down a rabbit hole of dead ends and wrong turns, never to escape. Like Grandma June.

Her grandmother's many field notebooks and research scribblings now sat on Ellora's bookcase that covered one wall of her apartment. She brushed her fingertips against their leather- and spiral-bound spines.

"Your grandmother's journals." Lanae's voice and sudden presence made Ellora jump.

Lanae handed her one of her favorites of her collected antique teacups, with lily of the valley painted on its delicate sides, and nodded to the shelves. "She was—*is* a born teacher, that one, isn't she? But an explorer first."

Ellora nodded and sipped the tea, a burst of berry and hints of floral from her new favorite huckleberry blend. "She taught me to love history. To find secrets behind what's already known." The words turned her voice wistful. "To dig deeper and never settle for what's on the surface. But—" her throat constricted "—her passion for historical truth is probably what…"

Lanae laid a hand on her shoulder. Lanae's hand slipped from her shoulder as Ellora lifted her arm.

"Maybe if I had gone with her, I could've saved her from whatever happened to her. Maybe she'd still be here…"

Lanae swallowed her mouthful of tea. "We don't know that. You can't keep doing this to yourself. Whatever happened to Grandma June isn't your fault."

Ellora couldn't bring herself to agree.

With a jut of her chin, Lanae indicated the journals. "I just wish Grandma June had said or written in one of her journals where she was headed while researching or where she thought the lost manuscript might be."

"Me too." Ellora backed up to the arm of the couch and took another warm sip of tea. "We found some notes on her speculations. A couple of places she thought the manuscript might be hidden, but turned out to be wrong. Some scratched-out ideas she'd already tried. But none of it led to the actual manuscript or Grandma June. The police looked. The surrounding communities looked. I looked. Dead ends, all of it."

The rumors of another manuscript that didn't accompany the Lindisfarne Gospels to Chester-le-Street first, then Durham and on to their current resting place, the British Library in London, had fascinated her grandmother and Ellora too at one time. The regret of not accompanying her grandmother to England filled Ellora with a thousand winged creatures, beating and clawing against the inside of her stomach.

Her grandmother, the baby she'd only known about for two weeks, her dilapidated marriage—the losses seemed to pile up like stacks of unopened bills. She was afraid to "open" them, to look too closely. They threatened to bury her in a debt of her errors and internal damages so monumental the balance could never be repaid.

Lanae sank onto an overstuffed velvet chair.

"El, I know England holds a lot of reminders, and it's complicated because Alexander is there, but I also know you love England. Your affinity for British history and research is being wasted here. And just because you didn't find the answers about Grandma June there before, doesn't mean you won't this time. Especially if the letter is true and she left clues for you to follow. And, you know, your favorite friend will be there to help." Lanae's grin was as wide as the English Channel.

"It's just hard to think of opening up this wound again. What if this clue Alex found leads to another and another and then nothing ever comes of it?"

"Was the wound ever really closed?" Lanae tipped a brow but her half smile was warm.

Ellora blinked. "Touché." As she threw a hand in the air,

a growl made its way out of her throat. "And England *was* my dream, Nae, but I've got to think about how I'm going to support myself now. What I need to do for my future if Alex isn't in it. I've heard some positions will be opening at the university, maybe even head of the history department. That could be my new dream and a fresh start."

Even though the words came from her own mouth, they held an off note. Lanae was right. She loved England and had always imagined she and Alex would someday move there or at least spend part of the year there.

Alex had been her first introduction to Alnwick when they were both students. Later, with Ellora raving about Alnwick as well as the potential for historical research, she dragged her grandmother back for Christmas break. For Ellora, there had been more than just the beauty of Northumberland calling to her. It was a certain handsome Englishman with a dashing one-dimpled grin and eyes the color of a bright, sun-soaked green sea. The North Sea shallows on a calm summer's day. That trip became the start of Grandma June's quest to find the rumored lapis lazuli illuminated manuscript.

Ellora gulped back the last dregs of now-cool tea and set the cup on the bookshelf.

Lanae pulled her legs up on the chair. "You've wanted to live in England since we were kids. This has nothing to do with Alexander, though I still pray you two can somehow work it out. Maybe he'll come around on having children. Maybe you both can move forward after...what happened."

Ellora crossed her arms, studying the worn floorboards. "If I do come, it won't be for that."

"Fair enough," Lanae said. "But there's also Grandma June to consider. Maybe finishing her mission *will* lead to answers about what happened to her."

The girl with the wind in her veins. That's what her grandma used to call her. The lure to explore, to learn, to know had always been with her. When she'd arrived in England as a twenty-one-year-old wide-eyed dreamer, something inside of her finally clicked into place like two magnets finding their match. But then, she'd once said the same about her and Alexander.

Her friend's lips puckered. "Look, I want you to make the right choice for you. Okay? More than that, I want you to walk through the doors God opens for you, not the ones I bust down because I want my friend by my side."

"That's the big question. Is this a door God opened?"

Lanae steepled her fingers over her bent knees. "Sometimes we don't know until we're walking through it. But maybe the key Grandma June left for you is the one to open that door."

Lanae stood and touched Ellora's shoulder. "I know you go deep to process things. But I have a feeling, if you think and pray on it, you already know what the answer is."

Did she know what she should tell Alex? What if she agreed to go but being around him again proved a total disaster? What if she didn't find the manuscript her grandmother had searched for? What if she did and it led to the conclusion she most feared? Would it bring meaning to her grandmother's life, what she very well may have died for?

Lanae squeezed her in a quick hug before grabbing her purse. "I'll be praying for you too. Let me know what you decide?"

"I will. Thank you." She walked Lanae to the door and bid her good-night.

Though compact, her apartment felt big and empty when she closed the door and locked the three dead bolts behind Lanae. She washed the teacups and returned them to their hanging rack, then changed into soft pajamas. It felt so good to let her elbow-length hair loose from the bobby pins poking into her scalp. With just her bedside lamp on, she grabbed a text on early Christianity in Great Britain but then read the same sentence over and over.

She jumped up and paced, weighing her pros and cons.

Exhausted, she finally sank onto the rug from her grandmother she'd placed in front of the bookshelves.

One of Grandma June's journals, a beautiful leather-bound red volume with swirling gold leaf detail, stuck out to Ellora—almost calling to her. Inside, the date had been inscribed ten years prior.

She hadn't gone through all of her grandmother's writings for the sheer number of them. She and Alex had read through any dated the several years surrounding her serious search for the lost illumination.

The pages of this journal were filled with sketches of engravings, maps of cathedrals and abbeys, notes from texts and manuscripts her grandmother read at the Bodleian Library at Oxford, on and on. But when Ellora flipped to the last page, an invisible hand clamped around her heart.

Her own name in her grandmother's slim, slanted handwriting stared back at her.

All of this research is dedicated to my Ellora. The dreamer of dreams. The girl with the wind in her veins. There is a great big world out there, brimming with wondrous could-bes and what-ifs. Hope with wings, some might say. Go and catch them. Let God be the guide and your heart the net.

Ellora pressed her fingers to her trembling chin.

Before she'd gone missing, her grandmother had been

preparing reports to present to the Royal Historical Society in Great Britain and to the American Historical Association. But without all the evidence she needed, she'd been met with mostly scoffing and skepticism from the other historians in her circle of contacts. So, while Ellora believed her grandmother when she said it wasn't all about the historical community backing her up, she knew their disbelief hurt. Only her grandmother's good friend Thomas Bixby, a fellow history enthusiast and historical association member in England, sided with her theories.

Ellora jumped to her feet, the journal clutched to her chest. Maybe Lanae had been right. She *did* know the answer, and it wasn't for herself.

With the truth burning in her throat, she couldn't move fast enough.

She dialed Alex.

He grumbled a just-awakened "You checking up on me?" It was six in the morning there, and apparently he'd forgotten he said he'd call *her*.

She rushed ahead before she could talk herself out of it. "Okay, I'll come. I want to figure out what happened to Grandma June."

"Brilliant." His voice was suddenly alert. "We'll set up permanent housing, and I was thinking—"

She bristled. "I said I'd come to get answers about Grandma June and I *will* teach this summer. But this isn't permanent. I'll stay until the end of the summer session. That's it."

He grunted. "Not trying to ruffle you. I just meant I'll secure somewhere for you to stay whilst you're here."

It was done. *For better or worse. Humph.* If she and Alex had listened to those words in their vows, things would be much different right now. Like no ocean between them, for one thing.

They said goodbye.

She bobbed her head at the empty room, trying not to be the person who looked a gift horse in the mouth. Technically, this was her dream—teaching in England, going to the birthplace of her most favorite eras and locations in history, bringing it all to life for her students, solving a historical puzzle. Everything she'd ever dreamed of or prayed for. Besides, the closer she came to finding this manuscript, the closer she may get to discovering what happened to Grandma June. And yet...

This isn't exactly what I had in mind, God.

In her dreams, there had been no impassable rift between her and Alex, a missing grandmother, uncertainty about her future and where she belonged.

She huffed a breath, then apologized to God for taking that old gift horse to the dentist.

As she lay awake, a million tasks already formed in her mind. She'd only have two weeks to move into storage the belongings she couldn't take with her. But even the arduous tasks sent a *whoosh* of wind through her veins for the first time in a long time. The air sparked with the flap of unfurling possibilities and the tang of hope.

Chapter Two

Sheep dotted the rolling hills of the Northumberland countryside, mirroring the puffs of clouds set against deep azure skies above. Ellora couldn't deny that everything about this, even the vehicles driving on the other side of the road, felt like coming home. But that didn't stop the furious thrumming of her heart as they neared Alnwick.

She tried to delve into her *History of Illuminated Manuscripts* textbook for the millionth time. But none of the words soaked into her brain. This was the last leg in an exhausting journey over the North Atlantic. She now sat beside a dozing Lanae on a bus filled with students and other university staff.

Her body was still six hours behind, on Minnesota time. She should be sleeping too. But it was as if her body knew she would soon face Alex again after months of separation. Her palms slicked with sweat and her stomach somersaulted with the next bump in the road.

Two weeks had passed since she'd told Alexander yes.

She'd had to notify the university. She hadn't signed another contract and her last fixed-term contract had just expired. They weren't thrilled. She'd usually taught several summer session classes. But they couldn't argue since she was still teaching for the university, just not on campus.

"You checking off that list in your brain?" Ellora jolted at Lanae's groggy voice.

"Just trying to remember if I did everything I was supposed to. I stored my furniture and belongings—" she counted on her fingers "—I forwarded my mail, signed the house papers..."

"Are you nervous to see Alexander?"

"A little. I'm worried about the mix of emotions I'll have. Will I have that old reflex to kiss him or will I want to smack him?"

"Or both?" Lanae reached over and squeezed her hand. "I'm really proud of you for coming anyway. Even if this search leads to another dead end. Even if you and Alexander don't get back together—"

"You know that's not why I'm here."

"At least you'll have closure on both fronts, right? One way or the other." Lanae's warm golden-brown eyes studied her, concern creased at the edges.

"Did you say Alexander?" Maddie, one of the students Lanae had introduced, leaned closer from her seat across the aisle from Ellora and Lanae.

Her friend Willa peeked over Maddie's head. "Are you talking about Professor Lockwood?"

Both girls stared, mouths hanging slack.

Lanae found her voice first. "Yes, Alexander Lockwood, the resident coordinator of the Alnwick program."

Willa held a hand over her heart. Her long dark braids swung forward almost to her waist. "We call him the Super

Professor because he saved that woman. Plus, I heard he's like a master horseman, he fences and plays piano. One of my friends went on the trip last semester and told us about him."

Maddie nodded. "He's like the hero from one of those British movies."

"Here we go again." Ellora's words scraped over a constricted throat.

Yes, he had saved someone's life, and she wouldn't undo that for the world. But it was what happened afterward that she couldn't get past.

They'd split up in the store that fateful day. He'd gone to the food section to pick up something for dinner. She'd said she needed something at the pharmacy. He didn't know she'd gone to find a pregnancy test. The test two weeks earlier said positive, though she'd known deep down days before that. But she'd needed confirmation that night. If it weren't true, she wouldn't have to find a way to inform her no-children-ever husband that, like it or not, he was going to be a dad. And somehow, she'd have to tamp her excitement over that same news for the entire pregnancy and beyond if it *were* true.

She'd paid for the test at the pharmacy counter.

Ellora relived the next hours as she had almost every day since then. Alex was in line at the grocery checkout when two gunmen, one at the front registers and one at the pharmacy, chose that moment to rain terror on the place. Seeking drug money and narcotics from the pharmacy, later reports would say. Drugs already in their systems likely played a part in the violence of their crime, firing indiscriminately and killing several people, and stomping on Ellora for trying to use her phone. Chaos kept them from each other for hours. Because she was bleeding she'd been rushed to the hospital by ambulance. Alex was nowhere to be found. Only later did she learn he'd been taken there for minor injuries.

When she did find him at the hospital, after the doctor confirmed she'd lost the baby, Alex stood in a sea of reporters competing for interviews with him. He was the local hero who'd saved a woman's life. Alex had pulled a woman out of a bullet's path but hadn't noticed the young man behind him. The bullet had found a mark, in the young man's chest.

In front of the crowd, he had been his usual charming self. But at home, it was as if someone had replaced her husband with a removed, emotionless robot. He wouldn't talk to her about what had happened—the college kid who had died, the woman he'd saved—and had never seemed to notice how much pain she was going through. She hadn't found the strength to tell him about their loss. She couldn't face his relief or worse, his apathy. From his viewpoint, she bore insignificant bruises that were already fading. He had no idea what she bore internally—the emptiness, the soul-deep ache and the remnants of terror. She justified her silence. And he left for his Alnwick job several months later.

The memories sent a tremor through her. The college girls stared at her, waiting for more juicy details on their "hero professor."

Lanae's back straightened. "Girls, I won't put up with any inappropriate talk about our respected coordinator this summer." She sounded every bit the student adviser.

Both Willa and Maddie nodded.

"Of course not." Maddie's waves bobbed with her head.

Willa beamed. "But making a wish list of qualities for my future husband never hurt anyone."

Obviously, the girls hadn't overheard *everything* she'd said to Lanae.

Maddie chewed on her lip a second, staring at Ellora. "What did you say your name was again?"

A bump in the road made Ellora bite her tongue. Salt and copper filled her mouth. She swallowed, her stomach twisting.

She needed Alex to sign those papers and change back to her maiden name.

But before Ellora had to answer, the bus crossed the 1773-built Lion Bridge, the main entrance into Alnwick from the north, distracting everyone for the time being.

The castle came into view atop the hill to their left. The turreted towers fortified by stone walls sat like a crown upon a royal head. Its reflection, mirrored in the calm waters of the River Aln below. The statue of a lion, the symbol of the Percy family, who owned Alnwick Castle and much of Northumberland, stood sentinel over the bridge.

They drove the incline of The Peth and the bus stopped in the small parking lot at the front entrance to the castle.

There he was. Alexander. Alex. Tall, with dark, tousled hair that curled at the temples, reminding Ellora of those British heroes of literature and film, indeed. Perhaps a more outgoing, affable version of Mr. Darcy himself. A broad grin brought out the otherwise hidden singular dimple on the right side.

Lanae squeezed Ellora's shoulder as she stood to retrieve her jacket and backpack.

"Well, here we go." Ellora hated how her voice shook, as did her hands. The weight of jet lag landed heavy on her shoulders, along with something else. A mix of trepidation and anticipation cycloned together in the pit of her stomach. She swayed but pushed her feet forward.

"Let's try not to go with either the kiss or the smack. You

know, in front of the students." Lanae's voice was close behind her.

At least Ellora managed to paste on a smile as she descended the bus steps and finally stood in front of Alexander.

He kept his calm, except for a slight tightening in his jaw. "Welcome, everyone, to Alnwick Castle. I'm chuffed you've made it." His arms spread wide in his waistcoat. He'd always had a vintage flair to his wardrobe too.

A slideshow—like the media still preferred by the older generation profs—played before her eyelids. Her dreams shattered in the wake of his betrayal and abandonment. On its heels was the joy of their wedding day, walking into their first home together. Dancing in the kitchen, laughing over shared meals with her grandmother, the way his excitement matched hers when it came to history. Their first kiss. Their last kiss, which, looking back, had felt like goodbye before she knew it was.

A lifetime of ups and downs replayed in a matter of seconds.

Alex gave one loud clap. "We have our student adviser, Ms. Lanae Reyes. She'll be taking great care of you all and planning our field trips this session."

For the first time since she stepped off the bus, his gaze landed and stayed on Ellora. His expressions were often impossible to read. What was he thinking now? "And this is Professor Ellora Lockwood."

At this there was a trickle of whispers from Maddie and Willa: "*Lockwood?* Do you think they're related?" and "Probably his sister or cousin, right?"

Lanae shushed them and Alex kept talking as though he hadn't heard them. "Professor Lockwood is the brilliant historian who will be teaching you all about Alnwick and Northumberland's medieval roots. Take it from me, you do not want to face this woman in a challenge of historical trivia. You *will* lose."

The grin he lofted over the crowd made Maddie and Willa sigh while Ellora's hands clenched into fists. Really? This was what he had to say to her after seven months? Then again, they couldn't hash everything out right there.

Lanae took the list Alexander handed her and called out room assignments. They walked through the Barbican Gate, waving at the guard, Gus, who kept tabs on the comings and goings of the castle from the little room built right into one of the gate towers where once armed soldiers would've kept watch over the castle.

"Aw, Miss Ellora! Aren't you a sight for sore eyes." Gus stepped to the doorway of his office. "I've been asking this one—" he jabbed a thumb in Alexander's direction "—when he was going to get his beautiful bride across the pond. Glad he's finally managed it." He winked at her.

Heat crept up her neck, crawled across her cheeks. "Thank you. It's nice to be back." And she meant it.

Maddie whispered to Willa behind her hand but still loud enough for Ellora to catch it. "With the same last name, I thought she was like his fifth cousin, twice removed or something. She's his *wife*?"

Great. The pull to flag down the nearest black cab taxi and skedaddle back to the airport almost won over. Almost. If she weren't so tired and in need of the nearest bed.

They passed into the outer bailey, the walled grounds with a wide, lush green courtyard. Everyone's rolling luggage bumped along the cobbled stone path to the university living quarters. Students and staff stayed in parts of the castle once used as servants' quarters. While they were functional—with a small library/computer lab, kitchen and dining hall, classrooms, offices, hotel-like bedrooms, among other things—they weren't grand and nothing like the exquisite keep of the castle, where the Duke and his family still lived for half of the year.

Ellora lagged behind, her suitcase and shoulder bag heavier with every step. Lanae met one of the castle's resident assistants, Devon, and student aides at the ancient door to one of the university sections of the castle. When Ellora made to follow, Alexander tapped her elbow. She ignored the goose bumps that raced up her arm without her permission.

"I reserved a room near the gift shop for you, by the old stables. It's a second-floor studio flat. Never fear. They don't keep horses there anymore." His lips tilted in a crooked grin.

"I know, Alexander. I've been here before. But that's so far from everyone." She'd assumed she'd room with Lanae.

An invisible shadow fell over his face. "It's the best I could do on such short notice." From his pocket, he withdrew a paper with her room number and a key, handing them to her. "Can I help with your luggage?"

She gritted her teeth and shook her head. "No, I've got it. Thanks."

"Supper's at six. You know the way."

She started toward the second-floor guest hall above the coach house, restaurant and café, and gift shop on the ground floor of a smaller inner courtyard, formerly the stable yard.

"Ellora?"

She turned back, almost to the clock tower. "Yeah?"

He shifted on his long lean legs. "I'm glad you're here." With that, he shoved his hands into his trouser pockets, ducked his head and walked away.

Unbidden warmth flooded her chest.

The sentiment dissolved a bit as she lugged her suitcase and bag up the twisted staircase to her room. Was this *really* the only spot left?

The heavy door to her room didn't seem to appreciate the intrusion, but did give way after some pushing. What met her eyes made them well up. The usual stark accommodations had been spruced up with homey touches. A roll-up writing desk under the tall, slim lancet windows where he'd placed the letter from Grandma June beside a key. He'd even placed a beautiful floral-print antique dressing screen in the corner by the bed next to a tall, mirrored wardrobe. And the plush down comforter would come in handy as even in summer, the rooms remained cool and damp. Only one thing more would make this her home away from home for the summer—the rug from Grandma June. She dug it out of her suitcase and unrolled it onto the floor next to the bed.

In the middle of the bed lay a folded piece of paper and a small basket of assorted foods including a bottled water.

Inside the note read:

Ellora,
I wanted you to be as comfortable as possible while you're here. I hope you like the room. I'll be just down the hall if you need anything. Enjoy.
Yours,
Alex
PS Feel free to check up on me in person now.

His cheeky last line barely registered as her eyes caught on the word *yours* over and over.

But the truth was, he wasn't hers anymore. Their marriage had been severed beyond repair. She couldn't forget that with one nice gesture. And she had a job to do. Two, actually. Teach the students the joy of history and find out what happened to her grandmother. Neither of which had anything to do with Alexander or their broken marriage.

★ ★ ★

She was finally here in the flesh. The idea of Ellie just a wall away from his own flat clenched his rib cage in a vise-like grip. In a good or a bad way? Perhaps both.

Alex denied to his own reflection that he had taken extra care choosing his clothing—a button-down beneath the brown leather jacket Ellie had once said made him look like a "hunky professor."

The image of her yesterday afternoon dashed through his brain and pummeled his gut. Her hair, what he'd called rosy gold, knotted up in braids. He'd found his fingers itching to untwist it like he'd done long ago. Her round cerulean eyes staring up at him, though red-rimmed and wary, were still the most beautiful thing he'd ever seen.

Her eyes had always been an open book. When he'd read fear, worry and exhaustion, it took everything within him not to put his arms around her. Where she'd once fit so perfectly.

He'd done a right thorough job of mucking that up. He'd abandoned her, but then, she hadn't exactly been there for him either. Now he had to live with the consequences and the shambles of their marriage. Just like he'd lived so much of his life with the consequences of not being there for his brother, Beckett, years ago. Beckett's death was Alex's fault, as was that young man's who'd been shot at the store, Dylan.

After giving himself a mental shake, he grabbed the key to his room. The key to Grandma June's office wasn't where he'd left it last. Curious. He'd have to stop in his office later to find it. He locked his door before marching down the hall. Her door had opened and closed half an hour ago, so he didn't bother stopping.

The truth was, it didn't matter that seeing Ellora stirred these long-dormant feelings. They were just muscle memory of the life they'd once shared. None of the reasons he'd left had disappeared. She had never forgiven him for not being there for her during the shooting—as if he could help it. He hadn't forgiven himself either. And if he were truly honest, he wasn't best pleased with *her* reaction afterward.

Before the robbery, she'd suddenly decided she wanted to be a mom after all. That's not what he'd signed up for. They'd agreed when they married to stay child-free, travel the world and focus on their careers. The Lord knew he could never be responsible for another human being. Not ever again. Yes, he'd saved one person, but the faces of two others haunted his dreams. And yet, even though Ellie had been the one to go back on her word and the plans they'd made, *he* was the villain? She'd been the one to change her mind on the matter. Why was it his fault that he hadn't?

He raked a hand through his hair. Maybe he *was* the bad guy.

His instinct to ask God for help fizzled before the inner words formed. Could he truly ask God, the one who'd created marriage, for help with his disaster of a wedded union? The disappointment raining down—was it God's or his own?

He tipped his head and called "Cheers" to the castle staff and tour guides, many dressed in medieval period costumes, as falconers and archers. He made his way across the outer bailey to the field trip meeting spot just beyond the entrance to the inner bailey.

"Hey, mate." Oscar Machal, the stable master for the Duke's horse farm in Hulne Park near the castle, held a hand up. "You popping over for a ride later? I think Raven's been watching out for you."

"She misses me spoiling her with sugar cubes, you mean."

"That, and she told me about your stunningly clever wit."

Over the last seven months, Oscar had become a true

friend. Especially since Oscar had gone through an unwanted divorce several years ago. He knew that kind of pain, that sense of failure, and had been a sounding board as well as a voice of reason for Alex.

"I might come by. I'll see how much work I have this afternoon. After supper, then?"

"Text me. No problem either way." Oscar scratched the back of his neck. "You can bring Ellora if you like." There was a hint there.

He scuffed his boot against the stone walkway. "I'm not sure she's keen on spending any more time with me than is absolutely necessary."

"How is it—seeing her again?" Oscar buried his work-calloused hands into his jeans pockets. He had none of the pretentious airs one might assume of a stable master for a large estate. But then, Oscar said he'd lived on a farm all his life. It was his love and knowledge of horses that had landed him the job. Not family connections or a certain pedigree.

An answer stuck in Alex's throat. He lifted a shoulder. "Fine, I suppose. Or is it unbearable? Like someone slowly plucking at every nerve-ending in my chest as though strumming a guitar? One or the other."

Oscar chuckled. "I'm sorry, mate. Maybe it's a good thing she's here. You two need to sort out the past."

All Alex could manage was a hard swallow and a noncommittal sound in the back of his throat.

He motioned for Oscar to follow. "Come on, I'll introduce you."

They strode through the stone archway leading to the inner bailey. The group of students along with two other teachers, Ellora and Lanae gathered by the Lion Arch and Tower, the gateway that led out of the castle walls to Alnwick Garden.

Ellora shook Oscar's hand and sent him a shy but polite smile when introduced. It was the lingering glance Lanae gave Oscar that made Alex grin.

Oscar waved and with a backward glance, said, "Cheers. See you later."

Lanae muttered to Ellora as Oscar strode away, "Who's the English cowboy?"

Since Lanae had just arrived and never been to Alnwick, she handed over the tour reins to one of the resident assistants, Devon. He'd been living and working at the castle the last several years, so he enjoyed flexing his knowledge muscles for newcomers.

Devon let out an earsplitting whistle. "Listen up, ladies and gents. You are a reflection of the castle and your university, so while we're in the garden and anywhere on castle grounds for that matter, you must be on your best behavior." Unlike Oscar, here was a Minnesota-born twenty-something who did put on a harmless but arrogant facade as though straight from the King's stock. Complete with a faux-Brit inflection.

They set off as a group through the arched gateway.

Ahead, Devon gestured to the garden entry. "Alnwick Garden was the brainchild of the Duchess of Northumberland. It has over 120 water jets throughout the garden's giant water feature, three thousand English rose shrubs with two hundred varieties, including the Alnwick Rose named for—you guessed it—the Alnwick Garden." Devon flipped his hair out of his eyes.

Walking backward, Devon wiggled a finger at his audience as if they were primary schoolchildren. "But don't get any ideas with that poison garden. Keep your hands to yourselves."

Maybe he needed to have a chat with the lad. Have him tone it down a tick.

A couple of the female students glanced back at Alex, whispering something behind their hands. Perhaps he'd already made some faux pas he wasn't aware of. He took long strides to catch up with Ellora.

She regarded him with wary eyes. He'd never adjust to that. There had been a time she'd looked at him with adoration, love, respect and trust.

"Hey." Nerves weren't usually his thing, but the single syllable came out strained.

She squinted up at him as they passed The Treehouse Restaurant, the world's largest treehouse and restaurant. Did the sight of it bring back the memories of the night he'd proposed like it did for him?

"How'd you sleep? Did you find the room to your liking?"

"Yes, thank you." Her answer was courteous but formal, and she avoided his gaze.

He cleared his throat but kept his voice low after a scowl from Devon. "I was going to stop by my office after this to get Grandma June's office key for you. Would you like to accompany me?"

Something warred across her face, wrinkling the freckles spattered across her nose. "Sure. I do need to start on this search as soon as possible. Digging into her notes is probably the best way to begin. Just let me know when you want to head back."

With that she moved closer to Lanae, and Devon released the group to wander on their own. Unsure what to do with himself on grounds with which he was well familiar, Alex hung back and strolled the path to the Grand Cascade water feature. Though he didn't want—couldn't raise—kids of his own, he enjoyed watching the faces of children as the jets spouted water in synchronized movements. Alex sat on a bench at the bottom near two children following a family of ducks who made Alnwick Garden their home. The littlest girl squealed as the mum duck ate biscuits from her open hand.

Soon, Ellora and Lanae made their way to the steps at the top of the fountain. An older man blocked their way on the step just below them. The man's back was to Alex, so all he could see was the skeletal-slim build and his high, almost-pompadour coif of silver hair.

At this distance and with the noise of the water, Alex couldn't catch what the man said. But he didn't miss how Ellora had gone rigid nor how Lanae's lips had clamped tight together. Ellora might not appreciate Alex's interference, but his legs seemed to have a mind of their own, carrying him at a sprint up the stairs.

The relief in Ellora's eyes made warmth swell in his chest. "Alexander, this is Byron Hughes. He's Grandma June's—"

"I would say colleague, as I'm a historian myself, but that's a tad on the formal side. I prefer *friend*." The way he said the last word didn't sit quite right. Byron put out a hand toward Alex. His handshake was firm, bordering on aggressive.

Alex's own father taught him from an early age that one could learn much from someone's handshake.

"I'm Alexander. I'm—" He'd been about to say *Ellora's husband*. "Grandma June is like another grandmother to me. Very special woman."

Byron's hands had gone to his bony waist. "Indeed. A treasure. Her disappearance is a true loss to the historical world."

Ellora's fingers clenched at her sides.

Lanae squinted at Byron. "Not to mention her family."

Inclining his head, Byron sent her an indulgent smile. "Of course, of course. Goes without saying."

Alexander moved up to stand beside Ellora and Lanae on the wide step above Byron's. "Well, we should let you get back to the garden. Nice to have met you, Byron."

"Yes, likewise." Byron swept an imperious nod over them. "I'm staying in Alnwick awhile. Conducting my own historical research for my fellowship with Oxford."

He started down and waved over his shoulder. "I'll be seeing you around."

Why did it sound like a threat?

Lanae was the first to break the silence that followed. "What was with Mr. McCreepy?"

Ellora shushed her. "Stop, he'll hear you."

They climbed to the top.

"I should get back to the students. You okay?" Lanae squeezed Ellora's shoulder.

"Just fine." Ellora's tone wavered a bit.

When they were alone, Alex motioned her toward the exit. "Should we go back to the office for the key now?"

She moved without answering but stopped before they reached the gate, hands tight to her sides. "You know, I didn't need a hero back there. I'm pretty used to dealing with things on my own. You didn't give me much choice."

Really? She wanted to go there *now*? "Ellie—Ellora, you looked uncomfortable with that bloke. I was just trying to help."

She didn't seek to press the matter.

He cast a furtive glance her way.

"So, did you know that chap? What'd he say before I arrived?"

They made their way along the wide gravel path back toward the towered gateway into the castle's walled grounds.

She let out a quick breath. "No, I've never met him. He said he recognized me from a picture Grandma June kept with her." She shrugged. "He questioned me about Grandma June. Kind of pushy, honestly. He asked if I knew what happened to her, had she contacted me before she disappeared, if she'd had any new leads before she'd gone missing…"

"Hmm. That is odd, but maybe he's just lacking in social skills."

She seemed lost in thought as they entered the university section of the castle through the heavy wood door inside the Middle Gateway's arch separating the inner and outer baileys.

They walked into the familiar main-floor hall with mailboxes along one wall. To the left, down a hall, was a classroom and the clean laundry room.

"If you remember, it's a bit of a labyrinth to reach the resident coordinator office." He threw the words over his shoulder as he led her down the stairs next to the wall of mailboxes, through the door and several more steps into the expansive, vaulted-ceilinged dining hall.

They passed the rows of long tables and the now-unused fireplace big enough to stand in that servants once employed to cook for the Percy family. Then another door, short hall and finally the white staircase, at the top of which was Alex's office.

"We will reach your office before dinner, right?"

His laugh bounced back to him. "Almost there."

Her breath huffed as they neared the top. But before he even stepped inside his office, the hairs on the back of his neck stood on end. Something was wrong.

He rushed past Ellora. The door was ajar. Not totally out of the ordinary as he didn't always lock it. But someone had messed with his desk. His carefully curated stacks of work were tossed about.

Ellora stood beside him now, mouth agape.

"Someone went through my office."

The divorce papers that had stayed on his desk for months now lay at his feet. He swept them up and shoved them under a book on his bookshelf. She eyed him. Had she seen them?

"How can you tell someone tampered with your office?" She smirked.

"I've told you, it's an organized mess. And this is *not* how I left it." The hook by the door where he would've kept Grandma June's office keys was empty too. "Come on."

He sprinted around the corner to Grandma June's office, Ellora on his heels.

The door stood open. And though Grandma June had always kept her office a mess like his, minus the organization, it was evident someone had torn the place apart.

Ellora covered her mouth with her slim hand, taking in the haphazard display of books, journals and papers.

"Who would do this? Especially now, ten months after she disappeared."

"Perhaps someone who just found out Grandma June was onto something new before she disappeared?" Alex ventured.

"Did you mention the letter and key to anyone?" A hand had gone to her hip, and he didn't like the implication of her words.

"No, other than Oscar. But he's a friend and I know he can be trusted. Let me assure you, the man didn't even know what an illuminated manuscript was until I explained it to him."

He scraped the back of his neck. "I suppose there's no reason someone couldn't have been listening to our conversations. I was walking the grounds with Oscar when I told him, and when I spoke to you, I was in my office with the door open. I'm sorry. I didn't realize..."

"I didn't either. I'm starting to see that one of the biggest mistakes I may have made with Grandma June was not believing her when I had the chance."

Ellora clenched her fists at her sides. "I just want to know what happened to her. And why would somebody have been after her and her research then, and why now, after all this time?"

He racked his brain. If only he could answer those questions, fix this. "I know we've been through this, but during your last phone call a few weeks before she went missing, did she say where she was headed? Think back—did she say what these new leads were that she mentioned in the letter?"

She pressed her lips together then paced the room, stepping over the debris. "I—I was distracted, I'll admit. You know, after everything we were going through. But no, I'm sure she never said anything about either of those. Other than Gus seeing her leave the castle the day of our last phone call, no one the police interviewed remembered seeing her. Gus didn't see if she got in a cab or a bus or anything else. Then she wouldn't answer any of my calls and her cell phone was untraceable."

He crossed his arms. "Mmm-hmm."

This was going to be much more difficult than he'd thought. No matter what became of their marriage, he couldn't let anything happen to Ellie. This situation had become more than just a personal quest to prove Grandma June right and find the lost manuscript. This might be the key to understanding her disappearance.

Chapter Three

Afternoon sun peeked into the tall windows, which Ellora had thrown open to allow the warmth of early summer to seep into her grandmother's stone-cooled office. Who said it always rained in England?

The two full days of rest for all staff and students before classes started had sounded more than sufficient at the outset. But now, a day and a half had skipped by while they dealt with the apparent break-in, talked to security and sorted through the mess in her grandmother's office as Alex cleaned up his office. The castle guards hadn't noticed anyone suspicious enter, but how would they know if someone was "mucking about," as Alex put it, or was a student or staff going about their business?

She and Lanae had picked up the office, but it was impossible to tell if something had been stolen. The small office still felt alive with her grandmother's zest for history. Maps, an antique globe, leather-bound books and journals piled high on every available shelf, even atop the mantel of a blocked-over fireplace and Grandma June's 1914 Victor Victrola record player cabinet in the corner, and pictures of other medieval illuminated works, like the Book of Kells and the Lindisfarne Gospels, littered the desk and floor.

Lanae returned from the lower-level dining hall with two steaming mugs and placed one on the desk in front of Ellora.

"Thank you." She took a sip, the Earl Grey with honey burning the back of her throat, and kept her eyes on the piles she'd made of papers, journals and books.

Lanae spun, her prairie skirt ballooning out as she flopped onto a wingback chair across from Ellora. "Any idea what someone might have been looking for? You know, like that Byron guy…"

With a gust of air, she exhaled, sending up a small cloud of dust. "We don't know it was him. Though he did act strange." Ellora returned a journal to the stack. "If I had to guess, whatever they were looking for, they didn't find it here."

"Why's that?"

"These are old history books anyone can find at a library, random field notes, most of them pertaining to other subjects like the Viking Age. Nothing here about the Lindisfarne Gospels or the supposed lost manuscript."

"Maybe that's because her last research project information was stolen." Lanae played with the end of her braid.

Ellora propped her elbows on the desk, folding her hands together. "I don't think so. Any important notes she had about an ongoing research project, she kept in her master field journal, which she always locked in her old steamer trunk. I haven't seen either yet."

Lanae stood, arms over her chest. "If she hid her journal and/or the trunk, she would've made a way for you to find them. She trusted you more than anyone."

Guilt tasted bitter on her burned tongue. Ellora twirled the key that had accompanied the letter Alex found between her thumb and forefinger. "Well, I have a feeling this is the key to that—the trunk—literally. Alex said it's too small for the doors around here and it does seem familiar. But even when I came here right after we realized she was missing, I never found it."

"Okay, scan everything, the shelves, the books. Let's see if she left any clues about where to find it." Lanae's hands grasped her hips, what Ellora called "boss mode."

"Let's look for anything out of the ordinary."

A quick knock sounded behind them and Alex popped around the office door. "Cheers, ladies. Can I be of any assistance?"

"I think we have it covered." Ellora's words shot from her mouth without thought.

He breezed in and pivoted into Lanae's now-vacant chair with even more grace than her friend. "Really? Not even to serenade you while you work? Or dance for your entertainment? I'm great for keeping up morale."

Lanae laughed behind a closed fist, which she turned into a fake cough.

How the man could burrow under her skin but be so downright likable all at once. It was maddening. "I believe we can do this without your multitude of wit and talent. Thank you."

He shook his head and jumped to his feet. "All right then." But at the door, he turned and shot her a wicked one-dimpled smirk. "But you admit I *do* have wit and talent."

She rolled her eyes and threw an eraser, narrowly missing his head as he ducked into the hallway.

"He's back to rare form today, isn't he?" Lanae quirked a brow at her.

"As usual, nothing can keep down his charm." *No situation, no matter how terrible, can dampen his humor nor his apparent need for the spotlight.*

She ran her thumb along a battered soft leather-covered journal inside the desk drawer—the kind with long leather laces to close it. Etched on the front was Ellora's name in childlike block letters. A knot rose in her throat. It was the first field journal her grandmother had bought for her. Grandma June had taken her to local museums and historical markers, encouraging her to write about what she learned.

Ellora opened it to find her wide-eyed wonder on display, written in her sloppy eight-year-old handwriting. On the last page was her grandmother's tall slender script instead.

"Lanae." The words came as a breath. "Come look at this."

They both bent over Grandma June's message: "Ellora, for help: 5112924225." Lanae's expression warmed. "You were never far from her thoughts, were you?"

She managed a small smile.

Maybe it shouldn't have surprised her, since her grandmother often left her notes throughout her research books. But this one plucked at a stinging thorn in her heart.

"This has to be the clue to finding her field journal and the trunk. It's somewhere only I would look. Anyone else would see the childish handwriting and toss it aside. In fact, I must've looked past it myself, before, when I came to help search for her."

"What could the number be? A phone number? Maybe it's someone who can help us find her research or her trunk."

Ellora slipped her cell phone from her pocket and shrugged. "There's only one way to find out..."

Lanae leaned on the edge of the desk, never-quite-without-dirt nails clicking against the wood.

Ellora keyed the numbers into her phone. Almost immediately, the wrong-or-disconnected-number automated message played. "Nope, that's not it."

"What else could it be? A locker combination? Pin number? Lockbox number?" Lanae counted each one on her fingertips.

"What's something only she and I would know?" The possibilities seemed to swallow her.

Her memories went to her and her grandmother leaving notes for each other throughout Ellora's childhood. Little "I love yous" in her lunch bag or on the fridge. That morphed into messages on the bathroom mirror, only visible after a roomful of steam, invisible ink made with lemon juice and brought out by heat. Eventually, they moved on to harder and harder secret codes.

Her pulse drummed a new beat. "That's it!"

Lanae straightened. "What?"

"Grandma June and I studied coded messages and ciphers used throughout history. The codes used during the World Wars which are still used today, the cipher disk used around 1470 by Leon Battista Alberti and even the secret messages used by Mary, Queen of Scots. Coded messages go back centuries. We used to leave each other messages using different kinds to challenge ourselves and stump the other person."

Lanae chuckled. "That's what historians do for fun?" More serious, she pointed to the numbers in the journal. "So this is in code?"

"I think so. Probably because she didn't know if I'd remember these, she chose a relatively easy numerical code. See?" She ran her finger under the line of numbers.

"Each number corresponds to a letter, wherever it falls in the alphabet. *A* is one, *B* is two, and so on."

Lanae snatched a blank piece of paper and a worn pencil and scribbled the letters across the top.

Squinting at the results, Lanae rubbed her temples like she'd developed a headache. "E-A-A-B-I-X-B-Y. What were you trying to tell us, Grandma June?"

Ellora's mouth spread into a grin. "Part of this makes perfect sense. *B-I-X-B-Y.* Bixby. My grandmother had one friend here in Alnwick who she said believed her about the illuminated manuscript. Thomas Bixby, the owner of the tea shop in town."

Lanae's sigh fluttered the paper. "Wonderful. I thought we were gonna have to break out the machine that cracked the Enigma code or something."

Ellora had landed herself in trouble enough by going full historian/teacher on people. Instead of expounding on this bit of history, she said, "No need."

The letters *E-A-A* tugged on something in her brain. "I just wish I knew what she meant with these beginning letters."

"I think I can guess." Lanae tipped a brow and her head to the side when Ellora stared in silence. "You mean I know something Ms. Knows-Every-Historical-Tidbit with, apparently, a minor in code-breaking doesn't?"

"Come on, what is it?" Ellora grabbed her bag, ready to set out to Thomas Bixby's tea shop.

The playful expression on Lanae's face melted away. "I think it means 'Ellora and Alexander.' As in, Grandma June meant for him to be a part of this."

The proclamation walloped her in the gut. Grandma June had always loved Alex like a grandson. Of course she'd meant for them to do this together.

"Well, Grandma June didn't know how he'd abandon me." To be on the safe side, she flipped through the rest of the journal. No other messages from her grandmother on the pages, but from inside the pocket folder at the back a small note fluttered onto the desk. Inside read: "You'll find the trunk travels. But the rails it rides are 1/100th its original size."

She and Lanae shook their heads and shrugged at one another. Then Ellora motioned for Lanae to follow as she pocketed the trunk key and locked the office door behind them—a locksmith had come out to change the lock on the door and gave her a new key.

A burst of scents each vied for Ellora's attention as she and Lanae entered Thomas Bixby's tea shop, the Traveler's Tea Room, a ten-minute walk from the castle on Narrowgate. The tea shop sat among a row of connected stone buildings dating back to the 1700s. She inhaled the bouquet of earthy, citrus, floral and sweet smoke, like a dry autumn day—the aroma of a hundred different tea varieties mingling together.

Lanae whirled around, hands in her skirt pockets, and let out a quiet whistle. "It's like someone reached inside your brain and threw it all over the place."

"Gruesome metaphor, but yeah. I'd have to agree." She couldn't help but smile at their surroundings. "I can see why Grandma June liked this place. The proprietor just opened in the last several years. I've never been here on my other trips, though Thomas did come over to the castle when I was here last looking for Grandma June and the police were interviewing everyone who'd seen her recently."

The tea room was split into two distinct areas.

One side was a sit-down café-style restaurant with an eclectic array of antique tables, chairs and benches—just Ellora's style—with antique maps, old globes and knickknacks from around the world. The other side was devoted to a shop for all things tea-related with shelf upon shelf of tea tins, teapots, cups, a glass case of baked goods, as well as a few displays of antiques and globe-trotting treasures for sale.

Ellora picked up a teacup with lily of the valley on its side, so much like her antique set back home. But then, she didn't really have a home anymore, did she? All her belongings were in a storage shed. Like a life stashed away, put on hold.

Lanae moved to the glass display case. A sign above a button on the wall read Ring for Service. Lanae pressed it. It let out the double-blast whistle of an old steam engine.

Mr. Bixby—a squat older man with broad shoulders and round cheeks—pushed through the swinging door behind the counter. He held his head down, wiping his hands on his train-engineer microstriped apron.

"Cheers, loves. Care for a cuppa? We have a lovely afternoon tea spread if you're peckish." His impressive mustache wriggled like the bristles of a minibroom as he spoke.

Ellora stepped closer. "Hi, Mr. Bixby."

He finally glanced up, a wide grin fringed his mustache and he touched the brim of his hat. "Why, Ellora, dear. How are you? Please, you know you can call me Thomas." The irony once again of a "Thomas" wearing tank-engine-themed attire almost cracked what she hoped was a warm smile.

"I'm all right." It was the best she could muster.

His thick, gnarled hands clapped together. "I know we only spoke briefly when you were here last, but, oh, how often your grandmother spoke of you. She never tired of regaling me with stories of her Ellie. I had so hoped we could have tracked down something about her disappearance. I truly did."

His expression was kind, but the resignation in his voice left a mass in her throat she couldn't swallow, blocking her ability to speak.

Lanae came to her rescue, leaning over the display case to shake the man's meaty hand. "I'm Lanae, her friend. It's nice to meet someone who knew Grandma June. Do you have a couple of minutes?"

"Of course." Thomas rounded the counter and gestured to the dining area. "I'll have Gwen, one of my cooks, bring us tea."

He led the way to a table near the back.

They passed an old passenger car seat repurposed. A couple huddled close, talking, inside one of the two "train car" booths.

When Ellora slid into her seat, a toy train rumbled by on a track circling the room above their heads.

She found her voice again. "I love this place. It has all my favorite things—antiques, books, travel and, of course, tea. They're my grandmother's favorites too. No wonder Grandma June always spoke highly of the Traveler's Tea Room and you."

Gwen Evans, a sweet-as-could-be older woman in her early seventies, if she had to guess, brought their tea and insisted they each take a savory hand pie she'd just pulled from the oven. Though Gwen was probably around the age of her grandmother, they couldn't have been more different.

Grandma June had been hardened in appearance, athletic, and windblown with dirt under each fingernail from her fieldwork. Always, she accessorized any outfit with her trusty multipocketed canvas cargo vest she called her "explorer's vest," where she kept her compass passed down from her father, Ellora's great-grandfather.

Whereas Gwen was soft, pink-cheeked, dressed in a floral dress and seemed the sort to host a beautifully laid family dinner party.

When Gwen, finally satisfied they would eat the food set

before them, retreated to the kitchen, Thomas leaned over steepled fingers. "This place is to honor my late wife, you know. She loved popping into antique and curiosity shops. We traveled all over the UK and the Continent by train. In fact, in my office, I have an antique European map on the wall with little flag pins. Places we traveled to and places I still want to go."

A nostalgic glimmer stole over his jovial face.

"It's lovely. Isn't it, Lanae?"

"Delicious. I mean, yes, lovely." Lanae swallowed another bite of the pie's flaky crust. "And I noticed you sell fair trade and sustainable farm teas. Good on you."

Thomas pointed to the kitchen. "That'll be Gwen. She handles most of the ordering for the menu as well as the shop area."

A shadow passed over his face, his bushy brows drawing together. "Anyway, that was many years back now. Your grandma encouraged me to travel again. But I guess I realized I'd come to my last stop some time ago."

She cleared her throat. "Thomas, the reason we're here is because of the lost manuscript Grandma June was looking for. I came to Alnwick to continue her search and hope it will lead me to what happened to her. While looking through her things, we found she left us a message with your name."

His eyes widened. "She did?"

Ellora sipped her Earl Grey with a touch of sugar, the perfect blend of citrus, floral, with a hint of sweet. "I know she trusted you. She always said you were the only other person who took seriously her hypothesis regarding the manuscript being written by a woman and, you know, actually existing."

"Ah, yes." His gray eyes brightened.

Ellora leaned over her elbows. "Do you have any idea of

where she may have last looked for the manuscript? Or she mentioned 'new leads,' do you know anything about that?"

Thomas puckered his lips. "If June did, she never had the chance to tell me about them. And I don't know where she last searched. I'm sorry."

Lanae's face scrunched. "Then—not to sound impolite—why did she leave us your name? It seems like you don't know any more about this than we do."

He leaned back, his spine creaking as much as the worn chair beneath him. "I can't rightly say. Maybe she knew you could come to me as a trusted confidant in all of this. I'm a bit of a history enthusiast, you know."

"How about this?" Ellora handed him the little note about the trunk and rails 1/100th their original size. "Does this mean anything to you?"

His brows gathered then shot to the middle of his forehead, and his chair skidded behind him as he jumped to his feet.

"Well, this note has to mean my model locomotive that runs the length of the tea room, all day, every day, doesn't it?" He adjusted his hat. "She would've known I'd never get rid of that thing."

Excitement bubbled and brewed within Ellora as they rushed to the miniature replica steam engine train, complete with puffs of white "smoke" from its smokestack. It had just circled back to the pay counter. Thomas grabbed it before it zoomed away and struggled with the off latch. Ellora helped him wrestle it to the floor.

Lanae stood helplessly above, calling orders. "Maybe one of you hold it and the other turn off the pesky switch."

They still struggled as Alex entered the tea shop with his friend Oscar. Both wore riding clothes and leather boots.

The fake smoke from the train puffed into her face. The

acrid taste of burning plastic hit her tongue and filled her lungs. Her eyes watered. She coughed and sputtered. Finally, Thomas managed to turn the train off.

Alex was the first to move, reaching his hand down to her. "You all right, Ellie—Ellora?"

She nodded and took his strong hand. "We've come to retrieve something of Grandma June's she left here for me." She pointed to the toy train.

His brows dipped as though confused about Grandma June leaving her a child's plaything. "We just stopped in for a cuppa before we go out to the horse stables…" The corner of his lips tugged upward. "Unless you'd like some help with this. I've been told I can wrangle a toy train with the best of them."

"I can handle this." It came out harsher than she'd meant.

Ellora pulled herself up straight. "I mean, that's okay. We've got this."

Oscar tipped his head. "Although this does look *interesting*, we do have to get out there. I have a mare about to foal, and I need to check on her. Cheers, ladies." He sauntered on his ever-so-slightly bowed legs to the counter.

Alex hung back while his friend ordered. Thomas plucked something fastened to the underside of one of the cars. He held the small object in the air, triumphant. "June must've snuck this onto the train when I wasn't paying attention."

Alex took the steaming paper cup Oscar handed him and pointed with his chin. "That's a key to one of the doors at the castle. I'd know it anywhere."

Thomas held out the old skeleton key.

Lanae peered over Ellora's shoulder. "Couldn't the key be to any place around here?"

Oscar had neared Lanae's side, towering over Ellora's petite friend. "But you see here?" Oscar's calloused finger traced something on the head of the key—an ironwork letter *P*. "A *P* for Percy. The family who've owned the castle for over seven hundred years."

Thomas relinquished the key onto Ellora's palm as Alex added, "Most of the heavily used doors have been switched over to modern locks and keys. But there are still a few that have these old keys."

Ellora sucked in a breath, regretting it immediately. Mixed with the scent of tea was the fragrance of soap, leather and cedar—probably from the chest where Alex kept his shirts and jackets.

Waving to Lanae, Ellora thanked Thomas and moved toward the door. "Come on. There's still time before dinner. Let's see if we can figure out what door this belongs to."

Oscar raised a hand. "Wait, before we check on my mare, we could help. Would you like some—"

"Help? No, you heard them—" Alex took a long, lazy sip from his tea. "They've got this. They don't need any help. Even though the castle has over 150 rooms, many of which are off-limits to the public and university visitors..." With this, he pulled an innocent smile that used to irritate her to no end. Yup, still did.

She thanked Thomas, then whirled around and out the door, pulling Lanae behind her. She'd show him that he was the last person she needed anything from, now or ever. He could only hurt and disappoint her. She'd sooner rot in some forgotten cellar than ask Alex for his assistance.

"Would it have killed you to ask Alex for a little aid?" Lanae trudged the last stair to the top of the battlements above the Barbican Gate.

"I know what I tell students about the use of the word *literally*, especially in their test essays. But, yes, I think it may have literally killed me to swallow what little pride an abandoned wife has left."

"You two. Sometimes I wonder if I'm dealing with two more college students—only with the maturity level more at the grade school level."

They'd already been all over the university's section of the castle, ruling out any of the off-limits areas. Gus, the elderly guard, had let them try all the doors on the ground level around the gate and then permitted them to check the walkway above, called the "wall walk." Between the square stone merlons, the embrasures, or openings, allowed them a breathtaking view of the castle's inner grounds and the pasture land below the river-facing castle wall.

"It's not a question of maturity, Alex and me. Though I own that I do revert a bit when I'm around him. That's only because he knows how to push my buttons." Her fingers flexed until her thumb knuckle cracked. "This is about loyalty, trust, being there for the person you've pledged to stand by, in good times and in bad. If he can't do those things…"

Her shoulder lifted. "I'll always have a place in my heart that cares about him—a place I gave to him long ago and can't get back. But I won't allow him to hurt me again."

Lanae brushed Ellora's elbow with her own. "I'm *your* friend first, always, before Alex's. However, I wouldn't be a very good friend to you or him if I didn't acknowledge that he may not have stood by you when he should have. But did you stand by him? After the shooting? After the media coverage blew up the internet and the college student who died was all the news stations could talk about?"

Alex needed her strength? But she had barely been holding it together at the time. She'd had none to give.

Ellora's teeth clamped together as she strode to the end

of the wall walk. She tried the key in the door leading into another of the castle's towers. It didn't fit.

Golden-hour light bathed the valley and grounds below in glowing amber. In the distance, the outlines of two horses with riders raced across the expanse of meadows and grazing lands of Hulne Park. The castle cast long shadows from the lowering sun and it seemed an outward expression of the darkness stretching within her own soul, consuming light as it went.

"It's getting late." Ellora jangled the key. "I have one more place I want to check before we head to the dining hall for dinner."

"Not that this running through the castle trying different doors like Alice in Wonderland isn't fun and all," Lanae said, "but I feel like I should prep for my first real day as student adviser."

Lanae. Such a free spirit except when it came to her job duties. "Besides, I have to check on Steve. I'm not sure he made the trip all right."

"Gross, you brought that thing? Steve, as you call it?" She couldn't understand why her friend had to bring along her SCOBY—symbiotic culture of bacteria and yeast—used to brew fermented kombucha tea, let alone why she'd named the disgusting gelatinous disk.

"Well, you should've seen the look that airport security person gave me when he checked my carry-on. But there aren't any rules saying I couldn't bring him on the plane. Besides, would you rather I left it in my apartment to die while I'm gone for the summer?" Lanae put a hand to her hip. "You've just never understood nor appreciated Steve and his many health benefits. Be careful or I'll make you a SCOBY Sarah for your next birthday."

Ellora rolled her eyes, but couldn't help the smirk sliding into place. "Let's get going. We don't want to keep poor Slimy Steve waiting."

Ellora led the way through the university's main castle doorway down to the stone-encased stairway and hallway leading to the student-use kitchen, recreation area and TV room. The temperature dropped ten degrees in an instant as they entered the dimly lit, windowless corridor.

The stone walls gave way to whitewashed walls but remained still, cold and eerie.

"If the cold, clammy air in here didn't give me the chills, the bowels-of-the-*Titanic* vibe certainly will." Lanae hugged herself, rubbing her bare arms.

Ellora's laugh echoed against the walls. "When I was a student, we used to run down this hall to get out of it as quickly as possible."

"I can see why." Her head swiveled this way and that as if expecting something to jump out.

Ellora checked the time on her phone. Almost dinnertime. No wonder the hall and the kitchen/rec room beyond it were silent.

Lanae stayed close as Ellora tried a lock. There were only a couple to try. The key from the letter Alex had found—presumably to the steamer trunk she never traveled without—was tucked into Ellora's pocket.

"Hurry, please. This place is giving me the heebie-jeebies."

"Can you hold your horses?" Ellora grumbled.

Lanae's giggle boomeranged back. "Maybe I should use that line on Oscar."

"That English cowboy is pretty handsome, isn't he?" She turned, raising her brows at her friend. "Seems like a gentleman too. Don't you think?"

"You have a knack for stating the obvious, my dear." Though Lanae averted her eyes and blushed.

Ellora pushed the key into a lock midway down the corridor. It made a *snick* as the grooves fit into place. The ancient lock resisted at first, then groaned as it turned.

The door swung open with a loud hinge-squeal. She flipped on a light, a lone hanging light bulb from the ceiling. If possible, it was even colder inside what appeared to be a storage room and her skin prickled into gooseflesh. Old tools, broken furniture, boxes, et cetera had found their way inside and never left.

And there it was—her grandmother's trunk in the corner.

Lanae stepped into the room and Ellora let go of the door to follow. When Ellora reached the trunk, she ran her fingers along the familiar worn leather, the buckled straps, the patches from places like Switzerland, Italy, Spain and, of course, Great Britain.

Behind them, a loud slam sounded. She and Lanae ran to the heavy door. Ellora tried the knob. Wouldn't budge.

"Oh, no. Steve! We should have propped the door open." Lanae's voice came out a tense whisper.

"Not the time for jokes, Nae." Ellora pressed her ear to the cool wood. Silence.

"Who's joking? I have to feed him, not to mention myself." Lanae, usually laid-back, let out a growl. "By the way, maybe the place isn't haunted, there's just a bunch of abandoned staff down here. Like us."

She fished her phone from her pocket. "No reception. I shouldn't be surprised since we're underneath tons of stone and surrounded by thick walls. Your phone?"

Lanae checked her own cell phone. "Nada."

They banged on the door and yelled for help but only their own echoes answered them.

"I'm a little worried about our chances of rescue." Lanae drew a shaking breath. "No one knows we're down here."

They shouted and pounded again until their fists were red and their voices hoarse.

Ellora slunk over to the trunk. "Someone's bound to miss us soon enough."

"Hope so."

"Lanae, it's Alex. For once, I'm grateful he's nosy. Since we're in here, I might as well look through the trunk. Also, not the time to chide me for that."

Lanae patted her growling stomach. "Got it."

After opening the lid to the steamer, Ellora's heart fluttered at the bittersweet sight of her grandmother's most prized possessions and her secret stash of research. The things she didn't want just anyone to find. "This may be the road map to the manuscript and to what happened to Grandma June. All her secrets."

"Yeah, well, they may stay secrets and die with us if we can't get out of here."

Chapter Four

"Professor Lockwood! Wait!" One of the girls who'd taken up staring at Alex like it was a sport—Maggie? Maddie?—called to him as he made his way to his flat after horseback riding.

He'd had such a good time he'd missed dinner. The mare Oscar had been waiting on had just started foaling when Alex left the stables. His friend and the stable hand on duty were in for a long night. He'd offered to stay, but Oscar told him there was no need. The "miracle of life," as Oscar put it, was both long and not much for them to do but check her progress, wait and pray.

Now, a hot shower and whatever he could conjure up in the small kitchen in his flat called to him. But, unfortunately, not louder than the student and her friend with the long braids close behind her.

He took a stab at her name. "Maddie? What can I do for you?"

"Professor, there's something creepy going on in that hallway leading to the student kitchen and rec room." Between the words, she huffed as though she'd run all over the castle looking for him.

Her friend—the name Willa seemed right—helped fill in the rest. "A group of students went down to play table tennis after dinner, but they all came running back saying they heard strange noises. Pounding and yelling. Like—" her hands went up as though grasping for an explanation "—it's haunted or something."

Alex held himself, including his face muscles, as still as possible. Not allowing the smirk that so desired to pull at his lips.

Instead, he dipped his chin. "There have been stories over the years, but it's best not to put much stock in them. It's probably some other students having a go."

He scrubbed at his five-o'clock shadow, itching to extract himself from this nonsense. "And anyway, not to put you off coming to me for help, but isn't this something you should bring to your student adviser, Ms. Reyes?"

Maddie put a hand up. Probably a student force of habit. "We tried. We can't find her anywhere. Or Professor Lockwood—I mean, Professor *Ellora* Lockwood."

The answer came like an electrical pulse to the brain. "I think I know who your specters are. If you'll excuse me, please."

He left Maddie and Willa standing in the outer bailey as his long legs made quick work to the stone hall.

Before he'd even reached the end of the white-walled passageway, where another door led to the student kitchen and rec room, the shouting and banging reached his ears.

He tried the handle. Locked or stuck. Of course. "Ellora? Lanae?"

They quieted.

"Alex? Is that you?" Ellora's question quavered, whether from wearing her voice thin, stress or relief, he couldn't tell.

"Yes, it's me. How on earth did you two manage to lock yourselves into a storage room?"

A growl of irritation emanated from the other side.

"The door slammed behind us. Grandma June's key fit in this door and her trunk is in here." It was Lanae this time.

He tried the handle, but it didn't turn in the slightest. "I think it's a self-locking door."

"Here, I'll pass you the key under the door." Ellora's words were smushed as though her lips were pressed against the door frame.

Grating metallic and then the tip of a key peeked out from under the door.

"Oh, no. It's stuck. Can you pull it through?"

The iron skeleton key was wedged tight. "It won't budge, I'm afraid."

"Why don't we push up on the handle and you see if you can wiggle the key out?" Ellora called.

"All right. One, two, three—go!" The key loosened as the women pushed upward.

He slid the key out, stood and unlocked the door in one fluid motion. The door flew toward him along with Ellora. She landed in a warm heap against his torso. His feet stumbled back, tangled with hers until they both fell to the ground. Pain shot up his spine as they hit the floor.

His arms instinctively wrapped around her. The scent of lavender, vanilla and tea washed over him. His head swam with a thousand memories. Back when he would've been free to brush back the wisp of hair over her eyes boring into his. So inviting. The pain in his back dulled to an ache, nothing like the ache roaring to life in his chest.

The moment was a lifetime yet only a few seconds.

Ellora was the first to break eye contact. He helped her sit upright.

She pushed herself to her feet without his offered hand. "You didn't tell me to let go of the door."

She brushed herself off, her mouth set in a hard line.

Did she actually expect him to apologize for helping her? Heat filled his stomach for a different reason.

"Thank you. For rescuing us." Despite the sentiment, the words seemed to drag from her throat unwillingly.

He stood. "I can't have any more reasons for the students to think this hall is haunted, can I? Besides, filling your job positions would be a beastly, tedious business now everything's set. One I wouldn't relish." He kept his tone light, teasing. But the recent feel of her against him, delicate but strong, still buzzed through his veins.

"Let's get this monstrosity up to your flat, yeah?" He shoved a block of wood under the door to keep it open this time.

The women agreed. They carried the trunk to the hallway, Ellora and Lanae on one side and he on the other. They made slow progress back down the hall. Wheels Grandma June had installed on the bottom of the trunk meant their job was made a little easier, except for the stairs. Once outside, they *click-clacked* along the cobbled path.

By the time they dropped it onto a luggage rack at the end of Ellora's bed in her flat, they were all red-faced and huffing air like they'd just finished a marathon. And they had, of sorts.

Lanae stood a moment by the door, wiping a hand against her brow. "That's it for me, folks. I've got to get back to Steve—"

He sent a questioning glance to Ellora, who waved it away.

"And shove something in my stomach while I go over my stuff for tomorrow."

After Lanae exited and shut the door, Alex hovered by the kitchen table. Would it be rude for him to leave too? Did he *want* to?

Ellora fidgeted, but her feet seemed cemented in place. Better question, did she prefer him to go?

She opened her mouth twice before making any sound. "Can I get you something to drink? I haven't had time to visit the shops, so it's pretty much water or the tea you bought me."

"Water is fine." He sank into one of the 1950s-style padded kitchen chairs.

She washed her dust-covered hands then filled two cups.

She handed him a glass. He took long, cold gulps. "Thank you."

Her chin dropped in response.

Leaning back in the chair, he clasped his hands behind his head. "So, can I help you with the search? You know, now that I'm personally invested by saving you two from an overnight in the dungeon."

She'd gone quite still, hand resting on the cup she'd placed back on the counter. "Sometimes the 'saving' comes too late."

"Too little, too late, yeah? Or was it just that in your mind I saved the wrong person." Not this again. He scrubbed a hand over the rough stubble on his jaw. "Does that have to be thrown back in my face at every turn?"

Her clenched fists and jaw, ready to take on this fight for the millionth time, set his own teeth on edge. How could he reconcile the sweet, thoughtful, generous person he'd fallen for with this bitter, grudge-holding woman before him?

"You didn't save the wrong person." Her voice came out a whisper. He almost missed it. "That was never why…"

But the misery etched into the creases near her eyes didn't speak of anger or disdain for others. Pain was written there.

He stood and closed the distance between them, at least physically. "Why did it hurt you so much that I saved the woman during the shooting?"

Her arms crossed. "Alex…"

Warmth, unbidden, spread through his chest when she said his name like that.

"It was never about that. It was just, I—"

"What, Ellie?" If she could use his nickname, he could do the same. "If we're going to be working near each other, I want us to get to at least a base level of understanding."

He didn't dare admit to himself that this had nothing to do with their working relationship and everything to do with the relationship they'd probably lost forever.

She pressed her temples with her fingertips. "I was so scared for you, for me. I needed to know you were safe. The not knowing, I couldn't stand it. All I wanted was to find you—"

Her feet unstuck from her spot and she began pacing. Never a good sign.

"—and make sure you were safe. And I needed you that night. You have no idea how much. I was terrified and alone. But you hadn't spared one thought for me."

There seemed to be more. Some war waged across her face, fighting to be heard. But in the end, her lips clamped together.

"How could I have known you were hurt? Everything happened so fast. The paramedics saw the blood all over me from trying to help Dylan, the young man who died." Alex's mouth dried. It had helped him and hurt him at the same time to learn the boy's name. Twenty years old, in school at the university for mechanical engineering, his parents had later said at the funeral. Should've had his whole life ahead of him. Just like Alex's brother, Beckett, long ago.

Alex studied his open palms like the blood was still there. The boy's blood had literally been on his hands. A permanent stain. "They thought the blood was mine at first. They whisked me away to the hospital." He could still hear the boy's wheezing last breath as Alex held him on the store's cold floor after the shooters had fled, waiting for the ambulance to arrive. Too late.

A dizzying swirl of memories that had nothing to do with Dylan swept him up and carried him back to the tragedy of his brother's death. Alex had been too late to help Beckett too. Alex may have been the younger brother, but he'd been the responsible one. The one Beckett, their parents' favorite, could always count on. His parents had blamed Alex and his mum had all but abandoned him afterward.

Ellora stopped and threw her hand up, snapping Alex out of his memories. "You had a phone. You didn't answer any of my calls or texts. I was worried sick."

He blew out a gust of air. "We could keep going around and around this same tree. I'm sorry now. I was sorry then, and all the millions of times in between. When can it be enough?"

Her eyes dropped, wouldn't meet his gaze.

"I did spare you a thought, by the way. I wasn't sure I'd make it out of there alive, and I just kept thinking I wished we hadn't rowed that day."

She did look up at him now. Two fathomless deep blue pools, her eyes blinked fast, as though staving off tears. "I remember. Truly one of the worst days of my life—our fight, stress from work, the robbery, the—"

Again, something passed over her face. Indecision mixed with pain.

Before he could press her to finish the thought out loud, she sighed. "I'd better do my prep for tomorrow. It's getting late and I don't want the first day to be a fiasco."

He tried to manufacture an encouraging smile, about as easy as smoothing over this disaster of a conversation.

"You know this material inside and out," he said. "It couldn't be a fiasco, even if you tried." He took a step toward the door and turned back. "By the way, for what it's worth, I really am sorry I ever made you feel I didn't care about you or that I'd abandoned you. I hope we can put our differences aside for now and work together to find Grandma June and her lost manuscript."

She moved to the door as he opened it. "I guess after your rescue, you do deserve a place on our team. Grandma June would've wanted it that way."

He quirked a brow at her from the hall. "Yeah? How do you know?"

Her smile was slow and slight but still curved her lips. "Because in the first clue she left for me, she included your initials with mine."

His throat tightened so he excused himself and bid her good-night. Grandma June had been like a grandmother to him as well.

His and Ellora's paths still touched. It was still undetermined, however, whether that meant they'd travel together as husband and wife. She'd been holding something back. She didn't trust him. But could he blame her?

Even if she allowed him to be a part of this journey, would their paths continue together afterward? Was that what he wanted when he couldn't give her the life she dreamed of? He couldn't be a parent when there was so much potential to cause harm, even unintentionally. What if something happened to his own child? Would he be there to save him or her? After his examples of parenthood from his parents, did he know how to love better than they had?

The questions mounted, weighing ever heavier on his mind as he returned to his flat. A busy first day of classes loomed in the morning. He needed rest. But the likelihood was abysmal.

He passed his piano, which he hadn't touched in so long, his fingers may have forgotten how to play. Slumping into his brown leather chair, he cradled his head in his hands as if that could stop the barrage of inner accusations.

Guilt, always present, sat on his shoulders. The shooting had brought back all of his failures, his not-enoughness, echoing back his parents' disappointments.

His mother's bitter words: "You'll never be your brother. No matter how hard you try. Why didn't you do something? Save him?"

She'd turned away from him then, slamming her bedroom door in his face. His father sat by, witnessed it, said nothing. His father's silence served as another confirmation of what nobody needed to say out loud.

If only Alex had died instead of Beckett, their golden boy.

That was why he'd needed to become a golden boy, a hero, good at everything, charm everyone into liking him. To "earn" his place among the living.

Well, this was his shot to show Ellora he wasn't the villain she thought he was, or at least that he was a former bad guy trying to reform himself. He may not be able to do anything to save their marriage; she'd made that clear by sending him those divorce papers—which he'd signed but had been unable to bring himself to send yet.

As he readied himself for bed, a resolve straightened his shoulders and spread new purpose through his chest. He wasn't sure he wanted to part from her, but if they must, perhaps they could at least part without her loathing the ground he stood on. Maybe even end things as friends. Though the word stuck in the back of his throat. But to do that, he would have to charm his wife's socks off. The trick was to do it without *irritating* her socks off.

"Alnwick has a long history, dating back to early medieval times. The seventh century, to be exact." Ellora circled the desk at the front of the classroom down the hall from student dorm-style rooms in an area known as Upper Fosse.

"But Alnwick really began its development into a town after Alnwick Castle was built around 1096 on this man-made motte overlooking the River Aln. During this summer session, we will be learning all about Alnwick in the Middle Ages and how it became what it is today."

Crossing her arms, she leaned back on the desktop and watched the students scribble notes. The sun reached through the long row of second-story windows behind her, turning her students' laminate shared worktables to glowing amber. The view of the grounds and river below could be a distraction, but she took it as a challenge instead to keep them engaged.

She grinned when a woman in the front row raised her hand—Natalie. A few years older than everyone else, a single mom, she'd brought her five-year-old, Teddy, on the trip. During the day, he attended a preschool summer program in the village while his mom attended the university classes.

Natalie leaned forward in her chair, eyes alight. "You said that Alnwick has been around since medieval times, maybe even earlier. Do you know if there's any evidence that Vikings came through or settled in this area? I'm really interested in Norse history."

The question caught Ellora off guard, but she considered it. "Alnwick isn't known for its Viking history…"

A creak sounded from the back of the room near the exit. Alex leaned against the door frame, ankles crossed like he owned the place. A lazy smile deepened his one dimple.

Heat prickled up her neck. She turned her attention back to Natalie, still waiting. "No definitive answer, I'm afraid, about whether Vikings settled in Alnwick or not. Though it would stand to reason as they made their way inland and south from Lindisfarne, they may have moved through the area." She'd stumbled over her words.

Natalie bobbed her head, a cascade of chestnut curls bouncing with it.

Alex pushed off from the wood frame and stepped into the classroom. "But one could say Alnwick has a long history that most certainly predates textbooks, and the Vikings didn't keep meticulous records. So, who's to say they didn't settle around here."

Pivoting on his heels, Alex stood next to Ellora. "Before the castle was built, Romans passed through, perhaps on their way to Hadrian's Wall, since Roman coins have been found around Alnwick. An Iron Age encampment has been found at Camp Hill. History abounds in this small village."

Annoyance tried to gain a foothold, but she had to admit she did love his excitement over history.

She held a hand aloft. "All right, everyone. Read chapter one from your medieval history texts for tomorrow and start thinking of your Alnwick in the Middle Ages project due at the end of the summer session. I'll need pictures of the medieval structures and details you find around Alnwick and from the field trips we'll be taking. So be ready with your cameras."

Ryan smirked. "You mean our phones?"

She shot him a withering look, but then schooled it into a more professional expression. "However you plan to take and then print the pictures is up to you." She turned a smile to the class at large. "All right, see you all tomorrow."

When they drifted out, Alex stayed rooted beside her.

She circled the desk again and sat in the old rolling desk chair behind it. "What's up?" She peeked through her lashes at him and grabbed the peanut-butter-banana-and-Nutella sandwich she'd packed from what she could scrounge in the community-use food in the dining hall downstairs. She really needed to shop.

He turned and leaned over the desk. "Still eating that primary school specialty?" One brow quirked, as did one side of his lips.

She rolled her eyes and reached for the stack of books from her grandmother's trunk she planned to look through over lunch. "Do you have something on your mind or did you come here to interrupt my class and insult my food?"

"Apologies." He slipped to the side of the desk and sat on the edge, hands lifted in defense. "I didn't mean to scorn your culinary prowess, Professor Lockwood. I came here to show you this."

He reached a hand into his sports jacket's inside pocket and retrieved a folded paper, handing it to her.

Across the top in bold print were the words "The Lost Artifact Society" next to a picture of a magnifying glass. Underneath were details of the meeting times—every Thursday at 13:00 to 15:00, the Traveler's Tea Room, open to "all history enthusiasts."

Tipping her chin back, she eyed him. "And? Don't we have enough on our plates and are already 'history enthusiasts'? I don't need to join a society to prove it. Besides, this is probably one of those glorified treasure hunter groups who make actual historians' and archaeologists' jobs more difficult by disturbing historical sites and handling priceless artifacts improperly." The skin on her neck warmed as her passion rose.

He crossed his arms. "I know and I agree. But I found this in a stack of papers on my desk—"

"It's amazing you could find anything in that mayhem." She flashed an innocent grin.

"Look at the back. That's Grandma June's handwriting, is it not?"

A laugh erupted as she read the words "Treasure hunters?" in her grandmother's handwriting, along with several dates over ten months ago.

"I guess she thought the same thing." He lifted a shoulder. "So, what do you say to a little recon mission and lunch? It looks like Grandma June may have attended some meetings."

Ellora tapped her chin. "Maybe we can see if they know anything about the illuminated manuscript, clues she may have been following, or even if she mentioned locations where she intended to look for information."

"Precisely. Shall we?" He jumped back to the floor and straightened.

A moment of hesitation passed. She had told him to be a part of this search, but was she ready to spend this much time together? With so much still unspoken between them? And, in some respects, too much spoken, in terms of barbed words and accusations.

Dry-mouthed, she opted for a nod as her answer. She put her sandwich back in its wax paper wrapping and grabbed her shoulder bag of books and notebooks from Grandma June's trunk. She dropped her bag at her flat but kept a notebook and pen for the society meeting. Soon they were walking into the tea-infused and travel-obsessed environment of Thomas Bixby's tea shop.

The owner himself popped out from behind the counter with a jovial grin. "Ellora! Nice to see you again so soon. Cheers, Alexander."

"Cheers, Thomas. All right?" Alex thrust a hand out to shake Thomas's after the usual British greeting.

"I can't complain. Here for a bit of nosh then?"

Ellora held out the flier. "We are, but also hoping to catch this meeting. Do you know if the other members are here yet?"

"Indeed they are. Over in the corner." Thomas tossed his chin to the side, gesturing to a mismatched group seated around two large square tables pushed together.

They seemed to have come from all walks and stages of life. A middle-aged man spoke animatedly with a metal detector in one hand, a wild Hawaiian shirt the only distraction from the sparse comb-over across his shining head. The woman next to him, the picture of English aristocracy—dressed in a smart sheath dress and pearls—crossed her arms and seemed to tune out the metal detector man's boisterous story. Others, including a teen-looking boy and Gwen, the tea shop cook, sat with varying degrees of interest.

Thomas nudged Ellora's elbow as Alex started toward the group. "Just so you know, I'm not entirely sure how helpful this group will be. June attended several times, thought perhaps she'd gather valuable info on local history. But, alas, nothing much to report. And I must say, having sat in on the meetings a time or two myself, a passion for history may not be the only motivation for some members."

Though his tone was warm, the warning didn't go unnoticed. "Good to know, Thomas. Thank you. I appreciate the heads-up."

He patted her shoulder as she turned to the table.

Alex motioned for her to sit beside him. "I'm Alex. This is my— This is Ellora. We understand that June Wiltshire, Ellora's grandmother, attended several meetings."

The man who'd brandished his metal detector like a wizard's staff stuck a hand across the table. "I'm Eg."

Ellora offered her hand in return, which he gave a vigorous jostle. "Egg? Like—"

"Right you are, like the breakfast food. But *E-g*, as in short for Egbert. No idea what me mum and dad were about naming me like they did. Bullies had me pegged, let me tell you. Between Egbert and the name for what comes out of a chicken, well, you understand. Between them, I chose Eg."

The well-dressed woman, perhaps in her early sixties, dipped her chin at them. "I'm Cressida Darlington. I remember your grandmother." Her narrow nose lifted. "She came to our meetings to learn what we knew about some rubbish story of some old lost manuscript but never reciprocated. Never told us anything worthwhile, did she? I voted to have her ousted from the group."

Cressida inspected her nails, and Ellora's stomach seemed to well up in her throat. Alex reached under the table and patted the back of her hand.

Gwen, at the far end, leaned over her elbows propped on the table. Her ruffled apron in place. A fashion statement or on a break from the kitchen? "Nonsense. June is a lovely soul, just focused on her manuscript. Means a lot to her, doesn't it?" Then she put a hand out as if to take Ellora's, but she was too far away. "I was so sorry to hear of her disappearance, dear."

Ellora's throat closed. She tried clearing it. "Thank you. We hope to find out what happened to her, possibly through continuing her search for this lost manuscript."

Thomas arrived with menus and an apology for taking so long. It gave Ellora somewhere else to look other than the pitying faces around the table. Though Cressida's haughty demeanor tamped down to a more somber expression, she seemed the least forlorn.

Alex ordered something beside her, though she had no clue what. Crawling beneath the table crossed her mind. To these people, Grandma June was a passing acquaintance. She didn't matter to them. Not really. Her light put out in the world made their lives no less bright.

But to Ellora, without that light, she felt lost in the dark.

Chapter Five

"What can I get you, love?" Thomas waited by Ellora's chair.

The thought of food turned Ellora's stomach as everyone looked on in silence. She pointed to something on the menu and handed it back to Thomas.

Murmurs, many heartfelt, of "my condolences" and "I'm so sorry" went up around the table. Though Cressida crossed her arms, shook her head and muttered under her breath, "I told that woman something bad would happen, wandering all over creation like that by herself."

Ellora's fingernails dug into her knees. Could she fault Cressida? Though arrogant and callous, she was right. Ellora should've been with Grandma June. Instead, she'd been all alone.

"I thought June was a jolly good sort. I loved her stories. The adventures she had all over the Continent as a historian." This came from the young man, possibly a teen, judging from his long limbs and sharp shoulders, as though he still had to grow into his tall frame.

Eg gestured to the boy. "That's my son, Freddie. Bit of a history buff himself, aren't you, my boy?"

Freddie ducked his head, a flush brightening his freckled cheeks.

Gwen ran to the back to retrieve their food.

She placed a plate of bangers and mash in front of Alex, one of his favorite meals. In front of Ellora, she set something with tiny fish tails sticking out at odd angles. Kippers on toast, a popular smoked herring originating from Craster, not far from Alnwick...something that turned Ellora's stomach even more than the conversation about her grandmother. That's what she got for picking without paying attention.

Gwen wiped her hands on her apron. "Not many Americans order our kippers-and-bits platter. Good for you, Ellora, for taking in local culture." She grinned and took her spot at the end of the table again with her own plate of fish and chips.

Alex cocked a brow at Ellora, glancing between her plate and her face, his lip twitching. Without prompting, he spooned mashed potatoes onto her plate and speared a sausage, adding it to the side. In one smooth action, he went back to eating the food left on his plate.

After a swallow, Alex gestured with his fork. "So, we're here to see if any of you might have an idea of where June was looking for the lost manuscript or if you have knowledge about the manuscript itself."

Ellora took a forkful of the mashed potatoes. Letting each fluffy bite work to calm her nerves.

"But I thought those were just stories." Gwen's forehead creased. "Like the rumors of Viking hordes in the area and the stories of the white lady. Legends, really."

"White lady?" Her appetite back, Ellora bit into another chunk of sausage. Alex smirked and placed another onto her plate.

Freddie bounced in his seat. "A local ghost story."

He seemed ready to dive into details, mouth open, when Cressida put up a hand to stop him. "Yes, yes, all well and good. But those all have one thing in common—fairy tales. Like Gwen said." Though it seemed to pain her to admit someone else might be right.

"What if it's not?" Eg scratched at his scalp beneath the thin comb-over. "I've heard of a man who was separated from the others escaping Holy Island in 875, who saved an illuminated manuscript of great value, dyed with lapis lazuli."

Ellora stilled, and placed her fork on a napkin. "You know about the Viking raids?"

"Indeed, I don't think anyone in Northumberland grew up *not* knowing the story."

"One thing's for sure, if that manuscript does exist, it would be worth a lot now." This came from Cressida.

Ellora and Alex exchanged a look.

When Cressida caught it, she straightened, her glance darting around the table. "I didn't mean it like that. Not to sell. I meant it would be valuable to the historical community. To historians like you, your grandmother, to the world."

As the lunch wrapped up and the others talked about different minor historical sites or projects they'd been working on, it became clear they had no further information on the lost manuscript. Or, at least, that they were willing to share.

Eg and Freddie seemed genuinely happy to invite them back to the next meeting and said they'd keep an eye out for anything they came across about the manuscript.

Slapping his son on the back, Eg tilted his head—shaped

much like an actual egg—toward Freddie. "Freddie will be attending a summer youth history program at Lindisfarne and said he'd keep a weather eye out for any clues about this manuscript."

Ellora and Alex thanked them both.

Although Grandma June had probably been to Lindisfarne a dozen times and never said she found what she was looking for, who knew? Maybe the boy would stumble upon something.

When she and Alex were again outside, a humid heat settled upon them and made sweat bead across her upper lip. She squinted up at Alex. "Thanks for that."

"For what?" He reined in his usual swift, long strides to match her shorter, slower ones. "Sharing my bangers and mash? It was a sacrifice, sure, but one I was willing to make to ensure you didn't honk all over that quirky lot." He winked in her direction.

"Well, I was referring to going to the meeting. But, yeah, thanks for that too."

Their steps along the sidewalk steepened. Almost back… She'd been about to finish the thought with the word *home*. But she needed to remember this was Alex's home, not hers. If he'd wanted her there with him, he'd have waited for her before moving. Included her in the decision to take the job in the first place.

"What'd you think of the Lost Artifact Society? Do you reckon they know more than they're letting on?"

She shrugged. "I don't know. Possibly. Their behavior at times was a little odd, to say the least. But then they're self-described history enthusiasts. Maybe we're all a bit strange in that category."

"We sure didn't gather much intel, did we? Sorry it wasn't more helpful. Bit of a faff, really."

"Not entirely."

They approached the Barbican Gate and waved to Gus as they passed through. Tourists milled about, as did students on their afternoon off. A Historical Grounds Tour was underway beyond the archway into the outer bailey. The tourists spread across the almost-too-vivid-to-be-real emerald lawn to listen.

"What do you mean, 'not entirely'?" Alex stopped in the small inner courtyard near the gift shop, where people stood in line at the ice cream stand.

"I mean, for one thing, we have a tiny clue from the story Eg told about an account of a man with a manuscript after the raid on Lindisfarne. Maybe we can trace that to its source."

"Smart Eg."

She smothered a smirk.

"Sorry, won't happen again."

"Anyway, I think I need to stop acting like we're Hansel and Gretel, trying to follow a trail of bread crumbs that may or may not exist through unreliable accounts."

"But I love wandering the dodgy woods, evading craggy witches with you."

She rolled her eyes. "Be serious." Her hand went to her hip. "What do historians do?"

"Stare really hard at old books, preferably wearing spectacles, saying things like 'My theory is…' and 'I hypothesize…' all while collecting almost as many paper cuts as scraps of near-useless historical minutiae?" His eyes widened, innocent.

She couldn't stop her hand from pushing his arm playfully. "Hey! You're a historian at heart too." Folding her arms over her chest, she shot him a glare. "I do *not* wear spectacles. Besides, you didn't mind the 'useless' facts when we used to team up for trivia night."

"Last joke. Promise." He shoved his hands into his pockets. "Let me buy you dessert to make up for it."

A promise from him? Even a small one let loose her pain at his other broken for-better-or-worse promises.

"Fine. But you can't always buy my acquiescence with sweets." They sauntered to the ice cream line.

He nudged her. "All right, so tell me, what *do* historians do? And you're one of the best I've ever seen, by the way. To rival Grandma June even."

She couldn't help the heated tingle that crept up her neck. "We research. Yes, we read. A lot. We search archives, historical accounts, church records. We ask questions of the right experts. Less a trail of crumbs than a puzzle to put together. Harder with pieces missing. But we can usually align enough to understand the bigger picture."

"Right you are. Use our resources. I'll help."

"Yes. But I do wish one of those resources was Grandma June's master journal."

They'd made it to the front of the line. She ordered a strawberry cheesecake flavor twist cone and he ordered plain chocolate. As they made their way up the stairs to their flats, he asked, "The master journal wasn't in the trunk?"

"No, I thought for sure it would be there, but it's not." Their voices bounced against the stone stairway. "She always kept a detailed journal of each project. Notes. Resources she was using. People she'd talked to, et cetera. But it's not there."

They stood before her door now. She caught a drip of ice cream with her tongue as she fished her key out of her pocket. Alex studied her lips, clamping down on his own.

She had to hold her breath to steady her heart.

His feet shuffled beneath him. "Ellie, can we talk? You know, about—"

Footsteps emerged from the staircase. "There you are. Where were you when a guy shooting a bow and arrow— unsuccessfully, might I add—out there was trying to get my number?" Lanae jabbed a thumb in the direction she'd just come from and strode with purpose down the hall, but faltered as she eyed their silent stance. "Oh, I can come back later…"

Alex popped the last bite of his cone into his mouth— somehow he'd managed not to allow one drip on his immaculate sports jacket or his fingers—then shoved his hands into his pockets. "That's all right. I have to go. Cheers." With a tip of his head to both women, he turned on his heel and moved down the hall to his own door.

Once inside, Lanae turned a raised brow to her. "How was it spending time with him?"

Ellora walked to the sink and washed her not-so-immaculate sticky hands. "It's not like we were specifically spending time together. We were attending this Lost Artifact Society meeting, looking for clues about the manuscript and Grandma June."

Drying her hands, she faced her friend. Lanae remained silent but put a hand to her waist.

"All right, it was a little weird, okay? But maybe the strangest part was how *not* weird it was. Does that make sense?" She tossed the towel onto the kitchen counter and threw a hand up. "It felt so normal in some ways, us together, talking. But then the memories would sucker punch me again, and it was like I was with a stranger."

"What was that little standoff situation I stumbled upon in the hall?"

"Oh, that. I'm not sure. He was saying he wanted to talk to me, but didn't say what about."

"Well, that doesn't take a genius, now does it?" Lanae

sank onto a kitchen chair and started sifting through a pile of books from Grandma June's trunk.

"I guess not." Ellora sat across the table and pulled a stack toward her. Opening her own journal, she wrote the date and set to work paging through the first book on medieval life in Northumberland. "It's just that talking about the messy time right before, during and after the robbery isn't going to help anything. It doesn't *change* anything. You know?"

She scribbled a note to herself to check the town archives and parish records for any mention of an illuminated manuscript being on display or used during church services as well as a church or an individual acquiring such a book.

Lanae reached across and stopped her hand. "It can't change the past, but it could change the present. El, you know I support most everything you do, praying all the time that the wind in your veins is the breath of God Himself. But Alex has a right to know."

Ellora slammed down her pencil harder than she'd meant to, snapping the lead. "He gave up that right when he left me in St. Cloud!" She stood, arms raised. "When he chose his own dreams over me. When he went from not only figurative walls between us, but a *literal* ocean."

Lanae's palms went up as if warding off an angry wild animal. The growling beast in Ellora's chest quieted.

"I'm sorry. I didn't mean to yell." Ellora's feet stopped their restless circular path around the kitchen.

"It's okay, I get it." Lanae stood.

"No, I'm sorry, but I don't think you do." Ellora's shoes seemed superglued to the stone floor now. "We'd said no family right from the beginning. Well, mostly Alex, but I went along with it because he was the man I loved and at the time, I thought there couldn't be anything else on earth

I'd want more than being with him. Even if it was always going to be just the two of us. I told myself that was enough."

Ellora swallowed and lifted a shoulder. "For a while it was. But then I thought I was pregnant. I was late and I was never late and nauseous. It changed my perspective, it changed everything. And I felt it down to my soul that I was no longer just me in here. I knew there was this other life, a miracle, growing inside of me." She clutched her abdomen where she could still feel the hollowness, the absence of that life.

Tears that matched her own swam in Lanae's eyes. Her friend nodded for her to continue.

"Suddenly, I had someone to protect, a future and a legacy. It felt precious, sacred. And for a moment, mine." Ellora's fist thumped against her chest. "It sounds so selfish now, but I knew the minute I told Alex he wouldn't be happy so I hung on to it for a little while. To enjoy the love that was already blooming for this little person. My dreams weren't just mine anymore. My dreams extended to this little one. And then...they were snuffed out. Just like that."

"You were going to tell him that night, weren't you? The night of the shooting?" Lanae took a few steps closer.

Ellora nodded. "I walked to the pharmacy in the store that night for another pregnancy test because I'd thrown the first one away, afraid he'd find it. I knew he would need the proof in front of him."

"Oh, El."

They both knew what happened then: she was thrown to the floor and kicked by one of the shooters while Alex was on the other side of the store trying to save those people. Her hurt was never about that. It had felt so lonely to ride to the hospital alone, already cramping and bleeding. Then leaving the hospital alone—truly alone, no child growing within her anymore, no more dreams for this life not yet lived.

And then she'd found her husband, the man who'd helped create the life they'd lost, and he'd been the hero. Interviewed all over for his bravery, for the life he'd saved. And she'd been the one who had lost a life and no one knew nor cared. No one mourned but her. Not that she'd shared it with anyone but Lanae. And that was only when her friend had pried it out of her months later. By then, she and Alex had grown so distant and she couldn't seem to find the words to tell him.

Though she'd raged, telling herself every reason she wasn't obligated to inform him, guilt gnawed at her heart. Scratching and scraping at her insides, devouring her resolve.

She let out a long breath. "I know I need to tell him. I will. Soon."

Lanae hugged her tight and pulled back. "Good. It'll be hard, but necessary. And, El?"

"Yeah?"

"If you are even considering trying to work it out, talk to him beforehand. Start with a foundation of trust."

Lanae's own parents had had a breach of trust, due to infidelity, that resulted in their divorce. It was the reason her mother had moved her and her sister to Minnesota when Lanae was a teenager. "I've seen firsthand what deceit could do to a marriage, even if, you know, I'm not married myself."

It was also the reason her friend was a free spirit except with her own heart.

Ellora walked with Lanae toward the door. "Hey, what makes you think we're going to work things out? I know he still has the divorce papers. I saw them in his office."

Lanae quirked a grin. "Because I can see how he still looks at you. *Annnd*...you, him." She shrugged. "Besides, if he was going to sign them, he would've done it already."

With that, she scampered through the door with a wave.

Thoughts of Alex and her miscarriage swirled in her mind until she made herself sit down with the stack of books. Research was always the perfect medicine for stress. She planned to lose herself down this medieval rabbit hole and leave behind all of this pain. At least for the moment.

Grabbing the book on medieval art history, she flipped to the first page and sighed.

"All right, Grandma. What do you have for me?"

History, legacy, the stories of the people who came before, passed down to their descendants through the generations—Ellora's life seemed forever linked to these things.

They spoke to her. Not in a literal sense. But deep in her soul, she was moved by them. Maybe the idea that there was a bridge to the past, a connection to those around us, the sense of a family tree, had always spoken loudest to a girl who'd watched her family tree cut down right before her eyes.

And it made the absence of the child she'd lost—a branch on her family tree, broken but not forgotten—all the more painful.

Ellora swiped at a tear trailing down her cheek, watching Alex from Grandma June's office window Monday afternoon, playing with little Teddy, Natalie's son. He tossed a ball to Teddy, then ruffled his hair. Alex left the boy with his mother and turned back to the castle. She'd never understood his rigid stance on not wanting children when he was so good with them. It was clear he didn't hate children, so what was the problem?

That was a question she'd wrestled with for years, but all she could ever get out of him was that he didn't want to have kids and the occasional allusion to something about being sure he'd "botch the job" of parenthood anyway.

"Hey, Somber Sally." Lanae leaped through the door frame. "It's beautiful out. We should get outside for a while. You never know when the rain will come back, right?"

Ellora stepped back from the window. "You're getting to know England and her temperamental weather pretty well, aren't you?"

"Yes, I believe I am. Of course, it can't be much moodier than Minnesota weather—am I right?" Lanae sauntered into the room, her long gauzy maxiskirt swirling around her legs with each step.

Ellora laughed. "Hey, it looks like you're getting to know a certain stable master too."

"Maybe…" Lanae traced the titles of the books on Grandma June's desk. "Oscar is really sweet. He showed me the horses and the stables in Hulne Park yesterday after church. I told him about the community garden I started in St. Cloud, so he said he'd like to take me over to the community project here at the castle gardens."

She and Lanae had run into Oscar and Alex as they returned to the castle from their riding lesson on Saturday. Oscar and Lanae hit it off immediately, especially as they gushed over their mutual love of animals, the outdoors and conservation. They'd all attended church at the little stone church just down the road from the castle on Sunday.

Joy for her friend abounded, but Ellora had squirmed through the church service feeling like a hypocrite in the hot seat. Like somehow, everyone could tell she and God were hardly on speaking terms, not to mention that she and Alex were on the verge of divorce.

"I'm so glad. He seems like a keeper." She laid a hand on Lanae's arm and tried to keep her lips from twitching with laughter. "Now, tell me, is it time for Oscar to meet SCOBY Steve? Or aren't we quite that serious yet?"

Lanae took it in stride with a twinkle in her eye. "Not yet, but any more talk about that recycling project he did with the students last semester and I might be looking at introducing them real soon. Dare I say—perhaps even giving him the new one that forms after this batch of kombucha?"

"The baby SCOBY?" Ellora put her hands up in mock outrage. "Whoa. You just met this guy." This talk about babies—even in this silly context—was a slippery slope but she kept her smile in place.

Lanae laughed. "Well, he seems special, but, you're right, I don't want to rush things. Besides, I'll be going back and forth to Minnesota. I can't permanently stay here with my temporary working visa, so I'll be spending at least part of the year back in the States. I still need to work that out with the university. And where Oscar is concerned, I really should be careful of letting my heart run ahead of me when things are so unsettled."

"The one thing I do know is that I don't think anyone could accuse you of being too cavalier with your heart. Don't be afraid to give it a chance—you never know what God can do."

Lanae tipped her head. "Ditto."

Ellora avoided her friend's gentle yet pointed gaze and opened the Lindisfarne history book she'd been reading, one from her grandmother's trunk.

She flipped to the page that caught her eye with her grandmother's notes in the margins. "Hey, you're planning the trip to Hadrian's Wall this weekend, right?"

"I was. The tour guide we were going to meet up with canceled. Plus, the weather looks like it's going to be terrible. I know we told the students to prepare for rain or shine, but I don't know if I'm ready to fly off one of those steep hills like Mary Poppins." Lanae twisted one of her two braids between her fingers. "I hope I can figure out an alternative in time."

"I'm sure you will. For being a self-described free spirit, you amaze me with your organizational skills."

Lanae stood taller. "I do like to think of myself as a bit of an oxymoron. A woman of mystery. You know, a juxtaposition of unique traits." She pointed, glaring down the barrel of her index finger. "And no wisecracks about the 'moron' bit."

She turned the book so Lanae could see the page about the Viking, or Norsemen, raid on Lindisfarne in 793 AD and the immediate aftermath as well as the eventual abandonment of the religious community there in 875.

"I wanted to show you this." Lanae picked up the heavy book as Ellora continued, "I've been reading about what happened to the Lindisfarne Gospels after they left in 875. And it looks like the men who escaped Holy Island with the gospels roamed but eventually settled in Durham to find safety for themselves and the priceless holy relics and manuscripts they carried with them."

"And you think maybe the other manuscript, the one your grandma was looking for, was brought there as well?"

Ellora raised a shoulder and tilted her head. "*If* it even existed and *if* it survived the attacks by the Vikings, it's not the most far-fetched idea that it could've been brought to Durham too, but that certainly would've been long after its creator had passed on."

The book puffed a cloud of dust as Lanae placed it back on the desk. "Where would we even start to find out if that's true? You're the historian, not me. That sounds like a needle in a haystack. Or rather, a pin in a stack of needles."

"Try one tiny dot of an *i* in the Bodleian Library's collected works." The thought of that famed Oxford library pulled at a wound in her chest.

Yes, Ellora had always loved Alnwick, but she'd dreamed of being one of the esteemed historians and research fellows of Oxford for as long as she could remember. Perhaps traveling between Oxford and Alnwick. The thrill of reading some of the most ancient manuscripts and books in existence and going out into the world to study and learn, to someday add her own little discoveries to recorded history, had captured her history-loving imagination.

Even though she happened to be on the "right" side of the pond now, that dream seemed further away than ever. She was supposed to think about her position in St. Cloud. Move forward with new plans, new dreams, once she was able to say for sure what had become of her beloved grandmother.

Ellora circled the desk and leaned back on it. "I can't stop thinking about something Eg said." She'd filled Lanae in on the Lost Artifact Society members. "He said there's a story about a man who was able to escape with the other manuscript, uniquely colored with lapis lazuli, but he was separated from the others with the Lindisfarne Gospels. What if he had caught up with them at some point during their wanderings and the manuscript was brought to Durham along with the Lindisfarne Gospels?"

"Maybe there's one of your fellow history experts in Durham you could speak with."

"Expert?" Alex stood in the doorway with shower-dampened locks clinging to his temples. Already the scent of his earthy spiced soap and mint toothpaste preceded him into the room. "There's sure to be one in every room, especially if I happen to be in it."

Her eyes nearly stuck in the back of her head like her grandmother had warned her about as a child with how far she rolled them.

"Only pulling your leg, love." His eyes widened as though he hadn't meant to say the *L*-word. Though she tried not to read anything into it as calling people "love" was a polite and common British pet name used on near strangers.

She averted his gaze, shoving down the whirl of emotions that little four-letter word brought on. Her feet carried her to the window again.

Lanae filled him in on what they'd been talking about.

"I have an old history professor who still works at Durham University. They have a great history department, with access to thousands of texts in their own libraries as well as the cathedral's archives." He'd planted a hand in one pocket of his trousers. "It's no Bodleian, but it holds its own as a center for rare and antiquarian books and manuscripts."

Lanae tapped her lips. "You know, since our plans to Hadrian's Wall fell through, we desperately need a close-by field trip destination for this weekend. Somewhere, preferably, that has some indoor activities. What if we take the students on this little manuscript hunt? While they tour in the cathedral, you two can talk to your old professor and check into the manuscript. What do you say?"

Alex agreed, but before Ellora could answer, a tingle dashed up her neck as though someone other than the two people in the room was watching her. She swung around, peering out of the small-paned window. Down on the lawn, amid moving groups and frolicking families, stood Byron Hughes. Unmoving. His gaze steady and concentrated on the castle, on her grandmother's office window. On her.

The tingle turned into prickled flesh. The words her grandmother spoke about being followed, that someone wanted the manuscript, reverberated back to her.

Chapter Six

High, clear voices filled Durham Cathedral to the vaulted ribbed ceilings, a dizzying height above Ellora's head. The youth choir sang an old Latin hymn, drawing people who'd lingered outside to wander inside and enjoy the beauty of both the music and endless display of craftsmanship.

Even with short notice, Lanae had managed to secure tours and an overnight rental for their group. It had turned into the perfect destination and only a little over an hour south of Alnwick.

Devon, their self-proclaimed resident tour guide, walked with confident backward steps, arms spread wide. "All of this began as a place to house the remains of St. Cuthbert, the famed holy man, teacher, sometimes hermit of Lindisfarne. The men there couldn't part with their beloved Cuthbert's body nor the relics and writings of the Lindisfarne Priory, so they packed it up—yes, wooden coffin and all—and journeyed throughout what was known as Northumbria, finally settling in Durham at the end of the tenth century. And the current cathedral structure was built between 1093 and 1133."

A smile stretched across his long face, seeming to touch each side. "So, you see Durham and Lindisfarne have been and will always be inextricably linked."

Ellora couldn't stop from raising her hand as though she were the student. "And the Lindisfarne Gospels traveled here as well with the body of St. Cuthbert and the other relics."

"Indeed, ma'am, they did." She tried not to be offended at someone less than ten years younger calling her "ma'am."

She added for the medieval history students, "They were housed here in Durham for many years, were even part of a private collection in the seventeenth century before becoming one of the foundational pieces of the British Library in 1753."

Though her knowledge of the time period and persons involved made her tongue itch to insert a few more details, she and Alex needed to be on their way.

As they passed the vibrant colors of the round rose window, Alex pointed to the stairway leading to the tower. "We could get a bird's-eye view if you like?"

His expression, a feigned innocence.

"You know how I feel about heights. Only the direst of circumstances could induce me to climb even half of those 325 steps."

A hint of a smile curved his lips. "Shall we make our exit then?"

They waved to Lanae and exited the cathedral's tall double doors. "So, this professor we're about to see, Ridgewater, he can be a bit ornery, high-handed. But when I told him what we were doing, he seemed more than happy to help us and said he actually met Grandma June."

Her 1930s-inspired sailor-button wide-leg pants flapped in the strong breeze. The weather, at least in Durham, hadn't turned out as bad as forecasted.

The Palace Green between the cathedral and the university spread out before them, a place once used as the town market in the Middle Ages and later, a place for leisurely promenades. Now it was a place for tourists to meander, stopping for pictures. College-age young men and women played ball, lay out on the grass or wandered in groups—probably those who chose to live in Durham year-round or took summer courses.

"So, he's the one with the painting Grandma June mentioned?"

Ellora had come across a note scribbled into the margins of her grandmother's art history book: "Professor Ridgewater" and "Look at the painting."

"I asked him about a painting and he said he does have one in his office, if that's the one she referred to. I've been to his office—I guess I never studied it. Did Grandma June say why we needed to examine it?"

"No, just those few words were all I found."

"We'll get there. Have a little faith."

Her hands brushed his as they stepped up to the Department of History situated inside a row of historic town houses on North Bailey and Palace Green. They'd been built in the seventeenth and eighteenth centuries as coffee houses and lawyers' offices. Alex opened the door and bowed his head like some kind of English gentleman, but an impish grin leaked onto his face. "After you, m'lady."

Inside, he took the lead, twisting through ancient halls until they stood in front of an office labeled Lionel L. Ridgewater, PhD.

He gave her a little wink before knocking on the door.

Why did that simple action still flip her stomach over? And why on earth did he insist on flirting with her, when they so clearly had more important things to worry about? Or was this just another manifestation of his natural charm, the kind that seemed to permeate from every smile, every pore, without any effort on his part? The door swung inward.

"Alexander!" A small man with a robust vibrato to his voice waved them inside. "There you are, chap." The many lines on his face creased in a not-quite smile.

Alex shook his hand. "Nice to see you, Professor Ridge-water. Thank you for helping us with this search."

Stepping to her side, Alex gestured in her direction. "This is Ellora, my—"

"Your wife, I know. I'd heard you ran off to marry an American. Well, and then I by happenstance made acquaintance with your grandmother, Mrs. Lockwood."

"Professor or Doctor, actually." She corrected him on her name but not the "wife" comment and wasn't sure why.

"Yes, of course. Apologies. A professor in your own right like your husband." Professor Ridgewater clutched his hands behind his back and circled the table. "I've dug up several documents and books you might find interesting. They're newer acquisitions to our Barker Research Library so I never had the chance to share them with June." He tipped a thick brow. "Though she certainly interrogated me as though we had more information on her lost manuscript than I was letting on."

Ellora's teeth clenched. It wasn't that he'd said anything she couldn't believe—Grandma June could be relentless when she was chasing down leads—but it was how he said it. So arrogant. So irritated with a woman who may have paid the ultimate price in pursuit of those answers. She tried to swallow.

"Though the Barker is closed on Saturdays, I pulled some strings for you to study there for a handful of hours. Provided you don't leave the library with anything." His tone was condescending, as though they weren't grown adults.

Alex backed toward the door again. "Of course, we'll leave everything as we found it. We have no wish to keep you if you're busy, sir. If you've no objection, we'll sift through the lot and then meet you back here."

"All right. I'll get out of your hair. As it happens I need to pay a visit to a colleague across campus. I trust you remember the way, Alexander?" Using his first name as though slipping back into their years-ago teacher/student days.

Professor Ridgewater tapped Alex's shoulder. "I'll be back in a couple of hours." He grabbed a leather shoulder bag and stepped toward the door. "Oh, and feel free to inspect my painting, if you like. I know you mentioned it when you called. Though, I don't believe it's anything of interest." His thumb pointed to a painting behind his desk.

Was this the painting her grandmother referred to in the margins of the art history book? It was the only one in Professor Ridgewater's office.

But she couldn't see why it had anything to do with their search for an early medieval manuscript since it depicted a hooded figure—possibly a man but the hood cast a shadow over the face—knighting someone outside Durham Cathedral, while villagers crowded around to watch. The hooded figure wore a Celtic knotted cross pendant, a common style of cross in the Middle Ages, around the neck.

But the intricate lace and beadwork both the noblemen and women wore, along with the ballooned breeches on the men, and the square necklines and wide skirts of the women, indicated the Tudor Era of King Henry VIII's reign. The figure held a book in one hand—a Bible?—and a sword in the other.

Ellora stepped closer, studying the delicate brushstrokes. "Do you know the history of this painting or where it came from?"

Professor Ridgewater's thick, dark brows raced to meet each other in the middle of his forehead. "This? I suppose I've a thing for historical misfits. Perhaps that's why your grandmother sought my expertise and why she was also taken with this painting. Her search for a manuscript supposedly written by a woman was its own sort of misfit, wasn't it?"

She wanted to ask in what way he meant that, but instead tapped the shallow divot in her chin while Alex joined them.

Professor Ridgewater continued, "All I know is that it was saved in an estate sale and later gifted to Durham Cathedral, since it's the cathedral in the background there." He pointed. "When they couldn't find its origins, the painting was given to the university and finally, I bought it. I'm sort of a magpie for things that don't seem to belong, you could say."

A scan of his office, full of historical trinkets and odds and ends, proved the point.

"We don't know who or what event this is depicting, especially since the Reformation happened during the Tudor Era of King Henry VIII. Churches, monasteries, et cetera of the time were stripped of valuables and sometimes burned to the ground. And although Durham Cathedral escaped total ruin, it was stripped of any valuables and the church wasn't exactly—" Ridgewater tipped his head toward the picture.

Ellora chimed in, "Hosting a knighting ceremony and the entire village and nobility to witness it?"

Alex crossed his arms. "Precisely." His lips pressed together. "Hmm…"

The Reformation and its destruction—all because a king had wanted a divorce. Maybe her own divorce wouldn't cause devastation so far-reaching, but what kind of havoc would it wreak on her heart?

Ellora arched her back and stretched her neck to either side. Stiff, sore muscles protested.

She caught him watching her from the chair beside her in the empty Barker Library. This was a dream come true—a library all to herself. But at the moment the quiet seemed deafening as his eyes bored into hers, more intense and serious than his usual jovial self.

A sudden rush of nerves propelled her to her feet. She moved to the glass-walled study room in the middle of the expansive space. To calm herself, she breathed deep of the historians' favored perfume—ancient parchment and vellum and aged-to-perfection leather.

Alex stood and moved next to her. They faced the words etched into the glass. Many different sayings, some in languages other than English, with an array of meanings. All to stretch the academic mind.

She crossed her arms. Again and again, a certain part of a quote stood out to her. A favorite poem of hers by British poet William Morris. "'Love is enough: though the World be a-waning...'" Her voice was a reverent whisper, loud against the silence.

"There's more. I memorized it when I studied here." Alex cleared his throat.

"And the woods have no voice but the voice of complaining,
Though the sky be too dark for dim eyes to discover
The gold-cups and daisies fair blooming thereunder,
Though the hills be held shadows, and the sea a dark wonder

And this day draw a veil over all deeds pass'd over,
Yet their hands shall not tremble, their feet shall not falter;
The void shall not weary, the fear shall not alter—"

She helped him finish: "'These lips and these eyes of the loved and the lover.'"

Their eyes locked for a moment, and her own gaze traveled to his lips. She turned back to the glass, whispering again, "'Love is enough…'"

Was love enough? The surety of these words, the steadfast tone, pulled at her own longing. But there was so much she still hadn't told him, so much he hadn't explained for himself.

"Perhaps it's not the only thing, but it's a good start." He'd answered her unspoken question. He angled toward her, standing close enough that the heat of his body seeped into her silky blouse. "I miss us."

"Me too" came out of her mouth before she could stop it. She hadn't meant to say it, but it rang true nonetheless.

"Then let's have out our differences. Talk it through. Row like bears if we have to. Figure it out and be done with the lot of it." He used a finger to tilt her face upward to his gaze above her. "Anything is better than pretending everything is fine like it is, that we can just go our separate ways once the summer is over. Like what we had didn't exist."

"It's not that it didn't exist. It's that it did. Yes, good. But so much bad. So much hurt. I don't know if we can get past everything that happened." She concentrated over his shoulder. "With so much in our past, how can we possibly have a future?"

He spun away, fingers curling into his hair. "I didn't realize there was an expiration date on our marriage."

"I'd say maybe the expiration date is about a year."

That seemed to deflate his anger. He turned back to her. "I know I left. I know it was idiotic. But you're my wife, Ellie. I forgive you. Why can't you do the same?"

Her fingers clenched into fists. "Forgive *me*?" But even as she said it, her indignation mingled with the humility she'd been taught by her grandmother as well as the grace of God's forgiveness in her own life. What she still hid from him nudged against her heart, an insistent poke that she shoved away.

He ran a hand over the back of his neck. "I only meant that we both said and did things we didn't intend."

She studied those sea-foam-green eyes. Every fleck as familiar to her as her own. "You're right. I guess there's blame on both sides." More than that, she wasn't ready to say, and admitting what she had brought her own sense of rightness snarling to the surface. Maybe she needed a little more help with her pride than she'd thought.

The intensity cranked up the longer his gaze linked with hers. He quirked his head to the side. "Can I get that bit about me being right in writing, love?"

They both let out a shaky laugh. But she needed a little physical distance to dissipate the tension. She wandered back to the table, staring absently at the opened book of hand-written letters.

Could this be the time to tell him about the life they'd lost without him knowing? Her heart sped up, beating against her eardrums.

His shadow fell over her right shoulder. "Ellie, I—"

He stopped, pulled the book closer and traced the words on one of the letters—a scanned copy of the original.

"What is it?"

"Here." He pointed. "Look, there's a bit about a lapis lazuli manuscript."

He read the letter, slowly. Though the ink had faded over the years, written in 1003 AD in Old English, Alex—who'd always been better with languages and translations than her—was able to decipher the meaning. It was written by a man who had originally thought to commission a Psalter for his wife, an early version of a Book of Hours with prayers for different occasions or even hours of the day, a calendar for holy holidays, Bible verses, a place for personal notes and often a family tree.

Alex interpreted, "The man's wife had admired a unique Book of Hours years earlier while in Durham from a group traveling through—a family heirloom, they'd said. The book's pages had been dyed with lapis lazuli and illuminated in brilliant colors and gold leaf. While the wife had been in Durham, during a pilgrimage with her family to see the relics of St. Cuthbert, there had been rumors of this manuscript having been saved from the Viking raids on Lindisfarne like the Lindisfarne Gospels many years prior. He'd wondered if the artist had taught these skills to an apprentice who could now create a similar piece for his wife."

Alex glanced up at her, their noses almost touching. "He asks if a strange rumor that a woman created it was true. It's sort of tacked on to the end of the letter and seems as though he doesn't believe it. See here?" He pointed to the end of the faded writing.

"Do you think he ever got an answer?"

They put their heads together and paged through the rest of the book of random letters from the Durham parish, examples of everyday life and commerce in the Middle Ages. The man had not received a reply, or it had been lost in the annals of history. Nor did they find a record of commission or sale from the scribes at the cathedral for a Psalter or Book of Hours in the same description or time period recorded in the cathedral finances.

With their phones they took pictures of the pages. Ellora also snapped a picture of the painting back in Professor Ridgewater's office, though it still wasn't clear why her grandmother made note of it.

On their way out and upon Ridgewater's return, the older man wished them well. "Come back anytime. I'm always happy to help out a history lover. Even an expat."

He winked.

When they were out of earshot outside, Ellora shook her head. "Why is he still bent out of shape about the American Revolutionary War? Over two hundred years isn't enough time to move on?"

Alex closed one eye against a beam of sun now peeking through heavy gray clouds and squinted in her direction. "Sometimes infinite lifetimes aren't enough to get over the one who got away."

They left the obvious unsaid between them. But while he might have meant her, she had to ask herself, even as hurtful as their recent past had been—was she letting *him* get away?

Chapter Seven

The rhythm of fiddle folk music carried through the restaurant Alex had suggested, which was right on the banks of the River Wear as it wound its way through the town of Durham.

The sunset bounced off of the water and set Ellie's rosy gold hair alight. Their group had taken over half of the restaurant's riverside outdoor seating. A local band played off to one side next to a space cleared for dancing. They'd eaten dinner, and the dishes had been cleared away.

Now, the group enjoyed the local music and a bit of a chin-wag after a long tour of the cathedral and town.

His frustration grew with each passing day. Why on earth had he ever thought he could stand being this near her and not long for things to be so different?

If he were truly honest with himself, he'd started to suspect he'd been an absolute dolt a little over six months ago, about the time it took for him to cool down and sleep off his jet lag when he'd arrived in Alnwick. Maybe even an idiot of the first order. Yes, she'd pushed him away after the store shooting. Yes, they hadn't seen eye to eye about having a family, and there had been a growing unease between them even before the shooting and Grandma June's disappearance. But he'd been a pride-wounded coward and left instead of fighting for his life. Because after his relationship with God, that's what she'd always been: his life.

Not charm, striving to be the smartest person in the room, bravado nor being the best at everything would help him now. These were the terms of his penance since childhood for surviving when his brother had died. His constant justification to his parents, to the world for being alive. But they wouldn't serve him where Ellie was concerned.

She needed honesty. So did he. There was something she wouldn't say. It tried to hide, but it lived right there behind her eyes where he could always read her.

He could pursue her like God had pursued him as a broken young man. Just the thought of the mess he'd made of his redeemed life made him cringe. All he could do now was let her know he wasn't satisfied with parting ways at the end of the summer. That word *friends* taunted him again. What if that wasn't enough for him? But he couldn't push her.

His knee bounced faster, out of beat with the soft folk song. Before he could talk himself out of it, he stood. He flashed a gallant smile and bowed to Ellie. All right, perhaps a *little* charm might help.

"May I have this dance?" He'd wanted to take her in his arms since she'd stepped off that bus in Alnwick. This was the perfect excuse.

"I..." Her gaze flickered from his face to Lanae's and the students'.

The students clapped, including the sweet boy, Teddy, who'd come with his mum. There was a chorus of "Go,

Professor Lockwood!" Though one of the young male students—Ryan?—leaned over to his friend and said over a snicker, "I didn't know old people could dance."

"Oh, all right." She blushed at the attention, taking his hand.

He led her onto the dance floor. The music turned into a lively jig and instantly he was catapulted back to the home they shared in St. Cloud, where she'd taught him all sorts of dance steps, some modern, but many from bygone eras. They used to move the furniture back to accommodate Regency Era reels and quadrilles as well as salsa, swing and even the occasional disco, which usually sent them into fits of laughter.

The cheers behind them bolstered his confidence and the moment the music washed over them, it was like their bodies remembered what to do, how to move in rhythm side by side. A flash of heat climbed up his gut as he spun her out and reeled her back in, her hips swaying, long legs sashaying around him in perfect tempo.

Their minds were in sync—combining different styles and keeping pace with each other, pivoting, parrying, almost like the give-and-take of fencing. Too bad they couldn't seem to keep in step with one another off the dance floor.

The surprised shouts of their audience told him what he already knew—they still had it.

"I can't believe you remember the steps." Her face split into a bright, broad grin. Her rich laugh rippled out and whirled around them as he lifted her in a spin across his back.

"Well, I had a brilliant teacher."

Standing beside her, he took her by the waist from the front with one arm and swept under her knees with the other arm. She grabbed on as he flipped her over his arm in the swing dance move known as the Charleston Flip.

People from inside the restaurant now gathered on the patio, adding their applause in time with the upbeat tune.

As the band slowed the music to a folk ballad, more couples joined them on the dance floor. He and Ellie panted for several moments, catching their breath.

"Thank you. I forgot how fun that is."

"My pleasure, I assure you."

The moment turned quiet. If he didn't save it, she'd return to her seat.

He slipped a hand to the small of her back, the perfect curve that seemed suited for the size of his palm.

With gentle pressure, he pulled her closer, ready to stop against resistance. But she didn't pull back. Instead, she placed an arm around his shoulders, the warmth of her hand grazing his neck. Did he imagine the tips of her fingers tracing the line of his collar?

This lit a blaze in his chest, as they clasped their free hands and began to sway to the song. No more fancy footwork, not even a waltz, as they moved in a slow circle. The muscles in her back relaxed. She watched the others from their group, as they filled in the dance floor—the nontraditional student, Natalie, in particular, with little Teddy. He had to admit that the boy was sweet and had taken a bit of a shine to him. And maybe vice versa. At the moment, Teddy was trying to spin his mum under his tiny five-year-old arm and giggling when she had to crouch beneath it.

Alex laughed at the boy's antics, but when he returned his attention to Ellie, her face was creased with pain. "What is it, Ellie?"

She plastered on a wobbling smile. "I could say 'nothing,' couldn't I? But you won't believe me."

"Of course not. I'm not that daft."

She angled her face away. "I need to tell you something."

Finally. Honesty. That's what he'd waited for. What they needed.

"You can tell me. I'm not going anywhere."

Though the promise must sound empty to her after everything that had happened.

She'd slowed to almost standing still. He edged them to the railing overlooking the river, sparkling diamonds of crimson and gold.

Pressing her lips together, she eyed the people dancing as though determining if they could hear her or not. But the people were too far away. Besides, the music would muffle anything they said. He stepped closer, blocking the dance floor from her view, to give them additional privacy.

She squared her shoulders. "Alex, I had a miscarriage." She'd blurted it, wringing her hands, and rushed ahead, "And being here with you, watching families and couples, and little Teddy, I can't help but wonder what would've been."

It was like a giant boulder had crashed through his rib cage and sank to the very pit of his stomach. He gripped the railing until his knuckles turned to the white outlines of the bones underneath and stood blinking for several long seconds. "What?" It was the single word he could push from his constricted throat.

"We lost a baby…right after the shooting." Her words were slow this time, and each syllable echoed through his soul.

He dragged his palm down his face. A million questions churned inside his brain, but one blinked like a red neon sign. "How could you not tell me?"

"I wanted to—I did." Her feet shuffled from one to the other. "It's just, everything happened so fast. I found out right after our last fight about having a family, a couple of weeks before what happened at the store. I was so scared to tell you. When I said I wanted to run over to the pharmacy the night of the robbery, it was to buy another pregnancy test to be sure. I knew I had to break it to you gently, but I had planned to tell you that night after dinner."

"I'm your husband. We're supposed to share life-altering information." A boiling stew of frustration, sadness and confusion turned his stomach so that his dinner threatened a quick and violent exit.

"I know and I am sorry. You have no idea how many times I wanted to say something, how many times I picked up the phone to call you." Her shoulders drooped. "But in the end, I told myself you'd be relieved and I couldn't handle that kind of reaction. It was so fresh, so new. I had just started to imagine what our lives would be like with a precious child of our own. How we'd be a family, the three of us, maybe more someday. How it might feel to hold this child, kiss their little brow, dance with them resting on my chest, teach them about history someday..."

His sense of betrayal that she hadn't told him dimmed, though certainly didn't disappear. But the searing-hot pain slicing through his chest couldn't be ignored. How could it hurt this much to lose something he never knew he had? Something he'd never wanted for himself.

She drew a juddering breath. "And then the spark of this new life and all of the scary and wonderful what-ifs were stolen in a blink."

"Do you know what happened?"

She wrapped her arms around herself. The temptation to pull her against his chest was still there but buried beneath a mountain of questions.

"One of the shooters knocked me down and kicked me in the stomach when I tried to use my phone. But it may have also been the stress of the situation. By the time I left the hospital, I'd lost the baby."

"I'm sorry you felt you had to go through that alone. But you're wrong—completely wrong about me, by the way—if you think for a second I'd have been relieved. I would never wish for you to be in pain, not at any cost."

"Then how would you have felt? First, to find out you were going to be a dad and then to have that snatched away?"

Her round eyes searched his. Perhaps looking for something that wasn't there because the intensity quieted.

He could only respond in kind, with honesty. "I don't know. I can't be sure."

The music, the people around them had disappeared. There was only this devastation, this place from which there may be no return. Perhaps she'd been right—after all, she'd had all of the information and he hadn't yet—maybe there was no going forward with this giant heap of pain from the past blocking their path forward.

Not that she blamed him, but Ellora couldn't get Alex to look at her for more than a couple of seconds for the entire trip back to the castle Monday morning after the awe-inspiring church service at Durham Cathedral the morning before and more sightseeing around Durham. He sat kitty-corner ahead of her on the bus next to the local British professor, who'd taken the post of British political science teacher for the summer session. Not once had Alex turned to look at or speak to her.

But she hadn't been able to keep the secret of their miscarriage to herself another minute. It wasn't great timing. What could she do? The longer she'd been in his presence, the more convinced she'd become that he needed to know. The truth was, if she could do it over again, she would've told him right after the robbery. But she'd been suffering from shock and grief. She couldn't turn back the clock.

When Alex left her, when it had been her alone with the holes in her life, it had been easy to justify keeping this wound to herself. Like he had no right to know.

But had he? If she'd shared this with him the moment she could after the news reporters had finally left Alex alone at the hospital, would things have been different between them? Perhaps opening up an opportunity for compassion on both sides?

At the same time, another thought kept niggling at the back of her mind—couldn't he see she'd needed him? Especially when they realized Grandma June was missing. Why had he stayed away all this time if he seemed so keen on making things right with her now? Well...maybe not now after the bomb she'd dropped on him.

Anger and resentment expanded in her chest. If she were honest with herself, these were her companions over the last year. They hid behind her calm exterior, her "I'm fines" to anyone who asked.

Lanae, who had shared a room with her at the Durham hotel, had asked what happened.

"I think I might have lost him. For real this time." She'd buried her face in her hands. "And I didn't even know I'd care. I spent this last year telling myself good riddance."

Lanae had placed a hand on her shoulder. "Sometimes we don't know how important something is to us until we've lost it." Ellora had thought of the baby she'd lost too. "But if I know Alex, you haven't lost him. He just needs time."

Now, Lanae caught her studying the back of Alex's head. "Hey, it's going to be okay."

"I hope you're right."

The bus stopped in front of Alnwick Castle. Alex stood

in front of her and with the jostling of people and luggage behind her, she bumped into his back. He turned, his gaze landing on her with a ferocity that made her step back and onto Lanae's foot.

"Ow!" Lanae yelped.

"Sorry," she said through the side of her mouth to Lanae. Then back to Alex, "Hey, can I talk to you? Later, when you've settled back in your flat?"

He disembarked and moved to the side, letting a group of students pass before facing her.

He scratched his brow. "Yeah, we can talk. In fact, I think we have quite a lot to talk about in private. Just let me run my things upstairs and put the kettle on."

"Sure, I—"

"Alexander!" The voice sneaked up on her right. "There you are." It belonged to his mother. There they both were, her in-laws, Marian and Reginald Lockwood.

"Mother, Father." Alex placed his bag on the ground to shake his father's hand and kiss his mother on the cheek, who did not reach up to embrace her son. "I didn't know you were planning a visit."

Reginald—a mostly pleasant fellow who seemed to go along with Marian's moods and ideas far too often in Ellora's opinion—took a bite of the ice cream cone in his hand. "Yes, well, you know your mother. Always planning a trip here, a holiday there. Thought we'd pop in on our way to Dorset for a seaside escape. Get out of this heat, I say."

Both of Alex's parents had retired several years ago—he from the world of finance and she from a successful career in marketing—and moved to the posh town of Leeds not far from Alnwick.

As Marian eyed Ellora, a grin etched in ice pulled at her plump, red lips. She was a short woman with big hair and an even bigger personality. It had been no secret to Ellora that her mother-in-law had never taken to her. But then the woman had let her own son believe he was to blame for his brother's death and had treated him with frigid bitterness for years afterward. So, she took her mother-in-law's opinion of her with more than a few grains of salt. His parents had been more involved later on in Alex's life, but to her knowledge had never apologized for the way they'd behaved when he was younger.

"So the prodigal wife returns." Marian clapped her manicured hands together. "What are you doing here, Ellora?"

"Mother." Alex's jaw flexed. "That's not—"

"What? I'm kidding." Marian threw her hands up. "I'm glad to see you both on the same bit of soil again. I am. Maybe you two can give me some grandkids before I'm too old to enjoy them."

Alex's skin blanched, his face stricken. The urge to take his hand was great, but that was probably the last thing he wanted.

Reginald didn't seem to know where to look. "Dear, that's between them. Let's not interfere, shall we?"

"Well, it's true, is it not?" Marian bumped Ellora's arm. "The old biological clock and all of that."

Was the woman insulting her age now?

Reginald shrugged like there was nothing he could do about his wife's behavior and continued eating his ice cream.

"Mother, that's enough." Alex's eyes had turned stormy. "I won't have any more talk like that. It's none of your business. Now, would you like to come up for some tea?"

She could hug Alex for his fierce protection.

Marian waved off the rebuke. "We actually wanted to see if you would like to have dinner—" She gestured to Ellora then continued, "Well, Ellora too, of course. We didn't know she would be here. If you're not up to cooking, I thought I could visit the shops and bring back some things to make for supper. What do you say?"

Alex caught Ellora's eye and started shaking his head.

What came over her, Ellora couldn't say, but she blurted, "Sure. But I'll cook." This woman had messed with her self-esteem in every possible way over the years; she wasn't going to let her win today.

She snagged Lanae's arm as Lanae had situated all of the students and was about to walk past Ellora. "And I'd like to make it a small dinner party if we could. My friend Lanae would like to come, along with…"

Her friend caught on. "With Oscar Machal." Ellora mouthed, "Thank you."

Alex's shoulders lowered as if relaxing. "Yes, my friend Oscar. You remember, the stable master."

Reginald inclined his head, a good-natured sort of smile on his face. Marian's drawn-in brows raised. "Of course, sounds delightful."

They agreed that the elder Lockwoods would visit the Bailiffgate Museum, which they'd planned to do while in town anyway, to give Ellora time to go to the grocery store and Alex time to tidy up his flat…and ensure he had a fire extinguisher. With her cooking, it might be necessary.

After Ellora had stowed her things in her apartment, Lanae met her at the Barbican Gate to walk into town. "What in the world are you going to make, girl? You've literally messed up boiling water. I can help you, but I sensed you wanted to prove something to your mother-in-law."

They started toward the little grocery store on Bondgate Within, a five- to ten-minute walk from the castle.

"I do. It's stupid and petty, but she never believed I was a worthy wife for her son. And she hated that he moved to

Minnesota for me." She rubbed her hands together. "So, I'm going to make—perfectly, might I add—a good ol' Minnesota delicacy, tater tot hotdish."

Lanae pressed her palms together. "Lord, help us all."

The smoke alarm blared for the third time, reverberating like a freight train in the small space of Alex's flat. Ellora pulled the tater tot hotdish—as close as she could get by making her own tater tots out of potatoes she grated on a cheese grater and then fashioned into little lumps—out of the oven and waved away the billowing black smoke with her oven mitts.

Lanae opened the window next to the dining area wider and used a kitchen towel to waft the smoke outside.

"Oh, man. They're going to be back any minute, aren't they?" Ellora slapped a hand to her forehead.

Alex and Oscar, who had been setting the table, approached with caution.

Oscar coughed into his elbow. "Sorry." He moved over to where Lanae chopped vegetables for a salad. They had a good rhythm as they worked elbow to elbow. Ellora's heart warmed for her friend as Lanae beamed at something Oscar said and tipped her head back to laugh.

Alex sidled up next to Ellora. "How's it coming along, love?"

At least as the afternoon went on, Alex had begun speaking to her again and the tension had subsided. For now.

"What? You couldn't tell by the three smoke alarms that dinner was almost ready?" She bit the inside of her cheek. So much for proving anything other than Marian right about her. Ellora had failed at everything, her marriage included.

Alex's grin turned wry. "Ah, yes. I'm like Pavlov's dogs

now. I hear the alarms and my mouth starts salivating. It's the dinner bell calling me to the table."

One of his brows arched when he caught her fixated on his mouth. His one dimple deepened. Did she mistake the blossoming heat in his own eyes?

"What am I going to do? What is your mother going to think of me?"

He started picking off the truly burnt bits on top of the hotdish with a fork. "Don't give what my mother thinks any space in your mind. I try not to, though I know she is a formidable woman. Besides, it'll be good for her to deal with something less than perfect."

An edge of bitterness crept into his tone.

Lanae brought the salad bowl to the table with tongs tucked inside, along with a balsamic dressing she'd made. "Here, we can have the salad. We can pick off the burnt parts of the hotdish and we have garlic bread. Voilà!"

"You mean the blackened garlic bread. I burned that too. I'm a hopeless cook."

Lanae, with rounded eyes and a somber expression, laid a hand on Ellora's shoulder. "Yes, my dear, you are. An absolutely abominable cook, a true force of ruin and havoc in the kitchen. It's actually kind of impressive. But you do have loads of other amiable qualities."

Ellora's grim frown cracked into a smirk.

She held up her glass of lemonade. "I'll cheers to that."

Everyone clanked glasses and sipped, lips puckering at the too-sour lemonade she'd made.

They took in the chaos around them and burst out laughing.

The change in mood continued as Alex's parents arrived. Marian didn't try to hide her disgust, and her pinched features made all of them clamp their mouths shut to keep from snickering. Ellora's eyes watered by the time she passed the tater tot hotdish to her mother-in-law and Marian tried as gracefully as possible to extricate a congealed spoonful onto her plate.

It fell onto her plate with a sickening *shlop*. Marian picked at the "food," her down-turned lips never lifting. "I never understood why Minnesotans insist on calling this a 'hotdish.' Isn't every dish that you cook hot?"

Reginald held his fork aloft like a conductor's baton. "Yes, what exactly constitutes a *hotdish*? Seems to me just left-over Sunday dinner thrown together." He seemed genuinely pleased with his observation and plopped a bit of unburned veggie into his mouth.

"Something like that. Similar to a casserole here," Ellora answered.

Marian's nose wrinkled as she pushed potato mush to the other side of her plate.

"Will you pass the hotdish down here?" Oscar put the last forkful of potato from his plate in his mouth, seeming unfazed by the blackened entrée everyone else picked at politely. "I quite like it. Not sure what you're all on about."

A grateful warmth filled her chest. She grinned as she passed the dish down to Oscar. "Well, you're all right, aren't you? You might be the only fan of my cooking."

Lanae too smiled in Oscar's direction when he took another bite of his new helping and gave a thumbs-up.

The rest of them ate mostly salad and picked off the blackened edges of the bread to make it edible.

After Marian dabbed her lips with the napkin, though she'd hardly eaten a morsel, she leaned over the table. "You know, your father and I saw something that might interest you, Alexander. About the Vikings. I know you always loved studying the Norsemen history of the area."

Reginald wiped his mouth with a napkin as well. But if she didn't know better, she'd say he'd spit food into it. "Ah, yes. Fascinating stuff, that."

From Ellora's memory, it was rare that his parents took an interest in Alex's passions or career since they thought he should have followed his father's career path like his brother had wanted to.

Alex stopped sliding a somehow undercooked yet charred bit of improvised tater tot around with his fork. "Oh? Yes, I'm very keen on that bit of history. And Ellora and I, that's part of why she came. We're looking for a lost manuscript from the Viking era her grandmother had been researching."

"Indeed?" Marian's eyes shifted to Ellora. "Well, the Bailiffgate Museum. They have a traveling Norsemen exhibit right now."

Reginald sat up, elbows on the table. A spark of excitement lit his forest green eyes, reminding Ellora of Alex's reaction to history and Viking history in particular. "Loads of old rocks they engraved and such. Writings, jewelry, pottery and the like. You'd love the weapons area, and they have a partial hull from one of the ships."

Alex matched his father, propping his elbows. "Really? I hadn't heard they were hosting a Viking exhibit."

"Oh, yes." Marian seemed pleased to inform him of something of interest to him. "And, do you remember, Reggie?" She gestured to Reginald. "There was that story the curator told of a little lore accompanying some artifact or other. She told of a highborn Englishwoman who disappeared after one of those Viking attacks on Lindisfarne. She was taken by the Viking chief and his clan, never to return to her family."

Why was she sharing this random bit of information? Maybe she and Reginald were trying to show more regard for their son's life and his love of history. Ellora could get on board with that.

Marian fixed Ellora with a calculated look. "It's kind of like when you kidnapped my son and brought him to the States. But in our case, he came home to where he belongs now. With his own people."

Nope. Maybe not.

"Mother, enough." Alex stabbed a cucumber with his fork, the metal scraping against the plate with a high-pitched screech.

The rest of the meal was eaten in silence save for a few cordial spots of conversation. Poor Lanae and Oscar carrying most of it.

Ellora's body sagged in relief as they bid his parents goodbye.

Despite Marian's declaration that she was happy to see them in the same place again, her comments told a different story. But one thing her mother-in-law probably hadn't expected—Marian's plan to scare her off had instead induced the opposite reaction. It had only reignited compassion in her heart for Alex and what he'd endured over the years.

While they still had much to discuss, much more forgiveness on both of their parts, she squared her shoulders at the challenge.

"So, next stop, the Bailiffgate Museum?" Ellora sent a glance Alex's way.

He dipped his chin. "I'm going where you are, love."

Chapter Eight

It wasn't that Ellora didn't want Lanae and Oscar along on her and Alex's excursion to the Bailiffgate Museum in the heart of Alnwick; it was just that she and Alex had so much to talk about. Was it possible he didn't want to be alone with her, didn't want to discuss the miscarriage or their relationship? Wednesday now, mid-June, and they still hadn't had that "row" Alex suggested, or even a conversation.

Of course, it had been a busy week so far. She'd been lesson planning, grading papers and took the students to see a couple of relics of the Middle Ages right there in Alnwick—including the Church of St. Michael, Hotspur Gateway and the ruins of Hulne Priory on the expansive 3,000-acre grounds of the Percy family's Hulne Park. So, perhaps it had been a timing thing, and inviting Oscar and Lanae had been in appreciation for sitting through the awkward and unappetizing—in more ways than one—dinner with her in-laws, like Alex claimed.

She studied Alex's profile as they walked to the 19th-century church-turned-museum. Lanae and Oscar were ahead of them, discussing all things farm animals and gardening with animated gestures. Even in such a short time, "smitten" was painted across both of their faces. Ellora needed to make a point to have a gab session with Lanae. What would her friend do if this job didn't pan out to become long-term? Or the long distance when she inevitably had to go back to Minnesota, at least for a while, became too much? Would she and Oscar be saying goodbye at the end of the summer like Ellora and Alex?

And her own unstable situation with Alex made her feel like she was the man from the Bible parable with his house on shifting sands. She lifted a quick prayer for direction, though for years now, she'd felt a distance from God. Like He wasn't there when she needed Him the most. Kind of like Alex. With each loss, God had seemed to inch further away from her. Or had *she* inched away from *Him*? The thought dragged at her soul and her feet slowed.

"You coming?" Alex waved her up the steps of the museum.

"Yup." The twinkle in his eye gave her hope that they could clear the air yet.

Nostalgia coursed through her mind in mental pictures of her time in Alnwick as a student as they strolled through the local history exhibit.

Then they entered the special installment about Viking history in Northumberland.

Two familiar faces rounded the corner—Eg and his son, Freddie, from the Lost Artifact Society.

"Hi there, you lot!" Eg rushed over, giving each person, even though he'd never met Oscar or Lanae, a vigorous handshake. He wore another loud Hawaiian-print shirt.

"Come to see about the Viking stuff, eh? It's brilliant. Absolutely brilliant. You'll see what I meant about the story of a man who escaped after the monks and scribes escaped Lindisfarne Priory, supposedly carrying a bound book. They have a bit of a write-up on it in the next room, but my son and I were looking into the name. We're almost dead sure we've discovered the name of the poor soul. He may have died shortly after the Viking attack. Aelfgar."

Eg had spit all of the words out in one long breath. While he sucked in a lungful of air, Ellora took the opportunity to lay a hand on his forearm. "Eg, will you let me know if you find anything else?"

Freddie bounced on his heels. "I'll look into it too, Ms. Lockwood. I'm leaving for Lindisfarne next week for the history immersion program. Even if I can't figure it out before I leave, I'll be in the best place to help you find information once I'm in Lindisfarne."

Eg beamed and ruffled the teen's mop of hair. "That's my boy. Well done. I'll do what I can to help too, of course."

"Thank you, both of you. We appreciate it."

Alex nodded his agreement. Out of the side of his mouth, he muttered for her ears alone. "The royal 'we,' eh?"

She gave him a playful nudge. "Shh."

Eg and Freddie tipped their heads. As they started to step away, Eg held up a hand and turned back. "Oh, our next meeting for the Lost Artifact Society is tomorrow at Thomas's tea shop. Do you think you'll drop in?"

She exchanged a look with Alex. The first experience hadn't been the best, especially with that Cressida.

Shifting on her feet, she finally answered. "We'll see if we can make it."

The father and son waved goodbye, and she and Alex

walked through the exhibit to join the other two, who had started to peruse the displays.

Lanae and Oscar examined a glass case of various Viking artifacts—metalwork belt clasps, engraved rune stones, chalices, necklaces and brooches. It had always sent a thrill of curious wonder through Ellora looking at physical pieces of the past like this. To imagine the people who would've used them, what their lives must've been like.

Ellora smirked at her friend. "Isn't SCOBY Steve old enough to be in here?"

Lanae planted a hand on her hip. "Steve is hardly that old. Though I've heard of a sixty-five-year-old sourdough starter in the Cotswolds. Just celebrated its birthday."

With a toss of her long beachy tresses, Lanae set her jaw, daring anyone to question her knowledge of these "crunchy granola" facts.

Oscar grinned. "I love kombucha. And I eat a lot of things other people think are abhorrent. Mostly natural stuff like quinoa and flax seeds, but also things that grow in the community garden—kale, brussels sprouts, lima beans... You should come out there with me tomorrow. I have a few things to check on."

"I'd love to. I'm having the students help me with a community project at the Alnwick Garden."

Alex nodded to their surroundings. "Well, what are we looking for?"

"We can start by finding that account of the Englishwoman abducted at Lindisfarne your parents told us about." Ellora tapped her foot.

"And don't forget the man who may have been carrying a manuscript after the raid."

Oscar chimed in, "Should we split up to cover more ground?"

Lanae cocked her head to the side. "Let's go in pairs."

Alex lifted a brow. "Subtle."

Ellora pulled Alex away and tossed over her shoulder, "Come find us if you see something of interest."

They found the picture etched into stone with crude outlines that depicted a man escaping Lindisfarne, Vikings in the background with axes and swords pillaging the priory. He did hold a book under his arm. Part of the stone had broken off, but in the foreground, a group of etched men and monks remained.

"So, this must be the man Eg was talking about. Why did he think this was the lost manuscript we're looking for?" Alex's arm brushed hers as he inspected the stone behind the glass.

"I'm not sure. But this certainly looks like a man escaping the raid and this edge here—" she pointed without smudging the glass "—where you can see the group of men running away. This man was left behind."

Left behind.

"This chap missed the memo it was time to go, didn't he?"

It was just a picture carved into stone, cold and not alive. And yet, it told the story inside of her own heart. Left behind. Pushed back. Others running away from her. Fending for herself.

Alex's smile faded. "What is it?"

"It's silly." Alex squeezed her arm with gentle pressure. "It's just, I guess I can understand what that's like. Feeling left behind."

"Because I left?" Pain creased his eyes, folded his forehead. "I've been wanting to talk to you since the weekend. Since I found out…"

"I want to talk to you too. But it's not just that. People have been leaving me all of my life. My mom, my dad, then my grandma." She held up a hand. "I know Grandma June didn't mean to. But much as I know she loves me, the next project, the next historical puzzle is always more important. Something else is always chosen over me. You know?"

Alex had moved to shield her from a couple and their small children tearing through on their way to the kids' exhibits, no doubt. Ellora caught sight of a tiny newborn in a baby sling, nestled against the mother's chest. Every happy family begged the question, "Why not me?" Had God left her behind too? Was He still listening, still there, sitting through this grief with her?

As the space quieted again, Alex's face hovered near hers. So close his presence warmed the sudden chill creeping through her limbs. "Ellie, I never wanted to be another wound on your heart. I bungled everything up."

"Me too. I should've told you about the baby right away. I should never have—"

Lanae and Oscar stepped around the corner.

Motioning with her hand, Lanae beckoned them. "We have to show you something."

She and Alex followed as they led the way to a painting. There was considerable damage to the middle right side of the painting, making it difficult to see all of the details. A person standing in the middle? Part of a knotted cross pendant, still visible, hung around the person's neck. The other people, villagers perhaps, were standing or kneeling and gathered around this central person. Praying? And the crowd seemed to be dressed like Vikings—warriors with their weapons stowed at their sides and backs, women in long dresses and pinafores, and children in their tunics.

There was something familiar about the painting, the way the characters within it were composed.

Her head snapped up, eyes widening. "Why does this remind me of the painting we saw in Durham?"

Excitement poured from Lanae's bouncing extremities. "Because it *is* like it only the people are dressed differently, right?"

Oscar inserted, "It looks like the picture you showed me on your phone, mate." Ellora had shared the pictures with Lanae as well.

Ellora exchanged a glance with Alex.

A museum guide walked by. Alex held up a hand to signal her over. "Excuse me, ma'am. Can you tell us a bit about this painting and where it came from?"

The woman, probably in her midfifties, seemed pleased someone wanted her help. "Of course. This piece was given to the museum as something that would not sell from a local auction. Most of our pieces are donated by the community. The estate it came from wished to stay anonymous. But we do know that it has been through a fire."

Ellora cocked her head to the side, studying the composition again. "Do you know what that building is in the background? A church?"

The guide polished her glasses on her cardigan, next to a name tag that read "Katherine," then placed them on her nose. "We think so. And some believe that with the Roman-looking fort on the hill in the background and there appears to be a river snaking through, that this is Chester-le-Street."

She exchanged a glance with Alex. She filled in Lanae and Oscar. "That was the first resting place for the monks and scribes who escaped Lindisfarne in 875. They wandered for several years and then settled for a time in Chester-le-Street around 883."

Alex added, "They brought the supposed uncorrupted body of St. Cuthbert, the Lindisfarne Gospels and other holy relics, and even erected a wooden church there before leaving in 995 for Durham."

"Do you know when it was painted?" This came from Oscar, who was appearing more and more intrigued.

The guide furrowed her brows behind her glasses. "I don't."

Alex jumped in, all debonair smiles. "Kathy—can I call you Kathy?"

Katherine hesitated. Alex continued, his eyes sparkling and dimple on full display. Irritation bristled up Ellora's back. He couldn't just do anything he wanted because he happened to put on his most devastating grin.

"We're continuing the noble work of my wife's—" Alex's widened eyes locked with Ellora's, but then returned to cool and collected "—grandmother, June Wiltshire. She is a historian and—"

"Yes, I remember June." Katherine fussed with a lock of her short curls. She didn't seem taken in with Alex's charm, just...a little agitated. "In fact, she came in here about a year ago." Her lips pressed together for a moment. "She asked to see this painting as well."

Could this have been one of the final places to see her grandmother alive?

"I can take it down if you'd like." The painting hung behind glass that Katherine unlocked from the side. She slipped on a pair of white cotton gloves and lifted the painting down.

All four members of their little team leaned in, but there wasn't much more to see on the front. When Katherine turned the painting over, there was the date 1535 next to some odd symbols, etched into the frame on the back.

Katherine brushed her gloved finger over the date. "Because of the date and Tudor-era painting style combined with an early medieval subject matter, we've wondered if this is actually a reproduction of an earlier work. Though we know Vikings did convert to Christianity over time, I've not heard of a large pilgrimage to a Christian site like this. But art doesn't have to contain fact, does it?"

"Hmm," Ellora mused.

The symbols next to the year seemed familiar, like she'd seen them somewhere before...

She gasped. The etching in one of the journals—she'd taken it as nonsense. "My grandmother had a rubbing of those symbols. Did she do that here?"

Now the woman shifted from one foot to the other, glance darting between the four of them. "We told her she could examine it in a back room, but...she managed to take it with her out of the museum. I'm sorry to say, we almost had to call the police."

Ellora's hand flew to her mouth. "I'm so sorry." The same old embarrassment and hurt surfaced again.

"It all came out right in the end." Katherine shrugged. "The next day, June showed up with the painting, undamaged. Well, as undamaged as it was already. I'm still unsure what she hoped to find."

After Katherine allowed her to take a picture of the front and back with her phone and locked the painting behind glass again—lest June Wiltshire's granddaughter decide to pull a fast one like her grandmother—Ellora and the others returned to the overcast afternoon outside.

"I wish I knew what the symbols meant," Ellora said.

"I do. Or at least I will." Alex's head tipped toward her. "I didn't want to give all of our secrets away. Can't be too careful."

All three of them said, "What does it say?"

"It's Futhark, the written language of the Vikings. Katherine may have known it too, but she didn't offer it up. So, I'll look at it and make our own interpretation. The language is notoriously tricky, especially because there can be multiple meanings for each symbol. Plus, it appears both Elder and Younger Futhark are being used here. So I'll have to consult my Norse linguistics texts."

"Finally, we're getting somewhere. Have I ever told you you're a genius?" A light, joy-filled balloon seemed to fill her chest. "But don't let it inflate your head."

"We make a good team," Lanae threw over her shoulder, her steps bounding along next to Oscar's steady strides. "What's next, Lost Manuscript Society?"

Lanae glanced back. "I thought we could borrow a page from that quirky Lost Artifact Society group and narrow our focus."

Ellora dipped her chin and set her shoulders straight. "Now, I say we contact Professor Ridgewater at Durham University, to see if he knows of any connection between these two paintings. Something strange is going on there."

"And let's double our efforts to find Grandma June's master field journal." Alex's jaw set.

The journal was the key. But she'd already searched every square inch of her grandmother's office and all around in the trunk. How would they unlock the doors to the answers they needed without the key?

Alex had never wanted to be a father. He'd known it from a young age, but more so after his brother's death. He'd touted it as an anthem for his life. It dictated what he pursued in his career, how he approached and planned for his future—not that his best-laid plans had always turned out the way he'd wanted. And this mindset, this absolute truth as he saw it, had informed who he chose as a spouse. This person had to be on board with not having children. That person had become Ellora, or so he'd thought.

So, why couldn't he stop thinking about the fact he'd almost become a father? And, in fact, he'd had an unborn child without knowing it.

He crumpled the edge of the paper in front of him. He'd come to his office early to decipher the Futhark letters they'd found on the museum painting.

So far, if he took the literal meaning of the Elder Futhark symbols, it pointed to a vague place—the ice lake or the lake of ice? But then their words for *year* and *hail* were thrown in there too. It didn't help that someone had mixed in Younger Futhark, used in the ninth century and beyond, which was slightly different than the older version of the language.

But concentration was hard-won.

Thoughts of everything that happened after the shooting pushed all else from his mind. Knowing what he knew now shed new light on the matter. Images of how broken and withdrawn Ellora had been after they'd returned home from the hospital rushed back to him. He'd taken it as the final straw, that she didn't love him anymore. That she wouldn't try to support him in his own turmoil over Dylan, the young man who'd died. He'd been so encased in the memories of his own brother dying to notice what she was going through.

But what if this giant spiked lead ball sitting in the middle of his chest, puncturing his lungs with every breath, and these thoughts on repeat, ran even deeper than his concern for Ellora? Or Dylan? There was another life extinguished that night.

Shaking his head to clear it, he checked his phone again for a call from Professor Ridgewater. Thursday morning had rolled into lunchtime in a quick spurt as he'd researched the symbols and tended to his work duties.

He'd called Ridgewater about the painting in his office. He'd shared his theory that perhaps the Tudor-era setting of the professor's painting wasn't the original, but was instead a scene from a much earlier time period.

The professor was intrigued and said he was fond of the painting, but not attached to it. Ridgewater planned to pull some strings with an art restorer at Oxford who could give an expert opinion on the matter. The art restorer had access to a handheld X-ray machine used to scan artwork of antiquity. This allowed them a glimpse beneath the top layer of paint to see if anything lay hidden underneath. Alex had sent a picture of the fire-damaged painting from the museum and was waiting to hear if this art restorer would help them.

He did a double take at the time on his phone. He was late. He'd promised to meet Ellora, Lanae and Oscar at the tea shop for the meeting of the Lost Artifact Society—sort of a little recon for their own newly formed Lost Manuscript Society.

Grabbing his waistcoat, he threw his arms into the armholes and fastened the four buttons. He couldn't bear the suit jacket on this humid day. This would have to do. He straightened his tie, grabbed his phone and locked the door behind him.

He dashed to the castle gates. The air left his lungs with an "Oof!" as little Teddy barreled into his gut.

"Promesser Alex, sir." He'd told the boy to call him Alex, but it probably confused him because his mother, Natalie, called him Professor Lockwood—confusing, in general, since Ellie was called by the same name.

"Just Alex, Teddy. What can I do for you, little man? I'm afraid I'm running a bit behind schedule."

The boy's big brown eyes rounded. "I don't know what shed-jool means. You sound funny when you talk. But I talk a lot. People tell me all the time. Sometimes it hurts my feelings." He stomped his trainers on the cobbled stone castle pathway. "That's why my mom says to be kind to people no matter what. Don't worry, I won't make fun of your funny talking." The words had rattled along together so fast, that Alex had to concentrate to catch them all.

Teddy beamed.

"Thank you. I appreciate that." Alex couldn't help the dry humor leaking into his tone.

His mother caught up to Teddy.

Her breathing came in gasps as she skidded to a stop. "I'm sorry, he got away from me when he saw you out the window."

As he understood it, Teddy's father had left her when he'd found out she was pregnant. Now, she had taken the opportunity to study abroad and complete the degree she was never able to, being a young single parent when Teddy came along. It squeezed another measure of compassion for this boy and his mother from Alex's heart. It also set something straight in his mind—although he'd never intended to have children, he could never abandon a child nor Ellora.

He waved off her apology. "Quite all right. We were just having a chat. Weren't we, Teddy? No harm done."

She bent to Teddy's eye level. "Teddy, you can't run away from me like that. You scared me."

"Sorry, Mama. I just wanted to give this to Promesser Alex." He dug a crumpled piece of paper from his back pocket and handed it to Alex.

Complete with scribbles and sticky fingerprints, inside was a flier for the Alnwick Fair, a yearly summer staple in Alnwick. This year the theme printed at the top was "Fair Maidens and Noble Knights: A Dalliance in Medieval Times."

Teddy had colored in the cartoon outline of Alnwick Castle, women in long medieval dresses and men in knight's armor.

"Are you going to the fair? I'm going. Mom said I can catch candy at the parade if I don't run out into the street and get squished." His face was so matter-of-fact as he smooshed his cheeks together with his little hands.

Both he and his mom clamped their lips to keep from laughing.

After clearing his throat, he managed, "Yes, I believe so, buddy." The paper listed activities for the day. "Besides, I have to see how I get on as a knight-in-training with this fencing competition, don't I? You know, in case there's anyone who needs saving."

The word *saving* gave him pause. He'd made a terrible hero, had never wanted to be one. But he'd done what he could...which hadn't been enough in the end.

He bent his head toward Natalie. "I'm sorry, I must be on my way."

"Of course. Thank you, he's quite taken with you."

Alex tousled the boy's hair on his way past. "The feeling's mutual. See you later, Teddy."

He turned one more glance over his shoulder. Teddy waved vigorously with one hand and his mother kept hold of his other lest he scamper away from her again.

What a handful. What an absolute delight. That same rush of questions with no answers spun around in his mind. What if? Would he have had a precocious son like Teddy? Maybe a sweet and spirited daughter who took after her mother? They'd never know.

Along the way, his phone buzzed in his pocket.

"Cheers, my boy." Ridgewater's voice rang out on the other end.

By the time Alex arrived at the tea shop, he couldn't wait to find Ellora and tell her the good news.

Byron blew past him in a hurry to leave the tea shop. If Alex wasn't mistaken, Thomas appeared out of sorts, but Thomas smiled and waved when he spotted Alex.

He found their group of three on one side of a long table made up of two smaller tables. The smile Ellora lifted toward him as he pulled out the chair next to her hit him square in the chest. One word came to mind—devastating. In the best possible way.

The rest of the Lost Artifact Society browsed menus and chatted among themselves at the other side of the table, so he leaned closer to Ellora to catch Lanae's and Oscar's attention too. Though, he had to admit, breathing in Ellie's scent of lavender and vanilla was reason enough to move closer.

"I have some good news, Lost Manuscript Society." He rested an elbow on the table. His mother would be appalled. "Professor Ridgewater has an art historian and restorer contact at Oxford. She's agreed to travel to Durham to inspect and scan Ridgewater's painting to see if any secrets are hiding underneath."

"That's amazing. Thank you." Ellora reached over and grabbed his upper arm. His muscles tensed at her touch. She rolled her eyes as though he'd meant to flex for her. Raking a hand through his hair to play it off, he winked and shot her a wicked grin.

Lanae pivoted in her seat. "So, what happens if they see something is hidden beneath that top layer of paint?"

Alex scratched the stubble filling in along his jawline. "Good question. Dr. Ridgewater is willing to have the art historian take the painting back to Oxford, if necessary, to complete a process of removing the top layer of paint with chemicals. But that's a painstaking process and can't be rushed. Otherwise, the bottom layers can be destroyed as well."

Oscar scratched his razored-smooth head, appearing a bit out of his element. "What are you hoping to find?"

Bless the man, he was taken with Lanae. If Alex had to guess, Lanae was more than half the reason his friend had agreed to join their little Lost Manuscript Society.

Ellora turned to Oscar. "I'm starting to suspect that the painting Professor Ridgewater has is a replica of the one damaged in the fire at the museum or vice versa. So, potentially, if they can remove that layer, we'll be able to see the true picture underneath and what the burned painting was supposed to show us."

When the four of them quieted, the rest of the table had gone silent.

Cressida narrowed her eyes as though she'd been listening to their every word. "So, Lost *Manuscript* Society. Is there anything you'd like to share with the class? Why you visited the museum? If you're not here to share, then you're wasting our time."

Though the other members' eyes widened, some seeming in shock and others in embarrassment, no one argued.

Alex gestured with his hand. "We're still working on June's search, but really, nothing to report yet." They needed to be careful about who they told, especially when they still didn't know the cause of Grandma June's disappearance.

Their smaller group excused themselves when it was polite to do so. He trusted Eg and his son, who had outright defended them to Cressida. But as all of those pairs of eyes studied them, not for the first time did it occur to him that any one of these people could be connected to whatever happened to Grandma June. Or at the very least, knew more about it than they'd let on.

From now on, they needed to keep their leads close to the chest. After all, it appeared more and more with each passing day that Grandma June may have been right. Someone had been after her and what she'd sought. Maybe even killed her to get it.

Chapter Nine

A chime woke Ellora from a restless sleep, full of stress and fear, nightmares of faceless evil chasing first her grandmother and then her. She sat up.

Still dark outside.

The reason she'd been dragged from slumber dawned on her. She grabbed her cell phone from the side table beside her bed. Just after 3:00 a.m., Saturday.

A message waited for her. She swiped the screen to read it. The words made her throw a hand over her mouth.

Learn from your grandmother's mistakes. Be careful digging into the past, or history is doomed to repeat itself.

A ripple of goose bumps raced up her back. Even the damp hair at the nape of her neck stood on end.

Could the text, the number listed as "Unknown," be from

someone who knew what had happened to her grandmother? Could this person have had something to do with it?

She jumped to her feet but froze to the spot. With only her eyes moving, she checked the corners of the room. When nothing jumped from the shadows, her body thawed and she flew into action. She grabbed her robe and phone, though she turned it off as if the phone itself had been watching her.

Fear gripped her stomach, and her heart pummeled her ribs so hard in her chest it left invisible bruises. The need to feel safe was the only driving force. She prayed that God would replace her fear with peace, but she couldn't stop herself from envisioning Alex. His presence had always been her safe place. Well, at least for a long time he'd been that for her.

It was a ridiculously early hour. She couldn't call him. But the other day he'd given her a key to his apartment when she'd wanted to drop off a stack of textbooks in his apartment but he'd been busy in his office a while longer.

Before she could change her mind, she snatched his key from the kitchen counter as well as her own. She closed and locked her door then crept down the hall. Every creak made her stop, scouring the nooks and crannies of the moonlit corridor.

She made it to Alex's door. Another moment of hesitation passed, her jittering hand poised in a fist. Should she knock? No. They both had a long day ahead of them with the Alnwick Fair. Instead, she fitted the key into the lock and turned it as quietly as she could. Though the screech of the hinges as she shut and locked the door behind her was like a bomb going off in the hushed space, nothing stirred within.

She shuffled forward.

Memories of the story of Ruth in the Bible came to mind as Ellora tiptoed farther inside, her fears ebbing away with

Alex's slow breathing off somewhere ahead. Was this the way Ruth had stepped through the dark, trying to find Boaz so she could lie at his feet?

There was much debate out there about what it all meant, but to Ellora, it had seemed a beautiful picture of trust and a pouring out of oneself. Ruth had put herself, her reputation and the fate of the only family she had left—her mother-in-law, Naomi—in the hands of the man she'd come to respect and care for.

Ruth had lain at Boaz's feet on the threshing floor, hoping he would accept her for who she was, her social standing, past and all. Which, of course, he did, wholeheartedly, and became what was known as a kinsman-redeemer.

And here Ellora was, Alex had already chosen her and she, him, but it had fallen apart. Their threshing floor—where the harvest was brought to separate the usable grain from the unusable hulls—had revealed all of the worst kinds of chaff. Selfishness, distrust, hard hearts and, perhaps worst of all, a loss of hope. They'd given up. Was there still any healthy grain left from the winnowing of their marriage? Anything on which they could nourish a life together as husband and wife?

Did the Great Thresher of Souls, her heavenly kinsman-redeemer, who could separate her from the chaff of her iniquities, still find grains worth using in her? She'd blamed Alex, blamed God, time and again. Had they fought for her when she needed them most? Had they stood by her and loved her when she was at her most unlovable?

Her chest ached with the questions pointed away from her, but also with what pointed back at her.

If she were honest with herself, she hadn't fought for their marriage either. She hadn't dealt with the baggage that had followed her into their marriage in the first place, which had made the added weight of the miscarriage unbearable to hold. She'd let go instead.

Her big toe bumped into the leg of a side table. She'd reached the living room. She sucked a breath through her teeth and tried not to cry out as her toe throbbed. She didn't have a threshing floor, nor did she care to sleep at Alex's feet, but she had a couch.

The threshing floor was a place of surrender, a "not my will but Yours be done." A place to swallow her own pride and where she hoped Alex would do the same. Could she do what would be required to move forward?

It was a tall order, especially for someone who'd learned early on to keep her guard up lest someone get in, love her, then leave her. And that's exactly what had happened with Alex. She let the silence wash over her, broken only by the sound of his breathing. Just the scent of him nearby slowed her heartbeats.

Perhaps he was right; she had to let his sorry be enough. Because she did believe he regretted leaving.

Feeling her way around to the front of the couch, she lowered herself down and drew her robe tight around her.

Maybe, if he wasn't upset or creeped out that she'd sneaked in—her heart gave a little tug—she'd like to have that conversation about where they could go from here as he'd wanted to days ago. Hopefully, he hadn't changed his mind after hearing about their miscarriage. She didn't know if it would all work out between them, but the alternative of not trying suddenly sounded so much more terrifying.

Truth be told, the warmth beside Alex called to her. He was a furnace when he slept and she'd always loved that.

He'd yelped more than once when she'd pressed her icicle toes to his legs during those frigid Minnesota winter nights.

They were still married, after all. They'd shared a bed for years…but not in seven months. Somehow those months had changed everything. She made herself a blanket of couch pillows and stayed put.

The strange text message and the reason she was there, safe in Alex's presence, seemed a distant memory as her own breathing slowed and she drifted off.

"Ellie?" The soft but surprised voice broke into Ellora's shallow sleep. "Is that you, love?"

Ellora pried her eyelids open. She blinked. "Mmm-hmm."

Alex stood above her, peering over the back of the couch, hair disheveled, glasses on, looking as handsome as ever. Behind his head, the clock read 5:45 a.m. So, maybe he was going to wake up early after all.

He pulled the pillow mostly covering her face back and quirked an amused grin. "Usually, if one breaks into a flat, they make off with the electronics or the good silver. Seems you've fallen asleep on the job. I must say you make an adorable bandit, but you're not a terribly successful one, are you?"

Ellora slid the pillow partially covering her face down to her chest and wrapped her arms around it. "I'm sorry I snuck in." Suddenly self-conscious, she shoved herself up to her feet and finger-combed through her tangled tresses. "There was this text last night and I got scared—but I didn't want to wake you, so…" She grabbed her phone from her robe pocket and turned it to show him the text.

"Possibly someone having a go, but with everything that's happened, we should take this seriously. We'll call the inspector on Grandma June's case after a bite of breakfast, yeah?"

"All right." It lightened her shoulders to have him share this burden. She returned her phone to her pocket and busied herself with drawing her robe tighter around herself.

At least she was in her extremely modest 1800s-inspired cotton nightgown with lace trim that Alex had affectionately named her Little House on the Prairie nightdress. But given the tender, heated way his eyes pierced hers, she didn't feel as though she wore this most unflattering of garments.

"I wanted to tell you that when that happened last night, the first person I thought of was you. I wished you were there with me. I've always felt safe with you, protected, and I knew if I could just be in the same room I'd be okay. But I'm sorry I used your key without asking."

He moved around the couch in long strides and pulled her into his arms, pressed her to his chest. Smoothing her hair down her back, he held her and rested his cheek against the top of her head. His heart beat a steady, familiar rhythm.

"Don't be sorry. Whatever is mine is yours." His words, whispered into her hair, were punctuated with a kiss to her head. "And I hope you will always come to me. With anything. Your hopes, fears, a pesky hangnail, whatever. I'm here for you and I'm working to show you that you can trust my words. Trust *me* again." The last words rumbled deep in his chest.

His fingertips brushed against her jawline. Their faces were so close now.

She hadn't planned a kiss. Hadn't weighed the pros and cons. Hadn't even brushed her teeth or hair...

A loud knock made her jump.

"Hold that thought, love."

He jogged to the door. Oscar was on the other side,

dressed in his fencing clothes. "Hey, mate. I thought we were going to practice before we help set up the sparring grounds for the fair?"

Then Oscar's gaze traveled over Alex's shoulder to Ellora. For some reason, even though this was her husband, having Oscar catch her there in her pajamas flooded her neck and face with heat. She hugged her middle with one arm and waved with the other. "Hey." The word ended on a squeak.

Oscar shared a significant look with Alex, who didn't seem embarrassed at all. On the contrary, his smile radiated the room like he'd just discovered the Viking artifact of the century. "I'll get dressed."

He rushed around the kitchen, put on the teakettle, handed her a scone and grabbed a banana for himself before running to the bathroom to change.

Ellie nibbled on the scone after adding jam and clotted cream. Oscar declined breakfast.

Alex returned fresh-faced and dressed. "Ellie, I'd like it if you came with us. I don't think you should be alone until we can figure out this text."

They showed Oscar the text and he sided with Alex.

"It's okay. I'll call Lanae to come over and get ready with me."

Alex seemed reluctant to let her out of his sight but agreed only if he and Oscar waited until Lanae arrived.

Ellora called Lanae, who said, "Of course, I'll be right over. Just let me check on Steve," in a still-sleepy voice.

They'd need to call the police to let them know. The detectives hadn't ruled out foul play, but they also didn't have any concrete evidence to say one hundred percent either way. And one text wouldn't change that.

Alex scrubbed at his just-shaved jaw. "It could be that we're on the trail of something, getting close to the lost manuscript, and someone means to scare us off before we get to it."

Ellora crossed her arms, still acutely aware that she had bedhead and wore a nightgown in front of an almost-stranger. Though a relentlessly cheerful one and one who obviously had amazing taste if he liked her best friend. "Well, why haven't they just taken the manuscript if they want it so badly?"

Oscar's dark brow furrowed. "Maybe they haven't quite found it themselves. And they don't fancy us getting to it first."

Lanae arrived in a flourish, her clothes on hangers and bags of toiletries in hand, still in her horse-printed pj's.

"Well, this is a party, isn't it?" Lanae fiddled with her braids, coming out in several places, and rubbed sleep out of her eyes before pulling on Ellora's arm. "Let's leave these two to their knights-in-shining-armor practice."

Oscar tipped his head, giving Lanae a lingering look.

Alex grabbed Ellora's hand and squeezed. "I'll find you later, all right?"

She managed a nod before she and Lanae were in the hallway, Lanae whispering, "You're so going to tell me why you were at Alex's in your Little House on the Prairie gown." Then out of the side of her mouth, "And thanks a lot for warning me Oscar was here too."

Finding Ellie on his sofa that morning had been a shock, but not an unwelcome one. If a moment more had passed before Oscar had knocked, would he have finally felt her lips on his again?

Another jab into his side from Oscar's sparring saber brought him back to the present. A ripple of applause went up from the crowd they'd started to draw from the castle tourists.

The whole male and female fencing club would participate in the fencing competition. He'd also agreed to help Oscar with pony rides for the children before the "knights-in-training" tournament.

Oscar lifted his fencing mask. "You're not even trying, mate."

With a little bow and wave to the people watching, Oscar indicated they were done for now. The crowd dispersed, and he and Oscar took a water break.

"Sorry." Alex pulled his own mask up to wipe sweat from his forehead. It was expected to be overcast but it was always hot in his full-body fencing suit. "I've got a bit on my mind."

"A bit? Like strawberry blond hair and a brain even more in tune with history than yours?" Oscar tipped a brow at him.

"Yes, but—" Alex gulped water from his water bottle to avoid Oscar's teasing smile and leaned against the castle's inner bailey wall "—give me some credit, I'm also concerned about the message she received. I don't like the idea of someone watching her, wishing her harm or knowing her number like that. I'm worried they're not bluffing."

Oscar's forehead creased, his expression turning serious. "It's a bit dodgy, isn't it?"

"Mmm-hmm." He removed his helmet now, allowing the breeze to cool the back of his neck. "How can I make sure I'm in the right place at the right time, if needed? The police are looking into it, but they can't be there every second."

Alex scraped his nails against his sweat-dampened scalp. "Everything feels so out of my hands and I don't like it. Any one of these people could have been the one to do something to Ellora's grandmother and is trying to do the same to her." He jutted his chin toward the people milling about.

"I understand, but you're not alone, all right?" Oscar clapped him on the back. "We'll all try our best to stay vigilant and keep an eye on Ellora. And, thankfully, God *is* in control. He's taking care of her."

"Yeah, I know. Of course." Though he couldn't keep the doubt from his tone.

He'd phoned the detectives who'd worked on Grandma June's case. They worked hard but didn't have definitive answers and this text didn't constitute any evidence. It didn't sound promising.

He and Oscar both returned to their own respective flats for quick showers and they were to meet in Alnwick's medieval-built town square to help set up the tournament area and begin the pony rides. Oscar, along with his stable hands, would load the animals into a trailer out at the stables in Hulne Park and drive them into town.

Of course Ellie wouldn't be there any longer, but he couldn't help the disappointment when he entered his empty flat. Her presence had seemed right. He imagined he could still smell her light lavender scent as he gathered his things to jump in the shower.

Minutes later, he jogged down the stairs in much more casual attire than he usually wore—jeans and a T-shirt with a picture of a medieval lance that read Freelancer: A Self-Employed Medieval Knight. He had to have something that would be easy to wear under his fencing gear, especially on such a warm day.

He'd also been informed that if he made it to the last round of the tournament, he'd have to wear chain-mail armor for the last match. Hopefully, the sun would stay behind those clouds if it came to that.

A warm, rich laugh carried over the market square, greeting him as he stepped into the space surrounded by stone buildings, shops, the tall presiding shadow of the town hall's clock tower and an eight-step octagonal plinth from the medieval period. The cross atop the plinth was a nineteenth-century replacement of the original, and was not unlike the knotted cross from the paintings they'd found.

He'd know Ellie's laugh anywhere. Not simpering, not restrained. She'd always belly-laughed at his jokes, even from their first date. He'd loved the honesty and pure joy of it.

She'd been like no one he'd ever met before. This quirky girl who loved antiques and everything vintage didn't laugh at just anything. She tended to be more intense and passionate, a little on the serious side at times. He'd had to work hard to hear her laugh and he'd made it his job to bring out her lighter, sillier side.

She and Lanae laughed over something as they set up a table where people could pay to play games. The proceeds would go to a scholarship program for the youth in the community to study with the university students as well as to the community garden, which helped feed those in need in the area.

She, Lanae and a handful of students, including Natalie and Teddy, would help with the ticket booth and the games.

He passed the band setting up onstage in front of the town hall. The smell of candy floss, popcorn and something fried already clung to the late-morning air in anticipation of the crowds that would start arriving in earnest within the hour.

But he couldn't help scanning the crowd and the darker

alleyways. Ellora was either extra safe in this crowd, or...she was in even more danger because the confusion and noise would make it easier for someone to get past him.

Chapter Ten

"How in the world did I let you talk me into doing the dunk tank, Nae?" Ellora eyed the watery torture device.

"Remember, you were the one who said if everyone received a ninety percent or higher on their last test in your class, you'd let them dunk you." Lanae looked official as the games organizer with a clipboard in hand and a pencil stuck through her artfully messy bun, accented with a tied bandanna.

"This is what I get for encouraging good grades," Ellora grumbled.

"I'm sorry, Professor." Natalie, who'd helped fill the tank with a hose, laughed. "But, on the bright side, I've never seen so many people stay in and study before. They've been razzing me that I'm far too boring, even for a single mom. But they were bringing their books to breakfast, even out to dinner." She held Teddy's hand as he begged to visit the ponies for another ride.

It had squeezed Ellora's heart to watch Alex swing the

boy into the little saddle time and again earlier that morning, laughing and chattering away with him each go-around.

Maddie and Willa stepped over from the ring toss game, a lull between players at the moment. Maddie shrugged. "I have no aim, if that helps."

"Not really. But thanks anyway." Ellora drew a breath, grateful the dunk tank didn't open for another hour.

The others busied themselves with decorating their booths.

Natalie stepped close to Ellora and let Teddy run to Oscar and Alex, both calling the boy over for another ride. The young woman's smile turned wistful. "I know how some of the other students look at me, wondering why I'm here. More important, why he's here." She jutted her chin toward Teddy.

Ellora had heard as one does in a small group like theirs that Natalie's significant other had left her when he'd discovered she was pregnant with Teddy. Compassion wrung her heart. "My grandmother always used to say that we could waste our entire lives worrying about what people think of us, but then we're not really living our lives."

Natalie smiled. "I like that." She shuffled her feet. "The truth is people look at him sometimes like he's my baggage. They feel sorry for me because I'm alone and because of what his father did. They think I shouldn't get to do what I'm doing because of Teddy."

Teddy made a face and waved at them from his perch atop the pony. They laughed and waved back.

Eyes shining, Natalie continued, "But he's no burden. He's my pride and joy. I'll never regret him no matter what his father chose. I chose Teddy, and I'd choose him again— and do—every day for the rest of my life."

Ellora hadn't succeeded in keeping a rogue tear at bay. She swiped at it. "That's beautiful. You're right where you should be, and Teddy has a wonderful mama taking care of him. You should be proud, of him, of yourself."

"Thank you for not treating me different." She bobbed her head. "Well, I better go get him or he'll stay there all day."

As Natalie bounded across the square, the question rolled through Ellora's mind—would Alex have done the same to her if he'd known she was pregnant? Maybe he'd have left either way. But then if she *had* told him and he'd stayed, and they'd had a healthy baby, would he have always felt their child was baggage? Like becoming a parent was something he had to endure instead of cherish? That was something she could never stand. Because even now, she would give anything to hold her baby, to care for and love her child. To make a lifetime of memories together.

The crowd started to gravitate toward the sparring circle to the side of the open courtyard. Alex, along with Oscar, had helped organize his fencing club members as the participants.

Lanae wandered back to her side. "I hate to tell you, but it's time." She gestured to the dunk tank.

Ellora growled. "Oh, all right. I guess it was for a good cause." Lanae shrugged an apology and shooed Ellora up the ladder. Ellora slid onto the seat hovering over the water, her bare toes dipping into its cool surface. She let her gaze roam over the growing crowd. Byron stood out among the throng; his height put his silver-haired head above those around him. He'd tried his hand at the archery stand and then spoke with two guys she'd call shady. If only she could hear what seemed to be a terse conversation.

But she wouldn't let him ruin her day. She waved at Thomas, Gwen and Eg and his son, Freddie. Even Cressida, looking as miserable as one would expect her to look in the middle of so much frivolity, passed by. Cressida seemed to consider the sign by the tank, Dunk the Professor, but continued on.

Alex jogged over, his fencing mask pulled up over his forehead. He bent a noble bow. "Fair maiden, how did you get yourself into this precarious predicament?"

She feigned interest in the scalloped edge of her shirt, trying not to laugh. "You could say I put myself in a lose-lose situation." She mock-glared at her students.

Continuing with his chivalrous charade, Alex covered his eyes as though scouring the crowd. "There must be a villain about who has caused this calamity."

"Hey, we resent that." Maddie crossed her arms.

The band played a trumpet to call the "knights-in-training" to arms after a short break in the action. Just as many women as men were dressed in their sparring suits.

Alex tipped his chin. "That is my cue, m'lady. I shall return a victor for thee."

He returned to the sparring ring.

"Ladies and gentlemen. Can you all see my lovely bride?" Alex's voice boomed over a loudspeaker. This sent a flush of heat up Ellora's neck but she waved. "She's sitting in imminent danger."

The crowd laughed and cheered.

"I would like to make a proposition for your consideration."

Again, the crowd applauded.

Now in his element, Alex walked back and forth on the small dais set up for the event. "If I win this competition, my last opponent will take my fair lady's place in the tank. If I lose, I will. But you must leave her dry upon her pedestal until then. What say you?"

The agreement was loud and unanimous.

Ellora covered her heated cheeks with her palms while the first match commenced.

Maddie, with Willa trailing behind, sidled up next to the tank, and shielded her eyes to look up at Ellora. "So, what's the deal with you and Professor Alex anyway?"

Her mouth opened and closed trying to form a response with dignity. "I— We, uh—"

Willa scrunched her lips as if in thought, laid a hand on Maddie's shoulder and said, "If I had to guess, their social media relationship status is 'it's complicated.'"

Lanae swooped in, shushing them and sending them back to their booth like a mother hen herding her chicks.

Ellora muttered under her breath, "You have no idea," and tried to bring her attention away from her and Alex's "complicated" situation. The sparring sessions were a fun distraction. Finally, they'd come to the last round.

A man who'd introduced himself to the crowd as the fencing club manager pulled a microphone to his mouth. "Before we settle this last score, knights, do you wish to collect a small favor from someone in the crowd?"

Ellora had just taught her students about medieval knightly favors—someone, usually a lady, could bestow a favor on a knight on the tournament circuit, usually a detachable sleeve, a handkerchief, a ribbon or a scarf. She then tied it to the knight's arm, belt, or pinned it to their shoulder.

Alex ran over to her and held out his hand. "M'lady, would you honor and oblige me with a favor?"

She undid the small red silk scarf she'd worn around her neck to complete her '60s-inspired outfit. Then she tied it around his arm, playing along. "You may, Sir Knight. Pray, take this favor and return it to me, along with yourself, sound and whole."

He moved off with a bow to the sparring ring.

A *thunk* brought her back to her precarious situation. Maddie had thrown a ball and missed.

"Sorry, had to try it." She beamed up at Ellora. "Told you. Bad aim."

Ellora gave her a thumbs-up.

The fencing club manager announced again, "Don't forget! The winner of the knight's tournament will receive a delicious three-course meal package for two at The Treehouse Restaurant and will have the opportunity to invite someone to join them on the parade float this evening." The man threw his hands in the air. "The last round is about to begin between Sir Lockwood and Sir Machal, if all of you gentlemen and ladies would like to see who will walk away the champion, head over now."

People steered in that direction.

Alex and Oscar faced each other in the ring. Around Oscar's arm fluttered the rolled bandanna that had been in Lanae's hair.

It was a fierce competition. They were evenly matched. Each scoring points back and forth with cobra-like strikes. She and Lanae cheered for "their" knights, as did the crowd. Even little Teddy waved and shouted from the other side of the ring, his mouth forming the word "Alex!" over and over again.

Alex jabbed Oscar with his saber, the first to score fifteen points, which meant he'd won the match. Then the fencing club manager called the last "Hit!" and the crowd cheered and chanted, "Sir Lockwood! Sir Lockwood!"

It was stupid, of course. But Ellora had to push away the thoughts that crept in—of Alex seeming to crave the spotlight.

Alex raised his saber into the air in triumph then bowed to Oscar, who pulled his mask up, his face in a wide grin. They shook hands.

The manager walked into the circle with his microphone. "Well, Sir Lockwood, have you a fair maiden in mind or a squire who would like to join you in the parade?"

Alex's eyes locked with hers across the square. Then he whispered something to the announcer.

"We have a special request to have a Lady Ellora join Sir Lockwood on the float as well as his young squire, Teddy, provided his mother says it's all right."

Warmth swelled in Ellora's chest as Teddy jumped up and down next to his mom. "Can I, can I, can I, Mama?"

After Natalie agreed and was invited to stand on the float next to her son, the crowd started to move toward the dunk tank with the last announcement that the parade would start in two hours.

Alex, face flushed and breaths coming in gasps, ran to Ellora still awaiting her fate. Fortunately, no one had decided it would be funny to dunk her in the meantime. Oscar plodded along behind, clearly in no hurry to be dunked himself. Both shed their suits, now in their simple light clothing underneath.

"I am here to save you, m'lady." Alex's hand went up in a flourish. He stood near the target now.

"Best get on with it then."

He chuckled. "Indeed, I shall not keep you waiting." With that, he threw his arms out, but his hand hit the button.

The next thing she knew, she was falling and *sploosh*! Unprepared, her mouth and eyes filled with cold water. She came up sputtering and coughing.

Alex's rounded lips and eyes showed his surprise and horror. "Ellie, I—"

"Help. Me. Up." She punctuated each word through her teeth. But her cheek twitched, containing a bubble of laughter.

The crowd hooted and oohed.

He climbed the ladder, leaned over the water and put his arm out. "Ellie, love, listen. I can see by the look on your face that I'm sorry."

Grasping his arm, she pulled him into the water. After a big splash and sputtering of his own, he surfaced, his face a mask of amused shock.

She pulled him close, amid cheers. The silly T-shirt he wore clung to his chest, and the warmth of his shoulders seeped through the cold fabric to her fingers. The crowd outside seemed to melt away. Those internal magnets had seemed to reactivate within them, but maybe it was safer to keep her distance. What if she was sucked into the intense pull, let down her guard, and he abandoned her again? What if she told him she wanted to see if things could work out between them and he didn't feel the same way?

Ellora was only too happy to relinquish her dunk tank duties to a rotation of three male students. They'd shown mercy to Oscar, saying they'd take his place in the tank.

He'd thanked them for their "sacrifice" with a grim face twitching with held-back laughter.

Lanae had brought a small stack of towels, which helped her and Alex dry up a bit. Alex ran back to his flat for a real shower, claiming the quick dunk wasn't sufficient.

They were told they'd all dress up for the parade, courtesy of the costume shop in town. They'd meet at a tent near the parade starting point close to the entrance to Hulne Park.

She'd invited Lanae since most of the games had all been packed away in anticipation of the parade.

As she and Lanae walked to the tent, Lanae eyed her. "Is it just me or am I seeing a little hope blooming between you and Alex?"

"Maybe. At least, I'm warming up to the idea, but I'm

not sure he's on the same page and I don't know if I want to open myself up to that kind of heartache again." Ellora's sandal caught on a crack in the pavement, but she righted herself before falling. "I could ask the same of you and Oscar, couldn't I? Is there something blossoming there?"

Instead of the girlish blush, this time Lanae's face tightened. "Yes, but this bloom is just for the summer."

"I get it. Long distance was difficult for Alex and me back in college before he moved to the States. But you never know…"

Lanae nodded, a half-hearted gesture.

The little cottages filling the lane, Ratten Row, with its low stone wall and intermittent wooden fence border, gave way to views of the rolling green pasture lands of Hulne Park. One could almost imagine they'd stepped through time into Ellora's beloved medieval era.

Ellora reached inside her purse for her cell phone to snap a picture of the idyllic countryside and stone arch entrance to the park. She fished around. Not there. She tried her back pocket, where she sometimes slipped it in a hurry. Nope.

"Have you seen my phone?"

"No, did you leave it at the booth?"

"I'm positive I put it in my purse for safekeeping while I sat in the dunk tank." She turned in a circle as though it would appear on the ground, panic setting in. "It had pictures of the paintings on it and some voice notes I recorded about our findings so far. You don't think it was stolen, do you?"

"Do you mean regular stolen or 'creepy after you and the lost manuscript' kind of stolen?"

Ellora lifted a shoulder but her heart raced. "Either. Mostly the second one."

"I'll go back and look, okay? You stay here in semipublic. No going anywhere on your own."

Soon she was whisked into the tent and the capable hands of the costume shop owners and hairstylists. But she couldn't stop thinking about what happened to her phone.

Finally, she stood before a full-length mirror, and Alex ducked inside the tent. Her reflection was as close to a medieval lady as modern clothing and finishings could achieve. The stylists had meticulously braided the top of her hair into a crown while the back was left down and curled into long cascading waves. The deep blue of the gown had indeed brought out her eyes as the costume shop owner suggested.

"Have you seen Lanae?" She straightened the gold braided belt, her long, flowing sleeves trailing behind as she moved.

"Yes, she filled me in. She hasn't found your mobile yet. I've tried calling it, but it goes straight to voice mail."

She sighed but more to release the anxious tension than resignation.

Alex placed his hands on her shoulders, his face above hers in the mirror. "There's a lost and found set up by the castle entrance. We can check there later. Maybe there's nothing ominous about this. It could've legitimately fell out of your bag and someone will turn it in."

"Yeah, I might be letting my imagination run away with me because of that text message."

She took in a steadying breath then turned, holding out the skirt of her dress. "Well, what do you think? Do I pass as a medieval maiden?"

"Indeed." Alex took her hand and kissed it, soft lips lingering a moment longer than necessary.

"You don't look too bad yourself." They'd decked him out in a white tunic, chain mail, belt with a sword tucked into a scabbard to one side and dark rough-hewed trousers. He held a helmet against one hip.

The makeshift styling team shooed them out of the tent,

including Natalie and Teddy, who'd come in for minimakeovers. They'd dressed Natalie in a mauve-hued dress, and Teddy wore a child-sized tunic and breeches with a small leather belt.

The parade director gave them a quick rundown of how everything would work as they walked to the float—a flatbed trailer pulled behind a large tractor and decorated with a tall cardboard exterior castle tower complete with drawbridge and moat, silk flowers and an array of trees, some repurposed Christmas trees. Several people behind the float would maneuver a long dragon "chasing" after them.

Pointing to the tower with his clipboard, the parade director said, "Fair maiden—" he indicated Ellora, and Alex smirked "—you're going to be standing inside the castle. It may be covered with cardboard and chipboard on the outside, but inside, it's a heavy-duty hydraulic-powered stand with a railing. When the parade starts, all four of you will be on the float, the maiden in her tower and the knight below, trying to save her."

Ellora gritted her teeth. "I'm not sure if this maiden needs saving. Perhaps the knight can be the one in the tower. The *maiden* is not fond of heights." She crossed her arms.

The parade director stuttered but formed no words.

Teddy pulled on the man's arm. "She's the queen, mister. You don't tell the queen what to do or—" he drew a line over his neck with his thumb "—off with your head."

Natalie gasped. "Teddy!" To everyone else, she shot a red-faced grimace. "I never should've let him watch *Alice in Wonderland*. I'm sorry."

Ellora covered her smile with her hand and agreed to go into the tower.

"The lad's not wrong though, is he?" As Alex touched

the small of her back, the warmth spread through the fabric of her dress.

He kissed her hand and lifted her onto the float trailer before jumping on himself. Teddy grinned up at Alex like he truly was some hero of old.

Natalie and Teddy sat toward the front, where they would wave and throw candy.

Ellora climbed into the contraption inside the tower.

"I don't remember this being part of the deal."

Alex assured her he'd be right there, and she'd be all right.

Inside the tower of cardboard reinforced with a wooden frame, it was much darker than she'd anticipated. The air close and unmoving. The trailer lurched forward and she had to hold the circular platform's railing to keep from toppling over. They would send her up and down several times during the parade route. *Great.*

She'd never thought of herself as claustrophobic before that moment. Despite the noise of the tractor and the other parade participants—which included the youth band from the primary school and the spectators—Ellora's heart drummed a frantic beat in her ears.

The noise, the dark, the close space. A prickle of familiar fear raised the hairs on her arms. A trickle of sweat trailed down her temple.

Like a dam bursting, the memory rushed back, nearly knocking her off her feet. The night her mom and dad were taken to jail for the last time. It wasn't the only time, but it was the time that had sealed all of their fates. Her mom had never breathed another free breath of air after that night. It was also the night Ellora had gone to live with Grandma June permanently.

Her mother and father had started not just consuming drugs, but making and selling them out of their little trailer.

Up until that night when she was six years old, there had been no escape for her. But then, would she have taken an escape? She'd had the innocent love a child has for her parents despite their failings. She loved who they used to be. She'd loved who they could be, wanted them to be.

That night an explosion ripped a hole through the trailer. Ellora had been hiding in her tiny closet because her parents had been fighting while making their "special recipe" in the kitchen. When the explosion shook their little home, she'd closed her eyes and covered her ears.

It was only when a firefighter found her that she looked up. She could still feel the cold that seeped through her pajamas as an officer took her from the firefighter and carried her out of the only home she'd ever known in the middle of the night. Her parents, she'd found out later, had survived but were injured and would later be sent to prison for their crime of making and selling methamphetamines.

They received twenty-five years. Her mother only lived to serve two of those years before she died in prison. Her father had a reduced sentence for good behavior. But months after his release, he'd run right back to the substance that had ruined his life. He was still in prison the last she heard.

The drive to the police station that night was the loneliest moment of her life. That is, until she'd lost her grandmother, her baby and her husband in tight succession. And it had seemed, with all of that loss, perhaps God had abandoned her too. If everyone had left her, how could He have possibly still been by her side?

A knock on the side of the tower snapped Ellora's attention back to the present. "Are you all right in there, love?"

"Yes." She hadn't meant for it to come out as a yelp. "It's a little dark. How much longer?"

"Just a minute, I believe." His face must've been close

because his voice was muffled. "The bloke out here oper-
ating this contraption said we have to turn onto Narrowgate and then he'll pull the lever to raise you up the tower.
Hang in there."

"Okay."

"You're a good sport, Ellie."

She *humphed*. Her curled hair began to stick to the back
of her neck as the seconds ticked by. She plucked them away
from her damp skin and fanned herself.

Finally, the circular platform started to screech upward at
a painfully slow pace. The opening at the top of the faux-
tower let in the pale light of the overcast day. As she neared
the top, a blessed cool breeze bathed her face.

But before she could enjoy it, the platform made a sharp
metal shriek, another reminder of the night her home ex-
ploded. As she emerged to the open air, the stand started
to tip. The hydraulics made another earsplitting groan and
a *snap*!

Screams filled the air, including her own. She clung to the
railing, now on its side, as she dangled over the road below.

Her hands slipped on the metal rail. "Help!"

"Ellie!" Alex's terror-filled voice rent the air. "Hang on.
I'm coming for you."

He ran to the front of the float, shouting to the tractor
driver to stop. But with the lurch of the brakes, Ellora swung
back and forth.

"I can't hold on!"

Alex leaped over obstacles and ran to the back of the trailer,
about to jump off when her fingers slipped the last inch.

Her body plummeted and hit the pavement with a sickening thud that radiated pain through every nerve-ending.

The sharp pain mixed with the throbbing so that she
didn't know where one pain started and another ended.

She'd tried to land on her backside so as not to break a foot or leg, but at the last millisecond, instinct threw her hand out to catch her fall. Her right wrist screamed in agony, as did the back of her head. Had she hit her head too?

Alex's face appeared above her, blurry and spinning. "Ellie, my Ellie. I'm so sorry, my love. This is my fault. All my fault."

She tried to calm him by placing a hand to his face and sitting up, but it hurt too much. A wave of dizziness and nausea hit so hard she had to lay her head back down. He held her head gently in place. "Hold still. Don't try to move."

But when one of his hands came away with a bright crimson stain, he yelled to the people gathered, "Someone, call the ambulance!"

Everything grew fuzzy and far away, but before Ellora embraced the warm darkness rushing toward her, the words "Hey, someone sabotaged this thing! This was no accident," reached her ringing ears.

Chapter Eleven

Alex held the tips of Ellie's fingers. Her face, so relaxed where she stretched out on her bed. The front of her body so unscathed from her fall, he could almost forget what had happened. Almost.

The Alnwick Infirmary medical center had done immediate CT scans and an MRI of her head as well as X-rays of her wrist. Her right wrist was sprained. Scrapes covered her elbows, the back of her head had an open wound—now stapled shut and bandaged—and she had a concussion. But after the doctors were satisfied there was no swelling or bleeding around the brain, she was allowed to return to her flat.

Seeing her usual distaste for everyone fussing over her told him she might be all right. A big deal after being sure when she'd lost consciousness that she was dying in his arms and, not for the first time, he'd had a profound sense of helplessness. Powerless to do anything to stop it. Just like he'd been powerless with Dylan and Beckett, before that.

He bent his head over the bed. "I'm sorry, Ellie. I meant to be there for you, love."

A wave of primal anger arose at whoever rigged the hydraulics to malfunction. A line had been damaged as well as part of the metal scaffolding under the platform. The person had wanted to hurt her, had nearly killed her.

But the blame kept circling back to himself. He'd been too late. *Almost* in the right place at the right time. But almost didn't cut it. Never had. Déjà vu.

His older brother by a year, Beckett, had been the sports star, the good-looking football and cricket player, who made decent grades, and the girls fell over themselves to be near him. Alex, on the other hand, was the quiet one then. Had never even asked a girl out.

What their parents hadn't known was that Alex had been the reason Beckett received those "decent" grades. It wasn't that Beckett was unintelligent. But he was as scared of disappointing their mother and father as Alex—with his awkwardness and disinterest in sports—and had started falling behind in his classes.

One night Beckett ditched Alex for a party with his friends. An inebriated Beckett called, again and again, to tell Alex to come to the party. Meanwhile, Alex was at home studying for a test and piecing together a project for Beckett. He vowed this was the last time he'd do Beckett's homework.

Later, he noticed another missed call from Beckett. As he'd let the voice message play, his heart sank.

"I can't drive, Alex. Will you come and get me?" The words had slurred. "If I don't hear from you, I'll ask around. Sorry I didn't stay home with you. I'm sure you're mad at me. Don't mean to disappoint ya. Mum and Dad either. Love ya, bruv."

By the time Alex sneaked out of the house and started

the drive to Beckett's friend's, Beckett wouldn't answer the phone. Everything seemed to move in agonizing slow motion as police and ambulance lights pierced the dark country road.

Beckett had indeed found another ride...with someone as intoxicated or worse than he was. That person had wrapped the car around a tree, killing himself, Beckett and another passenger in the back seat on impact mere minutes before Alex arrived.

He hadn't made it in time. Too little, too late.

That was the hardest phone call he'd ever had to make, to tell his parents Beckett was gone. He'd never felt so alone, so responsible. All he could do from that day on was fill his brother's shoes as best as he could.

Alex pressed a kiss to Ellora's hand, then leaned farther to dust her forehead with his lips. He wouldn't make the same mistakes with Ellora. Not again. He would be there for her. He wasn't going anywhere. Their future and whether they would remain together wasn't clear. But he wouldn't leave her side now; he would protect her in this quest. Not a good showing of that in the last twenty-four hours. Would she blame him when she awoke to catalog her many injuries? Would she tell him to get away from her? If so, this was one time he couldn't listen.

This search had grown dangerous, far more dangerous than he'd ever expected.

"You don't have to baby me. I'm perfectly able to get out of bed." Ellora couldn't help her disgruntled tone nor the scowl that tugged at her brows.

"How enraged, on a scale of one to ten, would you be if I reminded you just how adorable you are when you're any combination of hungry, sleepy or grumpy?" His one-sided smile warmed.

"An eleven. What am I, one of Snow White's dwarves?" She groaned, her bruised muscles protesting as she stood.

Just like the previous three days since her great fall, every part of her body ached as she moved like she had indeed been Humpty Dumpty and they hadn't quite put her back together again. Her knees wobbled but held her upright.

She shuffled to her wardrobe and flipped through the options. "I'm sorry for being a crabby patient. You and Lanae have been wonderful." He hovered nearby as though she would collapse at any moment.

Alex hadn't left her side since Saturday night. He'd insisted she take a few days off. A retired professor from the village was more than happy to fill in. It had been Alex's turn to sleep on her couch. Lanae had brought food and entertainment in the form of papers to grade—at Ellora's insistence. Lanae had even called the new phone Alex bought for Ellora to check on her. Ellora's old phone hadn't turned up.

The police were looking into the apparent sabotage of the float—interviewing the people who'd been around the float that day as well as the parade director, who'd said someone must've messed with it after his safety inspection. Nobody saw anything, or so they said.

By late afternoon Wednesday, restless energy buzzed through her veins. Waiting to heal. Waiting for answers.

Turning her neck sent a sharp twinge through the back of her head. She winced but managed a small smile. "Thank you. For being here, for everything. Really."

"Where else would I be? And you've been a perfectly lovely patient…for a growly bear."

"Oh, stop." She laughed, which she regretted. Pain radiated around her rib cage.

"Getting dressed today?"

She nodded. "Bathing too."

Tapping her chin, she surveyed her options. She'd want something soft, but not pajamas. She'd spent too many days in them already.

Running over to the kitchen, he filled a cup with water and grabbed one of her pain pills. "You need food with this. I made you some of that disgusting mushy avocado toast you love so much. Tea too. Maybe we should do that first."

"Mmm-hmm," she managed while she swallowed down the pill.

After her delicious toast, despite his protests, he ran the bath for her and hung the clothes she chose on the back of the door.

"I'll be out here doing a little work if you need me," he called after she'd shut the door.

It was glorious to let her sore muscles, all of her aches and pains, ease in the depths of the claw-foot tub. The warmth soaked into her very bones. And Alex had added her favorite lavender vanilla bath bubbles. But try as she might, she couldn't seem to wash her hair one-handed to any degree of success, especially as she tried to be careful with the wound.

She did her best to rinse it, wrap it in a towel, then dress in her soft stretch-cotton shift dress with a cherry print. The small line of buttons was a challenge but she'd managed. When she emerged with a mass of towel-wrapped unruly hair, Alex put aside a stack of papers and raised a brow.

"Can you help me with this?" She held out her hairbrush.

Pulling the towel from her head, he puckered his lips to the side. "I don't think you want me ripping through these knots with the brush when you've got those staples on the back of your head. Besides, you've still got loads of soap in here."

She groaned. "I'm not getting back in the tub."

"Come on." He picked up a kitchen chair with one hand and waved her over to the bathroom.

He indicated for her to sit in the chair, which he'd pulled up to the sink.

She hesitated, but finally sank onto the seat. "Be careful for—"

"The wound. Of course, love." She swallowed and laid her neck back against the towel he'd rolled and propped against the ledge of the wide pedestal sink.

"Just relax." His deep voice reverberated against the tiled walls.

His strong yet gentle fingers lathered the shampoo, careful to avoid her injury. Her scalp tingled, sending goose bumps down her neck. He rinsed then finger-combed the conditioner in, rinsed again, letting her hair slide between his fingers. He shut off the faucet and squeezed out the excess water then massaged her scalp near her temples. She let her eyes close.

There was a soft, warm brush of skin against her cheek. His lips.

Her eyelids snapped open meeting his intense, anguished gaze.

"I wasn't there for you. Again." His words came out of the blue, in a low rasp.

"What do you mean?"

"At the parade. I should've caught you. I tried." He seemed to be short on breath and the pulse in his neck had a visible and fast-ticking beat.

She reached up, placing her fingertips against the frantic thumping. "Alex, don't say that. There's nothing you could've done—"

"Of course there was. I thought I was going to lose you. There was so much I needed to say, so much I wanted to tell you…"

His thumb rubbed a circle beneath her cheekbone. "But

it all boiled down to this—to lose you would be like losing part of myself." Each word powerful, deliberate. "I should know. I've been living as but a shadow of myself the last seven months without you."

She lifted her good arm, hooking it around the back of his neck to draw him down toward her. They were nose to nose now. "I've felt the same way, like a piece of my heart had gone missing."

Then his hand slid between her neck and the rolled towel, cradling her, as his lips came down soft and warm against hers. She could feel his restraint. Due to her injuries? Perhaps out of uncertainty. That wouldn't do. She moved to stand up with his help.

She circled his neck with both her arms, despite her damp hair spilling down her back and her wrist brace. Fear and wonder tumbled together within her chest. Wasn't there still too much keeping them from a future together? Shouldn't she stop this to address that first?

But when his hands splayed against her back, and his voice came in a low rumble, "Be care—"

Her lips crushed against his, silencing his warning. There were no more worries, just the thrill of being back in her husband's arms, feeling his warmth, his closeness. Everything else melted away. It was only his fingers weaving through her wet hair, caressing her face. And her own good hand raking through his now-tousled waves, holding his strong jaw.

It was their first kiss and their wedding kiss, their two best, rolled into one and then times ten.

When air became an absolute necessity, they parted but he kept her pressed to his chest.

"Did I hurt you?" He searched her with his eyes, and put a hand to her cheek. "I may have gotten a little carried away."

She grinned. "No. Of course, I probably wouldn't notice another fall from a tower right now."

"I'm positive you could push me in front of a bullet train right now and I wouldn't feel a thing." His smile *was* slightly dazed. "But don't test the theory."

The room spun for her and she stumbled back a step, but his arms were there to catch her. "I'd like to think my kiss made you weak in the knees, but I think it's that concussion acting up. Let's get you back to the living room."

He held her elbow and escorted her back to the living room and lowered her onto the couch.

He bent to place a quick kiss on her lips. "All right, I'm making you dinner tonight, which has absolutely nothing to do with you being a near-invalid at the moment. But is the safest choice for us all."

"Are you sure you don't fancy another round of my famous Minnesotan tater tot hotdish?"

"Quite." His nose wrinkled.

He brought her grandmother's trunk closer, and plopped a stack of books onto the coffee table in front of her.

His hands clapped and rubbed together. "You sit tight, do a little research—like you've been begging to—while I rustle us up some grub like you Americans like to say."

As time-consuming and frustrating as their search had been so far, she had missed the chase of it during the last several days. Her concussion made her eyes blur after too much reading and her head throbbed. But for as long as she could stand, she wanted to dig back in and see if they could make some headway.

She flipped to another sticky-note-flagged passage in a Viking history book. This one spoke of a female Viking warrior, Hilda, known for leading her people after her husband died. This was the second time Ellora had come across the name.

She swallowed a grumble building in her throat. "What does that have to do with anything, Grandma?"

"Hmm?" Alex turned, large spoon in hand. The steam from whatever bubbled away had curled the hair falling over his forehead.

"Oh, nothing." She rubbed her temples, willing the dizziness away along with the ache forming behind her eyes. "I feel like I'm missing something. A lot of something. And I wish I could find Grandma June's master field journal for this search. I can't believe it wasn't with all of these books and other notes in the trunk."

"Have you dug all the way to the bottom?"

"As best as I could anyway." She shrugged. "But no harm in having another look."

She moved aside the remaining items covering the bottom of the trunk. A pen rolled into view from beneath a leather satchel of miscellanea she'd already gone through.

"My grandmother's special pen." She plucked it out and smiled at the heavyweight engraved metal pen. "I had kind of forgotten about this thing." The letters J.W. were etched on the side for June Wiltshire and the Latin words *Veritas Vos Liberabit.*

Alex bent over her, spoon still in hand. A waft of his culinary creation close behind, making her stomach growl. "'The truth shall set you free.' From John 8:32, I believe."

"Yes, that was one bit of Latin I knew. Grandfather had this made for her a long time ago. Her life motto, I suppose." She ran a fingernail over the words then the notch her grandmother had once told her opened and held the replaceable ink. She would have to refill it now. This brought another pang in her ribs that had nothing to do with her injuries.

She shrugged. "Though a lot of good that does us now. For someone who touted the wisdom of finding the truth, she sure didn't make it easy on the rest of us to find out what that 'truth' is." She placed the pen up on the table.

"We'll figure it out yet, you'll see." He walked back to the stove, stirred and turned down the burner.

With her braced arm propped against the side of the trunk, she used her good hand to sift to the bottom. When that came up empty, she scooted closer to the lid, which had pockets and small drawers for the bygone-era traveler to store jewelry, toiletries or undergarments.

"Have you ever heard of a Viking leader named Hilda?" She glanced up from yanking on a stuck drawer. "Grandma June noted passages about her several times. But I don't know if or why she'd have anything to do with the search for the manuscript."

Alex pulled a baking sheet from the oven and set it on the stove. "That was a pretty common name in the Middle Ages. But yes, that does sound familiar. Did it say she took over after her husband died and inherited some of his plunder from the raids he'd done in the north of England?"

"I'm not sure. I didn't get that far." She crisscrossed her legs despite the ache in her lower back and pulled the book into her lap. She traced her finger along the words.

"It says that she was thought to possess many enviable riches gained by her husband's exploits along the eastern coast of England. Something for which she had to defend her people. Other clans wanted to steal them, and the Saxons wanted them back. It says she returned the riches to the people they were taken from to be rid of their curse, all but one small parcel. It was rumored that only her closest family were allowed to see what it contained and thereafter it was passed down from generation to generation."

The next page showed Hilda's partial family tree except for her parents and ancestors. It only listed those who came after her—her children, grandchildren, et cetera. Those filled-in branches gripped Ellora's heart with a now-familiar ache.

She couldn't help but think about how drawn she still felt to Alex, especially after his tender care for her the last several days and the kiss they'd shared, but the same problems hadn't evaporated. He still didn't want children. She did. She wanted her own full family tree.

A pinch formed between her brows as she set the book back on the table. "What if the thing this Hilda kept for herself and her family was the lost manuscript? It's a stretch, but I can't understand why Grandma June would highlight this woman's life otherwise. Who says the lost manuscript wasn't taken by the Vikings at some point even if not at Lindisfarne?"

"Perhaps. It's certainly a leap, but not one without common sense."

"Thanks," she said dryly.

He winked. "We'll have to set about proving it. I'm sure we can find mention of her elsewhere in these books or, you know, using the modern historian's best friend, the internet."

She mock-scowled. "The internet isn't often peer-reviewed. It's hard to find the truth there."

One by one she placed the contents of the trunk scattered around her on the floor back inside.

He knelt beside her, taking the stacks from her hand. "The truth depends on the one telling the story, doesn't it?"

"I suppose…and on which side of history you find yourself."

The phone rang, his cell on the counter. He brushed his thumb against her cheek as he rose to answer it. While he did, she placed the last book into the trunk.

But before she could sit for dinner, she had to try the stuck drawer one more time. She stood and gave it another heave.

Alex strode over, a bounce in his step. "You're not going to believe it, love. That was Professor Ridgewater. He and the art restorer from Oxford found something using X-ray fluorescence spectroscopy, or XRF. There is indeed another layer below the current painting. They're sending us the image they rendered with the scan. Now the restorer wants to begin the process of physically removing the overpainting, which Ridgewater wholeheartedly consented to. She's already seeking approval for the time away from Oxford."

He grasped her face between his hands. "This is huge. He said the painting looks to be a much earlier work than he'd originally thought, possibly even from the Middle Ages."

"Wow, that's amazing. Can we go see it?"

"When they take off that first layer of paint and have something to show us, yes. They're starting with the hooded figure because they said something was definitely below that and they want to see what."

He let go of her face when something in the trunk seemed to catch his eye. "What is that?" He bent and reached for the corner of the inside lid where she'd been trying to open a small drawer. "Did your grandmother ever mention the trunk having secret compartments?"

"No, but then, she apparently has loads of secrets I knew nothing about."

A bit of paper poked through where the fabric-covered thin wood of the lid's interior met the actual thicker wood and leather-covered outer lid. With a gentle wiggle, the inside lid backing with the attached drawers came away from the trunk.

Alex caught it with both hands and set it on the couch. Inside did not hold her grandmother's master journal like she'd hoped, but instead an ancient-looking stack of papers, held in place with four leather strips at the corners. One page had slipped free, the one peeking out from the backing.

On the other side of the secret compartment, there were a couple of scrolls, tied in place to the real lid with long ribbons. "Secrets indeed," she muttered to herself.

Had she known her grandmother at all?

Their dinner still simmered on the stove all but forgotten while Alex untied the scrolls and Ellora retrieved what looked like a partial manuscript. They both were slow and careful with the old paper.

"What did you find?" On the table she laid the stack of handwritten pages. Alex was trying to unroll the scrolls without destroying the ancient paper.

His brows dipped in the middle. "They look like family trees. Do you recognize them?"

She leaned closer. Some were just names with lines drawn to connect them; others were a true tree shape.

One seemed familiar. She snatched the book she'd been reading about Hilda and flipped to the family tree. It matched. "This is Hilda's family tree. The rest, I'm not sure."

He indicated her stack of papers. "What's that?"

"It looks like a religious text, passages from the Bible. If I had to guess, from the early Middle Ages." The historian in her felt perhaps like she should be wearing gloves; this was obviously a very old document. Though there was some debate about the oils from people's hands actually being beneficial to old paper to keep it from drying out and cracking, especially vellum like this—made from the hides of animals.

She carefully flipped the pages, then sucked in a breath as a beautiful illuminated picture came into view. It was a painting of the angel Gabriel appearing to Mary, the mother of Jesus, the night she was told she would bear the child of God—a common depiction in illuminated manuscripts.

"Where on earth did Grandma June get this? If this is authentic, it's worth a lot of money." Her words more breath than substance.

"Do you think it is—authentic, I mean?"

Biting the inside of her cheek to contain the sheer terror and excitement at the prospect, she brought the illuminated page within a couple of inches from her face to inspect the brilliant blues, reds, greens and glinting gold. "Everything—the aging of the vellum, the pigments, the picture styles—certainly looks to be genuine. I'd put it on the same or similar time line as the manuscript we're looking for. We'll have to call on the experts at the Bodleian or elsewhere."

"You *are* the expert, love. But yes, we can certainly consult for second and third opinions."

She traced a finger along the edge where holes ran up the side at regular intervals. "This used to be in a bound book. This is one 'quire' or section of what was probably a whole manuscript and was threaded together. See? This is where the pages were sewn."

Her finger was over what looked like random markings or doodles near what would've been the crease of the book when assembled, hardly visible to the reader. But the letters didn't spell anything she was familiar with.

Ellora pointed. "Is this another language?"

"I don't recognize the words, but we can check. A code perhaps? Or the author's scribbles."

She tapped her chin. "It was a long and arduous process. Scribes were sometimes known to doodle, complain about the weather or scriptorium conditions, or even about the task at hand in the margins."

For safekeeping they opted to place the scrolls—now lying somewhat flat—and the partial manuscript in a leather portfolio. But they would, at least for now, still lock it inside of the trunk until they thought of a safer place for them.

They sat down to what might have been a romantic dinner otherwise, both lost in thought.

Alex speared another asparagus with his fork and nodded to the trunk. "One thing's for sure, it seems Grandma June has left us Pandora's box."

"Let's just hope it doesn't unleash as much trouble as Pandora's box."

Indeed, what other secrets did the steamer trunk hold? For that matter, what else had her grandmother known and how on earth would they piece it all together?

Chapter Twelve

More questions and no answers. Ellora had had about enough of it. But the stubborn part of her, the part that had never backed down from a research question nor a historical puzzle in her life, refused to quit.

Thursday morning she was ready for the day, but after a late night studying the partial manuscript, she let out a long yawn that made her eyes water. It was still too soon to head over to her classroom, so she gulped tea and waited for her brain to defog.

Her body ached along with her head, but she longed to step back into teaching. Besides, Alex would work from his office again that day and they'd both feel better if they were in the same building after everything that had happened.

It had moved from mysterious and vaguely threatening with the veiled threat by text to actual physical harm.

After a last gulp of strong tea, she turned one last time to the trunk. She squinted at that thing, wishing not for the first time it could talk and tell her all of its secrets.

"All right, you. What else are you hiding?"

She knelt in front of it, tracing a finger along its seams. Inside, she tried the stuck drawer again. When it finally opened, it was empty. But with some tapping and prying, the bottom of the small drawer came free—a false bottom. Inside was a rolled note that read, "The truth shall set you free."

The pen sprang to mind. Ellora retrieved it from the coffee table. Going on pure instinct, she clicked the lever on the side. Only it wasn't for refilling ink. Instead, a mechanical folding key popped out like the Swiss Army knife of pens.

She inspected the entire inside of the trunk for a keyhole. None. But among the many stickers and patches in the lower left outside corner, her grandmother had etched the Latin equivalent of the "truth" phrase...right next to a small jagged hole she'd mistaken for wear and tear.

Ellora placed the small key inside and turned. There was a metallic moving of gears and then a little drawer popped open at the bottom of the trunk. It swung open in an arc and inside, sure enough, there was a brilliant blue leather-bound journal with leather straps to close it and a gold-embossed tree on the cover. Inside, "The *Lost Manuscript of Lindisfarne*" was written on the first page.

Her grandmother's master journal.

"Yes! I knew it." She did a little dance but winced at the pains jabbing her head and arm.

Fighting the urge to sit and pore over it right then, she tucked it into her classroom bag along with her lecture notes and locked up the trunk. She also placed the partial manuscript in a top-closing folder, unable to leave it behind.

When she arrived inside the university wing of the castle and at Alex's open office door, she dug the journal from her bag and dashed inside.

"I found it!"

His head snapped up from whatever he'd been working on, brows rising.

She waved the journal back and forth. "It's my grandmother's master field journal. It was in a secret drawer on the outside of the trunk."

Coming around the desk, he hugged her in a gentle embrace. "That's absolutely brilliant!"

She laid it out on his desk. On the second page in her grandmother's slanted scrawl it read, "Clever girl." A short but sweet message just for her.

Sliding around the desk, she plunked down on his chair and pushed the open laptop back to accommodate the journal. She paged through it, names and dates spilling forth in a tide.

"It's certainly an 'organized mess,' like Grandma June used to say."

Alex chuckled. "That was a point we could always agree on."

Several times the name Mildrythe came up. She traced her finger along one instance.

"Look at this." Alex braced his hands on the chair's armrests, his cheek nearly touching hers as she read, "'Mildrythe and the partial manuscript scribe/illuminator were taught by the person who created the lost manuscript? Or did Mildrythe do the teaching? See illuminations. Coded message in margin of partial manuscript or reused vellum or author scribbles?'"

"Grandma June was trying to figure out the same things we are."

"Paper was difficult and time-consuming to make, so this partial manuscript paper could've been reused from something else. Hence, the scribbles. But it very well could be a coded message too."

Alex pivoted and leaned back on the desk beside her,

crossing his arms over his chest. "But what made her believe this artist of the partial book trained the same person who illuminated the lost manuscript?"

"Well, we do know this partial manuscript was completed around 874, about a year before Lindisfarne was abandoned and the gospels moved. I studied it front to back last night, and toward the back, there's a date."

She reached across the desk to retrieve her bag and withdrew the manuscript, turning it to the last page to show Alex.

"But how did she guess that this Mildrythe taught the person who scribed the lost manuscript? And how could studying the illuminations help if we don't know what the lost manuscript looks like?"

Ellora scrunched her lips, thinking. "Maybe she's making an assumption because the artist here—" she tapped the edge of the partial manuscript "—relied heavily on lapis lazuli and the rumored lost manuscript supposedly had a dyed lapis cover as well as pages. But that's still a stretch of the imagination there, especially for Grandma June. She was on the eccentric side, but she searched for truth above all else…"

After a moment of silence, she sighed. "I have to get to my classroom, but we can go over the journal later. If you want."

"Of course. And if you leave the partial with me, I'll take a closer look while you're in class today. You know, in between my most important work of approving the lavatory necessity budget and fielding about a million questions from fretting parents." He gave her a wry grin. Though he joked, his tone held deep affection for his job.

As she started to close up her bag an email subject line on his laptop caught her eye: "Please Give to Ellora! Job Offer!" It was from the head of the School of Arts and Humanities. Her history department answered to them. It was dated two days ago.

"What's this?" She opened it and scanned the contents. They'd been trying to reach her, but she hadn't checked her email since her accident. It said the head of the history department position was vacant. A career-changing kind of job. The kind she'd said she was working toward. They had recommended her for the position and needed to know soon if she'd be interested before moving on to other candidates.

Her eyes found Alex's. He shifted. "Ellie, I was going to tell you about that. It was just that you were hurt and I didn't want to add to your stress. Really. Today, I was going to speak with you."

"They want someone in place by August 15 to get acclimated before fall semester starts. I would need to answer within a few weeks. Were you really going to say something?"

His shoulders snapped back, gaze darkening. "You think I would keep this to myself? Why?"

"I don't know, would you?"

"How could you even ask that?"

But would he? Perhaps to keep her from going back, stop her from pursuing her dreams—wait, *was* that her dream?—or to keep her from the spotlight he seemed to gravitate toward? She bit her cheek, a slither of worry tunneling through her mind. She pushed away the suspicion, the toxic thoughts that drew her back to their relationship foundation's first cracks.

Her feet dragged her to the other side of the desk as she shouldered her bag.

Alex followed. "Hey, I was going to tell you. I'd be lying if this didn't concern me, but of course, I was going to tell you. The only reason I hadn't was because of everything that happened. I didn't want you to worry about something like that while you were still in so much pain and healing. All right?"

She tried to smile. A million questions ran through her mind in an instant. Did she want to accept? Would he want her to accept? What would that mean for them and the mending of their relationship? Would he move back to St. Cloud with her? What if he didn't?

But a quick glance at the clock on his wall told her she didn't have time to dig into those at the moment. She had to navigate the maze over to her classroom.

"Okay. I have to get to class, but we'll talk about it later."

After he brushed her cheek with his thumb and another promise to look at the partial manuscript, she hurried down the hall, swatting away doubts like a swarm of the famed Minnesota state birds—i.e. mosquitoes.

Propping a textbook in the crook of her good arm's elbow, she read from it as she crossed the classroom.

"An Anglo-Saxon chronicler wrote about the time just before and after the first great attack on Lindisfarne. Listen to this. 'Here were dreadful forewarnings come over the land of Northumbria, and woefully terrified the people: these were amazing sheets of lightning and whirlwinds, and fiery dragons were seen flying in the sky. A great famine soon followed these signs, and shortly after in the same year, on the sixth day before the ides of January, the woeful inroads of heathen men destroyed God's church in Lindisfarne island by fierce robbery and slaughter.'"

She glanced up. "Can't you feel his anguish and terror over what had happened? The people and valuables they'd lost?" Murmurs and nods, minimal glazed-over faces. Always promising. "Now historians tend to agree the reporter of these incidents made a typo—possible even in the ancient world—by writing January. June is assumed to be the month the Vikings attacked."

Crossing the room, still gazing between the book and her students, she continued, "And listen to this writing from a holy man of the island. 'The ebbs and flows against these shores can never cleanse this place of the spilt blood and horrors it befell. Though we ask the gracious Lord to rain down His justice upon the heathens who have wrought this atrocity and heal both our hearts and our land, just as the scriptures say, we fear even as we flee for our lives that we will not again set our eyes upon this once peaceful sanctuary of God.'"

She placed the book on the desk, leaned back and braced her aching forearm atop the other across her chest. The students had been so kind and helpful about her ordeal, offering to help carry her bag and books, pulling out her chair, et cetera.

Looking up to their expectant faces, she went on, "This incident, among others, started a long history of strife between the Vikings, often known as the Norsemen or Danes—though they weren't all from Denmark—and the Anglo-Saxons of England. The Vikings came for the wealth of this country, to explore new lands, for fertile soil and to claim a piece of it for themselves. As time passed, the Vikings settled in different areas of the then-kingdoms of England. It may be hard to believe with the accounts I shared of the Vikings' violent beginnings in this land, but many eventually converted to Christianity."

She lifted her good hand, palm up. "Sure, some converted for political alliance or were forced to as part of the treaties signed with the king Alfred the Great in his attempt to keep the peace. But others embraced Christianity as a new beginning and truly believed."

Natalie raised her hand. "Do you think that the Vikings ever felt part of the culture of their new home? Or do you think they always felt separate from them, even the ones who became Christians?"

Knowing how Natalie felt as a single mom alongside the younger and just plain-old single college students and how this often left her feeling isolated and an oddity among the other students, her question seemed to take on a deeper meaning.

Ellora took in a slow breath, letting her answer form. "You know, that's a great question. If I had to guess, because that's all we can do as Vikings didn't tend to keep great records, I would wonder if they felt sort of set apart from the people born and raised here. Probably torn between two lives. Pulled in two different directions—from what they knew and what was right in front of them. Between two different sets of ideals, dreams and plans for their lives. Between what was considered right and wrong."

Natalie nodded, seeming satisfied with the answer. And for Ellora, the answer she'd given held a double meaning for herself as well.

The class time ran out and as the students gathered their things, she was unable to separate what she'd expressed on the behalf of those long-ago Vikings and what was happening in her own heart. With this job offer, it felt like she was being asked to choose between her career, her dreams and her husband. But if she took this job, wouldn't that almost certainly seal their future…apart?

Alex stared again at the words of the email meant for Ellora until the letters blurred and lost all meaning. Or maybe the stark black letters against the white meant *too* much and blurred everything he'd been trying so hard to work on with his wife. Had complicated everything when the last thing they needed was another obstacle.

No, he hadn't purposely kept it from her, but if he was honest—and it stung his conscience to do so—he hadn't been in a hurry to tell her either. He should've told her the first day she felt well enough to hear it. He prayed for forgiveness and mentally kicked himself. Their lack of communication and habit of omitting the truth had spiraled them into this mess in the first place.

But was he down to a choice of integrity or his marriage? It didn't matter now anyway. She knew and the choice was in her hands. He had a choice too. If she took this job, which could well be her dream career, would he leave this, *his* dream career, behind to see if they could work on their relationship?

He answered a couple of pressing emails, then several less pressing ones—like a parent who wanted to ensure her son was wearing enough sunblock and staying hydrated like he was a child at summer camp instead of a legal adult and college student. Alex had to admire her care for her son though. He typed a polite reply.

He shut the laptop with a little more gusto than he'd meant and pulled the partial manuscript toward him. He'd better work on it like he'd promised Ellora.

"What are you looking so grim over, mate?" Oscar stood in the doorway.

Alex waved him in with a sigh. "I'm trying to look like I know what I'm doing for my wife. The way to her heart is through history, you know."

"Much like her husband, I think." Oscar chuckled. "I came to return the saber you loaned me for practice. Mine is back from the repairer. You know, after you about tore it to pieces in that match at the fair."

"Not at all." He sounded distracted even to his own ears.

His friend sat the saber in its case by the bookshelf and leaned over the manuscript spread out in front of Alex.

Alex pointed to the scribbles in the margin of the intricate carpet page. "The scribe of this partial manuscript may relate to our search for the lost manuscript. At least, that's what Ellora's grandmother thought."

"And you think what was written in the margin here is a clue?" Oscar's hand went to his belt loops.

"I hope so." Alex rubbed his forehead, studying the letters he'd assumed spelled Old English or Latin words, but hadn't been either. Then there was a string of Roman numerals. "I'm supposed to be the language expert, but I can't figure this out."

Oscar scooted a chair to the side of the desk. "Let me see if I can help you, mate. I know horses and animals are usually my gig, but I'll give this a try. Sometimes coming at it from another angle helps."

"You sure are taking an interest in medieval history all of a sudden."

Oscar's smirk said it all. "What, a bloke can't take up a new hobby now and again?"

Alex scratched his chin. "Sure, sure. And this wouldn't have anything to do with spending more time with Lanae, right?"

Oscar gave Alex the briefest glance then continued studying the letters and numbers on the vellum. "It might. She's amazing but, mate, she might not be able to stay in England for more than a few months a year. Maybe six at the most. And I haven't told her…"

"What? About your divorce?"

His friend dipped his chin, shoulders slumping. "She told me about her parents' divorce when she was younger. I get the feeling she's pretty careful about relationships because of that and if she hears I've been divorced—never mind that I did everything I could to stay with my wife, but she was determined to leave—Lanae will probably drop me faster than Raven does a bad apple."

Oscar leaned over the desk, elbows on his knees.

Alex clapped him on the back, but all the while he had to ask himself—would that be Ellie and him soon enough? He blew out a breath, focusing back on Oscar. "Lanae is a pretty understanding person. And what I'm learning, rather painfully might I add, is that honesty and the whole truth right away will save you from bigger problems down the road. No matter how hard that truth may be."

After a solemn nod from Oscar, they both continued to study the partial manuscript margin.

Oscar pointed. "What if the numbers correspond to the pages and words?"

Alex straightened. "A code similar to the one Grandma June had used to start this whole thing? Let's try it."

As he and Oscar gathered the letters from the pages and designated lines, the word "Mildrythe" appeared.

"Hmm." Alex mused. "What do you suppose this other gibberish is?"

Oscar scratched his head. "You're the language expert, remember?"

"I don't think that will serve me here, unfortunately." Then he examined it again in a new light, not as a language aficionado but as a person searching for a hidden message. That was it. The letters seemed to realign, moving into place in his mind.

"It's another code. She shifted all of the letters back one."

He dictated to Oscar, who wrote down the translated letters. When they were done, Oscar read, "'To my teacher, I give my thanks. From one woman and most treasured friend to another, reading and writing have opened a door that shall never close. Your own work of lapis lazuli shall live on in Lindisfarne, from dear St. Cuthbert's Island, long after we are gone even if we two alone know it was our toil which brought them into being.'"

Oscar leaned back in his chair. "So, Mildrythe taught this woman how to read and write as well as illuminate manuscripts? From her wording here, it makes you wonder how many women actually were the scribes and artists behind these written works."

Alex stood and held the notebook with their translation, going over the words again. "So true. Sadly, most of them probably didn't get the credit. Right cheeky and brilliant of this woman to ensure she received the recognition she was due, at least, in the margins."

For some time, the research and the manuscript's origins had seemed to lead them to Lindisfarne. He gathered the papers into a stack and placed them back inside Ellie's portfolio.

"Right then. Lindisfarne it is." A wild flicker of hope sputtered and burned to life in his chest. Maybe this would be the final epic conclusion. Could it be that the lost manuscript wasn't lost at all but had come to rest at its beginning, the place where it was created in the first place?

"Thank you, my friend." Alex shook Oscar's hand.

"Anytime." Oscar backed toward the door. "You had it all along. Sometimes you just have to get out of your own way and stop overthinking things."

They bid each other goodbye.

Perhaps if they had success in this search, Ellora would want to stay. A selfish thought perhaps, but a truthful one. But if they continued with their marriage, would she ever be satisfied with not having children and be content, just the two of them?

Or once this mystery was solved, would she consider her work done and return to Minnesota and expect him to hand over the divorce papers?

He lifted up a prayer for wisdom as he gathered the manuscript, eager to share their discoveries. He'd also managed to uncover the meaning of the Futhark on the museum painting. He'd been overthinking that one too. It wasn't a place. It was a name. Futhark symbols not only had different word meanings, but each was also assigned a letter. When translated into straight letters, they spelled "Hilda."

Now they needed to figure out what these two ancient women had to do with one another. What was their story? And if Grandma June's disappearance was connected somehow to this search, where had she fallen off the edge of this trail?

But he couldn't help the slight dread in the pit of his stomach. As they drew closer to the end of these women's stories, they may be drawing closer to the end of his and Ellora's story.

Chapter Thirteen

Ellora dug the fingers of her good hand into the rich, fragrant earth. She let every crease of her knuckles, every unique only-hers swirling line of her fingerprints, the crevice beneath every nail, fill with life-giving soil.

A smile tugged at her lips as she tipped her face toward the sun before it slid behind another white puff of cloud. An action that would've been unbearable with the stapled wound and concussion just ten days ago, but now, with the staples gone and her on the mend from the concussion, it only twinged.

"See? Told you gardening is good for the soul." Lanae sank to her knees at the vegetable bed next to where Ellora tended the mustard plants in the herb section of the Alnwick Garden's community garden. "Did you know that touching soil lowers your blood pressure and lifts your mood?"

Ellora shaded her eyes from the sun. "Even if the science is a little circumstantial, I'm going to agree with you. Or, at least, I'm believing my own anecdotal evidence on this one."

They had the place to themselves, which added another layer of peace to the moment.

Lanae grinned, digging into the weeds. "Kind of makes me think about the life God breathed into Adam, you know? Making him from the humble dirt of the ground. He used the lowliest of substances to create life. The first life, even. Do we each have a speck of that God-breathed ground inside of us, passed down through the generations?" Lanae sat back on her legs.

"That's a deep thought for a Monday afternoon, but I like it. There have been times I wondered if He'd left me. But maybe in ways I can't even see, He's been there all along. His breath already in my lungs, His love already a part of my DNA."

It was a beautiful thought, though a little hard to believe.

One of the ungerminated mustard seeds, discarded, forced to give nutrients to the ones who'd made it, rolled across her palm. A mustard seed forgotten and almost invisible against the soil. A seed never allowed to grow, to reach its full potential. A promise unfulfilled.

"What's wrong?" Lanae studied her.

She held it out for her friend to see. "This was how big the baby was when I—when I... The doctor said he was the size of a mustard seed."

"He?" Lanae crawled closer and laid an arm across her shoulders.

"Yeah, I had a feeling. Besides, I was tired of thinking and saying 'the baby' all of the time." She turned a quivering smile to Lanae.

Her friend ran a forefinger over the round seed. "So small, and yet— Do you remember the passage your Grandma June liked to quote from that old Bible?"

Ellora laughed. "Yes, the big family Bible. She loved the verse in Matthew 17, '...for verily I say unto you, If ye have faith as a grain of mustard seed, ye shall say unto this mountain, Remove hence to yonder place; and it shall remove; and nothing shall be impossible unto you.'"

"Makes sense she liked that version with its grand historical-sounding verbiage, huh?"

"Mmm-hmm. And it seemed to put vigor in her veins, not that she needed much convincing to believe she could cast aside mountains. But I think it reminded her that it was actually God behind the moving."

The gravity, the weight of the seed, nearly pushed her hand to the ground. "How can something—a *life*—so small carry a mountain's worth of hopes and dreams? How is it possible that the loss of something the size of a mustard seed left a hole the size of Mount Everest in the middle of my chest?" Now she couldn't stop the tears falling, wetting the earth, watering the seed that would never grow.

Lanae wrapped an arm around her again and laid her head against Ellora's shoulder. "Because, El, your baby was like a seed. He was a seed planted in your heart, and without knowing why or how, a mother's love sprouted and bloomed. And just because the seed died doesn't mean your love did."

She closed her eyes a moment. "Thank you. That's what I needed to hear." The word "died" was a harsh, invisible blow, but she found it healing too. It acknowledged there had been a life and now there wasn't, after feeling like she was expected to get over it. Like the life lost didn't matter to the world. Well, he mattered to her.

In the same way, her grandmother's life mattered. She wasn't stupid. The world had told her to face facts about her grandmother as well. To admit she was gone. But the heart was a complicated muscle, a stubborn, love-holding, hope-when-all-hope-is-lost kind of place. And she didn't have the strength to tell her heart anything different.

She made a little divot of soil, placed the seed inside and covered it over. Giving it a pat, she stood—but not without a groan for her stiff, still-sore legs.

Lanae jumped to her feet with little to no grumbling.

They finished their herb cuttings—Lanae planned to make Ellora more of her healing tea, which tasted like the clippings from a lawn mower mixed with the bitter dregs of a cuppa steeped too long. They moved toward the larger garden exit.

"So, are you packed for the trip to Lindisfarne tomorrow?" Lanae held the gate for her, her basket of herbs in one hand.

"I'm ready. I've felt this search would ultimately lead us there and now with the message in the partial manuscript Alex and Oscar found, it just makes sense to check it out."

She squinted against the sun, peeking at her friend's profile. "How are things going with Oscar?"

Lanae's lips tightened. "He told me he was divorced a few years ago. Said he didn't want to, but his ex refused to reconcile."

"That's tough to hear, I'm sure. But I'm glad he was honest with you."

She nodded but it was slow and reluctant. "We already have so much weighing on us with the long distance, I'm not sure we can handle extra baggage like that nor the 'specter of marriage past.'"

"I'm not sure you're being fair to Oscar, Nae. He seems like a genuine, godly man looking for commitment. That's what Alex says too. If we held the mistakes of our pasts and the bad choices of others against each other, none of us would be worthy of love and marriage."

Ellora certainly wouldn't be. A little push within told her she needed to look at how she viewed Alex and forgiving herself and him for their pasts. "It's always going to be two imperfect people vowing to each other under a perfect God."

Lanae gulped. "You're probably right. I have a lot more praying to do, I guess."

It wasn't lost on her that her words had some truth in there for her and Alex as well.

Passing through the stunning rose garden, they came upon Eg propped on a little stool, painting the scene before them. The likeness to the garden, the twisting iron gates and brick structures behind it, was astounding, but Eg had added a woman and a little girl holding hands, their backs to the viewer.

Lanae and Ellora stopped to watch for a moment.

Eg caught them and gestured to the figures. "My wife loved these gardens—she could wander these paths for hours. Watch the fountain go, loved to see the bees and the butterflies about their business. She's been gone five years now. But her memory lives here in this garden."

Ellora inched closer. "What a beautiful tribute to her, Eg. I'm sure she would've loved the painting."

A fond but melancholy smile lifted just the corners of his mouth. He pointed to the girl. "That's our Gillian. We lost her many years ago now, over fifteen. Freddie was a toddler at the time. Gillian passed from leukemia, six years old."

"I'm so sorry, Eg." Ellora's throat seized. Lanae repeated the same words and sentiment.

"I like to think of them together again, under God's care now." He turned a watery expression toward them. "It was long ago, but you know? You never forget. You learn to carry the grief, shoulder it, every day. Then, when you're ready, you lay it daily at God's feet. And when you do that, give the burden to Him to carry, He gives something in return."

"What's that?"

"Hope." He shook his head and his paintbrush at the same time. Good thing she was already dirty from the garden as he spattered paint onto her shirt. "Now, I'm not talking about blind-eyed optimism. I'm talking about hard-fought, hard-won, hope. Born of a peace that only comes after a long battle, forged in the darkest mire you never thought you'd have to wade through. But you made it and you know that you never would've made it through without His help."

She exchanged a glance with Lanae. Such fierce words, still in his usual exuberant tone but with much more intensity. They stirred something within her, a longing but also fear. A fear of letting go. Even giving painful things to God meant she no longer had control. She couldn't prepare or plan. It meant having no walls around herself. If she let Him close enough to take the burden of loss from her shoulders, He could leave her at any moment. Abandoned. Alone. Defenses down. Vulnerable.

Thankfully, Eg sighed by way of segue. "Well, Freddie said you're off to Lindisfarne with the students?"

Lanae said, "Yes, we'll be touring the village, the priory ruins and Holy Island. And we're hoping Freddie will be able to help us with some more details we found about the lost manuscript."

"Oh, that he will. You can count on him helping in any way he can. He's a good lad." The love and pride he had for his boy warmed Eg's tone. And she could see why they were so close; they only had each other now.

She knew all too well the feeling of a dwindling list of loved ones, the connection to family disappearing. That had been part of the longing to become a mother, to not allow her family tree to stop with her.

They thanked Eg and wished him well as he finished his beautiful painting, which he said would be on display and for sale in a local artist section of the castle gift shop. It helped fund his son's trip to Lindisfarne and their historical adventures.

The more Ellora looked at the painting, the more she was drawn to it.

She had to toss one more glance over her shoulder before she and Lanae exited the garden. Something about the way the mother held her child's hand commanded Ellora's attention. Yes, it was meant to be Eg's late wife and little girl, but they seemed to symbolize so much more, something that felt almost personal. It spoke of gentle leadership, protection and love between parent and child. And it opened up the familiar pang of longing within her heart.

"Maybe you need to buy that painting, you know, when it's ready." Lanae cast a careful side-eye Ellora's way. "You could even let Eg know you'd like to buy it directly from him to make sure it doesn't sell to someone else."

She brushed the idea into thin air with one swipe of her hand. "How would I get it back to the States with me? It's enormous and it would be so expensive to ship. I couldn't."

Lanae shrugged as they made their way along the wide gravel path back to the castle, the River Aln and lush green spread out to their right. "Unless…you don't plan to go back and find a way to stay."

Ellora tried to swallow, but it stuck halfway down, turning into a cough. "I don't know yet. Alex and I are growing closer, but there's still a gulf between us. I have this job offer, and I'm not sure if Alex will ever change his mind about having a family."

They passed through the Lion Arch tunnel to return to the castle grounds. Lanae's sharp exhale echoed against the dim space. "Is that a deal breaker?"

The question, so simple yet so pointed, pierced Ellora in

the gut. "I—I...don't know. There's a longing in me for a family that I just can't let go of."

"I don't have the answers. I certainly don't know what it's like to go through what you've both gone through." She threw Ellora a pained glance. "Don't forget, I was there when you took your vows. When you pledged to be there for each other through thick and thin, even when life got rough and every dream didn't come true. I know it may not be any of my business, but I don't want you to live with the regret my mom and dad did after their divorce."

"I know you don't. But we're not your parents and when I said those vows, that was before I'd known what it felt like to carry a child." Ellora clenched one fist, but even as she said the words she couldn't help going back to what she'd just told Lanae about Oscar. Was she being fair to Alex? Was she refusing to work through their differences, their pasts? But then, he'd never made an effort to compromise his position on children either.

Staying meant her ultimate dream—far above being a historian and furthering her career—of being a mother might stay just that...a pie-in-the-sky dream. Could she even consider giving that up?

"I'm saying this as your oldest—well, not old but dearest—friend. You know that, right?" Lanae fixed her with sober eyes. "He never lied to you, El. He told you right away he didn't want to have children. You said you didn't care and you chose to walk up that aisle to him anyway. You chose to. You said you were sure. I understand that you've changed your mind on the matter, but can you fault him for not changing his?"

Each word, though spoken in a kind tone, was like a tiny barb jabbing into her heart. All the more painful because of their truth.

Ellora threw her hands out, the sprained one smarting. "You're right. He never misled me. But what did I know about starting a family then? I was young, in love and I thought all I'd ever want or need was me and him, the wind in our veins and adventure in our back pockets. I didn't know about this ache—" she clutched her chest "—this consuming desire to love a child, how I'd feel this ever-present missing piece in our lives."

Lanae's creased brow made Ellora try again to make her understand. "I know you're probably thinking this is a way to fill a void, with my parents long gone from my life, Grandma June missing and no other family. But you're wrong." Ellora's temples started to pulse. "It's—it's like discovering my calling as a historian, only more personal, more a part of who I am, deep down. I just know to the bottom of my soul, I'm supposed to be a mom."

"And if Alex knows to the depths of his soul that he's *not* meant to be a dad?"

A moment passed. The ache moved to her throat. "I don't know yet." She rubbed her forehead. "But thank you. I will pray on it. Like you. Promise. I'm not jumping on the next plane back to Minnesota just yet—you can be sure of that."

"Good. We've still got your grandmother to find, and you can't leave before I fix you up with my special kombucha blend. I made it from SCOBY Steve's significant other, Stacy. By the way, it seems serious. We could be looking at marriage."

"At least someone around here has this commitment thing figured out." Ellora's laugh echoed against Lanae's until they reached the outer bailey. "You're so weird. Does Oscar know? The sooner he knows, the better."

"That's why you love me." She sent Ellora a wide Cheshire

cat grin. "And yes, by the way, he does. Thank you very much. I've already introduced him to Steve."

This lightened the mood as they headed to their respective rooms to wash up for dinner and prepare for the trip to Lindisfarne in the morning.

Water poured down from thick, velvety gray clouds, welcoming them to Lindisfarne. They bumped along the Lindisfarne Causeway, which connected the mainland to the island village, in their rented coach bus. Even though a couple of students had become carsick along the way, Ellora had enjoyed sitting close to Alex during the forty-minute drive.

The topic turned to their search, which would overlap with the field trip. They'd all travel to the priory ruins and then the museum together, where she and Alex would meet up with Freddie to see if he'd learned anything about the name Hilda or Aelfgar, the man rumored to have escaped with a manuscript. She'd done a little digging and spoke with some of the local history experts in Lindisfarne as well. Extensive excavations had been done in the area already, and no manuscripts like she described had been found.

"I wonder if that reference to Lindisfarne in the partial manuscript meant that another clue could be found there or if the lost manuscript had been there for a time but later moved after that coded message to Mildrythe."

"It could be. The message was fairly vague. Did you bring the etching you found in Grandma June's master field journal?"

Ellora patted the shoulder bag in her lap. "I brought the whole journal. With everything that's happened, I didn't want to leave it behind at the castle."

She retrieved the journal from her bag and slipped the etching out.

Alex traced the lines with his finger. "This seems to be a rubbing of a stone carving of some kind. If I had to guess, it's from a rune stone."

"That's what I was thinking too."

Rune stones were markers used by Vikings, typically to commemorate important life events or as a gravestone. They usually said something about the person in Futhark and often had pictures.

Alex rubbed his chin as he studied the depiction of a carved woman holding a knotted cross. And there were some symbols, possibly Futhark, on the edges, but the charcoal rubbing hadn't captured the whole thing.

They arrived at the parking area for buses and tourists. "I hate to say it, but doesn't it seem strange a woman is shown in this way? This is almost like a great warrior's burial rune or that of a chieftain," she said.

"Indeed. Though there were female warriors among the Vikings, but to commemorate them in this way at their deaths wasn't typical." Alex folded the paper again and handed it back to her as everyone stood and moved into the aisle. "I'd have to translate the rest of the stone, but it seems to speak of great deeds."

Lanae led the way to the Lindisfarne Priory ruins from the car park. A constant sea breeze snatched Ellora's hair free from her loose twisted updo and brought with it a steady swirl of salt, fish and wet sand.

Huddled under umbrellas, they took a turn about the ruined priory—a place that should have been filled with peace in its wholeness but, instead, saw hundreds of years of attacks and power shifts. It was finally at rest in its decay. The beauty of the still-standing arches extended into the vault of sky above. One complementing the other.

At the priory museum, Freddie waved her and Alex over as the group moved through the exhibits.

Freddie tried to smooth his mop of hair back. He bobbed on his heels. "Hi, Professor and...Professor Lockwood."

They exchanged pleasantries. Freddie scanned the crowd. "My father's chuffed I'm here. Actually, he put together a last-minute field trip for the Lost Artifact Society. They should be here any minute."

"If we had known, we would have invited them to ride with us," Alex said.

Ellora agreed and then reached for the etching in her bag. "We don't intend to keep you long. We just have a couple of questions for you."

"Of course. Anything I can do to help." He straightened, his long limbs stretching to his full height.

Ellora showed it to him. "Have you seen the stone this came from around here or anywhere in your studies?"

"No, I'm afraid I haven't. There's the stone carved by the monks after the initial raid—the Viking raider stone, or Domesday Stone, but none like this."

Alex reached a hand, touching her forearm. "Have you found anything on that Aelfgar chap? The only one who supposedly misplaced the memo that the monks were leaving Lindisfarne and left on his own or was somehow separated from them? There was a story that he may have been seen with another manuscript on his way inland."

The young man scratched the back of his neck. "I looked into it and it seems like it's probably a dead end. There's one account that he did escape but died shortly after on the journey to catch up with the others. And another record of his death during one of the raids on Lindisfarne, just before the people abandoned Holy Island in 875. So, if he'd had the manuscript, it didn't get far."

"We'll have to hope it wasn't with him then." Alex ran a hand through his hair, giving it a tousled look other guys probably spent hours trying to achieve.

She was about to thank Freddie and move on, but the young man held a finger in the air. "Oh, I don't know if this helps at all or is relevant, but I discovered that Aelfgar was engaged, you know, betrothed to a woman named Mildrythe."

Ellora's mouth dropped open and Alex froze. They exchanged a glance.

Alex cleared his throat. "Do you know anything about Mildrythe and her whereabouts after Holy Island was abandoned?"

"That's where the story gets a little fuzzy, with some accounts saying she was kidnapped by Norsemen around 875, and was soon after presumed dead. But there's conflicting information on that."

Ellora was about to bid him goodbye for now, but Freddie nodded to a display of medieval writings. "There's a partial Psalter from the late 800s I thought you might find interesting."

She and Alex peered through the glass to a simple yet neatly written illuminated early medieval Psalter, much like the later medieval Book of Hours, with a variety of prayers, reflections, calendars and select passages from the Bible.

Alex read aloud, "'O most merciful God, incline Thy loving ears to our prayers, and illuminate the hearts of those called by Thee, with the grace of the Holy Spirit, that they may be enabled worthily to minister to Thy mysteries, and to love Thee with an everlasting love, and to attain everlasting joys; through Jesus Christ our Lord. Amen.'"

"It's interesting how there are historiated initials—" she indicated the larger, elaborate letters usually reserved for the first letter on the first word of a new section or chapter "—in multiple places throughout these two pages instead of only at the beginning."

Freddie pointed. "Exactly. Look closely."

Alex's forehead creased, lips moving silently. "If you put those letters together, it spells 'Mildrythe lives.'"

Her eyes widened. "What?" She leaned closer, careful not to touch the glass.

"There is some writing in the margins too. I'm not sure what it says," Freddie said.

Eg sauntered through the crowd with his ragtag group, arms and smile spreading wide. "There's my boy. The big history expert." He embraced his son. Freddie reddened but didn't pull away.

Cressida and Gwen greeted them next. Ellora said hello to Cressida, who appeared only mildly interested in her surroundings and more like Eg and Gwen dragged her along. Ellora asked Alex to take the photos of the Psalter pages so they could study the margins later, just in case anything happened to her new phone.

They thanked Freddie and said goodbye to the society members.

They found Lanae and the students watching a demonstration of Viking metal jewelry and weaponry making in a temporary ironworks shop set up outside the museum.

The heat and smoke of the fires, along with the loud clangs of the hammers, permeated the tented space and made Ellora's head pound in time with the metallic banging.

After giving her the details, Lanae asked, "Do you think this Mildrythe was the one who created the lost manuscript? And if she was, who would've taught her?"

Ellora tapped her chin. "The thing is, there was Cuthbert's predecessor, Aidan, who was known for encouraging women's education. He died long before Mildrythe would've been born though."

Alex crossed his arms over his chest. "But maybe it's not unreasonable to think there had been another more 'modern-thinking' man here at the time who chose to educate women on reading, writing, preparing paper, bookbinding and, of course, painting skills to use for illuminated bookmaking. Sort of following in Aidan's footsteps."

"You know—" Lanae leaned in "—since there have been a few mentions of a Hilda somewhere in this mix, could Mildrythe have learned from another woman?"

"Could be." Ellora puckered her lips in thought. "There were also families who did copywriting for a living. They copied books word for word by hand. Maybe Mildrythe learned from older family members, and this was their family business."

"Well, whatever is going on, I need to get these young adults fed, myself too for that matter, before we turn back into toddlers." Lanae ushered the students back to the exit to find lunch and wander the village now that the skies were clearing.

Just as Ellora turned toward the main museum, she spotted him—Byron. Not far off, one of those tough-looking men—with a buzzed haircut, thick arms, wearing all black—she'd seen with him at the Alnwick Fair, strode in his direction.

She elbowed Alex, who yelped. "Oops, sorry. Look. There's Byron."

Alex's eyes narrowed, searching the crowd. "Maybe this bloke and I need to have a little heart-to-heart."

An idea sparked. She snapped her fingers. "Call my phone."

His brows drew together and then lifted.

"Not my new one. My old one. Hurry. Please."

He dug his phone from his jacket pocket and pressed Call to her old number.

The loud, clear sound of "Dream a Little Dream of Me" sang out over the crowd. Byron's expression darkened and after a moment of people crossing in front of him, he was gone. How did he keep doing that?

"That thief." She gritted her teeth and took off through the wandering museum patrons.

"Wait!" Alex was on her heels at first but then she lost him.

She tried to follow the song. But with so many people and the echoing walls of the museum, she'd lost both. The guy dressed in black was gone too. Finally, she dashed for the front entrance. She swiveled her head but didn't spy Byron anywhere outside.

Alex caught up to her, huffing in and out. "And what—" each word punctuated with a breath "—pray tell, did you intend to do if you'd caught up with him, my love?"

"I have no idea." She'd been so focused on stopping him, she hadn't thought about that.

Something caught her eye on the other side of a rose-bush. Her stolen phone with an elaborate spiderweb crack on its face.

But the screen still functioned and had snapped an accidental picture of a shoe tip. A men's leather shoe. It had a slight blur, but it looked to be a black loafer. Just like the posh-dressed Byron Hughes wore.

Chapter Fourteen

The cracked face of her stolen, now-returned phone stared up at Ellora as she slumped onto her couch. If only its shattered mouth could speak.

Byron kept popping into her mind. He'd been there when she'd heard her ringtone at the Lindisfarne museum two days prior. The detective who had been handling her grandmother's missing person case had just brought by the phone and still, there was no true answer. The detective had finished dusting the phone for prints.

It wasn't a common practice for a stolen phone. But since she'd received threats on the phone and the thief may be connected to Grandma June, he'd checked. The only full print he could pull belonged to her. Everything else was indecipherable, smudged.

Now, she was halfway through the summer session and no closer to any answers. Time was slipping away and the end-of-the-summer deadline loomed.

She kicked off her T-strap heels, sore after a day of walking the uneven cobbled castle path and moving around the classroom.

Time had not given a denial nor a confirmation of her grandmother's death. Too long with no answers, only more questions.

And yet, not enough time—only five more weeks—to decide the rest of her life. She and Alex had yet to discuss the job offer she'd received or the fate of their marriage in general. But spending time doing the things they were passionate about did remind her of why they had fallen in love in the first place.

Without thinking about it, she'd taken out her travel jewelry bag. At the time she'd packed, she couldn't bring herself to leave her wedding ring behind. She laid it on her palm. The antique 1930s art deco design glistened in the afternoon sun reaching through the windows.

Inside the band were the words they'd said to each other from Song of Solomon: "I am my beloved's and my beloved is mine." His ring, wherever it was, had the same engraving. It was also the verse her grandfather had engraved on her grandmother's ring. And her grandparents lived those words. Through thick and thin they had been at each other's side. It made her ache with missing them but also with a longing to live this out with Alex again.

Her grandmother's ring. It wasn't the ring she'd been given at their engagement. Grandma June had lost it deepsea diving in Malta. But her grandfather had replaced it with an antique sapphire ring. Grandma June had never gone anywhere without it. Whatever had happened to her grandmother, wherever she now was, undoubtedly the ring rested with her. A little comfort in that, but still another loose end.

A knock on the door made her jump. She returned the ring to the jewelry bag, and hurried to the door.

Alex stood there, forearm resting above his head on the door frame, looking so much like the front cover of a British men's magazine with his textured three-piece suit and roguish dimpled grin. "All right, love? I missed you."

He could still manage to send a thrill of butterflies—more like giant flamingos—flapping through her stomach. Heat ebbed through her cheeks and down her neck. "Hey," she managed.

"I missed you too." It sounded dull to her ears, but the way his grin widened told her he didn't think so. She opened the door farther to let him in. "I've hardly seen you since Lindisfarne."

Before she'd hardly pivoted to face him, he'd swept her into a firm embrace and took her face, kissing her soundly on the lips.

"I know our future is uncertain, but I can't stand having this wall—as in a literal wall—" he gestured to the wall that separated their flats "—between us. One of the best parts of being married to you was that no matter what kind of day I had or how busy, at the end of it, I came home to you. *You* were home to me." He cradled her face between his hands, his eyes searching hers. "Does that make any sense?"

She reached up and brushed his cheek with her good hand. "That's the way I've always felt about you. No matter what was going on, I could come home to you and it was like my heart, everything, breathed a sigh of relief. Like whatever had been missing in my day had finally been made right. But..."

Drawing a breath for strength, she pulled back an inch. A flash of something crossed his face—hurt? Frustration? And her gut echoed the sentiment.

"Alex, I wish we could move forward instead of looking back. I do. More than anything. But there are some major issues still between us. I'm afraid that if we just jump back into our life together without dealing with these things, pretending they're not there, our marriage will implode for good. And there won't be any coming back from that."

He swallowed, squeezed her good hand. "Right now, I don't know what the answers are, and I don't want to force it. We both have decisions to make. For now, are you still all right with us working on it, albeit with a wall between us?"

He quirked a smile, but there was something vulnerable and hopeful behind it.

"It's better than an ocean." She reached up to kiss his cheek, but he turned his head to catch her lips instead. A impish grin spread. "How about this? If we're missing that end-of-the-day conversation, let's commit to checking in with each other and spending time together after work every day. That way we won't have to miss each other so much."

"Yes, I knew I married you for your brains."

She giggled at the ticklish sensation as he buried his face in the crook of her neck and held her close.

He extricated himself to plunk down on her sofa, which was a little on the short side for him, so his long lean legs bent like a grasshopper's.

Grabbing Grandma June's field journal, she joined Alex on the couch. She swung her feet onto his lap, like she'd always done at home after a long day.

He massaged her calves—he knew how ticklish her feet were. "Let's start this end-of-the-day chin-wag right now. Have you found anything else about Mildrythe?"

She sighed, resting her braced sprained wrist across her abdomen. "Nothing other than what we've already learned or suspected. But I did see another mention in here—" she held out the page in the journal "—about Hilda. See? It says, 'White lady... Hilda's ancestor?'"

"White lady? Where have I heard that before?" His brows drew together.

"It was at the Lost Artifact Society, remember? Somebody was talking about a local legend. A white lady that haunts an estate or something."

"That's right. That Cressida woman." The way he said her name was like he'd tasted something bitter.

"Mmm-hmm. Eg mentioned it too, I think."

"Why would Grandma June suspect this white lady was the ancestor of Hilda?"

Ellora held the journal close to her face like the thing would shout the answer. When she flipped the page of the soft leather-bound journal, something in the margin caught her eye.

Alex traced a finger over what Ellora had thought were absent doodles. "Those are the same type of markings the woman who wrote and painted the partial manuscript used to write a secret message. May I see it?"

She handed it over and sat up next to him. He dashed to her desk and returned with a pencil and scrap paper. Going between the scrap paper and the margin, scribbling furiously, he finally raised his head with a smile. "Grandma June used the same method of code the medieval woman scribe did. The one who had named Mildrythe as her teacher."

"What does it say?"

"It says, 'Proof is in my office. You will know by the music in your ears.'"

She grumbled. "That woman and her riddles. If she were here..."

But she let it trail off because if Grandma June were there, they wouldn't be running down this never-ending path of clues. And perhaps the reason Grandma June felt the need to be so secretive about her findings was also the reason she wasn't there.

Alex reached over and squeezed her knee. "One part was pretty clear—it's back to Grandma June's office."

They dashed out the door, down the stairs and out to the quieted castle grounds—the last of the tours done and guests gone for the day.

Once Alex unlocked Grandma June's office door, Ellora blew out a breath and turned a circle in the middle of the room, unsure where to start.

"Any ideas?" He propped a hand on his waist, scrubbing at his stubble with the other.

She wandered the perimeter.

"Hmm." His long fingers slid over the spines of the books on a bookshelf. "What did the note say? Something about music?"

She nodded. "It said we'll 'know by the music in our ears.'"

"A clue in a music-related book, perhaps?"

"Maybe. Though, I can't say as I ever knew Grandma June to be much of a music connoisseur."

They scoured the shelves anyway. No music-related books, no loose sheet music, nothing.

Alex pointed to the corner, where more books were piled on top of the Victor Victrola record player cabinet. "Hey, there are more books over here."

After lifting each one to inspect it without success, a little buzz of adrenaline shot through her veins. "Alex, music in our ears? We're busy looking for a music history book because that seems like her, but what if she's being more literal than that?"

She tapped the side of the cabinet, where the top held the

turntable while underneath had a cupboard and pull-out leather albums to store the records.

A grin lit his face. He gestured with his hand. "You do the honors, love."

She opened the front of the cabinet, then the little double doors of the cupboard. Inside, behind and partially hidden by a vinyl record cleaning kit, was a small box. The size of a jewelry or music box. Even though the detailed carved dark wood was in beautiful shape, it was obviously of antiquity. Unless it was a skilled replica, Ellora would place it in the Tudor or Elizabethan era. She'd have to inspect it further to know for sure.

"We'll know from the music in our ears." Alex lifted the corner of his mouth at the same time as he lifted the small box out of the cabinet. He ran his hand along the bottom edge, where carved symbols ran around all four sides. "It's the Younger and Elder Futhark alphabets."

He laid it on the desk. Ellora tried opening it with one hand, but couldn't. Alex tried with two hands, but it was firmly locked and a solid little thing. Heavy too. They checked the rest of the record player. No key.

"Of course." Ellora pursed her lips. And the opening for the key was a shallow, odd shape. "What kind of key would even open that?"

"Not any I've ever seen." He turned it over in his hands with careful, slow movements. "Hey, look at this."

On the back side of the box, carved right into the wood, was a unique knotted cross.

"That's the same cross from Lindisfarne and the paintings." Her heart pumped again.

"So, if the white lady was supposedly Hilda's ancestor, does that mean this box belonged to the white lady?"

"Could be."

Ellora's head shot up. "What day is it?"

"Thursday, why?"

"The Lost Artifact Society meeting is today! They're doing a supper meeting this time." Ellora moved toward the door with the box under her arm. "Let's see if anyone—even if it has to be Cressida—can tell us more about the white lady. Maybe we'll figure out why she's important in all of this. And Hilda, for that matter."

He pressed a fierce kiss to her forehead. "The brains. I love them."

Alex locked the door behind them.

They brought the box back to her flat and locked it in the trunk and were about to leave when Alex's phone chimed. "It's pictures from the art restorer. What she has uncovered so far."

He turned the screen so she could see too.

Hello, Professor Lockwood squared. I thought you'd appreciate seeing the progress my team and I have made so far. It's coming along nicely. Let me know if you have any questions and I'll keep sending photos as we uncover more of the original work.

Using his thumb and forefinger, he zoomed in on the pictures. A woman with two long braids had been revealed instead of a hooded figure, like in the overpainting, an intricate knotted cross hung around her neck—like a blend of Celtic and Christian artistry, and the woman held a book... of brilliant blue. The color of lapis lazuli.

Ellora nodded to the trunk. "That cross looks just like the carving on the side of the jewelry box."

They'd also just started to uncover a bit of the background. He rubbed his chin, bent over the screen. "Hmm. That doesn't look like Durham Cathedral in the background, does it? It's just a small piece so far, but it looks far too simple to be the cathedral."

"Right, it looks more like a small building or church."

"Maybe this is supposed to be Chester-le-Street like we suspected of the museum painting."

"Well, if this is the really early medieval artwork we think it is, that makes sense since Durham Cathedral's first stone wasn't even placed until 1093."

"I was thinking the same thing. But we had best run if we want to catch the meeting."

They locked up and sprinted toward the tea shop.

They were quite late, but as they jogged the last block, it seemed they weren't the only ones. Cressida spoke to someone in the narrow alley between a little thrift clothing store and a bits and bobs gift shop. Their tones were crisp and full of strain.

All Ellora could discern was a "We'll see about that" from the person with Cressida.

Then that "someone" who'd been shrouded by the alley's shadows ducked out into daylight and almost ran into Ellora. Byron.

His widened eyes quickly narrowed. "You had better watch out, Ms. Lockwood." And both his ominous tone and his choice of words, so close to the texted warning, sent prickles up her forearms despite the warm day.

The question she'd pondered for days popped out of her mouth. "What were you doing in Lindisfarne?"

His nose turned up. "The same thing as the other museum patrons, I expect. Learning about the history of the area. I needed to check on some things for my research. That's not a crime, last I checked."

Alex glowered at Byron. "How about taking something that doesn't belong to you? Say someone's phone?"

The older man's expression was unreadable, but seemed somewhere between indignant and confused. "I haven't the slightest idea what you're on about. Now, if you'll excuse me."

Byron brushed past them, his long legs carrying him down the street and around the corner. Alex asked, "Are you all right?"

Cressida nodded, putting on a stiff smile. "Are you on your way to the society meeting?"

They both said yes and she urged them forward with a curt jut of her pointed chin. "Come on, you lot, we're late."

Ellora had to hand it to her; the petite woman had speed. Cressida's clipped steps brought back memories of being taken to the principal's office in grade school for highlighting her favorite passages in the library's history books and writing her own corrections in the margins.

"Cressida, wait." Ellora quickened her stride. "I'm sorry, I know we don't really know each other—"

"You've got that right."

Ellora cast a pained glance over her shoulder. Alex clamped his lips together. But she pressed on. "It's just, can I ask how you know Byron Hughes?"

"You can, but that doesn't mean I must answer you." Cressida's jaw tightened.

Ellora gritted her teeth and looked back at Alex again. Instead of him offering his natural charm, he dipped his chin as though to say *You've got this.*

She tried another tactic. "I'm not trying to be nosy. Really. I only want to extend the kindness of saying please be careful."

Cressida's small lips all but disappeared, pressed together. They'd arrived at the tea shop, full with the late-afternoon tea and early dinner crowd. Alex opened the door for her and Cressida. Ellora continued in a quieter tone meant just for Cressida, "I have reason to believe that Byron may be dangerous. He has harassed me about my grandmother. I also think he may have—"

They'd reached the table with the other society members, who were already deep in discussion. Cressida whirled around. "Don't you think I know that? Byron Hughes was my husband." Her voice carried, stopping the society meeting in its tracks and making the two closest tables stop and stare. Cressida slumped into a chair, her imperious air deflating. "Now he's my ex-husband."

Alex pulled out a chair for Ellora next to Cressida and he took the one next to Eg, normally occupied by his son.

Ellora tried placing a hand on the older woman's shoulder, but Cressida flinched away. "I only meant to help."

Cressida took in a deep breath. "Many of you know Byron in the historical community, with his work at Durham University and Oxford as well as his articles published in historical journals." There were nods around the table. "What you may not know is that he and I used to be married. And what you most definitely don't know and needs to stay confined to this table—" she pinned each person with a pointed glare and waited for agreement before continuing "—is that Byron had a gambling problem and often took to alcohol when the bets didn't go his way."

"I'm so sorry." Ellora clasped her fingers together to keep from reaching out again.

Cressida held up a hand as though to ward off the sympathy. "The further in debt we became, the worse his drinking became. He jeopardized everything we had, even our home, his ancestral estate de Clare Hall, not far from here."

Eg wiggled a hand in the air. "De Clare Hall? Isn't that where the stories of the white lady come from?"

"Indeed it is."

Sounds of surprise went up around the table.

Ellora leaned closer to the older woman. "What do you know about the white lady?"

"Just what I was told by Byron and, you know, the old stories and such you hear in the area. She was a woman who lived at the manor in the Tudor era. She was rumored to have come with a great dowry, wealth passed down through her family, but her husband was much older, violent and not the person she would've chosen."

Ellora's shoulders slumped as Cressida went on.

"Though women didn't usually get to choose in those days, of course. Her husband had dwindled away much of her wealth and heirlooms. The white lady had a plan to hide away some of her most treasured possessions handed down to her from her mother somewhere secret on the grounds. With the help of a trusted set of guards, she stashed away the valuables and planned to leave with them the next week. But, alas, the woman died in a fire on the estate before she could make her escape. She's said to haunt the halls of the manor in the white dressing gown she died in. Though I lived there for years, I never saw a thing."

Cressida continued, "But Byron lost the estate after we didn't have two pennies to rub together. So in debt we were with the bank. Then some rough-looking chaps started coming by the house. I could hear raised voices from Byron's study. They wanted something from him. He owed them money, no doubt."

Ellora nodded to encourage her to continue. She obliged. "When we lost everything, Byron was manic. Obsessed with recovering the estate—his family's legacy, he said."

Cressida tucked a piece of perfectly coifed silver hair behind her ear. "Anyway, he would stop at nothing to recover what he saw as his. But by that time his drinking... and abuse—" she swallowed "—were too much for me. I left and divorced him." Her lip trembled for a moment—a crack in her usual cool demeanor.

Alex leaned forward, across from Cressida. "Do you know what he's doing in Alnwick now? He mentioned to us that he doesn't live here and is here for work. But we suspect he may be here for other reasons, possibly to find the manuscript June was looking for. Has he mentioned anything to you about it?"

Cressida shook her head. "The only thing he has been harassing me about is some *thing* of value he thinks I took from the manor before I left. A family heirloom. But for one thing, he never told me he wanted it, and for another, I took only what was rightfully mine when I left.

"Besides, the valuable heirlooms in the story of the white lady could be anything. He doesn't even know what they all entailed or if they even truly existed outside of rumors and legends. I don't know why he'd think I'd be able to find them after he and practically his whole family tree before him tried to find them without success. And can you imagine me digging around in dank underground cellars? Absurd." She sniffed.

The whole thing was absurd indeed. "You said he'd do anything to regain his estate. How much *anything*? Like going to the trouble of sabotaging my grandmother's work—" she had to keep herself from saying *kidnapping or hurting my grandmother* "—so he could perhaps sell the manuscript to the highest bidder?"

Eg raised a hand. "Could he find a buyer? It belongs in a museum."

Cressida turned a slow incredulous smile to Eg. "For the right price, everything is for sale." When she received raised brows in return, she added, "That's what Byron always said. There is a black market for stolen artifacts and valuable pieces of history. That's a fact, unfortunately."

Cressida pinned Ellora with a piercing look, a look that cut her to the bone and chilled her right down to the marrow. "So, in answer to your question, Ms. Lockwood—I wouldn't put anything past Byron Hughes."

Chapter Fifteen

The light scrape of paper sliding beneath Ellora's door was stark and unsettling, enough to wake her from a restless sleep.

She shivered as she tied on her robe and tiptoed to the door. A folded piece of paper stared up at her. For a moment, cold sweat swept across her forehead. But Alex's neat scrawl greeted her and warmth replaced the chill, spreading through her chest.

Although she couldn't make out most of it—he'd written using the pigpen cipher—it was signed "Yours, Alex" underneath. Along with that, a "PS. Before you say it, I'm aware this code method is the most easily broken and used in children's books. But it has history which I thought fitting."

And it did too, thought to have originated during the Christian Crusades.

She threw on a pullover dress, brushed her teeth and twisted her hair into a low chignon. After just enough makeup so as not to scare her students, she grabbed her bag, her grandmother's journal tucked inside, and the note to puzzle over as she ate breakfast.

The clatter of dishes and chattering students and staff filled the stone-vaulted dining hall as Ellora grabbed a tray of food—a full English breakfast. Alex was nowhere to be seen.

"I saw him run in, snatch a cup of tea to go and said he had to talk to Oscar," Lanae supplied before Ellora could ask. She was studying papers spread across the table. Again, without looking up, her friend pointed at the note in Ellora's hand. "What's that?"

"Has anyone ever told you that you'd make an excellent teacher? Or mother, for that matter. You've got the whole 'eyes in the back of your head' thing down."

"It's all of those years I spent as a teacher's assistant and resident assistant in the dorms."

Ellora tapped the paper. "Alex put this under my door this morning. It's in code. I haven't had time to figure it out yet."

Lanae squinted at the apparent symbols. Lines, some angled, some straight, and boxes—some with dots, some without. "I can't make anything out of this gobbledygook."

Ellora grabbed a pen from her bag and started drawing out the cipher to help them read the message, which was a set of grids containing the letters of the alphabet, part of the alphabet on grids like tic-tac-toe boards and the other part on big Xs, some containing a letter and others, a letter and a dot. She tapped her drawings. "See? In the message, the letters are then replaced by fragments of the grid itself based on the letter's placement on the cipher."

Lanae tilted her head. "If you say so."

But her friend was a quick study and they worked together to solve it. Ellora read, "'My dearest Ellie, would you do me the honor of accompanying me to dinner this evening?

A second "first" date, if you will. Perhaps this time you'll answer the phone.'"

Lanae glanced up with a crooked grin. "What's he talking about?"

Ellora's cheeks still heated with the memory. "I had spent weeks hoping Alex would ask me out. Well, you remember."

Lanae blew out a whistle. "I seem to remember a certain someone obsessing over it, unable to talk about anything else, until another certain someone—" she cleared her throat and jabbed her thumb into her own chest "—thought she'd scream if she heard the words 'Alex' and 'date' in the same sentence again."

Rubbing her forehead, Ellora grimaced. "Of course, he did finally ask me out. It was during spring break while you were back in California visiting your dad. The night came for our date. The phone rang, him calling to let me know he was downstairs, at our apartment."

"And?" Lanae propped an elbow on the table.

"I was suddenly terrified. I second-guessed everything from what I was wearing to if I was the most irritating person on earth. Or worse—the most boring. I was frozen, like I get. And I couldn't bring myself to answer the phone."

"You never told me. So, what'd you do?"

"I called him the next day and apologized. He teased me about it a little and asked if we could still go out and we agreed I would pick *him* up instead. We went and the rest is history."

"I'm surprised he hasn't used this to tease you at least a little bit over the years."

"Oh, he has, but I made him promise to keep it between us."

"Want my help getting ready?" Lanae eyed Ellora's arm— still sore with her small muscle movements, but healing.

"Would you? That would be amazing."

"Of course. I don't want you injuring yourself again. Girl, you're getting a bit of a track record here for accidents and injuries. But I'll give you that one." Lanae gestured to her wrist. "It was that Byron Hughes."

Ellora finished her last bite and stood. "Now, hush. We don't know that for certain...yet."

Lanae *humphed*. Ellora had filled her in on the conversation with Cressida too.

They made a plan for Lanae to meet her at her flat after classes.

Ellora hurried to her classroom. So focused, already thinking ahead to the evening, she didn't notice the shadow in her peripheral vision until someone's arms circled her waist. She shrieked.

"It's just me." Alex had swept her into her classroom. "I wanted to see if you'd found my note earlier." His eyes twinkled, more of an emerald green with the shadow over his face.

"I did."

"And?"

A twinge of uncertainty made her pause, but she heard herself say, "Yes, I will. Where are we going?"

"That's a surprise." He straightened, dimple deepening.

She started backing toward her desk. "Can I at least know what time?"

"Nineteen hundred. Seven o'clock, for you Americans." He winked. "You'll come to the door?"

"If I never have to hear about that incident again..." She raised a brow.

"I'm not sure I can guarantee that." He put a hand to his heart. "But I'll do my best."

Her smile lingered as he spun on his heel and disappeared through the doorway. The smile persisted throughout her classes. Even the students noticed.

Maddie raised her hand. "Professor Lockwood, you haven't stopped grinning the entire class period, even when you were talking about the Black Plague. Did you find that book you were looking for or something?"

Willa chimed in, "It was a manuscript, remember?"

Maddie opened her mouth, about to respond to her friend.

Ellora held a hand up to stop them. "No, ladies, I did not. But we hope to soon."

Maddie faux-whispered to Willa. "Maybe she's got a hot date with a certain 'superhero professor.'"

Ellora straightened her blouse and put on her most dignified expression. "Or maybe it's a lovely day. Why not smile?"

Maddie and Willa slumped in their seats, obviously hoping for something juicier.

When class ended, she raised her voice above the scrape of chair legs and chatter. "Don't forget to read chapter ten through twelve for Monday. And keep that end-of-session project on your radar. We only have about four weeks until it's due, and we finish up to return home."

A groan went up as they exited the room. A groan her own heart echoed. When she'd said "return home," referring to Minnesota, an immediate contradiction warred within her. A place that questioned where her home was now that everyone who'd made her home *home* was gone.

After a quick trip into the village after classes, Ellora returned to her flat, where Lanae waited to help ready her for the date.

"When I ran into the village, I had this feeling like someone was watching me. Like there was a set of eyes in each alleyway following my every move." Ellora set down her purse and couldn't help the chill that still clung to her spine.

Lanae had her sit at the kitchen table, while she twisted and plaited sections of Ellora's hair and pinned them in place.

"Maybe it was all the talk about Byron the other day and Cressida's story of the white lady."

"Yeah, I don't know. I guess it could be that."

"But it doesn't hurt to stay vigilant. Obviously, after what happened at the parade, we can't be too careful."

What kept tumbling around and around in Ellora's mind was—who was behind the not-so-veiled threats? And were they getting any nearer to the truth about Grandma June and this supposed manuscript or were they chasing down something that would always be just out of their grasp—like the wind?

Lanae pinned one last piece then handed Ellora a small mirror for inspection. "There, finished." It was an elaborate low updo of braids and twisted hair but in a loose style that left a few tendrils to frame her face.

"I love it. Thank you."

"You're welcome." Lanae stretched her fingers and slipped into the chair across from Ellora. "So, do you know where he's taking you?"

"Not a clue." Ellora stood and went to change behind her vintage dressing screen. "But he did say to dress up for dinner and pack something comfortable for afterward, including 'something for your feet other than your usual torture devices.'"

"That sounds interesting." Lanae chuckled.

"So, how are things with you and the English cowboy?" She smiled to herself.

Lanae was quiet a moment then answered, "We're just taking things one day at a time. But I'm trying to take your and my own advice, going in with an open mind and grace-filled heart."

Ellora sighed. "I get it. Same here."

Ellora slipped on the sunflower yellow to rosy gold to

crimson ombré chiffon dress she'd packed. At the time, it had been a whim. She'd had to hang it in the bathroom while she took a steamy shower to rid it of the wrinkles.

"You look like a sunset," Lanae gushed, clasped hands over her chest as Ellora stepped around the screen. "And it brings out the red in your hair."

Ellora smoothed the dress in front of the mirror. "Alex always said the same thing."

Ellora checked the time on her phone just as it played "Dream a Little Dream of Me," which she had uploaded to her new phone. Alex's name appeared on the screen.

She let it play several times, then smirked as she swiped the face to answer. "You worried I wasn't going to answer again?"

"Well, I think you've given it away that you're in, love. I can hear your ringtone through the wall." Warmth curled up between each word like a steaming cuppa.

His voice echoed from the phone *and* the hallway outside her door.

With a last flourish of blush, Lanae declared her done and magnificent. Lanae grabbed her supplies. "I'm heading out, but, El?"

"Yeah?" Ellora retrieved her bag with the change of clothes, her shawl to go with her dress and her purse from the table and followed Lanae to the door.

"I'm praying for you, friend. Listen to each other." Lanae reached out and gave her a one-armed hug.

She opened the door to Alex waiting in the hall, dapper in a charcoal suit and a tie the color of his eyes. He had a leather backpack slung over his shoulder. They said goodbye to Lanae, who winked and bid them a good evening.

Alex kept glancing her way as they set off.

"What? Didn't I dress appropriately for your plans?" She smirked.

"It's not that. You look—" his hands gestured, mouth opening and closing "—incredible."

"Thank you." She bent her head and put a hand to her updo.

"I'm also concerned about those shoes. We have to walk a bit to get to the place I have in mind."

"Oh, you know me. Beauty is pain and all that, especially when it comes to the right pair of shoes." She slowed and gave a dainty little point of her toe, admiring her red T-strap heels. "By the way, what place *did* you have in mind?"

She'd followed his lead and found that they'd crossed the inner bailey to the Lion Arch.

He stopped in the tower passageway. "Well, as I'm thinking about this, perhaps this was a foolish plan. I made reservations at The Treehouse Restaurant, partly because I won that meal for two from the tournament." His lips stretched into a grimace. "But will this bring up too many bad memories for you? You know, with our engagement."

"They're good memories too, you know." She took his hand, but she couldn't help the tremor that ran through her own hand and up her arm.

Could the good memories outweigh the painful ones?

He stopped, swinging around to face her. "It's not too late to go somewhere else. Anywhere you like, even the take-away fish-and-chips shop."

But this night was for hope. For facing the hard things. It was supposed to be a date, a romantic one it seemed. And while she could appreciate his efforts, that did not negate the major obstacles they still had to overcome. Hopefully, this would be their chance to finally discuss everything they needed to. Because without that, there would be no moving forward together.

She pulled him ahead. "We are going to The Treehouse Restaurant. Come on."

She pushed away the doubts as they strolled the rest of the way.

Truth be told, her toes had gone numb by the time they arrived and she couldn't wait to be seated. Although she didn't know what they were for yet, she was grateful the comfy canvas sneakers awaited her for after their supper. She might just slip them on at the dinner table.

They walked through the main indoor dining area, a rustic, magical place that seemed to have climbed out of a children's fairy tale. And the tree limbs curling and climbing around the tables, up the walls seemed ready to reclaim the place for the surrounding forest.

They passed young couples holding hands, families with children laughing and placating impatient little ones waiting for their food, as well as older couples enjoying their time with grown children and grandchildren. They were all of the stages she and Alex had been through and all of the stages she'd hoped they'd reach one day.

A sweep of sadness held her throat captive.

He turned back. "I reserved a special table on the deck."

She managed a nod and small smile.

Lanae's words came back to her. What if he truly never wanted children? Could she be content with that now that she'd had a taste of motherhood? Could the agreements she'd made before her heart had been changed forever hold up now as they stood at the crossroads of their marriage?

Maybe she needed to root out the reason he didn't want to be a dad. Searching for truth in history came naturally to her. When it came to people, not so much. But he'd never given her a definitive answer, and she needed to understand.

The hostess left them at a table tucked into a private corner of the wraparound deck lit by a golden-hour sun poking through the canopy of trees surrounding them and by the hundreds of twinkling lights draped around the support beams. It was breathtaking.

Alex pulled out a chair for her.

When the waitstaff arrived, Ellora gestured to Alex. "You go ahead and order for us."

He studied her a split second then complied.

As they waited for their food, they were surrounded by the sounds of evening's early embrace.

But not even the birds settling in for the evening, the frogs beginning their night song, crickets chirping nor the squirrels and chipmunks scampering among the branches could block out the impatient snarl from her stomach.

She shot Alex a sheepish grin just as the server placed their food in front of them—pork belly with gravy, leafy greens and crispy potatoes, her favorite when they'd visited before. He'd remembered.

She took several bites to quiet the growling monster in her stomach then paused to address the unspoken elephant in the corner. "If we decide to build a new foundation for our marriage, we'd need to build it on something other than our own strength." This was it. She had to take this chance to talk about the tough stuff.

His forehead creased as he finished chewing. "I'd like to think so. Like the man who built his home on the rock instead of—"

"The shifting sands. Yeah. In the book of Matthew." She twisted the napkin in her lap. "Well, part of this new foundation needs to be more open, honest communication, wouldn't you agree?"

"Yes, I couldn't agree more…"

"Then I need to know what's behind your self-imposed rule about never having children, Alex. I need more from you than just 'no' or telling me over and over again that you've always promised yourself you'd never become a father. You almost were." She clutched her chest. "I was almost a mother. In my heart, I already was. It awakened something in me I can't put back to rest."

He took in a slow breath, eyes on the fireflies now beginning to blink through the treetops. "Your childhood, my childhood, were so difficult. I'm glad you had Grandma June and for a while your grandfather. But I didn't have that. I had no one once my brother died. It was like my whole family died the night my brother was killed."

"That must've been horrible. I'm sorry you went through that. I am." She reached out to his forearm. "But I don't understand what that has to do with not wanting to be a father."

"It has everything to do with it." His jaw tightened. "After Beckett died, I had to be the golden boy replacement. But see, I never quite lived up to it." His voice growing vehement now. "I saw firsthand how easily parents through their expectations and careless words can hurt their children."

His flat hand tapped the table for emphasis. "I never had a desire to potentially mess up a child, leave them lonely or hurt, even unintentionally."

"But you could never be like that. I know you couldn't."

"My parents weren't ever extremely affectionate and they had high expectations, but they'd been decent enough parents before Beckett died. And then it was like Dr. Jekyll and Mr. Hyde, mostly for Mum." He scrubbed his forehead. "I don't know. Maybe we're all just one tragedy away from be-coming our own worst nightmare."

He took her hands in his firm but gentle hands. "And I don't ever want that to be us, our children left to deal with the fallout."

So many thoughts piled up in her head, she could hardly keep them all from spilling out of her mouth at once.

He glanced to the deck ceiling. "What if something hap-pened and I changed? Or on the flip side, what if something happened to our child? I watched those parents after the shooting—they arrived just as I was being loaded into the ambulance. They were devastated. What if I couldn't save my child from illness or injury or, like my parents, a brutal accident? How could I live with myself?"

The piece of her that was still hurt by his inattention after the shooting, when she'd been shattered by the loss of their baby, reared up, indignant and roiling with pain. They had already lost a child. Didn't he get that?

He hadn't been there for their child or her. And instead of making things right, he'd run off. Even now, he could be thinking of ways to compromise. He obviously cared enough about potential children that he didn't want to see them hurt or alone. But he'd made it about how he couldn't control the outcomes of having children in their lives. Another part of her, the part that feared many of the same things, who desperately wanted to bring her life under her own control, was right there with him in this mire of worry. Ready to shut the door to the unknown as well.

But... God.

She gazed fully into his passion-filled eyes. "None of us knows what tomorrow holds, but we know that God holds all of our tomorrows in His capable hands. And I think it's how we live with the unknown that matters and will help us find peace with what only He knows. We live by leaning into His hope, trusting because of the good He's already done and what we know of His character. And we hold on to the ones we love, appreciating each and every moment we're given with them."

His nod was slow as though digesting what she'd said. She tried to process and believe them too. Knowing the words were true in her head was different than believing them deep in her soul. The only nagging thought was that she wished he cared half as much about the actual, real child they'd lost as he did the made-up, hypothetical child he'd conjured in his head.

Maybe if he did, he'd see how important motherhood was to her and consider parenthood as the next big dream. For both of them.

He leaned closer. "Ellie, I—"

But whatever he was going to say was drowned out by something whistling past their heads, followed by a *crack, thunk*!

Ellora pushed back from her chair with a yelp, while Alex toppled his chair jumping to his feet. To the side of her head, an arrow stuck out of one of the wooden support pillars. A piece of paper was rolled around the shaft of the arrow.

"What in the world?" Ellora's gaze met Alex's.

They dashed to the railing. A shadow moved among the trees below but disappeared among them.

"Hey, you there!" But hurried steps and the *snap* of breaking branches faded.

Alex pulled out the arrow and unrolled the paper.

In large messy handwriting, the hooded figure had written, "The missing manuscript is mine. You will find it and turn it over to me or the only people you have left will be eliminated. Instructions are forthcoming."

The note was at once formal and menacing. If the person had wanted to hurt either her or Alex, they could've easily done so, but he or she hadn't. This person or persons didn't know where the manuscript was any more than she or Alex did. Otherwise, they wouldn't have to tell Ellora and Alex to find it for them. And undoubtedly, their plans for the manuscript were for personal gain.

She and Alex blurted at the same time, "We need to get to it first."

And after they paid a little visit to the police station, that was exactly what they planned to do.

Chapter Sixteen

"You all right, love?" Alex propped his elbows on his knees, which still had a slight tremor from the close call with the arrow. Inches from Ellora's head.

He pushed the what-ifs away, tried to ask God to protect her like he by himself never could.

"I'm okay. I just don't understand who is doing this and how much further they're willing to go." Though he knew her strength, her sitting on her bed, legs tucked underneath her—she'd changed into her Little House on the Prairie nightgown—she seemed so vulnerable.

"I know. And all for money? I guess people have been motivated by less." He drummed an irregular beat on his thighs, where he sat on a kitchen chair pulled to her bedside.

They'd given statements to the police and shown them the arrow and note. The police were out at the restaurant and bridge walk looking for any possible witnesses. They'd put an officer outside of their apartment building, just in case. He and Ellora told Lanae and Oscar about what had happened. If the person following him and Ellora knew their friends had helped with the search for the manuscript and her grandmother, they all needed to be extra cautious.

He scratched at his five-o'clock shadow. "Do you feel like there has been a bit of a mixed message though?"

"What do you mean?"

"Didn't the text you were sent say something more like stop trying to find the manuscript and leave it alone? This note said to basically find it for this person, and they'll contact us about how to give it to him or her."

She jumped to her feet. "You're right. That is odd. Maybe they're getting desperate because they think we're close to finding it, so if we get to it first, they want to make sure we hand it over to them."

"Maybe." Something still didn't add up, but he couldn't put his finger on what.

"No matter the reason, it's more important than ever we find the manuscript before they do. We have to somehow put these puzzle pieces together." She walked the length of the sitting area and ran a hand through her hair until her fingers tangled in her elaborate coif, still in place.

Bracing his hands on the back of the couch, he added something he'd meant to tell her earlier. "Speaking of puzzle pieces... I knew we were looking for more information on that etching, the probable rune stone it came from, et cetera."

"Yeah?" Her eyes lit.

"I researched rune stones sighted in the area and I found a news article about a hiker who'd discovered a Viking rune stone near here at Wooler Common Nature Preserve. I was able to track down the hiker. He apparently sent Grandma June the etching of the stone at her request. He also sent me a picture of the rune itself. I think you're going to want to see this."

He scrolled to the picture and handed the phone to her.

"It's the same kind of depiction—" she glanced up "—a figure praying over a group of what looks like Vikings. And…it does looks like a woman, doesn't it?"

Alex inclined his head in agreement. "And do you see here?" He pointed to the top where there was an etched design. "It's the same knotted cross we've seen elsewhere."

"The jewelry box." She breathed the words.

It was her turn to point at the bottom of the picture.

"These markings. Aren't they just like the ones you translated on the back of the painting at the museum?"

He squinted and enlarged the photo with his thumb and forefinger. "It's Futhark, that's certain. Let me look at the translation again." He slipped the notes he'd given her from the portfolio on her desk. Studied the Futhark symbols he'd written there, finally nodding. "It is the same symbols. The same ones I interpreted as Hilda."

Their eyes met over his phone.

Ellora wandered the sitting room—her "thinking stance" that he used to tease her would wear a hole in their wood floor. He gripped the back of the sofa, trying to fit the pieces together.

She sank onto the floor in front of the trunk and started sifting through it again. "I don't know, maybe something will strike me differently now that we have the tiniest bit more information."

"Right. Sometimes something can be right in front of you, but until you have the information you need, you can't see it." He sat beside her and lifted out the jewelry box. They hadn't found a way to open it yet.

He studied the grooves of the carved Futhark letters all

the way around the bottom edges. Each symbol had a carved square around it. Some of the squares seemed to have a little more wear and the divot a little deeper.

"I wonder..."

He pressed a sequence of the Futhark letters, the same ones that spelled Hilda. The wood carvings pushed inward and there was an audible *click*, but stiff and creaking like the carved-letter "buttons" hadn't moved for centuries— probably because they hadn't.

Ellora gasped beside him, leaned in.

The top popped open with a gentle nudge of Ellie's fingertips. It didn't sing, but then, it appeared to be over five hundred years old. Automatic music boxes weren't invented until 1770. Inside lay a necklace and a folded piece of yellowed parchment, thick and aged. She handed it to Alex. "Will you read it?"

After unfolding it, he scanned the contents. "It's written by a woman named Sibilla de Clare and dated 1536—"

Ellora put a hand to her mouth. "That was the beginning of the Reformation, when Henry VIII ordered the destruction of churches, monasteries, priories, any religious building, and destroyed or seized anything of value or religious importance inside."

He smirked. "You went one hundred percent professor on me there."

Her cheeks rosied to the same hue as her hair. "Sorry, continue."

With a wink, he went on, "She says she lived on an estate, de Clare Hall. Not far from here, near Tynemouth."

Ellora held a hand up like she were the student now. "The estate Cressida lived on with Byron?"

He rubbed his chin. "Must be the very same."

Bending over the letter once again, he continued, "Sibilla tells of a manuscript that has been passed down to the women in her family—a manuscript of brilliant lapis lazuli."

His head snapped up.

She sucked in a sharp breath. "Keep going."

"The manuscript was created by her ancestor, Mildrythe, she says, 'a woman who far surpassed her time,' and bequeathed it to the daughters of her family."

"So, who was this Mildrythe? And I guess we know that if she was captured by Vikings like some stories say, she wasn't killed outright or she never would've passed on the manuscript, right?"

"Indeed not." He scanned the next several lines. "She doesn't go into great detail about Mildrythe. Sibilla gives a enigmatic hint that Mildrythe had two names, one at birth, another at her rebirth, born into a new family. Whatever that means." He blew out a short puff of air and read the bottom of the page. "Sibilla goes on to say that her own daughter died tragically, and she was therefore not able to pass it on to her. But here's where it gets interesting."

Ellora grinned at his hand gestures.

His feet shuffled underneath him, intrigue building. "She says her husband had a jealous eye on the manuscript and felt she didn't have the dowry he'd deserved, so he planned to sell the manuscript for money. She knew he'd try to claim it as a work of a monk or other religious man because no one would've believed it came from the hands of a woman. And if they did, they likely would find fault with it and would not want to purchase it."

Alex wandered around the kitchen table and then back holding the letter, taking a page from Ellora's habit of pacing. "With the beginnings of the Reformation of Henry VIII, which she refers to as 'the discord between the crown and the church,' she put away the thought of donating the manuscript to the local church. She didn't want it destroyed along with the many other holy relics, buildings and artifacts."

So close. They were so close.

Ellora knelt on the couch backward, arms resting on the backrest. "Does she say what she did with the manuscript?"

He held up a finger, lips moving silently to translate from the Tudor-style English. "Sibilla says she plans to hide it in the tower of de Clare Hall, a spot in the manor she alone uses 'to escape the demands of her husband and behold the beauty in this land and dream of the freedom below.' She mentions a loose stone. But she doesn't specify where in or on the tower. 'I leave this knowledge for my cousin who lives at the priory.' Again, she doesn't specify the priory or the cousin's name. She says she 'hopes he will see to its safety, but barring that, perhaps someone of goodwill shall come upon this note and find the manuscript, not for personal gain but to value the account within, and to find the love passed down through her family's generations and spread it to those around them.'"

Alex set down the letter and Ellora retrieved the necklace from the bottom of the box, now sitting on the table.

She laid the heavy-looking metalwork pendant flat on her palm. "It's the same knotted cross from the outside of the jewelry box and the paintings. It probably *is* the necklace Mildrythe wore. Do you think it's the same necklace worn in the paintings?"

"It very well could be. I think the probability is great that it's all connected. But what do you think about this estate? Are you thinking what I am?"

They both said at once, "Cressida."

Approaching midnight with everything that had transpired on their second "first" date, they agreed to get some rest and track Cressida down in the morning.

When Ellie walked him to the door, he stopped, bracing an arm against the frame. "Even though this night didn't go as I had planned, I had a nice time. You know, before someone shot an arrow at us. I'm glad we talked about everything that we did."

"Me too."

He had a sense that there had been more to say, on both sides, before they'd been rudely interrupted. But the shadows beneath Ellora's reddened eyes as well as the massive yawn building in the back of his throat told him that those words would have to wait.

She giggled at his loud, obnoxious yawns as he pressed a kiss to her cheek and wished her good-night.

A heavy sky and the sweet, earthy scent of impending rain clung to the morning breeze and drove the Saturday-morning Alnwick crowds into the shops up and down the busy street, including Thomas's tea shop.

People waited inside the door to be seated. They received disgruntled glares and mumbles from the patrons waiting as though they intended to jump the queue.

Finally, they caught the eye of a harried-looking Thomas. He delivered a tray of food and teacups to a table, then wiped his hands on his apron. "What can I do for the Lockwoods today?" He clapped his meaty hands together.

"We're looking for Cressida. Have you seen her or know where we might find her?" Ellora gestured to the packed café.

A flicker of something flashed in his otherwise jovial eyes—distaste for the woman? Well, Ellora couldn't exactly blame him there. The woman's abrasive personality didn't endear her to many. Though, after Cressida opened up about Byron, Ellora's heart had begun to soften to the woman.

Cressida had been through a lot, kind of like Ellora. Sometimes hard circumstances hardened people. Ellora had been fortunate to have the love of her grandparents and Alex to keep her heart from turning to stone.

Thomas tipped his head toward the back of the café to the old train car table. There Cressida sat with a man Ellora didn't recognize.

They thanked Thomas and he bustled back to the kitchen. After a quick wave to Gwen, they moved toward Cressida.

The man she was with, as though by some silent signal, stood, doffed his cap to them and strode to the door.

"My financial consultant. All of that estate nonsense," Cressida said by way of explanation. She gestured to the long bench seat across from her. "Please, sit."

Alex did so and lifted a brow. "Financial consultants work on Saturdays?"

"Mine does." Cressida's smile turned smug.

Compassion. Compassion, she reminded herself.

Ellora explained why they came, but tried to keep the details to a minimum. She indicated Alex with a tip of her head. "Alex and I would like to see the place for ourselves if possible. With what we've discovered so far, it looks like there may be a clue about the manuscript hidden at de Clare Hall. We wondered if you still have any pull there, and perhaps could secure a tour for us."

It was a long shot since de Clare Hall didn't belong to Cressida as Byron's spouse anymore, but they had to try.

"This—this—" Cressida tapped a finger on the table "—clue, does it refer to the white lady?" She seemed to veer off course from Ellora's question, but Ellora didn't want to upset her when they were asking for a favor.

Not wanting to divulge too much, she shared a nod with

Alex and replied simply, "It might. We're still trying to figure that out." It was still the truth.

Cressida's brows arched. "It would certainly fill in the gaps of what she was protecting—perhaps the manuscript after all. Part of the story goes that when her husband couldn't produce the promised money nor anything of great value like he'd promised to his creditors—perhaps the manuscript, which he couldn't find because Sibilla hid it—the people he owed money to set fire to the estate."

Alex turned to Ellora. "Wasn't the painting at the museum in a fire?"

Ellora drummed her fingers, itching to find the next clue. "That's what the museum volunteer said. And it came from a local estate."

Cressida hung her head. "The painting was one of many of the estate's belongings sold at auctions and donated. All of our beautiful things. So much family history...gone." There was a real pain etched into each word.

"The carved box where we found our last lead." Ellora cast a glance at Alex. She probably shouldn't divulge this information even to a fellow Lost Artifact Society member, but suddenly the box didn't feel like hers. Guilt took over. "My grandmother purchased it at an auction. I think it may have come from de Clare Hall. You should have it, really. She didn't know it had belonged to you or she would have."

Cressida held a hand up. "No, you are a fellow history lover, as was your grandmother. It is safe with you and I have no attachment to any jewelry box. Keep it."

"Thank you. I will take good care of it. I promise."

"I guess that brings us to the next point." Alex folded his fingers together on the table. "Do you know if we can get permission to look in the tower where the white lady may have hid the manuscript?"

Cressida snapped her fingers. "I can do you one better. I'll take you there myself. I know the caretaker and owner who took over when it became a tourist trap instead of a home. But we're on good terms. He'd be fine with us looking around. I'll go give him a ring right now."

Alex grabbed her hand under the table and squeezed.

This could be the breakthrough they'd been waiting for.

A fine mist coated their faces and eyelashes as they stepped from Alex's sedan—rarely used as he lived and worked in the same place and most things in Alnwick were within walking distance. The clouds had gathered only to burst apart into a million minuscule droplets instead of the downpour Ellora had anticipated earlier.

"This way." Cressida waved them forward.

They passed an informational sign for de Clare Hall that had the years the estate had residents, ending several years ago. That must sting for Cressida to see.

She caught Alex's eye. Should they even dare to hope? After so many years, after a fire, and weather, and who knew what else?

And yet…a sliver of hope remained. Like a mustard-seed-sized faith planted in her heart, it refused to leave.

They passed window after window of the grand estate. An Edwardian update over the older Tudor-era build. It was vast with many cold and silent chimneys puncturing the sky, ornate stonework, sprawling gardens and a glass conservatory.

Off to one side rose a tower, a proud head above the rest of the manor.

They followed Cressida to a side entrance off of the well-kept garden.

A man stepped out of a small outbuilding—a groundskeeper garden shed? He seemed familiar, but Ellora couldn't place him.

Cressida introduced him as Glen Arbuckle. He'd combed his mousy brown hair back, but it seemed determined to stand up straight and be noticed. Glen shook hands all around and motioned them inside the wide glass double doors.

"Welcome, welcome. My home is your home."

As they moved inside, Cressida hissed under her breath, "*Your* home used to be *my* home."

Glen must not have heard because he went on in a joyous tone. "I understand you want to take a look at the tower?"

He showed them inside to a little hidden door off a sitting room, told them to feel free to look around, then excused himself to work on another part of the house.

The place looked like a museum. Quiet. Still. Perfect. Cold.

Cressida caught Ellora's eye. "It doesn't look lived-in now because Glen didn't buy it to live in it. He lives in a guest house on the property and uses the manor as a place for tourists to visit."

Was that wistfulness or bitterness in her voice?

Cressida opened the small door to reveal a curving stairway much like the one to her and Alex's flats at the castle. They landed in a rounded space at the top with a door that appeared newer than the stones and stairs, but still cut with the heavy panels and iron handle and brackets of antiquity.

The air was unmoving in the cramped space with only small window slits to the outside. Many of the stones were blackened, though some were newer.

"Let's get a little light in here, shall we?" Cressida tried to open the door but it wouldn't budge.

Alex shoved it with his shoulder and it finally grated open, letting in the cool, damp air.

Ellora pointed. "The blackened bricks, are those from the fire in the white lady's time?"

"Mmm-hmm. We did some renovations while I lived here, but we kept as many of the original stones as we could. The home was in a bit of disrepair back then. I have to say, we never saw anything hidden behind any stones or anything unusual."

Alex craned his head, inspecting the outside of the tower. "Let's look for old stones, loose stones, anything that would indicate her hiding spot."

Ellora's heart sped up as she peeked through the door. They were up high. "I'll look inside the tower."

Alex cocked his head to the side. "You've already conquered your fear of heights after the parade though, right?"

She sniffed. "Or it's scarred permanently into my soul. Whichever."

"All right then, I'll look outside." He winked at her and disappeared out the door.

Cressida seemed to lose interest or perhaps wasn't keen on the work, so she stood back and let Ellora do most of the looking inside the tower while Alex searched the outside.

Ellora ran her fingers along the time-smoothed soot-stained stones. None seemed loose. None had been marked or written on.

After several minutes, Alex called for them. "Hey, Ellie, come look at this."

He stood on a stone ledge and pointed to something. The sight of him only one wrong move away from falling to the ground three stories below sent a flash of panic through her chest.

"Be careful up there. Please, come down."

She edged closer. Her knees shook, protesting. Between

that and Alex clinging to the outside of the tower, her heart leaped into her throat.

He clung to a small stone, blackened like many others by the fire but turned a dull gray from the wind and weather. "Here, do you see it? The symbol? It looks like the stone has been moved before."

Ellora kept a hand to the tower wall and shuffled nearer.

Cressida marched toward them, much steadier than Ellora in her steps. "What is it? Did you find something?" Her voice was eager.

Ellora squinted. Etched into the side of the stone was the knotted cross that seemed to tie everything together, the same one in the paintings and on the jewelry box.

"This might be her hiding spot. I can't believe we found it."

Cressida brushed against her, hurrying to get a look and making Ellora wobble even more. "I didn't know about this. I've been in this tower plenty of times and never saw a thing." She seemed irritated with them like it was their fault she never saw it. "Well? Does the stone move?"

But before Alex could answer, a car pulled into the driveway. Glen had closed tours for the day so they could look undisturbed. Cressida growled and muttered something under her breath and dashed for the stairway.

"Cressida, what's going—"

But she was already gone, saying something about "I told him to keep out of my business…" Her words trailed down the spiral stairway.

"What's she on about?" Alex asked over his shoulder, his fingers still pulling at the edges of the stone.

"I'm not sure." She peeked over the edge toward the car. A tall, slim, gray-haired man had exited the car. "Byron. He's talking to Glen."

The conversation was animated, but she couldn't hear what

they were saying. The memory struck her as she watched them converse from afar. "That's where I know him from."

"Who?"

"The caretaker/owner, Glen. I thought he looked famil-iar. He was just out of context." She edged closer, but kept a hand on the tower. "I saw him talking to Byron a couple of times. Once near the gardens and then again at the fair. Only then I thought he looked shady. I don't know what it was. His demeanor or something."

Cressida rushed out of the manor below and over to the two men. Ellora couldn't hear her either, only a raised-voice "mumble."

"I'm not sure what's going on down there, but we should probably go find out."

"We will. In a moment." He gritted his teeth, digging his fingers into the small crack between the stones. "I think this stone can be removed without damaging anything. You can see scrape marks like someone has done this before." Alex shifted the stone, pulling it toward himself. "I don't under-stand how your grandmother could do this. She would've had to have help."

Something fell from the crevice behind the stone. It glit-tered even in the dull daylight. "I've got it." One hand went out to catch it but with the stone in one hand, it set him off balance.

"Alex!" She reached for him, snatching his jacket and pull-ing him toward her. The stone he'd freed narrowly missed her face, dropping beside her head, while his body landed on hers. He sucked a breath in through his teeth.

"Ow," they said together as he rolled onto his back.

"We really need to stop almost falling to our deaths." Her heart drummed in her ears.

"That would be a nice change of pace, wouldn't it?"

The thing he'd tried to catch from behind the stone must've fallen to the ground. "I wonder what that was."

"You mean this?" Still panting, Alex held out his hand for her to see. They both sat up. On his open palm was a large ring. She'd know it anywhere.

"That's Grandma June's."

She took the ring from Alex's outstretched hand.

Turning it over and over, she examined the large sapphire set in a heavy, filigreed white gold. The engraved verse, inside.

"I never saw Grandma June without her ring." His voice held the same suspicion growing in her own heart.

"Never," she agreed. "Only the direst circumstance would've made her take this off or made it fall off."

"But the way it was wedged in between the rocks makes me think she put it there on purpose."

"Right. Why would she want to hide the ring? And if it came off accidentally while she was looking behind the stone, she wouldn't have willingly left it there."

The word "willingly" prickled up her back. The chill was quickly replaced with anger and frustration. Someone here knew something. She glanced down at Byron. Someone who wanted this property back. Someone who wanted the manuscript and for them to either find it so he could sell it or didn't like them getting in the way of him finding it. And regardless of his intentions, he would probably just as soon get them out of the picture by any means necessary. Had probably done the same to Grandma June.

Alex put the stone back. Nothing else hid in the crevice behind the stone.

She placed the ring on her own finger for safekeeping and started toward the stairs. His steps echoed after hers.

As soon as Byron's gaze alighted on Ellora, his brows

dipped low. He sent her a sharp glare. "You. Didn't I tell you to watch yourself? What are you doing here like this? Snooping around alone."

Alex had caught up and stayed a protective distance from her. "She's not alone. And I've had about enough of you threatening my wife."

"Threaten?" Byron's eyes widened. "Me? It's her. She's the problem—" he pointed at Cressida "—she never should've brought you here. And this is my property. You shouldn't be messing with my property—"

Cressida put a hand to her throat. "How dare you? This isn't your property anymore. And why? Because *you* lost it!"

Glen crossed his arms and the lighthearted person he'd introduced himself as disappeared. "Right you are." He turned a glare to Byron. "I'm the caretaker here now, and I say you need to leave, Mr. Hughes."

Byron bared his teeth. But then his shoulders fell in defeat, though the scowl never left his face.

Before she lost the chance, Ellora held out her hand to show the ring. "What was Grandma June doing here? And why did we find the ring she never went without behind a stone on the tower?"

Byron's eyes flickered with something—recognition?—for a fraction of a second before darting to his ex-wife and Glen then back to her and Alex. "I don't know what you're on about. I've never seen that ring in my life." But something in his tone said otherwise.

His mouth opened once more with no sound, but then he turned on his heel and strode to his car. He muttered, "No good deed goes unpunished."

They made their goodbyes to Glen—though she and Alex had a vigilant eye on the man—and planned to call the police with this new lead on her grandmother's disappearance. Again, the feeling that someone watched her continued. She even imagined a black SUV followed them most of the way back to Alnwick, but then it turned off before Lion Bridge.

Probably ridiculous. But after finding the ring and knowing that on two separate occasions she saw Glen with Byron, she couldn't stop the question—how many people were involved in Grandma June's disappearance?

Chapter Seventeen

The wall Ellora had built within herself edged closer, another stone added. It crushed her lungs and made her wonder if it needed to come down.

She sat at the small desk in her flat, twisting her grandmother's ring around and around her finger. The deep blue sapphire captured the light from the window. She'd always admired the ring's intricate scrollwork and interlocking initials along the cathedral archway setting beneath the stone. The initials *J* for June and *G* for George, her grandfather. At least, that's what Grandma June always said it spelled. Though in truth, she'd always found it hard to decipher the swirling antique calligraphy. Like the knotted cross they kept finding, the design had no beginning and no end.

As they'd shared the new information about finding her grandmother's ring on the estate with the police, the looming and probable reality of Grandma June never coming back had started to sink in like never before. The ring was one more piece of the great puzzle—so much more important than the manuscript they were searching for on her behalf.

She'd experienced her share of ambiguous losses. The kind of wounds that never healed. Could discovering what had happened to Grandma June begin to close those wounds, grow scar tissue over them? They'd never disappear, but perhaps like any scar they'd lighten over time.

Of course, that's what she'd told herself about her parents. And losing her baby. But each new loss seemed to rip right into those scars. Kept her mired in fear, confusion and pain.

And she had yet to decide if she'd return to St. Cloud for the job she'd thought she'd wanted. If she did, she and Alex might as well sign the divorce papers still in his office.

The prospect was terrifying and heartbreaking, but so was the thought of staying and trying with him, only to have him later change his mind and have him desert her once again.

She let out a long, deep breath but it did nothing to lighten the weight pressing against her chest.

"God, where are You in this?" Had He forsaken her too? Why did He feel so distant when she needed Him the most? When everything seemed to be falling apart.

With what they'd learned, they had all but given up on the manuscript too.

After all, the only known hiding place for it had been burned in a fire five hundred years ago. The manuscript itself would've been almost eight hundred years old during the Tudor era and if it still existed would be almost twelve hundred years old. In all likelihood it was long gone, burned, stolen or who knew?

Then again, the Lindisfarne Gospels had made it out of Lindisfarne and still existed at the British Library in London. So had the Book of Kells and many other medieval illuminated manuscripts.

She needed to get out of her lost Alice in Wonderland mindset and think like a historian once more. It was a long shot, but she'd reached out to her grandmother's old contacts at the British Library. They might be able to help.

Besides, at the estate, there had been no evidence that something burned behind the secret hiding stone. No trace of paper or binding or ashes of any kind.

Maybe Sibilla had realized the danger she and the manuscript were in and had moved it before the fire. Perhaps there were even more accounts of the estate. That was one of the things she loved about the Brits as a historian and general history lover. They didn't get rid of anything and were meticulous record keepers.

Just as a call came in, there was a knock. She answered the phone. "Hello?"

Too bad these old doors didn't have peepholes. No matter what the inspector said, she didn't trust Byron and wouldn't put it past him to show up at her door.

While the person on the other end of the phone said, "Hello, Dr. Lockwood? This is Dr. Phyllis Wade, from the British Library," Alex's voice came from the other side of the door saying, "It's me."

She opened the door, waving him in. Propping the phone between cheek and shoulder, she strode back to her grandmother's opened journal on the desk, where she'd added notes of her own. "Yes, thank you for calling me back. I saw from some of your online archives that you have a book relating to an estate in Northumberland. De Clare Hall. I'm not able to read it in its entirety online. I'm wondering if you'd be able to look for references to the residents there around the time of the Reformation era."

"Yes, my colleague informed me of what you're looking for and I found some passages I think you'll find helpful."

She gave Alex, who'd slunk down into a kitchen chair, a thumbs-up. "Oh, wonderful."

Ellora put the phone on speaker and held it out so both she and Alex could hear.

There was the faint whisper of pages turning. "This is a little-known book written about the lesser nobles of Henry VIII's court and it has a section on the Northumberland gentry. It's not much, but there's a passage about the quick rise and fall of a noble family from nowhere and who, in particular, bought the estate they named de Clare Hall in the 1500s. They were not of a noble bloodline but, for special services to the king, received a noble title and lands. This happened often with the royals' favorites."

"Mmm-hmm, that makes sense." Ellora pressed a finger to her chin and nodded for Dr. Wade to continue as if she could see her.

"The lesser noble and owner of the estate at the time quickly became in debt. This book cites the reason as his 'spendthrift ways' and he decided to marry well for a handsome dowry. A woman named Sibilla."

Ellora swallowed. Okay, so this wasn't all in their imaginations. This woman did exist.

"There was rumor that she came with more than a monetary dowry, something of great value, but it doesn't say what. It didn't take long for her husband to spend most of her money. He planned to sell her possession of great value, and boasted of it to the wrong person. This someone worked for the king and said it was of great religious value. Well, this was right in the middle of the Reformation and the king would not stand for it. The estate was subsequently ransacked and the tower was set on fire. Though it was never proved that the king sent the men, this is me reading in between the lines—"

"The king sent the men…" She murmured the answer.

"My thoughts exactly." Dr. Wade made a clicking sound. "But the story told was that the nobleman's creditors had set the fire."

"What about Sibilla? How did she die?"

"It says she died in the fire, having been up on the tower at the time. Later, people would claim they saw her in her nightdress standing on the roof near the tower."

Ellora nodded. "Hmm, that must be how the stories of the estate being haunted by the 'white lady' began."

She exchanged a glance with Alex, then thanked Dr. Wade for her time and help.

When she turned to Alex, she shook her head, shoulders already drooping. "Well, you heard her. I don't see how it could be any clearer that the lost manuscript is truly lost. Sibilla probably carved that sign, intending on putting the manuscript in the space behind the stone, but never got the chance. The place was set on fire and she and the manuscript perished together."

Alex stood and put his hands on her shoulders. "We don't know anything for sure yet."

Her chest constricted, making it hard to breathe and form the words that she didn't want to say. "Yes, I think we do."

She turned away. "I feel so stupid. I can't believe I actually thought we'd find it. Not at first, but after a while, I really thought we were onto something. I thought we'd follow this trail and there would be my grandma at the end of it. It's so dumb. It's not as if she was off sipping tea somewhere just waiting for me to open the right door, but I—I don't know what I thought…" She covered her eyes with her hand.

"Hey—" his words and hands gentle as he turned her to face him "—you are not stupid. Do you think I'd marry a dolt?"

This pulled at her lips until they lifted at the corners.

"You are brilliant, just like Grandma June is. Even if this means the manuscript truly is gone, at least we can rest assured that it *did* exist. Your grandmother was right. All of those naysayers, her colleagues who ridiculed her, were the ones who were wrong. The stories, everything she said was true. And if we don't find out precisely what happened to Grandma June, we can rest knowing that she was doing what she loved. I don't think she'd have had it any other way."

A bittersweet lightness lifted her spirits but formed a lump in her throat. "You're right."

He tipped his head, a mischievous grin stealing over his face. "There we are again. Can I get that in writing, love?"

She smiled back, but it wobbled. "Grandma June would love this. Us working together. On a historical scavenger hunt. And I think she'd be relieved someone finally believed her. I just feel bad that I didn't while—while…she was here. You know?"

"She would be so proud of you. She always was."

Alex sat on the desk chair and pulled her into his lap, arms sliding around her waist in an embrace that both bolstered and comforted. She nestled her head into the crook of his neck, before she straightened and shrugged. "Now what?"

It felt odd to not be looking for something, to not have a continuous niggle in the back of her mind.

He watched her fiddle with the ring, glance flickering to the box still on the desk. His lips parted. "Ellie…"

She stood. "What?"

He grabbed the box, turning it to one side where there was a pattern of carved little ovals. His head came up. "Can I see Grandma June's ring?"

He held it up to one of the carved openings she'd always assumed were part of the design. He pressed the stone setting inside the middle oval...and it fit, perfectly, as though meant for this precise thing. But the ring band kept slipping in Alex's grasp.

She tried it while he held the box. The ring turned like a key followed by a meshing of gears and a *pop*.

A sliding drawer opened on the very bottom, much like the trunk. Perhaps the jewelry box had inspired her grandmother to modify her steamer trunk.

A folded paper lay inside the drawer. She held her breath and opened it. Her grandmother's writing. Alex set the box down, waiting.

She read, "'My dearest girl, if you made it this far, I'm not at all surprised. Both by your abilities and the fact that I'm likely not there beside you. I'm proud of you—'" Alex rubbed her shoulders as the words cracked with her tears now falling "'—I'm piecing together this puzzle, and I apologize that I've had to remain ambiguous and often vague.'"

Ellora *humphed* a laugh. "'Sometimes it has been because I truly do not know the answer yet or because the answer must remain hidden to those who would seek to find the manuscript for their own gain. My granddaughter with the wind in her veins, you have always been more clever than you give yourself credit for and more resilient than you ever deserved to be. I'm sorry I'm not there. If I were, the trail I set up for you as the contingency plan should something happen to me wouldn't be necessary. I'm sorry that because of the past, you may have felt left behind, abandoned. But you are never alone. Now, as to the next leg of this journey...'"

Ellora skimmed the note, then glanced up. "She's giving us the story of the fire and Sibilla."

But then Ellora landed on something they'd only heard in a passing mention. "Grandma June says that she read an account of someone who tried to help Sibilla hide the manuscript. 'Sibilla knew she and the manuscript were in danger, so she enlisted the help of her cousin. The one she later said lived at Hulne Priory—'" She looked up.

Alex pressed his fingers into his chin. "So that was the nearby priory Sibilla mentioned in her letter."

She dipped her chin, swallowed and continued reading, "'Sibilla's cousin led her through tunnels underneath and away from the estate to the North Sea, coming out near the rocky shores of Tynemouth Priory and Castle. I don't know if Sibilla would have tried to hide the manuscript in the tunnel itself, perhaps planning to come back for it. But, of course, we know she didn't come back for it because she died shortly after in the fire. There are stories from locals that the white lady is also rumored to haunt a certain cave near Tynemouth—the echoes within are her cries for help. I'm going to the sea cave, and either it'll be successful or not. But if you don't hear from me, this may confirm for you that something has happened to me. I feel someone is on my heels. Always watching. I've had some threats. But nothing I can prove which is why I've arranged all of this for you.

"'If I'm not there in person, know I'll be there in heart. This certainly wasn't the plan—my plan, Ellie…'" Her voice caught but she pressed on. "'But then His ways are not my ways. "For I know the thoughts that I think toward you, saith the Lord, thoughts of peace, and not of evil, to give you an expected end." And should I meet my end because of this search, I know it was His plan. All I can pray is that you continue it, see it through to the finish line, and know all the while that I love you and God loves you. Even when it feels as though He's silent or has left you, He hasn't. You have Alex's help, too. That dear boy.'"

She glanced up with a watery smile just as Alex swiped something from his cheek.

She continued, "'Trust each other and in the Lord. May your love for one another be the greatest adventure of your lives. Love, Grandma June.'"

The verse she'd heard often growing up, a favorite of her grandparents', pounded against the wall she'd built around her heart. The one to protect herself from being left and abandoned again. Where the stubborn, fearful place within her railed against trusting anyone else's plan for her life—even God's.

She met Alex's gaze; the whirlwind of emotions in his likely matched her own.

She focused on the piece that would keep them in motion. "Looks like the search is back on."

Her phone sang its song again.

The police inspector's direct line.

She had made another phone call to the Alnwick police station earlier to see if they'd checked the grounds of de Clare Hall and questioned Byron. Fury still burned through her gut, thinking of that guy still out there walking around when he clearly had something to do with her grandmother's disappearance, maybe even her death.

When she answered, she rushed ahead before the inspector said more than "Hello."

"Inspector, I hope you have news for me. Have you arrested Byron Hughes yet?"

He stuttered, but finally answered. "I'm sorry, Miss Lockwood." She didn't correct him. "Byron was not in possession of the estate at the time of your grandmother's disappearance. We've verified it with the bank who owned it at the time."

Ellora paced and fidgeted with the hem of her blouse. "But he still could've gone to the estate—"

"I know, but he also has an alibi that would put him out

of the area the several days surrounding your grandmother's disappearance."

She growled. "What if he had somebody else do it? That— that—" her agitation took the words right from her brain "—caretaker/owner. Glen something. I saw him with Byron twice before. Maybe he's in on it. I feel it in my gut— something's not right here."

"Perhaps, but that's all speculation." The strain and frustration in his tone told her he didn't like the loose ends any more than she did. "I'm afraid we need much more than gut feelings, as strong as they may be. We need evidence. And we have nothing for which we can arrest Byron or Glen at this point, ma'am."

She tried to control a slow breath. "Yes, all right. Thank you for all you've done."

As they hung up, her heart was heavy in her chest. With the waiting and not knowing what had happened to Grandma June, the weariness of it all seemed to catch up all at once, dragging at her very soul.

Would they ever know; would she ever get the answers she so desperately needed?

All she could do was coax one foot in front of the other with what seed-sized faith she still had, trying to trust in God's wisdom and guidance. He'd not given her the fully lit path ahead, only enough light for the next step.

But that's all she needed.

She prayed with every ounce of that faith, asking Him to multiply it for what came next, that it would lead to finding something much more important than an old manuscript. That it would lead to the truth about Grandma June. After all, that's what her grandmother had lived for and possibly died by—finding the truth.

The question was, would it set her free?

★ ★ ★

A walk on the beach with his wife sounded like a romantic pastime. Especially under blue skies, to the sound of rolling waves and the scent of brine and sand in the air. But they'd trudged along, trying to find the sea cave Grandma June referred to in her note. The bright day seemed to darken with their task.

So far none of the little alcoves seemed to be deep enough nor connected to the estate about a mile away. They'd decided to start on the beach instead of the estate, both because they didn't want to be under the watchful eye of Glen—whom they didn't know if they could trust—but also because Cressida said the tunnels beneath the estate had been blocked off years ago.

He handed Ellora a water bottle from his rucksack. She thanked him and tipped her head back for a long drink.

"Are you sure you want to do this?" He shielded his eyes against the midday sun.

She wiped her mouth with the back of her hand. "Yes, I'm sure." Though there was a slight quaver in her voice. "I have to do this. It's not only about finding the manuscript in Grandma June's honor. It's about finding out what happened to her. And the closer we get to the manuscript, the closer we get to figuring out just that."

He had to agree with that. "Let's crack on then."

The majestic ruins of Tynemouth Priory and Castle upon its rock throne watched their backs, while the sun spokes reaching over passing clouds made a trickle of sweat run down his neck. The constant breeze cooled his skin and then the process started over again. He took the water bottle back, downing several gulps before returning it to his rucksack.

They'd waited several days before making their way to Tynemouth. It's not that it was far and Ellie had certainly been anxious to come, but they'd had responsibilities with the university and the students.

Now it was Saturday and, he couldn't believe, the second week of July. The end of the study-abroad session quickly approached. What would he do if she decided to take the job in St. Cloud? Was it necessary that one of them had to give up a dream for them to be together? Perhaps more than one.

What about the dream she now held close, to become a mother? Could he change his mind about fathering children? If he told her yes, would it feel like giving in, the definite precursor to resentment? Children had never been part of the plans for his life. But then, he'd never considered how his plans would affect her or how she felt about them. Nor did he ask God what *His* plans were for him. The verse she'd read from Grandma June's letter sparked the question, were God's plans for Alex's life better than his own?

It was legitimate for some people to not want children. Not everyone was called to be a parent. He'd always considered himself to be one such person. But perhaps his reasons didn't hold up like they once did. He did enjoy children, after all. Maybe he'd allowed fear of becoming his own parents to dictate his decisions for too long. And though he'd been blindsided by the miscarriage, knowing he'd almost become a father had planted a seed, whether he liked it or not. A seed of what? He couldn't rightly say, only that it sprouted something protective within him as well as opened a space of an unfamiliar feeling—longing?—he'd never known existed.

"Let's try this one." Ellora threw the words over her shoulder, and then the wind whisked them away.

As they entered the cooler space within, he had to pause a moment beside her as he allowed his eyes to adjust to the dark cave.

"Did anyone from the Lost Artifact Society say if they

were going to come out and help us look for clues that Grandma June had been here?" He retrieved his phone and turned on the torch feature.

It lit up the small tidal opening in the rocks set into the bluffs overlooking the North Sea and near what was known as King Edward's Bay.

"Yeah, I think so. I know Eg said he could bring his metal detector." Her lips turned up in a fond smile. "Thomas was going to try to make it too."

Already, Oscar and Lanae were scouring the beach in the other direction.

"Do you think this could be the one?"

He hooked a thumb under his pack straps and took in the deep but narrow vaulted sea cave with a small rivulet of water running through its length. "Could be. With the iron gate on the outside like that, it was obviously an entrance to something. But there were hidden entrances to Tynemouth Castle as well."

"Let's keep looking to see if we can see anything related to de Clare Hall or Grandma June leaving us another clue."

They ventured farther in and it became clear that the cave was formed by both nature and man. At the very back there was a "blowhole." When the tide was high, water would spout out of the hole like a whale. Behind a tall rock formation, he pointed to a heavy-looking iron door. He tried pulling it but it didn't budge.

"Do you think this is the entrance to the tunnels that lead back to the estate?"

He tried once more and grunted before dropping his hands. "It could be, but it could just as easily lead back to Tynemouth and therefore have been closed up."

She pointed to near the top and bottom handle-side of the door. "Look, it's been screwed shut."

Spinning away from it, she held her own phone's torch high, shaking it when the light started to flicker. The battery probably wouldn't last much longer. "Then we have to find evidence. That's what the police keep saying."

He wandered to the back of the cave and felt the rock wall for anything unusual. "So, they searched the estate?"

"Yes. Nothing came of it, but I'm glad they had enough probable cause to at least look around." She pointed her light where he stood.

The roar of the surf seemed closer. "I think we had better see ourselves out, love. High tide is closing in." He checked his phone to confirm the time.

She laughed and it reverberated against the rock wall. "A little water? What's that in the face of potential murder investigations and priceless historical artifacts?"

He slid closer, letting her warmth melt into his skin. "I like this Dr. Brave you've got going on here, but like it or not, soon this cave will be full of the North Sea, it waits for no one, and we don't want to be inside it when it is."

His light landed on something over her head, a drawing on the back rock wall. A swirling design. Not the knotted cross they'd grown accustomed to.

Ellora held up her hand with Grandma June's large ring, which dwarfed Ellora's slender fingers. "Hey, that looks like the interlocking initials on Grandma June's ring."

He held her hand up to compare the two. But a loud *clang* shook the air, interrupting. Ellora jumped. He ran in the direction of the sound.

The iron gate was down, trapping them inside. A shadow moved and then was gone.

"Come back here!" he called but no one answered.

"Oh, no." Ellora's voice was faint but full of terror.

They both pulled on it, but it was firmly in place. Water

already rose from the rivulet and spilled over the rock walkway. "I'll see if we can go under the gate. Here, hold my phone."

She took it, letting out a shaky laugh. "Good thing you bought me a waterproof phone. But I didn't expect to put it to the test."

He hopped into the water.

"Alex, be careful," she called.

The rivulet running into the cave hadn't looked more than waist deep when they'd arrived but now it was past his chest and rising. He dunked under the freezing water, feeling to the bottom of the iron gate. And it did stretch to the ground, no gap. He strained, trying to pull up on the bars. Again, no movement. He surfaced and took in a lungful of air.

He shook his head as he climbed out. "We can't get out that way. We'll have to find another way out."

They backed away from the gate, now pouring seawater in a torrent. He squeezed her hand. Her breath came in gasps. "It's going to be all right, Ellie. We can call for help."

After all, Lanae and Oscar couldn't be far. She tried to open her phone but it fell from her shaking fingers. Since they were on an incline and the height of the cave was taller at the back, the water level only reached their ankles where they stood. She retrieved her phone.

He grabbed his phone too. "No service," at the same time.

He ran a hand through his wet hair. "It's probably the thick rock around us."

They tried the door to the side again. It wouldn't move.

Minutes ticked by and the swirling black depths rose higher and higher, now past their chests and climbing. They were at the very back and highest point they could be. Even in summer, the water wasn't above twelve degrees Celsius. Their teeth chattered. Ellora was ghostly pale in the dim light.

He shouted "Help!" several more times, his voice raw. But instead of panic, a juxtaposed sort of anguished calm stole over him.

He propped her on a boulder, where she teetered on the tips of her toes. The water, now up to his chest standing on the ground, thrashed him from side to side. Over her shoulder, something moved—cloth?—with the churning of the water, caught behind another large rock. The light from the blowhole hit the spot, revealing the cloth's frantic motions as though desperate to be found. Not that he could spare the energy, but he couldn't help it. Something about the fabric seemed familiar. "What is that? Behind you."

"Wh-what?" Her teeth clacked together.

"It looks like something caught in those rocks."

Her brows drew together. "I think we have bigger problems right now."

He couldn't explain—nor take the time to—why he had to know what it was. But his gut wouldn't let this go.

He managed to crawl onto the rock beside her, but they just barely fit.

She finally growled and with slow movements and his free hand steadying her as much as he could, she turned to the cloth. With a few tugs and close calls, the mystery cloth was free. Ellora held it out, mouth hung slack. She'd gone very still, as still as the waves allowed.

He guessed even before he asked, "What is it, Ellie?"

"It's Grandma June's explorer vest. At least, I think it is."

Before he could say anything in response, she unbuttoned the two buttons still fastened and slipped her arms through the sopping, torn canvas armholes.

"I don't want to lose it."

She clung to him then with one hand and tried to grasp the rock wall with the other. The water had reached their waists while standing on the boulder. He did all he could to keep her still. With the heavy, wet vest around her now, her body shook so hard he could hardly keep hold of her. "Ellie, listen to me." Each word was punctuated by heavy breaths. "I'm going to get you out of here. When the water rises a little more, we'll be able to reach the hole in the ceiling. I'll push you up as far as I can so you can pull yourself out. But the force of the water through that opening could be deadly. We'll have to time it just right, while the water rolls out to form the next wave. All right?"

He didn't know what would happen to him after that, but it didn't matter as long as she was safe.

She grabbed his shirt, hauling him close. "Keep your feet on this rock, Alexander Lockwood. This is not a Jack and Rose situation, all right? I'm not going to let you sacrifice yourself for me."

The reality of their circumstance sank in as the water reached their shoulders. They were staring their own mortality in the face, weren't they? He prayed. He didn't have any words, just a swirl of fear and desperate pleas to save his wife. But surely God would understand. He would be there for her this time.

She huffed air as did he. His limbs had gone numb from moving his arms to stay balanced atop their rock, but now he was mostly treading water. They struggled to stay on their perch while the water rushed in, trying to knock them off.

"Look, I have to tell you something, all right?" He pulled her close as best as he could.

Her chin wobbled, from the cold or fear, he didn't know. "No, don't do that. We're going to find a way out of this."

He silenced her with a kiss. "I'm praying we do, but in case—in case…" He let that trail off, cleared his throat, the tang of seawater on his tongue. "Ellora, I love you. I wish I could erase everything I've done to hurt you. If I could do it over again, well..."

He'd what? Have a family with her? Not have left when she needed him most? Sought God's counsel on the way his life should go instead of listening to his own fears and hurts of his past? Probably all of the above.

"I'd do things so much differently," he finished, wishing so much that he could express what he felt properly.

"I would too." She held his face with one hand. "But none of that matters. If God can forgive and wipe the slate clean for me, I can do the same. And my record isn't free of blemish with you or with God. I'm so glad I decided to get on that plane. I should've done it sooner."

"And I shouldn't have left without you. I'm sorry I was a coward." He pulled her closer. "I'm not ready to let go." His voice broke though he'd tried to stay strong for her.

Tears trailed down her cheeks, mingling with the beads of seawater. "It's not really letting go if we're holding the hand of God."

Her lips turned up in a heartbreaking smile as another wave hit and the tide rose higher.

She started to slip from his grasp. Her eyes widened and registered surprise as she fell from the rock. He dived into the dark depths. No hesitation.

He turned and squinted all while being pushed by the water's churning current. Only when he thought he'd pass out did he come up for air.

No! This couldn't be happening. Now it was his turn to panic.

"No, Ellie! God, help me."

He dived back down. Finally, there was a faint glow ahead. He struggled to get to it.

It was Ellie's phone lit up in her pocket. He closed the last meter of distance. She was still moving, fighting her way toward him. Taking hold of her middle with one arm, he swam with the other and kicked his legs with all his might until they broke the surface. Both gulped air. She coughed and wheezed but was able to help tread water. So out of breath, neither could form words for several long seconds.

"Our only hope is to get you out of that hole." His lungs burned.

"No," she panted.

He was thankful that was all she could argue.

Finally, she agreed, but said, "I'll reach down for you. I'm not leaving you."

He nodded to comfort her, but it wasn't realistic. She'd never be able to pull him up after using all of her strength to swim and pull herself up. It was all right. If his last act on this earth was to show her how much he loved her and finally live out his vow to be there for her, never abandon her, in sickness and in health, to his dying breath, then so be it.

He dunked beneath the water and pushed her up with all the force his kicking legs could muster, but still she couldn't reach the hole. He tried and tried as his energy dwindled. He prayed harder. *God, please!* He just wanted this one thing—to save her.

Suddenly, a hand appeared through the roof opening. "Give me your hand!" a voice shouted. Thomas's voice?

Alex said a silent thank-you to God. They had to hurry; the big waves could tow her under again or worse, knock her against the rocks. Using the last of his strength, he pushed her in the direction of the hand, which caught her raised arm before she could slip beneath the water.

He let go and peace swept through him, knowing she was going to be all right even if it wasn't him who had saved her.

Suddenly, another arm reached down and grasped his hand in a viselike grip. It was Oscar and he wasn't letting go.

Soon more than one set of hands hauled him up and over the edge, dragging him a safe distance from the hole, and laid him on his back next to Ellora.

Lanae, Oscar and Thomas stared down at them with a mix of confusion and worry.

Neither he nor Ellora could speak as they gulped sweet sea-perfumed air. Pure gratefulness sprang from his chest, for the woman beside him, their friends and for the God who had made a way where there had seemed to be absolutely no escape.

He rolled over to her, pulling her head against his chest, trying not to think about how close he'd come to losing her—and not for the first time. He could only hope and pray it was the last time.

Chapter Eighteen

Warmth poured from Alex's car's heat vents as Ellora, Alex, Lanae, Oscar and Thomas crammed into the small sedan to recover from their near-drowning.

Alex had given her a jacket he'd had in the boot of his car, which she wrapped around her shoulders, still heavy from the vest she wore. Alex had dried himself the best he could with an extra button-up shirt he'd thrown in the back seat.

Thomas smoothed his broom-head mustache. "So, was that the cave we've all been searching for then?"

Her teeth chattered, but she managed, "Y-yes."

Alex turned in his driver's seat. "Just before—" he paused, probably overwhelmed with the memory of almost drowning like she was "—before you lot rescued us, we saw the calligraphy letters from Grandma June's ring on the rock wall. But then there's this." He gestured to the vest.

Lanae leaned forward from the back seat. "Is that what I think it is? Grandma June's explorer vest?"

"I think so." Even though it was like wearing a soaking wet sack, she gripped it tighter around herself. Ripped in a spot and missing a couple of buttons, it still looked just like her grandmother's vest.

Thomas's jaw set, studying the garment. "Have you checked the pockets? How do you know it's hers?"

She shook her head but patted them and undid the zippers and buttons on the pockets. Empty, until she got to the chest pocket over the heart.

A round object, cold and metal, met her fingertips. She pulled it free. "Her compass."

A soft gasp from Lanae broke the silence.

Ellora's hand tremored as she turned it over in her palm. She'd know this anywhere, another element to what made her grandmother her grandmother, who never left on a historical hunt without it. Grandma June's initials were carved into the back.

"She always said she kept it nearest her heart—" Ellora had to clear her aching throat before she could continue "—because it reminded her that just like in exploring we need a good compass to find our way, so does our heart need God's guidance, His 'true North' for our lives."

Alex reached over and wrapped one of her hands in his, warmth and solace injected into his grip.

"What does this mean?" Oscar asked, his tone tentative. "Do you think she died in that cave?"

They all exchanged a thoughtful glance.

Ellora's head bent, shoulders dropped as she stashed the compass in her purse. "I don't know. Just another question to add to our growing list."

She shoved her hands in front of the heat vents, rubbing them together to coax warmth back into her fingers.

Alex tapped on the steering wheel, facing forward now.

"Otherwise, this vest washed in from somewhere else. Or was left there intentionally by Grandma June. I guess those are our options, aren't they?"

Lanae piped in, "At least now we have physical proof she was here."

Oscar bent over his knees, elbows propped. "I see nothing for it. We have to keep going, find answers."

Thomas reached a thick hand forward to squeeze warmth into Ellora's arm. "I'm sure we'll find the manuscript, my dear. Then all of this can be put behind you."

He meant well, but no. This could never be put to rest even if she could find what her grandmother had died to find and preserve. Even if she was eventually able to put her grandmother to rest. The pain would live on, as would the love she had for her grandmother. Grandma June hadn't been perfect, but then, she was learning that no one was. They were destined to disappoint one another as humans—especially those closest to each other—perhaps so they would look vertically for the perfect kind of love only God could give.

But Grandma June had been there for her, filled in the space her parents had vacated with her kindness, her flawed but oh-so-big love. She'd believed in Ellora, had towed her along on adventures around the world, and had encouraged Ellora to dream bigger than the sky. After all, Grandma June had said you could never outdream God.

Of course, her grandmother had also reminded her that dreams needed to be sifted through God's hands. Maybe that's what she'd forgotten along the way—to allow God to shape and mold her dreams into His will. Like the verse from Jeremiah she'd shared in her letter. "For I know the thoughts that I think toward you, saith the Lord, thoughts of peace, and not of evil, to give you an expected end."

Something she'd read a million times and her grand-

mother had quoted often, but she'd missed the most important part. She'd been focused on the longing for peace, for
good things, like her own dreams fulfilled. But the quota-
tion wasn't "For Ellora knows" Ellora's plans, was it? It was
for *He* knew the plans *He* had for her life. He knew better
than her. Because He created her and saw her life from beginning to end.

She thanked Him silently for saving her and Alex. She
studied Alex's clenched teeth, his hands gripping the steering wheel even though they were parked now. He had to
be freezing. She put the coat over him despite his protests.

"I've warmed up now anyway."

Lanae babbled away about finding them because they'd
finished their search and started walking to the other side
of the ruins and down the beach.

"And then we had this sinking feeling because the tide
was coming in and we couldn't see you anywhere. And, let's
face it, your track record hasn't been great when it comes
to disasters, El."

She pursed her lips at her friend and then held out her
hand with the ring—another prayer of thanks it was still
there—to show them. "This little symbol was drawn onto
the wall in the sea entrance cave. It's the curving interlocking letters of my grandparents' initials."

Lanae grabbed her hand to inspect the ring. "But you already found out the secret with the ring, right? It opens the
jewelry box. Do you think Grandma June just didn't expect
you to figure that out by now?"

"I don't think so. She told us to go to the cave by leading
us to open the box with the ring, and her note inside was
adamant. So if we had made it to the cave, we would've almost one hundred percent have had to figure out that the
ring fits in the box."

Alex held a hand out. "May I see it?"

She handed it to him, her finger feeling so light without its weight.

"Isn't this the center design of the knotted cross?" Alex asked.

"What?" She hadn't meant to sound so shrill in the enclosed space nor to snatch the ring away in such a hurry. "I thought those were initials. There's no way. I've seen this ring a million times—"

But as she held it close, slanting it this way and that, the image seemed to transform, becoming something she hadn't noticed before.

"I think you're right." She met his eyes over her still-lifted hand.

"Again, anytime you want to get that in writing, my love, would be brilliant. Let's have it notarized. Framed even." He winked, a little sparkle coming back.

Lanae tapped her heels against the floor. "So, we need to go check that necklace you found in the jewelry box, don't we? I mean, we've been seeing that thing everywhere. It has to be significant to this search, right?"

Ellora replaced the ring on her still-shaking finger while Alex and Oscar agreed.

"I think I'm going to stay. Let the other society members know what happened." Thomas opened his door. "If you wouldn't mind me tagging along on the end of this adventure though, I'd love to meet up with you all later. I'll be driving back to Alnwick soon with Eg and his boy."

"Of course." Alex twisted in his seat to shake the man's hand. "Thank you, again."

Ellora jumped out of her side and ran around the car to pull the older man into a hug. He stood unmoving a moment then patted her back. She stepped away and grinned.

"Thank you, Thomas. If it hadn't been for you, we'd have been goners. I know Grandma June would be so glad you're helping us and that you were in the right place at the right time today."

He seemed uncomfortable with the attention, waving it away, his gaze landing anywhere but on her face. "Oh, now. Don't make a fuss."

They said goodbye and he had her promise they wouldn't embark on the next leg without him. "It would mean a lot to me to see this through. I wasn't able to be there for June in the end—" he sighed "—I'd like to be there for you."

"Absolutely." Ellora shivered in the breeze coming off the water. "We'll call you the minute we know anything. And I'm hoping this will be the last of the clues. This search has the potential to be the death of me, quite literally."

He gave her a grim nod and she returned to the passenger seat.

Alex handed her the coat as he'd warmed up well enough to drive. She would need to let the officers know about what had happened in the sea cave. They were probably weary of her penchant for calamity too.

She took her phone, thankful it was still in her pocket and that the waterproof cover had worked. She had to roll her eyes—*now* she had reception bars.

As soon as they returned to Alnwick Castle, they each ran to their prospective rooms to take hot showers and throw on dry, warm clothes. Then Alex invited everyone to gather in his flat for steaming cups of tea and to check out the necklace.

But before she could join them, she had to check in with the inspector. She filled him in on their latest danger-filled escapades, including them finding her grandmother's vest.

She walked the length of her flat and ran a hand through

her wet, tangled hair. "Look, I know you deal with absolutes or at least theories beyond a reasonable doubt. So do I as a historian. But I'm telling you, something happened in that cave. Sometimes we have to go with our gut when there's not enough evidence, don't we?"

The inspector was quiet a moment. "Right you are. Some of the best police work starts out as a hunch."

"So, you'll check out the cave?"

The detective agreed and said they'd form a team to investigate the cave and the coastline if needed. He'd call her when there was news, one way or the other.

Ellora joined Alex, Lanae and Oscar in Alex's flat. Her nervous energy and stomach twisted in knots—what would they find in that cave?—wouldn't let her sit like the rest of them, huddled in warm clothes and blankets after their run-in with the North Sea.

She stood with her steaming mug held in both hands, letting the heat seep through her palms, ebbing through the rest of her body.

Everyone else sipped their tea except Lanae, who'd brought a mug of her home-brewed kombucha. The jewelry box sat on his round coffee table, with the necklace beside it.

Alex stared into the depths of his tea. "Do you think Grandma June's clues may have unintentionally led us to the place she was hurt...or killed?" The last words came out a hoarse whisper.

They were the thoughts she couldn't quite form out loud. They were so harsh to her ears.

She pressed her lips together then let out a gust of air. "I don't know. I don't want to believe it, but I have a bad feeling about that cave. I just spoke with the inspector. They're going to search the cave and surrounding area for—for—"

she could not say *a body* or *remains* "—any clues connected to Grandma June."

"Tell them to watch out for that high tide." Lanae's forehead creased. Oscar reached over to squeeze her hand.

As anxious as she was to see if there was another clue related to the manuscript, possibly through the necklace, it also seemed that the chase was coming to an end. Was she ready for that? Or what if the opposite was true? What if this clue led to another clue and another and another? Or it all came to a screeching halt with a dead end to beat all dead ends? Her spirit was already so drained. In some ways, the search had made her face the heartache of feeling abandoned by her grandmother and Alex. It had been frustrating and difficult. Heartrending, at times.

But it had also been exciting and reminded her why she loved history and the research aspect of her chosen career.

The search for the lost manuscript had led her here. To spend time with her friend, to make new friends along the way and, of course, to be with Alex again. It had helped to reignite what she loved about him. To bring them face-to-face once more and confront the pains of their marriage but also see what had drawn them together in the first place. And not only that but see that there could be something new and wonderful built upon what they already had if they stopped trying to build it with their own meager strength and abilities.

She blew out a cleansing breath and retrieved the necklace. Everyone scooted to the edges of their seats, watching.

"This center symbol on the ring does seem like it's identical to the middle circular portion of the cross. What does it mean? It still looks like looping or interlocking letters of some kind. It's kind of dusty, like dirt particles have collected in the crevices."

Alex jogged over to the kitchen, and retrieved a soft flour sack dishcloth for her.

She rubbed at the slightly raised or domed center of the cross. Suddenly it gave way with a little *pop*.

Her own widened eyes matched the expressions of everyone in the room.

A little crevice inside held a small many-times-folded piece of paper. She carefully unfolded it. The pure white paper and the handwriting told her it was not of antiquity and she recognized the writing right away—her grandmother's again.

She swallowed and said, "Grandma June wrote 'Mildrythe' then an arrow to 'Hilda.' Then she said, 'I will check the estate, though I feel deep down the manuscript can't be there, and after that, the sea cave. I conferred with a fellow historian, and must rule out these places. Ultimately, I believe the answer may begin and end in Alnwick. But, Ellora, if you're finding this, I caution you to be alert. And trust your gut. Better yet, trust God's leading. I know you can do this even if I cannot.'"

Lanae held up a hand. "So, she went to the estate first and then the cave? We must have found these clues out of order then."

Ellora chewed her lip, gathering her thoughts. "It does sound that way. Maybe our original assumption that the estate was the connection to her disappearance was incorrect. I think something *did* happen there though. And maybe Grandma June left me the ring in the tower because she was worried she wouldn't be coming back from her next stop— searching the cave."

Oscar crossed an ankle over his knee. "And it was this Byron bloke behind it. We're all in agreement there, yeah?"

They all nodded. Alex raked a hand through his hair. "No matter what happened, she obviously never made it to this other place after the cave, where she thought was the actual hiding place for the manuscript."

Everyone shook their heads.

"And what does that mean with the Mildrythe and Hilda thing?" Oscar downed the rest of his tea and set the cup on a side table.

"It may mean they're related or that perhaps one or both of them held on to the manuscript at one time." Ellora paced, holding the necklace. "Okay, where in Alnwick could Grandma June be referring to?"

"Maybe a better question to start with is, who was the only person Sibilla could trust?" Lanae jumped to her feet too.

Alex put a finger into the air. "Wasn't it her cousin? She mentioned it in the letter we found in the jewelry box."

Ellora stopped pacing, froze a moment, then dashed for the box, heart already thumping in her ears. She retrieved the letter inside written by Sibilla. Alex was always better with language than she was so she handed it to him. He opened it and scanned it.

"Yes, she says she can only trust her cousin, but she was vague about what priory. But it was in that other note in the bottom drawer of the jewelry box from Grandma June where she mentioned it was Hulne Priory. She must've found the evidence or narrowed it down as there were only so many in the area at the time. This was before the priory would've been destroyed and disbanded during the Reformation."

"Would it have been possible for the cousin to still hide the manuscript there?" Ellora crossed her arms over her chest.

Oscar squinted, as though trying to see something invisible over Ellora's right shoulder. "If he hid it well enough. Or maybe he would've waited until after the priory had been destroyed, found a secure place, figuring now no one would come looking or snooping around for anything."

They all agreed that had to be the place. But Ellora hoped they wouldn't be let down with another empty clue.

Alex said he would talk to the estate manager, who would in turn need approval from the Duke himself in order to look around and potentially dig or move stones.

He'd have to use Oscar's phone or hers, having lost his cell phone to a watery grave. "I hope they'll speed the process along as many people in the Alnwick area and northern England have grown up hearing the rumors of this manuscript, though most had felt it was just that—a story. Much like the tales of lost Viking hoards. Or the white lady haunting de Clare Hall—though, I suppose part of that turned out to be true." Alex used big gestures as he spoke. "But with the clues we've found, could anyone, even the Duke and Duchess, deny that there's a very real chance the manuscript has been right here in Hulne Park all along?"

Oscar, who worked close to Hulne Priory, shook his head in wonder. "What a great find that would be and it would bring even more tourists to Alnwick."

Lanae tossed a hand to her hip. "And not only is this supposed to be a unique and beautiful sight over twelve hundred years old, but it was also created by a woman's hands."

Oscar threw his phone to Alex so he could call the estate manager and whoever necessary for them to secure permission to look for the manuscript. They didn't know what that would entail yet, so this would take some convincing no matter how much evidence they had to support their claims.

But every minute they waited, the chances of someone getting to the manuscript first increased. They needed to hurry. To "get a move on," like the British would say.

If it had been up to Ellora and laws hadn't been involved, she'd have gone to Hulne Priory the minute the trail of clues led them there. But as it was, there were strict rules about these things. So, Alex made sure they worked with the proper people and procedures to search the priory.

She grabbed her shoulder bag from her wardrobe, stuffing Grandma June's field journal inside. Today was the day. They'd waited four days—which had been rushed as a favor to Alex as the resident coordinator for the university program—and now their official permission to move forward with the search had arrived.

The inspector hadn't contacted her yet about their plan to search the cave and the coast. She'd called, but he said it had been a process to get a team together. Today was the day for them too though. He could call anytime with news on their search. Her blood pumped loud in her ears. Hope that they wouldn't find anything tugged at the back of her mind. Not that she didn't want an answer, but now that it came down to it, could she handle whatever the truth may be?

She straightened her spine, pushing those worries down for now.

Sunbeams flickered against the window panes as clouds passed by. A perfect day to settle this search once and for all.

After the estate manager and the Percy family knew they had a significant lead on a piece of Northumberland history—though somewhat hearsay—they granted permission to look with a couple of guidelines. First, their search had to be as noninvasive as possible. For example, they couldn't take down a whole section of wall but could remove a stone or two as long as it didn't damage the structural integrity of the wall.

Second, they could dig in the ground within a certain measured circumference if they were as certain as possible they had a reason to do so.

Third, they must turn in anything they found to the Alnwick Castle estate and the estate would, in turn, contact the Portable Antiquities Scheme, run by the British Museum. This was the place to report findings of nontreasure artifacts of historical or cultural value. They would also have to contact the local coroner—that's just how they did things in England when something of value and antiquity was found on one's property. The hope was that the manuscript would be moved out of anyone's reach who had harmed Ellora's grandmother and wished the same fate for her. If it found a home in a museum or something, it would allow people to enjoy its artistry and history.

Alex had given the students, who'd been working hard at their final projects and studying for end-of-term tests, the day off.

Ellora grabbed sunscreen and a water bottle, shoving those into her bag as well, then headed for the door, locking up as she went.

Emerging in the courtyard, she spied their little search team. She'd kept the location they would be looking a surprise and they wouldn't know where they were headed until they were about to set out—she'd rather this than think of it as a secret from Thomas and the Lost Artifact Society. She'd been quick to assume they could trust every one of them. But the estate manager and the police made her, Alex, Lanae and Oscar agree not to tell anyone outside of the four of them. The inspector made a good point that someone was still after her and the manuscript, maybe killed for it. And even if the people in the group were trustworthy, they may let it slip to someone who wasn't.

"Ready to make history?" Lanae beamed at her, pulling her backpack straps onto her shoulders.

Ellora nodded, a sudden thrill zipping to her toes as they

made their way through the gates to gather with the other society members and Thomas, now an unofficial member.

They would divide into two groups: one would drive, while the other would walk. No vehicles were normally allowed inside the park. They'd received special permission to use Alex's car for the equipment.

Alex strode toward her after explaining what would happen to Eg, Gwen, Cressida and Freddie. Eg and Cressida seemed to get along well, and though the woman had been pricklier than a pear on their first couple of encounters, Ellora had warmed to her. Especially after hearing about what she'd endured with Byron and having faced him herself. Perhaps both Eg and Cressida would find a second chance at love with each other.

"We're about to take off, my love. Are you ready?" The way he'd started saying the personal "my love" again instead of the general pet name "love" made the back of her throat clog.

"I think so."

A slow smile lifted his lips as he caught her staring at his fitted black T-shirt, a rare look for him with his usual three-piece suits. She stopped herself from pressing a finger to his dimple.

She reached into her bag to check she had everything. "Ugh, I think I left my phone in your flat. Can I run up and get it?"

He'd invited her over for an omelet breakfast that morning.

"I think we may need to find you a lanyard for your phone." He winked and tossed her the keys. "That's fine. I have an issue the university wants me to handle before we can leave anyway."

She loped through the gates, waving to the guard, Gus, again. Inside Alex's apartment, she turned in a circle. Where had she left it?

That's right. She'd placed it on Alex's desk near the window. Picking it up with a swift swipe toppled a haphazard stack of papers. One fell to the floor. She reached to pick it up, but something caught her eye. The paperclipped pages on top of the stack—she read their names at the top and then "Petition for Divorce (without children)."

Her heart had been breaking as she'd sent it to Alex. And the "without children" had been an extra punch to the gut.

She picked up the papers.

He'd moved it from his office. Why? She'd assumed he'd forgotten about it in his office and would perhaps throw it away at some point if they decided to give it another go. At least, now she hoped he would.

She flipped over the multipage document. There on the signature page...his initials and signature. She'd signed her part before mailing it.

It was like someone had just kicked her right in the stomach, not unlike the night of her miscarriage. Her breath left her lungs with an *oomph* and she stayed like that, staring, chest aching until her phone chimed a text notification.

Alex had typed, **Did you get lost?** followed by a wink-face emoji.

She licked her suddenly dry lips, tried to swallow but it stuck halfway down. Had he been playing her for a fool this whole time? Was he just being nice to ease the blow of consenting to the divorce as he packed her off to the States again? Had it all been a lie? Was his expression of love in the cave just a spur-of-the-moment declaration because he thought they were about to die? She told herself to calm down. She didn't know the circumstances around it yet. But she couldn't think straight; the room spun like the first several days after her concussion.

Her throat ached from holding in sobs, but she had no

choice. She had to go and face the search team. She couldn't discuss this with him in front of everyone.

Just make it through today.

She squared her shoulders. Blowing out a long breath, she replaced the papers on his desk and jogged back to their group.

She tried to smile when he teased her again about losing her way. This was going to be a long day regardless of what they did or didn't find.

Chapter Nineteen

Perhaps sensing her shift in mood, or maybe he was back in his element as the center of attention, Alex took charge at Hulne Priory. He separated them into three groups to cover more ground. She, Alex, Thomas and Gwen would search inside the partial walls of the picturesque ruined priory. Eg, Freddie and Cressida would search outside the walls. And Lanae and Oscar would take the more intact walls of the infirmary.

As her little group gathered, she told herself to give Alex the benefit of the doubt, but she couldn't erase the image of his name signed in black ink on those divorce papers. To know that at some point in time—since she arrived?—he'd been ready to call it quits cut right through her. Yes, she'd sent the papers to him. She'd been hurt and angry. But really, she'd wanted him to have a wake-up call, to ignite a fire within him to fight for her. No one had ever fought to stay with her. She'd never been worth it to them.

As the other groups moved to their designated areas, out of sight from their group, Alex reached for his ringing phone. He walked several paces away and within moments his fingers scraped through his hair making it stand on end. "Yeah, I...That's fine. I'll come...No, I should be the one to take care of it...All right. Cheers."

He pressed the screen to hang up then pivoted to face them. Thomas was busy chattering away to Gwen. The older man had been thrilled when they finally called to say they were going to go look for the manuscript. The jittery excitement, almost on edge, seemed kind of out of character for the laid-back man. But it had been a long search for all of them. They paid Alex and Ellora no attention as they both retrieved work gloves from their backpacks.

"I've got to go deal with some things at the castle. I need Lanae to come with me too. It's a student issue," Alex said, though it seemed to pain him to do so.

"What?" The two people closest to her wouldn't be with her at the end of this journey?

"I'm not any happier about it than you are. Five students and counting have come down with food poisoning. A few just thought they were a little under the weather, but it has turned serious. One of the student aides let the other faculty know and parents are calling as they can't reach their children and want to know what I'm going to do about it. There are several students who need medical attention, including Natalie and Teddy, and we have to contact trace in case it came from the food in the castle's kitchen... It's a disaster."

At the mention of Natalie and Teddy, worry did grip her, but this was too much. Alex not being here for this epic conclusion? "Do you really have to be the one to go? Can't someone else do this?"

He swiped a hand over his face. "It's my job, Ellie. It's my responsibility. Would you ask Lanae the same question?"

Guilt roiled in her stomach, but she pushed it away, irritation taking its place. It's not that she didn't care about the students. They were so dear, even the ones who tested her patience. But this was too important. Why did this have to happen now?

Her fingers curled into fists. "Well, I just don't understand—"

"No, you don't." The words were harsh but his expression was defeated, melancholy. "Look, I have to go get Lanae. I'll be back as soon as I can, all right?"

"Fine." She turned to the other two in their group as he jogged away.

Lanae frowned and waved to Ellora before they hopped into his car and were gone.

No matter how much she told herself she was being silly and selfish, she found herself at the crossroads of needing Alex and others needing him too. And he'd chosen them over her...again.

Was their need greater? Yes, probably. But her heart didn't believe her mind on this one. Her heart hurt. Did their need negate hers? Diminish it? Did it make her the most terrible person in the world to want him to stay when he needed to go? Or that it left her feeling abandoned, yet again?

Of all the times for him to choose something, anything else, above her and what they were trying to accomplish together, it chafed. He'd also been distant after the near-drowning. Maybe she was more trouble than she was worth, and that's why he planned to give her the divorce papers after they found the manuscript. Or maybe her vision over the entire situation was skewed by the fact that her emotions were raw and on edge about the other search happening right now at the cave.

Gwen and Thomas signaled her over.

Gwen squeezed her shoulder while Thomas inspected the stones in what used to be the cloisters. "It's all right, dear. He'll be back. No big deal. There's nothing for it."

Ellora bobbed her head and plastered on a smile. Why did it *feel* like a big deal then?

Alex or no Alex, they had a manuscript to find. "Sibilla and her cousin will have likely put the manuscript inside a container or box of some kind. So, that's where assistance from Eg might be helpful with his metal detector. If it's in the ground, that is. But if it's in one of the walls, we might look for an indication something is there. A stone that's marked in some way or another."

She'd hardly finished speaking when Thomas grabbed a shovel and thrust it into the air. "Let's crack on then, shall we?"

It was truly a clueless search. If the manuscript was there, they had no idea where it might be. But neither this nor the fact they'd lost two members of their team seemed to dampen Thomas's spirits.

Ellora wandered by herself, in and out of crumbling corridors, rooms once filled with cooking, singing and praying.

Soon she rounded a corner into a partially enclosed space, most of one wall overrun with vines and fragrant purple blooms. It was as though she'd wandered into the children's story *The Secret Garden*. A hush surrounded her. She so wished she could share this moment with Alex. The thought left her feeling even more alone.

One wall had still-intact low windows with a wide stone base underneath, big enough to sit on. Drawn to them, she moved closer. The stone slabs laid over the bases, like a window seat, were timeworn and smooth. But the slab on the right had moss growing in the center, irregular, almost like a pattern. The soft tufts of green came away easily from the depressions underneath her touch.

When they were cleared away, the image—as familiar to her now as her own face—emerged though it was faded. The knotted cross. The symbol that had led them through this search as much as her grandmother's clues. And now with a new perspective, the interlocking letters—could it be?—the letters on the ring she'd always assumed were her grandparents' seemed to change into something new. An *M* and an *H* popped out at her in the center of the cross. Mildrythe. Hilda.

"I think I found something!" A bubble of excitement rose in her chest.

The other two ran over. She pointed to the cross.

"Can we move it?" Gwen squeezed her hands together over her chest.

"I don't see why not." Ellora ran her fingers along the sides of the approximately three-inch-thick, flat, rectangular stone. "It doesn't appear to be holding up this window. That's these—" she pointed to the vertical stone frame "—but this stone at the base seems to just lay on top and is sealed with mortar."

Thomas leaned his shovel against a wall and retrieved a trowel from his backpack. "Let's dig in, shall we?"

Gwen opened her bag and pulled out an ice pick. Ellora's brows shot up.

"What?" Gwen's shoulder lifted. "It's what I could find."

Ellora retrieved the woodworking chisel she'd been able to get from a shop in town. "Maybe we should ask Oscar or some of the others for help to lift this thing. That stone looks really heavy, and my wrist still isn't one hundred percent."

Thomas, who dived right into scraping away the mortar, shook his head. "No need, no need. We've got it."

It took all three of them pulling, and eventually using the shovel as leverage, to remove the stone. Like taking the lid off of a box, underneath the stone was an open space.

Inside this humble hiding place lay a lumpy cloth-covered parcel. Ellora reached in and pulled it out with considerable effort, ignoring the sharp jabs in her still-healing wrist. Whatever was inside felt solid and heavy.

All three of them knelt on the grass, the parcel between them, in silent awe. Thomas's hand inched forward, but Gwen laid a hand on his forearm. "No, it should be Ellora. For her grandmother's sake."

She squeezed the older woman's hand. "Thank you."

To Ellora's surprise, a flash of irritation crossed Thomas's face before he smoothed it once more into a smile. "Right you are."

Inside a heavy, rough waxed cloth, the medieval version of waterproofing, was another tied parcel made of leather with its natural water repellency. She opened the leather and inside was a beautiful, ornate box of engraved and enameled copper not unlike the Chasse with the Crucifixion and Christ in Majesty—a French-made medieval rectangular "reliquary," or box, used to house holy relics. Scenes of Jesus's life were depicted around the sides while the top held a many-branched tree, all decorated in blues, greens, splashes of red and gold.

Gwen took in a sharp breath while Thomas rubbed his palms together.

A lump swelled in her throat. This was it. She looked up at Gwen and then Thomas, whose eyes gleamed with anticipation.

Sadness that Alex wasn't there washed over her. It didn't feel right.

"Maybe we should bring it back to the castle to find Alex and Lanae first. Open it then."

Thomas leaned in. "If this is what we think it is, it's been around twelve hundred years. It'll be around in another hour or so for him to see once he's handled things at the castle. It's not likely to change. So, let's have a look, shall we?"

Gwen seemed unsure, glancing between them. "Do whatever you think best."

Thomas pushed the air with his hands, a coaxing gesture. "Open it, then. Let's have a peek."

Guilt plagued her again, but so did her curiosity. Besides, Alex had never asked that they wait for them to return. With a held breath, she undid the latch and with gentle pressure opened the lid that likely hadn't been opened in about five hundred years.

She marveled at the box's interior. "Do you see here? They lined the inside with leather and—" her heart thundered in her chest at spying the thick rectangular shape in the bottom of the box "—they wrapped the manuscript, to waterproof it. Sibilla's cousin clearly knew the importance of keeping this precious document safe, not only from those who would seek to either destroy it or sell it to the highest bidder but also from the elements."

"Yes, yes…dear." Thomas's voice seemed strained and the "dear" added on as though to soften his impatient tone. "Open the leather. Get on with it then."

She tried to tell herself they were all anxious for the end of this as she lifted the covering off.

Time seemed to stand still. The brilliant blue cover made her heart jump.

Jewels bedecked the outside of the book and the lapis-lazuli-hued leather cover matched the blue interior of what were called the carpet pages—the highly decorated introduction pages to each chapter or section of the book. The interlocking *H* and *M* were on the first carpet page along with the cross, but the artist had added a swirling pattern along the top and upper sides so that the cross became a tree.

If only Alex was there to help her decipher, but she attempted to muddle her way through very old English. At least the author had learned to write in English and not Latin like many of the scribes of the day.

The first part of the book was a very early version of a Book of Hours, a Psalter. But as it went on, it seemed to change into a journal or a woman's account of her life.

Thomas bent next to her, checked his watch and the priory grounds. Perhaps searching for the others.

She scanned the words, careful not to handle it too much, reading a section to the other two.

Gwen's hand went to her heart. "That's amazing. Truly breathtaking."

She tried not to think of the emptiness because of the absence of the three people she'd have loved to share this with.

But she wouldn't let that ruin this moment.

She inspected the delicate hand that had created this manuscript. She should call the other team over to let them know the search was over, but the excitement and desire to marvel over each page took over. "Listen to this—she says her name is Mildrythe, originally from near Lindisfarne. She was a lowborn woman using her scribing skills to transcribe manuscripts as a means of a living wage after her father died. She learned from the monks and scribes at Lindisfarne. A wealthy man commissioned a book of prayers from her, but then became infatuated with her, later telling her mother that Mildrythe would wed him. Doesn't sound like he *asked* for her hand." Ellora glanced up, her legs beneath her shaking as she read.

Both Gwen and Thomas leaned in, as silent as the stones around them.

She wet her lips and went on. "To care for her mother, she agreed to marry him, but he told her she must give up scribing and illustrating even though she loved it. But before the wedding could take place, the Norsemen came upon Lindisfarne again. She says, 'raging against it like a tempest upon the shores of Holy Island.'

"The only thing of value she carried was the Book of Hours she had begun to create as a parting gift to her mother. It was the book her betrothed commissioned turned into her own personal volume, and he agreed to fund the expensive materials as long as she married him. But her mother was killed in this raid and Mildrythe herself was taken as their prisoner. Then she says—"

Her phone rang, snapping her out of her historical reverie. Already she felt she knew and had a kinship with Mildrythe.

"Maybe that's Alex." She met Thomas's eyes as she lifted the book over to Gwen and stood.

Thomas rose. "Yes, tell Alex we need the car back here. You know, to transport the manuscript."

It was the inspector's number. *Okay, here we go.* Maybe it was nothing. Maybe he was calling to say it was another dead end.

She walked a few paces, turning to answer. "Hello, Inspector."

"Miss Lockwood, I wanted to reach out about our search this morning. We went to the cave you told us about. We, uh—" He seemed to struggle to keep his voice even, professional.

She didn't like the ominous tone, like a portent of doom

sweeping in like the tide they'd encountered. She had no foothold. Nothing she could do to stop it.

"Ellora, dear?" Gwen's timid voice tiptoed from behind her. She put up a hand to indicate just a minute.

"I'm sorry, Miss Lockwood. We found your grand-mother's remains behind the door in the cave. Someone had, uh, disposed of her there and screwed the door shut. We've confirmed with our rapid results DNA testing, the body belongs to your grandmother."

Ellora's ears rang, a sharp, piercing whine. "No…" The word, just two letters, wasn't enough to stop the reality of what he'd said. Not enough to keep the sky from spinning, nor the choked sob from escaping her throat.

"I'm sorry, ma'am." The rest of what he said—something about signs of blunt force trauma to the head and an autopsy needed to confirm faded into the muffled background.

Her thumb pressed End Call. The phone slipped from her fingers, landing with a soft thud on the grass. Her knees threatened to give way.

A deep, abiding grief ascended to meet the filament of hope she'd still clung to, as absurd as it seemed now, that somehow her grandmother was still alive. Everything, start-ing with the center of her chest, went numb and spread through her extremities.

This was it. Her grandmother was truly gone. Her fam-ily tree had become a twig with no branches. And all she wanted was to have Alex hold her and tell her it was going to be okay, but he wasn't there.

Suddenly, a weariness clung to her bones. Pulling her tight against the earth. Like she wore a pair of these stones as shoes.

Just as Gwen said her name with more insistence, some-thing cold and unforgiving pressed into the space between her shoulder blades. Before she could react, Thomas's voice was in her ear as a whisper, "Don't say a word. Just turn around slowly."

She did so, already knowing the unbelievable truth—Thomas had a gun and it was pointed at her. Every emotion, every horrific memory of the night she'd been kicked and held at gunpoint, rushed back.

Instinct made her hands rise to chest level, palms facing out. "What are you doing, Thomas?"

"I'm getting what I deserve."

Gwen still held the manuscript and glanced between the gun in Thomas's hands to Ellora like she couldn't decide between fight or flight. Ellora's own legs had chosen for her—freeze. She couldn't make them move even if she knew what to do next.

Keep him talking. That's what they always said in the movies.

"Wh-what do you mean? Were you in this to get the manuscript the whole time?"

"Of course I was." His laugh was incredulous. "Do you actually think I cared about your grandmother? Or you, for that matter? You were both a means to an end."

That stung, but she fumbled for another question as he snatched the manuscript away from Gwen. He gestured with the gun for Ellora to stand by Gwen.

"But then, why didn't you just take the manuscript for yourself right away? Why did you let us continue with the clues, why let us get to this point at all?"

His gun waved and his face reddened with anger or frustration, perhaps both. "Because I didn't know where it was! As much as I loathed it, I needed you to find the clues only June's granddaughter could find. Why do you think I sent you that text? Dogged your steps in the shadows? To confuse you, to scare you into thinking someone was right behind you and spur you on to find the manuscript faster." He growled. "At first your grandmother's stories about a lost female-made manuscript were obsessive gibberish. But I soon realized she was onto something. She told me about getting that ring with her husband at an auction years ago and how the rumors of the manuscript soon seemed intertwined with it."

He laid the manuscript out on top of a nearby partial support column, and caressed the brilliant blue cover and the inset jewels. The excitement Ellora had thought she'd seen earlier glittered the truth now—greed.

"When I knew she was on the trail of something of great value, I was able to secure a large price for the safe delivery of the manuscript. In just a couple of days, I'll meet with my *investor* and will be ten million pounds richer." He sniffed. "I've been stuck in that dull little tea shop, working myself to the bone. I deserve to finally fulfill my dreams, travel, see the world."

Gwen's mouth hung open. "I can't believe this."

He sneered, let out an unpleasant laugh.

Ellora glared at this man whose whole face had changed in a matter of minutes. Unrecognizable. "If you needed us to find the manuscript for you, why did you almost drown us in the North Sea?"

He scratched the edge of his mustache. "That wasn't me, but I'm sure an accident like locking yourselves in a sea cave isn't too difficult for bumbling baffoons like you two. I was just there to keep an eye on you."

Thomas peered around the corner to the priory door. "I need to get out of here." Then he whirled around, pointing with the gun once more.

She forced herself to ask, "It was you, wasn't it? You killed Grandma June."

He shrugged. "Not exactly. Though, some would certainly argue I was the cause of her death. While I tried to coax her into finding the manuscript, which she clearly failed to do, someone else seemed to be trying to throw her off the scent. Like they wanted to get to it first. After she went to the estate like you did, someone told her to check the sea cave connected by tunnel to de Clare Hall. I already knew that was a dead end and told her so. But she didn't listen and went anyway. She had just started to seem suspicious about me and my motives after I slipped up, said something I shouldn't have—"

"I'm sure she did." Ellora's interruption earned her a glower.

"She wanted to leave the cave, she seemed in a hurry. I couldn't have her blathering on to the police, could I? I tried to stop her." His voice took on a pleading edge, as though to convince her he wasn't such a bad guy. "She wouldn't listen and started to run. I grabbed her arm to make her stay, to listen, but she tripped and hit her head on a rock. Nothing I could do for her then."

Fury and anguish crashed against each other in the middle of her chest. "So, you just left her there? Threw her in that tunnel door and what? Came back later to screw the door shut thinking no one would ever find out?"

He rolled his eyes. "Well, I couldn't tell the police about her death myself, could I? They'd never believe she fell and that would lead them to poke around in my affairs. And I burned all of the notes June and I took, that I could find anyway, about the cave and the connections she'd made to the manuscript. How did I know you'd find these—these—" he waved the gun hand "—secret clues from her field journal and elsewhere to come snooping around yourself?"

She exchanged a grim glance with Gwen, who said, "I just can't believe it, Thomas. All this time. I trusted you. We all trusted you. June was our friend. I'm your business partner, worked next to you for years…"

He shook then straightened his shoulders. "That's enough. I don't owe you an explanation."

"Well, what are you waiting for?" Ellora's voice rasped. "Go. You have what you came for."

He kept peering outside of their little hidden alcove. "I'm waiting for that imbecile husband of yours. He has the car and I could sure use a getaway about now."

"He's not going to hand over his car to you." Ellora crossed her arms.

Thomas spun the gun around his finger, not too smoothly either, and grinned. "Oh, I think he will."

And here she was again. Alone. Abandoned. Forgotten. The gravity of the situation grew, shackling her legs in place. Police sirens pierced the quiet countryside. But they were still a ways off. Thomas's eyes rounded. He turned his head this way and that from Ellora and Gwen to the manuscript, indecision written all over his face.

Finally, he leaped toward the manuscript. Protectiveness arose in her and her own feet became unstuck. They'd worked too hard. Her grandmother had paid too high a price for him to take it. She dashed for the manuscript too.

He was closer and snatched it before she could, but his rounded mouth told of his surprise.

She tried to pry the book from his one arm. His teeth gritted together as he said, "You know, I never wanted to use this, but I will." He finally wrested himself and the manuscript away from her reach and leveled the gun at her again.

For good measure, it seemed, he shoved her with the gun in hand and she fell onto her backside.

The sirens neared and with one last look at her, Thomas ran, abandoning his idea for a getaway car to go on foot. The motivation of the authorities closing in seemed to hasten him on to a shocking speed.

Oscar and Freddie stepped out from behind the partial wall of the infirmary.

Eg jogged, knees high, the metal detector held over his head. "Oscar let us know something had gone sideways with Thomas. He overheard the row between you from behind the infirmary walls. We've been lying in wait like one of those police programs but didn't want to jump out and startle Thomas into firing that gun. Freddie called for the police."

The police pulled in and flew from the car. They made sure everyone was safe and uninjured before they radioed for backup while two of the officers took off in the direction Thomas had run.

They returned shaking their heads. "We've lost the trail. But it looks as though a car peeled away on the gravel up the road."

So he had found a getaway car after all. The inspector she'd spoken with earlier showed up and made sure Ellora and the others understood they weren't giving up. They would search for Thomas and arrest him on sight. For now, there was nothing more to do at the priory. So, Ellora, Eg and Freddie worked together to move the stone back into place. The hiding place was empty now. A cold, dark hole lay within. That felt like her heart.

"I'm so sorry, Ellora." Eg put a warm hand on her shoulder. Deep lines crinkled around his eyes. "I know how much it meant to you to find that manuscript. Was it as beautiful as you had hoped?"

"More so." She tried to smile, but it faltered.

He patted her arm. "I know your grandmother would be proud of you regardless. You never gave up."

All she could do was study the ground beneath her feet. She couldn't even bring herself to nod. Her grandmother was gone. Like, *really* gone. That seed of hope turned to dust and scattered away in the wind. That shimmer of a prayer, that at the end of all of this she would sit with her grandmother and recount the tale of how she'd finally found the manuscript and breathe a sigh of relief, had vanished. This was the end of the line. Grandma June was gone for good and so was the manuscript she'd died to find and protect.

The officers placed the box that had protected the manuscript all those years into the trunk of the police car. They would keep it safe. Too bad she'd led the one person she shouldn't have right to the manuscript. She hadn't kept safe the contents of that box any more than she'd protected her baby all those months ago. Her one job. Nor had she accompanied and protected Grandma June on this quest in the first place.

The failure of one collided into the failure of the others. They churned together into one big swelling heartache.

As the others, shoulders slumped and disbelief still written into the lines of their foreheads, started to make their way by foot back to the long trail leading away back toward the castle—whoever could fit had ridden with the officers—Ellora gripped her middle, not able to move.

Just before pulling away in the second police car, the inspector said he saw no reason that Thomas would come back here; he'd likely try to lay low for a couple of days. But he offered to leave an officer behind to walk her back if she liked.

She shook her head. "That's all right."

Though Oscar didn't ask if he could walk her back, he seemed determined to do so. But he trailed behind her, silent, as though sensing her need to process her thoughts alone.

She hadn't made it far when Alex drove up the hill and skidded to a stop.

He had barely opened the door but she couldn't keep the hurt and the rage from spewing from her mouth as she shouted, "Where *were* you?"

The shrill wails of the sirens had cut right through Alex's chest as he realized where the police cars were headed.

Along with Lanae he had just finished speaking with some of the students who'd become ill. There were two who were sick enough to send to the medical center for IV hydration, while the rest would be monitored by student aides and their friends. That's when he'd heard the police sirens.

He and Lanae sped to Hulne Park, but they'd been made to wait as the police blockaded the entrance. The officers wouldn't answer any questions other than to say there was a gunman in the park.

He'd slammed his palms against his steering wheel and shouted in the direction of God's ears, "Not again! Don't let this happen again. Please, protect Ellora. Protect them all."

"They're all right. They have to be all right," Lanae had said in hushed tones.

Once again, he was not there for Ellie when she'd needed him.

A sea more cold and dark than the one they'd almost drowned in had closed in around him.

When the police vehicles exited Hulne Park and took down the barrier, he explained who he was to the officer posted at the gate, and he'd been allowed to drive through the entrance once again. He'd driven as fast as the dirt road allowed.

Relief poured over him when he spotted Ellora and Oscar close behind, alive and well. He'd nearly forgotten to put the car in Park as he'd slammed on the brakes and opened the door. So, when he was met with her stormy blue eyes, he couldn't hide the confusion bubbling to the surface.

Her hands had gone to her hips. "Well? Where in the world were you, Alexander Lockwood?"

The tone and the use of his full name reminded him so much of his mother's hateful treatment that his entire body tensed. His joy and relief quickly morphed into a shield of defense.

Lanae and Oscar, the innocent bystanders, kept quiet.

"I was doing my job, Ellora." He matched her tone as he slammed the car door and clenched his hands at his sides.

He'd always been embarrassed when his mother and father fought in front of company, but now here he was. Oscar crossed to Lanae, taking her hand before saying something quietly into her ear. "Mate, we're going to walk back. Let you have some privacy."

His neck heated, and Ellora's cheeks reddened.

Before slipping away, Lanae called, "I'm glad you're all okay. Come tell me everything when you get back. All right?"

Ellora agreed.

But her silence disappeared the minute their friends did down the hill. She threw her arms up, wincing with the movement of her right wrist. Her lips tightened into a straight line. "Once again I was scared for my life, alone, deserted, and you were nowhere to be found." She shook her head, a sardonic smile marring her sweet face. "No, I take that back. Once again you were playing hero for others, just not me. Your words have meant nothing. Saying you're there for me, that we're in this together. But when I really needed you, you weren't there."

Noises *clacked* in the back of his throat as he tried to form a coherent thought to speak out loud. Her words threw sharp daggers into the center of his chest. He had to stop himself from doubling over.

When the words did come, they came as a thunderclap and a raging fire. "I've done everything I could to show you that I care. I'm sorry if you can't go three seconds without getting into some kind of crisis. At what point and what else do I have to do for you to believe me? Hmm? Do I actually have to take a bullet for you? Maybe if I were martyred for the sake of your precious sense of security and equally precious lost manuscript, you'd finally get it—that I'm just a bloke doing the best he can."

Her lips blanched, almost disappearing as she clamped them together. A wash of shame drenched his forehead with cold sweat. But the anger still coursed through his veins.

"I hope you're happy then because the *precious* manuscript, as you put it, is gone." The grief of that statement drew weary shadows beneath her eyes.

"What? Where is it?"

He realized that with everything that had happened he hadn't even stopped to ask if she'd found it nor what had happened.

The stubborn set of her jaw said she didn't want to tell him, but finally she crossed her arms and said, "Thomas took it. He was playing us all along. He didn't want to help find it in honor of Grandma June. He wanted to find it so he could sell it to some black market dealer. He admitted that he caused her death."

Her chin wobbled. "And I—I got a call from the inspector just before Thomas showed his true colors... Grandma

June's remains were found in the cave, behind that door." She swiped a tear from her cheek then sniffed and sent her gaze over the hill behind him. "She's really gone, Alex. It's ridiculous. I've told myself for months, others have told me, *you've* told me, someone missing this long can't possibly still be alive, but some part of me denied it. I didn't want it to be true."

Her shoulders fell. "I half expected Grandma June to walk through the door any minute to tell me she'd been on an adventure in some remote part of the world with no way to contact me or something. She'd regale me with stories, we'd laugh and I would never again let her explore alone. I'd never—" her voice cracked and she swallowed "—abandon her again, because I know how much it hurts to be left alone by those you love."

He longed to step forward, to hold her, tell her everything would be all right, but her arms gripped tight across her chest. "I'm so sorry, Ellie." His own dashed hope that somehow things wouldn't end like this, that Grandma June wasn't truly gone, catching up to him.

"I love her, Alex. I miss her so much. She can't be gone." Her words were punctuated by sobs. "I didn't even get to tell her how much she meant to me."

She turned her face away from him.

"So, yeah. You basically missed everything important."

The impact of those words, all that he'd left her to deal with on her own, took his breath. Guilt piggybacked by grief so sharp, so keen, it sliced straight through to the bone. To the very marrow. It was so akin to the anguish he'd felt after Beckett died, it sent wave after wave of flashbacks that made the back of his throat clench tighter than his fists. But warring against that grief was his side of the story. She didn't understand.

"It's not as if I've been off on holiday, have I? People needed me."

She swallowed, studying the dirt road at her feet. "I get it. I do. It's just...so did—*do*—I."

"I've been paying for the things—" he had to swallow to continue "—I've missed all my life. I don't know what you want from me, Ellie. I'm doing what I can. If we're supposed to be building on a new foundation, *His* foundation, then why are you throwing every record of every wrong back in my face? We're supposed to forgive and *forget*."

Scuffing her shoe on the gravel. "What if I can't?"

Frustration leaked from his mouth in a growl. "From the minute you got here, I've done nothing but try to show you that I'm in this. I'm not going anywhere. But you won't trust me."

She thrust her fingers through her hair and spun around with an incredulous laugh, before turning back to him. "You're with me? You're *with* me? Trust you? No, a man who is with his wife, not giving up, doesn't sign divorce papers. I saw them, Alex, when I went to your flat for my phone. Signed and practically sealed and delivered."

Stricken, he swiped a hand down his face. "Ellie, I..." It wasn't what she thought, but how could he explain that in a moment of weakness he'd thought perhaps she was better off without him?

She put a hand up to stop him. "A man *in this* wouldn't have left in the first place, putting an ocean between himself and his wife. Wouldn't have eaten up the glory after being a hero to someone else while his wife lay in a hospital bleeding, losing a precious child, left her helpless and alone, never asking if she was okay. And for that matter—" she walked closer, pointing to his chest, teeth gritted "—never asking if she—*I*—wanted that baby. Never asked if I grieved for this tiny but significant piece of my heart that had died. Because I did, Alex." Now she sobbed. "I so wanted our baby. I want to be a mother."

"Ellie, that's not fair and you know it. I hated the attention after the shooting. It was agony to sit through those interviews. And I knew nothing about the baby or you having a miscarriage. I was beyond shocked, gutted really, when you told me. I admit it—I didn't know what to say."

He mimicked her move and scraped his fingernails against his scalp until it burned. "And if we're on the subject of who did or didn't do what. Who doesn't tell their spouse about having a miscarriage? That's pretty big news. You're supposed to be my wife, Ellie. Why was I the last to know? If we can't be honest with each other, how can we…?"

He let the statement trail off; sudden fear gripped him for where the answer may lead.

Her blue eyes pierced his. "That's just it, isn't it? We've not been honest with each other. Maybe not even to ourselves. Grandma June used to say love is a choice. But so is honesty. You can't have one without the other, can you? And we did not choose love. If we had, we would've been honest with each other. When it came down to it, we didn't choose each other at all."

The vows they'd said came back to him. The way she'd looked in her white dress. The flush of peach in her cheeks as she'd promised him the same things he'd promised her. He'd said them honestly. He'd meant every word right down to his core, his very soul. And yet, she was right. After that day, they hadn't really chosen each other. They hadn't chosen love or at least the type of selfless, truth-giving love they were called to as God's children and husband and wife to each other. And when they'd inevitably messed up, they did not forgive as God forgives, casting the offenses as far as the east is from the west.

She was already walking down the road. Their life, their marriage, seemed to be slipping through his fingers like water. He was losing. What could he do to make this right? But nothing came to him.

He jumped into his car, and she did allow him to drive her back to the castle, but the small console between them might as well have been the Atlantic Ocean all over again.

Chapter Twenty

"That's it, Nae. I'm leaving." Ellora threw another cardigan into her suitcase with a quick backward glance at her friend sitting knees to chest on the couch. "He's already decided our fate by signing the divorce papers—"

"Which you sent to him in the first place, may I remind you." She raised a brow.

Ellora groaned. Like she didn't know that? "I know, but I never thought he'd actually sign them. I think deep down, I hoped it would jolt us both back to reality and we'd rip them up together. Naive, I know."

But now, too much had happened and they'd said too much. The saying that words cut deeper than any two-edged sword had proved true.

Lanae walked over to where Ellora had her suitcase open on the bed. "Are you sure about this? Maybe you should slow down and give it another day or two to think about it. I don't need to tell you that the students need you and you're putting us in a jam if you leave, right? They've been through an ordeal too with the food poisoning."

"I know and I'm truly sorry about that. And I'm grateful everyone is recovering, especially Teddy. But I talked to the retired British professor who helped out after my fall and he doesn't mind filling in to give their final test and grade their end-of-session research projects. They'll be fine without me."

Lanae sighed.

"I thought I was going to stay. I really had considered it. But this isn't going to work." She stopped folding a silk scarf. "Besides, I've already given it four days." Granted, four days of mostly avoiding Alex, who seemed just as eager to avoid her.

She rolled her shoulders back. "Once I receive Grandma June's ashes and am cleared to fly with them, I'm going to go back and take the job in St. Cloud. The university has been a steady constant in my life since I was eighteen years old, unlike my husband." As well as God and anyone else she'd ever loved. The loneliness of that settled around her heart like a shroud.

"But what about the manuscript? You've worked so hard to find it. Are you going to give up now and let Thomas have it, sell it on the black market? Not to mention, we now know he's responsible for your grandma's death. You're going to let him get away with that?" Her honey-brown eyes beseeched Ellora.

She slumped onto the edge of the bed at the mention of the now-confirmed death of her grandmother. The grief inside kept knocking at her wall, the one that protected her heart. She hadn't opened the door. Letting it in would make everything more real. As it was, that phone call with the inspector had seemed a bad dream, especially with the surreal circumstances afterward. She didn't want to feel this loss. She'd had too many already.

"The police haven't seen anything of Thomas or heard about a nefarious gathering of black market dealers in the area. I think I have to face that he's gone and so is the manuscript. Maybe I can write for one of the historical journals, if they finally believe that it exists, about what I was able to glean from it."

"But didn't you say he let slip his plan to meet up with the black market artifacts dealer? Think. Where? Did he say when?"

She rubbed her chin. To think on it meant going back to the terror of being held at gunpoint, not for the first time in her life. "No, he didn't say. But then, it's hard to think when someone is pointing a gun at you." She hadn't meant to sound sarcastic. With an apologetic glance, she added, "Sorry."

Lanae ignored her acidic tone. "Let's go over to his tea shop and see if he left a clue of some kind about this meetup."

When Ellora gave her a skeptical tilt of the head, Lanae pulled her up from the bed. "Come on. What could it hurt?"

"Nothing, but I'm sure the police have gone there already."

Her friend was just trying to delay her leaving, but in the end, Ellora agreed to check it out. The police had allowed the tea shop to reopen after they'd gone through the place to look for any evidence. They hadn't realized Thomas, having faced financial issues of his own, had sold half of the tea shop ownership to Gwen, who was keen to continue on as usual.

But once Ellora was out of the castle walls, the bright early-morning sun and the bells from the church at St. Michael's called to her.

"Before we go to the tea shop and find the inevitable, as

in *nothing*—" she sighed, as she didn't mean to be a Somber Sally again but all truly seemed lost "—would you mind if we go for a walk? I need to clear my head."

Lanae's face warmed with a soft smile. "Of course we can."

Right now, she needed to be grounded in God's creation, be close to His house more than she needed the inside of that liar's tea shop on another likely fruitless search for something perhaps she was never supposed to find. They made their way down the hill to the stone church with the ancient graveyard, stones marking the passing of people for hundreds of years. It only made her think of her grandmother's ashes, which she would collect from the crematorium soon. What would she do with them? She hadn't wanted to face a burial and it seemed too permanent. Whereas her grandmother had been a free spirit a little like Lanae, going where the wind took her.

Ellora was like her grandmother that way. So, spreading ashes where the breeze, rain and creation's elements could move them as they would seemed the better option—though she knew her grandmother's body may be gone, her soul was safe and at peace in God's care now.

The full, rich sound of the people inside of the church singing "It Is Well with My Soul" met her ears before they'd finished walking the incline to the churchyard.

The people inside the stone building dating back to the fifteenth century sang the first verse again and she and Lanae strolled the pathway that wrapped around the outside grounds.

The united voices echoed out of the open doors, spilling out to the empty graveyard. "'When peace, like a river, attendeth my way, When sorrows like sea billows roll; Whatever my lot, Thou has taught me to say, It is well, it is well, with my soul. It is well, with my soul, It is well, it is well with my soul.'"

Was it well with *her* soul? God had called her to be humble, to trust He knew best, to love others more than herself, including her husband. To forgive as He forgave, keeping no record of wrongs. But when the sorrows of life like sea billows rolled over her, she'd allowed herself to be swallowed beneath their waves, one after another. She'd stopped trusting God had good intentions or anything resembling a loving plan for her life.

Lanae stopped at the low stone wall enclosing the grounds. Ellora leaned back against the cool stone. When the music had quieted and those inside probably settled in for the rest of the service, the noise inside of Ellora's head ramped up. A tumult of thoughts, pain, pleas to God. "Nae, one loss after another feels like too much. I don't know what to do. It's like this layer upon layer of grief—it's so heavy, so all-consuming. I'm cracking under its weight." Her nails dug into the grit of the stone beneath her. "And I just wonder, where is God in all of this? Does He still care about me? Does He still deal in goodness, in light? Because everything feels so dark right now."

Lanae glanced at Ellora, studied her, compassion written into the lines of her face.

"I think we often equate God's love with how well our lives are going." Lanae's words came slow, as if choosing them carefully. "And the more difficulties we suffer, the more our own plans go awry, the more we wait with unanswered prayers, the less we feel God cares for us. Because how could a God who claims to love us allow these things to happen?"

Her heart twisted at these words.

Lanae touched Ellora's shoulder then clutched at her own

chest. "But the truth is, there can be both. Life can be terrible and we can still have a good God. One doesn't negate the other."

Somewhere deep in Ellora's soul, an opening, a pinprick of light, an invitation sprouted. But could she begin to trust God again? Especially where her marriage was concerned and after everything that had happened? After He hadn't answered her prayer—at least in the way she'd wanted—for Grandma June to be found safe?

Leaning against the wall too now, right beside Ellora, Lanae let out a small chuckle. "After we spoke about Grandma June's love of the King James Bible and you showed me the verse she wrote in that letter, I've been studying that version for myself. 'For I know the thoughts that I think toward you, saith the Lord, thoughts of peace, and not of evil, to give you an expected end.'"

Lanae reminded Ellora of herself as she began pacing in front of her. "I know other translations have a different closing to the verse, but I love the words 'an expected end.'"

Ellora wrinkled her nose. "Why? Don't get me wrong, the idea that He has a plan, especially now that I have no clue about even one step in front of me, can be comforting. But He's going to give me an end? That doesn't sound promising. It sounds morbid, if anything."

Throwing a finger into the air, Lanae stopped and grinned. "Ah, but not just any end. Not a final *the end*—it's the culmination of all that God has planned for our lives. Like a painting, one color, one brushstroke at a time, that when it's complete we will stand with Him in eternity to admire."

Could this be true for her though? It seemed it might be true for others, but what about her? Even if she wasn't sure if the sentiment applied to her, Ellora stood and embraced her friend. "Thank you." It came out a whisper and it was all she could manage for now.

"What do you say to checking out the tea shop now?"

Ellora lowered her chin. "Sure. What could it hurt, right?" They started back toward the gate to the churchyard.

She'd been holding her pain so close it had become her armor. Could she let that drop now? Let Him in? Could she trust Him after everything that had happened? What would He expect her to do about Alex? And could He really forgive, keeping no record of her wrongs? She'd been so selfish, wrapped up in her own grief, she couldn't see the hurt she'd caused around her.

People started to empty out of the church as the service must have ended.

Suddenly, Alex was there, striding along the path, having just exited the church, Oscar behind him. His eyes widened as they locked with hers, but she couldn't tell if he was pleased, surprised or neither.

He stepped beside her and indicated for her to move through the gate ahead of him. "Divine appointment, much?" Lanae mumbled the words out of the side of her mouth.

Lanae slowed to walk beside Oscar.

She had no choice but to fall into step with Alex, but she had no desire to hash out anything in front of the other churchgoers. Plus, they'd clearly each said what they'd wanted. Though the acid-laced words that had spewed from her mouth were not exactly how she'd felt. She'd been reeling with the news of her grandmother and what had happened with Thomas.

Clasping her hands in front of her, keeping her gaze straight ahead, she said, "We're going over to the tea shop to look around. See if Thomas left anything about a meeting place for that black market dealer."

He shoved his hands into his pockets and turned a sideways glance at her. "Was that an invitation to tag along?" Though his one dimple deepened in a small cheeky grin, it didn't reach his eyes.

She bit the inside of her cheek. "If you'd like. I thought I'd give it one last shot before I finish packing." She wasn't ready to call this an olive branch. But the words "one last shot" seemed to extend to their marriage as well.

If Your plans are good then please help me trust You where Alex is concerned because nothing seems good between us right now.

Alex appeared to take it as an olive branch anyway and continued beside her as they turned onto Narrowgate. Lanae and Oscar were close behind them. "I'll go with you. I don't want to give up either. I'd like to do everything I can to save it if I can." His words also seemed to be about more than the manuscript.

Inside the tea shop was abuzz and busier than ever. The townsfolk had probably heard what had happened with Thomas by now and were hoping for a bit of news along with their tea.

Ellora found Gwen in the kitchen, flustered in a way she'd never seen the older woman act before. But at least several extra servers helped in the kitchen and in the café.

"I'm sorry, I don't want to bother you, but we'd like to look in Thomas's office if we could," Alex said.

"Of course, my boy. Go right on in. I hope Thomas is caught, the sooner the better. Shame on him for putting you all through this and for doing what he did to June."

They entered the office, still in some disarray from the police searching it. His datebook lay open on the desk.

Ellora flipped through it. "No notes in it. No dates circled. But then, he would've known that's the obvious place."

They each took a corner to search. When she'd gone through books, notebooks and random papers in her section, she tossed over her shoulder to the others, "Anything?"

They all called back, "No."

Ellora stood, hands on hips, with a view of the large map on Thomas's wall. It was marked with colored pushpins. He'd told her the white pins were places he'd been and the red were places he wanted to go.

"Hmm…" She ran a finger over the backs of three bright blue pins about an inch apart in a triangular shape.

"What is it?" Alex called.

"The blue pins. Those weren't there before and he told me he only used red and white ones."

Lanae and Oscar followed and Lanae pointed. "Isn't that the area you guys went to with Cressida—that estate Byron used to own?"

Ellora covered her mouth and spoke through her fingers. "Yes, if you triangulate these pins, that's right where the estate is." A whir of fear and anticipation renewed in her gut thinking of Byron. She'd been so sure he was the one causing problems and had something to do with her grandmother's death. So, she'd been shocked to find out it was Thomas instead. But maybe this was the connection to Byron.

"Perhaps Byron *was* in on it the whole time." Alex's words echoed her thoughts. "Maybe he's the black market artifact dealer Thomas is selling the manuscript to."

Lanae squinted. "The only thing is that if that were true, why would he have warned Ellora?"

Oscar scratched his head. "What if those weren't vague warnings, but instead thinly veiled threats? I mean, the chap did say, 'Watch out or you'll end up like your grandmother,' didn't he?"

"That's what I thought all along."

Ellora gestured to scribbled writing beneath one of the pins that read: "13/00/89 17:07."

"I think he tried to do a code here. What do you think? If that was supposed to be the British way of doing the date and time, there is no month of zero-zero."

She was still trying to wrap her mind around Thomas being a killer and a thief. It seemed ludicrous. Byron seemed more the sort.

They took up staring at the pins and writing underneath, each lost in thought.

Alex rubbed his chin. "What if Thomas was trying to throw off anyone who happened to see this and suspect something—like us—by mixing up the date with the time? As in, 13/00 isn't the date, it's the time 1300 or 1:00 p.m. for you Americans—" he winked at her "—and likewise, the 17:07 is the date. July 17."

They all stared at each other.

Lanae was the first to state the obvious. "That's today."

"What's the other number for?"

No one had an idea.

Ellora stepped away from the map and toward the door. "That's also soon. We don't have much time to get there."

"What about the police?" Alex said.

"We'll call them on the way. Most of them are in the countryside surrounding Alnwick today. I spoke to the inspector earlier to ask if they'd found Thomas yet. We don't have time to wait for them and we don't have time to explain it to them and convince them to go. We can't let Thomas and Byron get away with this."

The other three hesitated only a moment before dashing out of the door and the tea shop with a quick wave to Gwen.

This could be the most brilliant or the most stupid thing she'd ever done and she may not know until the "expected end" which was the case. She could only pray God was with them in this and she asked Him to surround them with His protection as they raced to do what she'd wanted to do all along. Save the manuscript and preserve it for all generations to come, even if none of those generations came from her.

To avoid being seen, they parked half a mile from the entrance to de Clare Hall, so they could stick to ditches and tree coverage. The iron gate between the two stone pillars was closed. The hours hung there indicated the estate was closed on Sundays, which was probably the reason Thomas and Byron had chosen this location and time.

Ellora had called the police on their way, but they were a ways from Alnwick in the opposite direction, so at least for now, they were on their own. Not that the inspector had encouraged them to pursue this on their own, quite the opposite.

Alex waved them to the stone wall surrounding the estate.

Oscar put his fist out for them to bump with their own. "The Lost Manuscript Society, unite."

Alex smirked. "You know that we may have just fist-bumped to our imminent demise, right, mate?"

Oscar shrugged. "Best to go in with a bit of confidence then, isn't it?"

Lanae rolled her eyes. "All right, let's get on with it. Crack on, as you would say, hey?"

Leading them to an outcropping of trees close enough to give them some coverage in their shade but not close enough to help them climb the wall, Alex stopped and turned. He jumped, grabbing onto the top of the wall, and pulled himself up until he knelt with one knee on the top. Oscar followed suit and both reached down for her and Lanae.

Alex's large hands encompassed hers. Once inside, thankfully they were shielded from view by another, thicker grove of trees on the estate grounds.

It was so brief and so soft, the brush of his thumb against her cheek, that she almost missed it before they sneaked forward, going from tree shadow to tree shadow, until they had a view of the house. There stood Thomas just outside of the garden, near his car, manuscript under his arm as though it was the day's newspaper.

This made Ellora's fingers clench as they crouched together behind a giant oak tree.

As Alex inched to the next tree toward the high-shrubbed garden path, another two people sauntered around the side of the manor. It was Byron beside Glen.

This was it. Both of the men responsible for her grandmother's death and stealing this important work of history.

"There he is. See? Byron's in on it."

Alex dipped his chin. "Let's stop them before they can make the deal and Byron drives off with the manuscript."

As they started to move, Oscar whispered, "Wait."

But she and Alex had already made it to the side entrance to the garden. Lanae and Oscar scrambled after them.

They crouched behind the shrubs.

Glen's voice rang out, not quite so jovial as the last time they'd met. "Look who I found skulking around the property? Acting like he still owns the place, he does."

The four of them bent and tiptoed forward.

Thomas guffawed. "But then he never really did, did he? It was hers."

The flash of metal in Glen's hand made Ellora gulp.

They exchanged a confused look. Lanae mouthed, *"She?"*

Glen poked Byron in the ribs with the gun barrel, but Byron, to his credit, glared right through the man. "I made mistakes. We were about to lose the estate, so I used whatever assets I could to save it, including hers."

"Well, you did lose it." Thomas's shrug was as nonchalant as when he'd spoken of her grandmother's death. "Along with your dignity. What could you possibly want now?"

"I want you to stop using the manuscript in this way. June was right, it belongs to everyone. It's—"

Thomas's broom-like mustache fluttered as his lips went *pffft*. "Important. Yes. Blah, blah, blah. Don't you think I've endured enough, weeks on end, of that drivel from that idiot granddaughter of hers and June herself until she so inconveniently went and hit her head, getting herself killed before she found me the manuscript?"

"Yes, and I'm sure you didn't have a thing to do with it." Byron's tone took on disgust and revulsion.

Clucking his tongue, Thomas threw a hand out. "Now, now. That was her doing not mine. Had she not put up such a fuss... Though, I can't say as I miss her constant babble about Holga and Mildred or some such."

Ellora covered her mouth to keep from crying out.

Thomas studied the nails on his free hand. "I'll get what I want—the funds to get out of here and start checking off the dreams on *my* list and she'll get her home back. Everybody wins."

Another henchman walked out of the manor, his white hair stark against his black clothing. "She's here."

A black SUV pulled up, now familiar after they'd seen it several times over the last weeks.

Everything Thomas had said, everything Byron had hinted at, the things she'd seen, everything clicked into placed as the henchman opened the back passenger door and out stepped…Cressida.

"*She's* the black market investor?" Lanae whispered to no one in particular.

The man who'd opened the door appeared to be a bodyguard as he wore a shoulder-strap holster with a gun strapped to each side, under his heavily muscled arms.

"Great, what are we going to do now?" Lanae huddled in close and kept her voice low.

"I reckon we wait for the police to arrive." Oscar's eyes and voice were tight. Not so much an adventure anymore.

Cressida glared at Byron. "Here to try to talk me out of selling the stupid manuscript again?"

Then turning her attention to Glen, Cressida gestured to their surroundings with a careless yet impatient air. "We saw that pestilent Professor Lockwood's car parked a kilometer down the road. I'm sure he and his irritating wife are around here somewhere thinking they can get their precious manuscript back."

Thomas whipped his head from side to side.

Cressida snapped her fingers at the bodyguard. "Check the grounds."

The man nodded to the driver, who exited the vehicle and they started searching behind trees and bushes, but on the other side of the garden. It was only a matter of time. Sweat trickled down the nape of Ellora's neck, her breath coming in short huffs.

Alex reached back for her hand and gripped it.

When Cressida returned her attention to Thomas, she tapped a foot and crossed her arms. "The police are probably not far behind. We need to get on with this." The last part was so quiet that Ellora leaned in to hear better.

But her foot slipped and made a sound as it scraped against the gravel.

Cressida's head shot up and her sharp eyes darted to the line of sculpted bushes they hid behind like she had X-ray vision. She snapped at the driver and bodyguard again, calling them back.

She pointed. "Over there."

Yup. This was it; they were done for. This was officially the dumbest plan ever.

They started to scramble backward. The driver, much more limber than he looked with his bulk and muscles, leaped over the shrubs and landed in the path, blocking their way, while the guard's voice boomed behind them, "Stop!"

They all froze.

The guard growled. "Get up and turn toward me, slowly."

Lanae whimpered. He gestured with this gun. "Get a move on. Over there."

The bodyguard pointed to the driveway and they filed out of the garden.

They lined up next to Thomas, who looked bored by the whole ordeal. Cressida sent them a dazzling smile.

"Well, doesn't this just tie up all of the loose ends? So efficient." Cressida turned a pitying smile to them. "Didn't you even wonder where I went after Thomas's pathetic escape with the manuscript? I thought maybe he'd spilled the caviar about me, but—" she flicked her manicured finger "—judging by your moronic expressions, I guess not."

She lowered her chin once to the men with the guns. "Take care of them."

Byron protested. "Cressida, you don't have to do this. There are other ways."

She threw her hands into the air. "You took every other

option from me, Byron. There is no other way and I *will* have my home back. I earned it. You *made* me earn it."

"But you don't have to kill anyone for it."

"Do you even know what it was like for me?" Cressida spun a circle and thrust a finger toward Byron. "To see my belongings at auction houses—like the jewelry box and ring her grandmother took away from me." She turned her thin finger toward Ellora.

The older woman's gaze turned dangerous. "And if that manuscript belongs to anyone, it belongs to *me*. It's as much a part of this house and the history here as anywhere. With that being said, I can part with it for the right price. I have an estate to buy back."

Glen leveled his gun at Thomas now, but Thomas clutched the manuscript to his chest. "Hey, now. What's all this then? We had a deal. Ten million quid and it's yours."

"Hand it over." Cressida opened and closed her upturned hand.

The bodyguard strode to Thomas and wrestled the book from his arms.

Cressida clicked her tongue. "Oh, poor, stupid Mr. Bixby. If I had ten million pounds, do you think I'd need to sell this manuscript on the black market myself in order to buy back this property?"

"So, you're not a black market dealer and investor? You—you…" Thomas's mouth opened and closed as though still floundering to piece together the truth.

"Yes, me." Cressida rolled her eyes then lifted her chin to the bodyguard. "Why do you think I sent a message to Ellora to find the manuscript and turn it over to me—though she didn't know it was me—with that arrow? I cut out the middle man, i.e. *you*. I was also tracking the manuscript myself, hoping I could cut each one of you out of the equation.

That's why I had her phone stolen and broke into June's office. But it was useless, all of it. Despite my impatience, I had to hang on to you all in case—even by accident—one of you stumbled upon the manuscript or a useful clue."

Cressida let out a long-suffering sigh. "But not anymore…" The gleam in her eye turned vicious.

But the sound of screeching metal and tires crunching on gravel tore everyone's attention to the entrance gates. Two police cars burst onto the property, busting down the gate with their vehicles.

Thomas jumped toward the bodyguard to grab the manuscript from his hands in the distraction. It happened so fast. A flash of silver as the bodyguard went for his gun.

Alex threw himself over her and curled around her body. An earsplitting *bang!* and Alex's body slammed hard against hers. He let out a groan.

"Alex? Alex!" She rolled over beneath him, face-to-face now.

His face contorted with pain. He sucked air through his teeth.

"Where?" was the only question she could think of.

But more blasts covered whatever he said.

She ever so slowly flipped him onto his back. He held his left arm where a hole had been ripped through his shoulder. Blood. So much blood.

She did the only thing she could remember about wound care from the teacher's required first aid course—keep pressure on it. She ripped off her cardigan, placed it over the injury and leaned on it. He roared and bared his teeth.

"I'm sorry, sweetheart. Just hold on. You're going to be okay."

Teeth still clamped tight, he managed a grimacing smile. "You haven't called me sweetheart in ages."

Glen lay across from them clutching his knee, blood flowing through his fingers. The police had already handcuffed the driver and were working on taking down the bodyguard. Thomas had made it out unscathed—being that the bullet meant for him had gone into Alex's arm instead. As they secured the dangerous persons, her fear lessened.

But Alex was losing a lot of blood. He held it in, but the sweat beading on his forehead and shallow gasps spoke of tremendous pain. "Help! Over here!" she called to the officers.

Alex put a hand over her forearm still pressing on his wound, the cardigan wet and warm with blood beneath her fingers.

An officer dashed to her side, helping to put added pressure. She took comfort that the officer's face showed practiced concentration but didn't appear grim.

"Is he going to be okay?" Her voice shook as did the muscles in her arms.

"He should be just fine, but we need to get him to the infirmary. The paramedics are on their way. Now, I have to check on this man over here. Can you hold this a little longer?"

Oscar and Lanae stumbled over. They'd managed to duck behind a bush when the fighting broke out. Oscar took a turn holding Alex's wound.

When the paramedics arrived she couldn't bring herself to leave him for a moment. Ellora sat in the back of the ambulance, clutching Alex's hand, marveling that he was alive. They were all alive.

"You didn't really have to take a bullet for me," she whispered.

He gave her a weary smile. "You know me, I never do anything by halves, do I?"

He had chosen her, put his life on the line for her. That

spoke in ways her heart had finally listened. Maybe that door could open. Maybe the wall could come down. But if it did, what else would she be letting in?

Chapter Twenty-One

Even the Duke and his family were subject to the laws concerning historical artifacts found on their property, especially this valuable. They turned in the information to the local coroner's office—as required by law for any potential "treasure" found on one's property, and to the special division of the British Museum that dealt with such things, to be on the safe side.

While the powers that be decided what to do with this exquisite illuminated masterpiece, they'd allowed Ellora—with her historian and university professor hats firmly in place—the opportunity to pore over its pages. Read and study the contents as though they were written for her alone.

She'd learned so much about Mildrythe, who had later taken the name Hilda, and her life in early England.

Her betrothed, Aelfgar, had two different rumors surrounding his life and death—one, that he'd been carrying the lost manuscript, and two, that he had died during the raid around 875. Both were untrue. He did live through the raid and saw Mildrythe taken by the Vikings. He couldn't let her go and attempted to hunt her down. Before the raid that took her mother's life, she'd started to see violent tendencies in her husband-to-be, and her mother warned her not to marry him.

Aelfgar became obsessive and possessive, vowing he would find Mildrythe, take her away from these Vikings and marry her. He scoured the countryside, becoming more frantic as he heard stories of an Englishwoman living among the Vikings now willingly, even taking one as her husband. Which was true. Eventually, Mildrythe did fall in love with the clan leader.

As Mildrythe, now Hilda, traveled with her new clan, bringing the stories of the Bible and prayers to life with her illuminated manuscript, even though half-finished, she taught people how to read and write. And wherever they traveled, villagers learned how to copy parts of her book to share with their people. People like the woman who had scribed the partial manuscript. But Hilda asked the new scribes to hide messages to pass on to her family still living, so they would know she was alive and well—like the sample Ellora and Alex saw in Lindisfarne: "Mildrythe lives." They also used these messages to alert one another if they'd seen Aelfgar.

What impressed Ellora about this woman was her resiliency and faith in the face of so much loss—she'd lost most of her family, the only home she'd ever known, even her own people, everything that made her *her*. She had to make a new land her home, strangers with strange customs her family. In this way, Mildrythe reminded her very much of Ruth.

When Mildrythe began using the second half of her Book of Hours as a journal, she'd drawn a family tree to remember and feel close to those she'd lost. Many branches remained empty. Then love began to take root and grow between her and the Viking chief who'd held her captive but later captured her heart. A slow-burn sort of love bloomed from mutual respect and admiration. He wasn't the monster she'd taken him for, and as his ways softened, she told him about her God, that there was a different way to live. He, along with his whole clan, whom she now saw as her adoptive family, turned to the Lord and converted to Christianity. She changed her name as a rebirth into a new life.

The paintings Ellora and Alex found were depictions of Mildrythe-turned-Hilda praying with her new brothers and sisters in the Christian faith, the Vikings, at Chester-le-Street about six miles from Durham and the first resting place for St. Cuthbert's remains, the Lindisfarne Gospels and other holy relics as well as the people who'd escaped Lindisfarne. Hilda and her clan had wandered after the initial raid in Lindisfarne just like the monks and scribes who fled Holy Island, eventually seeking out Chester-le-Street after their conversion not only as a pilgrimage to visit the holy relics and the rough wooden church built there but also as penance for what they'd done.

Even through great loss, Hilda didn't give up on God or say He had abandoned her. She hadn't closed herself off from her own capacity to love and be loved. Mildrythe/Hilda had written, and Ellora had practiced her translating skills to reveal: "Greater is the sorrow to lock away my heart and throw the key into the waters of the sea than to open my heart's gate to those whom I love. I would surely perish should I not seek and give love as the Lord Himself has commanded the greatest of these, speaking of His commandments, is to love the Lord your God and love thy neighbor as oneself."

Hilda had left her writings to the female line of her ancestors, Sibilla in the Tudor Era being one of her lineage. Hilda had become the leader of the clan once her chief husband had died and she was buried with honor as a chieftess in her own right—hence the rune stone and its carvings—when she passed away. One of her daughters had made the entry about it once Hilda was gone. Over the years, Hilda had been able to fill in the empty family tree and it was full to the last branch at the time of her passing.

Each page was bursting with hope and family history. From what could've been considered one tragedy after another, God had redeemed each and every one, creating beauty in their places.

Could He do the same for Ellora? Would He, after she'd chosen wrong so many times?

Alex would be released from the hospital today. She'd stayed at his side last night until the doctors assured her he would be all right; the bullet had shot through "cleanly," as they put it. Though clean was not what came to mind at the memories of warm, sticky blood covering her hands. There was a reason she was a historian surrounded by dry, dusty books and not a health professional.

The doctor's and Alex's insistence sent her back to the castle. Oscar said he'd drive Alex back sometime late morning, whenever the infirmary discharged him.

There had never been the right time to talk with Alex about anything too important with him being at the hospital. Her suitcase still sat half-packed near her bed. Undecided, like her mind.

Perhaps some fresh air would do the trick. Soon, she may not be surrounded by the peaceful beauty of this place. She had to soak it up while she could.

She thought about asking Lanae to come along, but the

solitude was what her soul thirsted for. A solitude from people but a closeness with her Heavenly Father.

Walking the paths through the Alnwick Garden, she again came to the community garden. The mustard plants' delicate green shoots and cheery yellow heads danced in the breeze. And the words her grandmother said long ago about love being a choice came back to her.

Even though she'd agreed with her grandmother, perhaps she had lived like love was a feeling, something easy, handed to her. When the reality of love and marriage was much more complicated, so much harder than she'd ever thought possible. But maybe so much more beautiful because of the hard work, the craftsmanship that went into it. A laying down of oneself upon that threshing floor. Her ego. Her pride. Her anger. Her hurt and selfishness. And choosing him, choosing them, but mostly choosing her Savior and His ways over her own. Choosing each and every day, even on the hard days.

Suddenly, her stuck fight-or-flight mode, her frozen feet, heart and mind pulled free.

She had to find Alex. She had to fight for who she loved.

Never much of a runner or athletic like Alex, she made a surprisingly quick exit, even in T-strap heels, and blazed a trail back to the outer bailey.

Before she could dash up the twisting staircase to see if Alex was back yet, she was stopped by the estate manager, a tall spindly man with small, twinkling eyes.

She tried not to be rude, but she shuffled from side to side, bouncing on the tips of her toes.

"You look like you've recovered from your ordeal."

"Yes, thank you."

He smiled brightly. "I'm so very glad Professor Lockwood will be all right. Jolly good news. Say, are you finished looking at the manuscript? I've been instructed to keep it locked up in the Duke's quarters for safekeeping. Can't be too careful, you know."

"Indeed, I do." Though she never wanted to be finished devouring its contents. She felt as though she knew Hilda now. Like a friend...who happened to have lived over twelve hundred years ago.

But she sighed and said, "Come on up. It's in my flat."

He seemed in no hurry, unlike her, and took the stairs at a leisurely pace.

When she opened the door, an envelope slid across the floor. "Ellie" was written on the front. Alex's handwriting. She picked it up but would have to wait to open it.

The estate manager wandered in, hands tucked behind his back. "You know, Professor Lockwood had to acquire special permission to paint this for you, update the loo and move this furniture in. He was quite adamant."

This information wasn't a surprise, but warmed her heart nonetheless.

"Yes, yes, and he's improved the university program immensely whilst he's been here. It's too bad that he has put in his resignation. He will be missed here, I'm most certain."

The shock dragged her mouth open, where it hung slack for several long moments.

"Oh, I apologize. Did you not know?"

She wet her lips. "No, I, did he say where he's going?"

Her mind raced. What did this mean?

"He didn't. But I told him I won't consider him gone until he's moved out."

She couldn't stop herself from opening the flap of the envelope in her hand. She didn't even need to see the full words of the heading. It was the divorce papers.

Her breath caught.

Finally, the kind but sometimes oblivious man seemed to catch on.

She thanked him for letting her study the manuscript and it felt like handing off a piece of herself.

"You're most welcome. You have a keen eye for history like your grandmother. We hope to house an exhibit right here of the manuscript and will need someone to write about it, perhaps even curate the exhibit itself. I can think of no one else who knows as much about it as you. Something to think about. And if that's the case, you can study it anytime as well."

Something lit in her chest at his words, but after he was gone, the light dimmed to a dull flicker.

Was this it? Alex's not-so-subtle way of telling her it was over? And where was he going? Was this like when he moved to England without telling her? His way of escaping her?

She ran to his flat. No answer.

She tried calling him but he didn't pick up.

Sprinting for the stairs, she missed a step and stumbled but caught herself as she burst into the courtyard. There was a commotion outside of the Barbican Gate. She couldn't make out what was happening but there was a buzz of voices.

When she peeked through the gate walkway, Gus the guard tipped his hat to her.

"What's going on, Gus?"

"Cheers, Miss. That'll be your Professor Lockwood. Town hero now, isn't he?" He grinned, but she couldn't return it.

Sure enough, when she emerged from the Barbican, Alex was surrounded by press, people snapping photos and clamoring to ask questions. And there he was, eating it up, smiling, being his charming, attention-grabbing self.

It was happening all over again. He got to be the hero for everyone else, while breaking her heart by leaving.

★ ★ ★

Alex lifted the one arm he still could to quiet the gathered crowd. His only thoughts were of finding Ellie. That's what he'd been trying to do since he'd arrived home. He'd been so eager to tell her what he'd been thinking the last couple of days, really the last couple of months, or year, for that matter. It had taken time to develop and grow.

He wanted to be with her no matter what that meant. Even now, in this din of voices, he silently thanked God for his wife, who she was, who she would become, her laugh, her smile, her kindness, her intelligence, the ways she inspired and challenged him to be the best version of himself, even her stubbornness because it meant she didn't give up. All of the qualities that made her a wonderful wife...and perhaps, God willing, a mother.

If he looked to the example of his Heavenly Father instead of his earthly parents, he would have all he needed to be the kind of father he would've wanted as a child and the kind of dad he wanted to become. The thought still gripped his gut and twisted it, worrying he wouldn't be good enough. But there was also a spark of hope and peace in his chest.

The reporters demanded his attention again. Maybe if he answered a couple of questions, they'd be satisfied and leave. Somehow a local news source had leaked the information about the shoot-out at de Clare Hall.

A journalist raised a hand and shouted, "Is it true that you were shot saving a twelve-hundred-year-old book?"

He laughed. "Well, when you put it like that, you make me sound like either the world's biggest idiot or history buff. I guess you can take your pick."

The crowd chuckled in return.

He cleared his throat. "But, no, honestly, I was shot trying to protect my wife. And I would do it over again any day, every day, to keep her safe." His voice had caught at the end. He took a breath. "That's not an invitation though, I promise."

A few more laughs mixed with "Aw."

That's when he spotted her, off to the side, her eyes wide like a doe frozen in fear on the side of the road. She held the white envelope he'd left under her door before he'd been too impatient to await her return and ran out of the castle to see if she'd walked into the village. But he'd run into the reporters instead.

Why did she look so stricken?

It hit him that this may be too much like the outside of the hospital after the shooting. But he didn't crave the spotlight like she thought. Truly.

He waved her over. At first, she ducked her head and shook it. But the journalists caught on and started snapping pictures of her.

"This is my wife, Ellora Lockwood, and if it were not for her, this lost early medieval illuminated manuscript would still be hidden underneath stone."

She finally took slow steps toward him until they stood shoulder to shoulder. After a wary glance up at him, she swallowed. "No, it's because of the incredible work of my grandmother, June Wiltshire. No one believed her when she told the historical community about her theory that the rumored lost manuscript of Northumberland was created by a woman and it was a Viking woman at that."

Her chin lifted and her shoulders straightened as she spoke of Grandma June and explained what she'd learned from the manuscript so far.

It made his own heart swell with pride.

Always the one to step back from the spotlight—though

he admitted he may have been so center stage at times that people couldn't see her in the shadows—she shone now.

"My grandmother always said to dig deeper, to never settle for the obvious answer, and to find truth even when it's not easy or popular. That we could all learn from the past." Ellora's eyes met his. Despite her apparent excitement talking about the manuscript, pain seemed to roil beneath the surface.

Was it her grandmother? They would receive her ashes from the crematorium the next day. The whole experience had been a difficult one, especially for Ellora. She hadn't even had time to properly let the grief set in, to face it.

If only he could hold her now.

Suddenly, he had no desire but to be alone with his wife. So, he waved his good arm and said, "All right, it's time to let this hero—" he gestured to Ellie, which made her cheeks turn the same color as her rosy gold hair "—and her assistant—" he indicated himself "—have a rest. You may contact the castle's estate office or the police for any further details."

They'd asked him if he could share anything about who did the shooting, who tried to steal the manuscript, et cetera, but he'd told them it wasn't for him to share since it was still an open investigation. He and Ellora knew and kept to themselves that Thomas and Cressida, along with her henchmen, were being held responsible separately for their part in everything that had happened.

As the crowd dispersed, he placed a hand on her back to lead her back inside the castle, but she pulled away and started down the hill on the road known as The Peth, leading toward the River Aln. The ivy-covered wall on the right buffeted by the breeze as he followed her.

"Ellie, wait! What's happened?"

When they reached Lion Bridge, she descended the little path along the riverbank. The castle reflected in the water created a majestic sight.

Ellie stood, arms at her sides with one hand still clutching the envelope.

"What's wrong?"

She held up the envelope with the signed divorce papers and his letter inside. "This is what's wrong." A rock seemed to sink to the pit of his stomach. Did she want to mail the divorce papers to the lawyer instead of what he'd suggested?

He waited. Unable to speak.

Her shoulders rose with a deep inhale as though taking in courage for what she was about to say. His chest tightened.

"Alex, I've had too much pride and fear to tell you the truth about what I feel. But, you know, feelings are fickle anyway." She pinched the bridge of her nose. "This isn't coming out right."

Her voice shook and even though he was certain she was about to break his heart, he laid a hand on her shoulder. "It's all right, my love. Just say what you need to say."

"I ran to find you. I needed to tell you—not what I thought you wanted to hear, not what is the least vulnerable thing so I don't get hurt or rejected, not more accusations. I've tossed those to the wind as I hope you will with mine... I want to be with you. If love is a choice then I choose you. Us. God as our foundation. Every day. But..."

His heart blipped then raced.

Again she lifted the envelope. "You didn't. You gave up. Do you really want me to mail this? Do you want out? And what's going on with your resignation? Are you leaving?" The implied *me* at the end of the last statement was clear from her impossibly blue eyes, filled with tears.

She blew out a loud breath. "If you want me to, it will be the hardest thing I'll ever do, but I will mail this. First, though, I have to hear it from your mouth." She waited, eyes rounded, and mouth clamped together, probably trying to hide the shake in her jaw.

"Ellie, did you open it?"

Her brows sloped together. With trembling hands she fished the papers out of the envelope, his handwritten note fluttering to the grass.

Ellora retrieved the letter from the ground. The movement made her head spin and stomach threaten to give way. She read:

My Dearest Love,

I choose you. I choose us. And the God who created us and brought us together.

Over and over again. In a million little ways. In all ways. Every day. I choose the love and life we've created together.

I know we'll muck it all up on occasion. (It'll probably be me. Just to save us time, I'm sorry.)

But there's nowhere I'd rather be than with you. Wherever you are that's home to me. I love you, bone of my bone, flesh of my flesh. Without you, I am missing part of myself. The best part.

I am my Beloved's (yours, my sweet Ellie) and my Beloved is mine.

I'll return to Minnesota with you, happily. I want to see your dreams realized. You deserve that. And it doesn't matter where we are as long as we're together. Always.

Your Alex

She wiped tears away. A burning desire to jump into his arms almost overtook her. But she remembered his arm.

"So, the resignation?"

He gave her one of his heart-melting one-dimpled grins. "I resigned so that I can come back to Minnesota with you. You said once that I never fought for you and you're absolutely right. But I am now. I will go wherever you go. I never want to be separated like that again. But I want you to do what you will with the divorce papers."

His words again brought back to her the story of Ruth. The vulnerable hope living in those sea-foam-green eyes she loved so well made her throat clog with the hope bursting from her own chest. "What are my options?" She stepped closer to him, putting a hand on his chest. His heart beat hard against her palm.

His eyes lit. "Hmm...we could burn them." He held up fingers on his good hand as he went. "Give them to the gardener's dog to chew up. Feed them to the paper shredder. Let me use a sword to hack them to pieces. Bake them into that truly horrid tater tot hotdish. Then there's the simple, yet effective, tearing them up by hand. Or...mail them."

"Any except the last one. Tearing is good. Burning even better. And how about we rethink that whole 'going back to Minnesota' thing?"

"Oh?" He barely restrained his look of anticipation.

She looped her arms around his neck.

"Yeah, I think I like it here. It feels right. Like—"

But he pressed her to him with his good arm and she was careful not to touch his shoulder as he lowered his mouth to hers, cutting off what they both knew she would say. He tasted of sweet beginnings. Of hope and love. Of promises. He tasted of home.

And that's just what it felt like in his arms...like she was finally home again.

Epilogue

Welcoming a new group of summer session students was an exciting prospect, but waddling her eight-month-pregnant self over to the castle gates from the little cottage she and Alex had moved into on the castle grounds was getting more difficult by the day.

She twisted her wedding ring, back on its rightful finger, a little snug these days. They'd renewed their vows at the cute little stone church, St. Michael's, to share their renewed commitment—their *choosing* each other—as well as asserting God as their foundation going forward.

Checking her clothes for paint in the mirror where she'd been adding finishing touches on the nursery, she passed the painting Alex had bought for her. The picture Eg painted of the mother and daughter in the garden. Her dreams fulfilled in one painting.

Grandma June's rug, a clash to the rest of the entryway colors, held her shoes. Her lips lifted in a smile as she slipped them on. Her feet were finally perfectly warm. Swollen, but warm.

Out the door, the bright and perfumed flower- and plant-lined cobbled walkway in front of their cottage greeted her. She'd planted mustard seeds among the blooms, and let her fingertips glide over their bright, sunny yellow heads. Her hand went automatically to the necklace Lanae had gifted her with a real mustard seed preserved inside a clear locket. Just like her love for her first child would be forever preserved in her heart.

Alex sprinted to her side. "My love, take it easy. Don't push yourself. You don't want to exhaust yourself or our daughter."

She laughed, her belly bouncing with each chuckle. They'd found out they were having a girl at their five-month ultrasound, and neither one could keep it a surprise. "I'm perfectly fine. It's good for me and Millie to be up and about." Their daughter gave her a swift kick in the ribs as though to heartily agree.

They'd chosen Mildrythe June to honor the two strong women. Hopefully, like Eg/Egbert, she'd grow to embrace the name they'd given her.

They walked to the parking lot in front of the Barbican Gate, where Gus had set a chair in anticipation of Ellora. She turned to wave and shout a thank-you to the sweet older man before sinking onto the chair. Her breath came faster these days after walking or her dancing exercises, which Alex did with her if she didn't try any jumps or swing dance moves. But she would take any discomfort necessary to keep her child safe until she made her entrance into this world.

Alex had proved himself a loving and attentive father already and Ellora knew he would continue to thrive in this role he was meant for when their Millie was born.

"You know, I think I'm ready." She rubbed her round stomach, at which Millie turned and ran a whole leg or arm underneath Ellora's hand.

Alex bent with wide eyes, putting a hand to her belly too.

"No, not that." A look of wonder spilled over his face when Millie kicked his hand. "I think we should spread the ashes at the river."

They'd kept Grandma June's ashes on the mantel of their cottage's fireplace, above where they'd burned the divorce papers in the fire below. Those months ago seemed like years in some ways. She'd never regretted telling Alex to immediately get his job back and see if there was a way for her to stay too—which of course there was, both as a teacher and as the now-famed *Lost Manuscript of Lindisfarne* exhibit curator and historian.

She'd had the privilege of writing for several historical journals to both educate people and clear her grandmother's name in the historical community. But by far the biggest fulfillment came from adding to her own family tree in the back of Grandma June's brilliant blue field journal.

He kissed the top of her head. "Then we'll walk down there tonight. Should I invite Lanae and Oscar?"

She smiled and nodded.

"Oh, there's the bus!" She could hardly wait for it to stop.

She jumped to her feet as quick as she could, considering. When the doors opened, Lanae dashed out and ran to Ellora. She hugged her close then pulled back to look at her rounded form.

"Did you eat a watermelon seed?" It was an old joke of her grandmother's.

They laughed and hugged again.

Holding up a baggie of her SCOBYs of various sizes, she squealed. "The whole family is back together again!"

Lanae was working on her visa and Ellora and Alex knew Oscar was planning to ask Lanae to marry him during this trip. Soon, Ellora wouldn't have to say goodbye every few months.

For every loss, a new seed of hope and beauty had been planted. God had been faithful to grow her in ways she'd never anticipated—and not just in the vicinity of her abdomen—painfully at times but for her good and His glory. And she'd chosen to love Him and place her life in His capable hands the same day she'd chosen to love Alex all those months ago, finally understanding her vows—for better *and* worse.

She'd opened the door to love, to hope and, yes, even grief. Letting it wash over her in a mighty tide. The grief only told the story of how deeply she'd loved those she'd lost. God had taken her grief and, not replaced it with, but given her joy alongside the grief. She could have both. Much like the joy given back to Ruth and Naomi after a long season of piled-up losses.

Life was like that—both beauty and pain. A giving and a taking. Life wasn't perfect for her or anyone. She still felt the keen ache of those she had lost, but God had showed her He would continue to carry her through every day of her life. And though she'd once believed Grandma June had abandoned her too, she could now see her grandmother's love and encouragement "illuminated" throughout her life, not just during her search for the lost manuscript.

Lanae had been right. God was creating a whole magnificent picture out of their lives. It was in the looking back that she could see all of the places He was there for her, where she thought things couldn't possibly turn out all right. But together, all of the beauty, all of the pain, everything she'd learned along the way, worked in harmony. He'd taken what she thought was beyond repair, all of her dreams she thought were lost forever, and redeemed every one. The wind was indeed inside her veins every bit as much as the Wind Maker was inside of her heart. He'd been guiding her to this very place of goodness and light.

A place He'd planned all along. To this expected end.

★ ★ ★ ★ ★

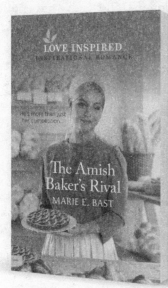